The Gilded Lily

The Gilded Lily

Helen Argers

St. Martin's Press
New York

Book design by Ellen R. Sasahara

ISBN 0-312-18571-5

First Edition: July 1998

10 9 8 7 6 5 4 3 2 1

To Astera,
    my sister, my role model.

And in memory of
    my mother, Carol-Calliope,
    and father, Thomas P.

And always, always, to N.N.—for love.

Acknowledgments

To the people of New York City, Philadelphia, and New Jersey, then and now. I particularly salute the New Jerseyites, south and north, who have a history of independence and more elegance than ever credited.

I am indebted forever, as are all readers, to the great authors of the Gilded Era who bequeathed to us all the manners, mores, and humor of their time—from Edith Wharton to Henry James to Mark Twain. The latter penned the term that captured and crystallized his time in three words: The Gilded Age.

Prologue

1876 was a time of the reign of the super-rich in America when the wealthy and privileged lived lives of exuberant excess. They did not merely "gild refined gold" and "paint the lily" but star-spangled it as well—especially during the patriotic celebratory year of the United States' Centennial Exposition. Yet excess and want are two sides of the same coin. The average American worker, earning a dollar a day, gilded his life by idolizing the moneyed class, reading about their daily spendthrift doings in the newspapers and spending from their little to purchase photographs of the beautiful heiresses. Some of the wealthy began to see the want in their lives and question their own excesses. Having too much is often very much like having too little, for when the core of life is at either edge, existence is unbalanced and leads to rebellion. One such rebellion began with the well-to-do women who refused to live in a gilded cage and sought freedom through the Women's Suffrage Movement. Other American heiresses rebelled by escaping to Europe. One beautiful heiress named Nina De Bonnard became a rebel in every way against her gilt-edged society and its veneer values, even risking ostracism. This is her story and the story of an American era with a "gilty" conscience.

The Gilded Lily

One

ina De Bonnard was the only lady at her family's garden party who did not have a parasol. That was unquestionable proof of her nonconformity. It showed that she was not only nonchalant about the dangers of the sun but also unwilling to rely on a parasol's proven assistance in dealing with another elemental force of nature: gentlemen.

Indeed, the language of a parasol had been perfected by generations of ladies and understood and accepted by generations of gentlemen. Closed, a parasol could effectively hold a gentleman at bay. Open but held near to the head, it blocked a man's advances. But lifting the open parasol higher demonstrated willingness to be approached. As for allowing a young man to duck his head under one's personal canopy—well, that was tantamount to an announcement.

But Nina preferred her hands free and her body unsheltered, refusing to accept the basic confinements of her set. Any messages she needed sent to a gentleman she would send in her own direct way. Thus she gave the illusion of being approachable, until a gentleman attempted to do so. Then it became quite clear that she had her own rules, from which her followers deviated at their peril. Today she was holding a long white rose and used that to anoint a favorite. A touch from it meant permission to come closer and converse. To her admirers, the flower seemed like an

1

extension of her own smooth, white-skinned hand; its touch was her touch and decidedly titillating.

Whether here at Oceana or during the winter months amongst the gilded set of New York City's elegant ballrooms, Nina's beaus followed her like a royal entourage. Heedless of the whispers from surface observers that the lady could not be satisfied by one gentleman, Nina used her entourage to protect herself from any individual gentleman.

Out of the corner of her eye Nina spotted a compelling stranger. His two immediate attractions were that he was not of her set and that he was older than her crowd by almost a decade, all of which he had apparently spent looking at ladies. At least that was what the amused expression in his deep, dark eyes seemed to indicate. Stopping midstep, Nina returned his look, her arched eyebrows lifting higher in a steady evaluation.

There was something about his cool, appraising stare that had Nina wondering whether he was keeping his evaluation on a gentlemanly level. A cold, discomforting sensation was spreading through her. She found herself wishing for her stole and sent one of her admirers to the house for one. Still, step by step, the stranger advanced. And step by step Nina retreated behind her admirers. The white eyelet wrap was brought and Nina had to wait through flowery comments about the young man's wishing he were the wrap upon her shoulders before she could use it. She rewarded her gallant with her bright unforgettable smile, and the gentleman felt more than compensated. Yet the wrap had no effect. She still felt trembles. Next moment the wrap was used to cover the décolletage of her dress, for the intruder's pointed stare had Nina rethinking her mother's admonition that the bodice was cut too low for an afternoon affair. Nina resented being made to feel so inhibited. She was usually neither embarrassed by her feminine attributes nor proud of them. Mostly she was unaware of her body, feeling herself a watcher, separated from her group and thus untouched by remarks—jealous or admiring—and certainly untouched by a look, tantamount to a leer, from an unknown and unintroduced gentleman!

Another annoying aspect of the gentleman was his attitude, lounging, laughing, languid: He had stopped his movement toward her and was resting his large form with one arm against an oak tree, as if he would not put himself to the trouble of moving from a choice spot. The small smile around his lips suggested that he was considering whether she was worth any further effort.

Piqued, Nina could not dismiss the attraction of his being an uninvited intruder to this select affair. That delicious fact could quickly be determined by checking with her mother, who had sent out the invitations. But Nina decided not to do so, lest that make her attraction too obvious, even to herself. And certainly her mother would question any special attention to a stranger. A lady never betrayed interest of the smallest kind in a gentleman until and unless she had been properly introduced to him. Only then, perhaps, could he enter into her thoughts. Yet Nina had long since gone beyond that degree of restriction. She liked to think of herself as a daring young lady in command of her life who would take chances, especially if the gentleman in question had chanced a great deal more by gate-crashing into her home.

The next moment the stranger was approached by two of her father's friends. Nina caught her breath, waiting for him to be uncovered and escorted off her property. When the conversation proved obviously friendly, she exhaled in disappointment. He had somehow passed muster. That instantly diminished his allure for Nina, and she turned away.

Actually, the gentleman was a stranger neither to Oceana nor to the De Bonnard family. He was Jordan Houghton Windsor, who had grown up in the same New York City upper-crust set but had left years ago and only recently returned. He had followed his mother and brother on their yearly migration from New York City to this New Jersey summer resort, not expecting a change of people but hoping for some slight loosening of their rigid patterns. Overall, Jordan concluded that this exclusive social set was rather like a snail, in that it carried along its own stultifying world wherever it went. Content in those cloistered ways, it moved at a slow, self-satisfied pace, leaving a smear to mark its glistening path. The movement was circular: where it began, there it ended. A small, tight set with gossip its main source of sustenance. A shell like that was too confining for his larger horizons, Jordan had decided, and he had taken off for Europe. He had an inkling the lady with the white rose might be a fellow rebel.

Persuaded by his family, much against his desire, to present himself at the De Bonnard party, Jordan hoped the ladies in attendance would reward him for his effort. They attempted to do so but failed. A thorough investigation of the young females present had revealed, much to his amusement, that they not only hung together in gaggles but jointly giggled. They even answered together: "Oh yes, Mr. Windsor!" "How exciting, Mr. Windsor!" Everyone was anxious to be singled out but fearful of standing out. Until the lady with the rose.

Looking in her direction again, he noted that she was completely enclosed by her supporters, so he set off for a walk on the long green lawn. Nothing could still the restlessness in him since his return. He must always be moving . . . seeking. Not far from here was the ocean; he could almost smell its salty tang. Confound, what had made him think that here on the open beaches and verandas some of the closed thinking and guarded manners of New York's brownstone confinements would similarly open up? Some slight memories remained of life being freer at the beach, but those were undoubtedly due to his own youth at the time. This week at Oceana reminded him of all the reasons he'd left. Further, and most grating, was a new element of national chauvinism, possibly a result of the coming centennial celebration. In Europe, a variety of opinion was not only expected but offered. Here, they all thought in unison. America, the beautiful. America, the all-powerful. And yet wasn't that what he'd instinctively believed throughout his youth? Indeed, on his arrival in Europe, he'd been shocked to note that the people there did not secretly wish to be Americans themselves. Now, back home, he could only look at the America-boosterism about him with a smile and a shake of his head. Enough, he groaned when a matron stopped to ask everybody's favorite question: Wasn't he relieved to be back in the good-old-USA? He made his usual false reply. He had been on the point of an early departure until the appearance of the lady with the white rose. What had first amused was the way her phalanx of young men moved when she moved, keeping her always surrounded, like guards around a treasure. But his smile froze when he noted his younger brother, Dick, in the thick of the pack. Putting together some of the heated conversations he'd overheard between Dick and his friend Bobby Van Reyden, he'd concluded that this must be their bone of contention, Nina De Bonnard. Even his mother had had several words of warning about that lady. Not once but several times she'd stopped to say she hoped he would not pay the slightest attention to that young miss, who was perilously close to being considered fast!

Naturally, that practically assured he would be on the lookout for her. And yet that lady had caught his interest before he'd realized she was Miss De Bonnard. As a self-noted connoisseur of women, Jordan had from first view rated Nina according to his own personal system of evaluating the fair sex. Beauty was important, but intelligence and, most of all, charm garnered the highest marks on his scale. He'd put himself to the fatigue of actually pushing his way to the outer rim of her circle for a closer evaluation of her particulars: gold-red hair hidden almost completely by the usual wide-brimmed lawn hat; nose, unremarkable; mouth, ordinary; height, average; carriage, too much of a preen to it. Altogether, he would have given her a median rating but for her eyes. They doubled her marks. Not just for their elegant shape and a copper glow in the center of the hazel tones, but for the life in them. And then, as she unabashedly kept her composure under his direct glance, calmly accepting his challenge of stares, he had to up his rating a point further, above any he'd given other women, for audacity.

Unable to resist a challenge for long, Jordan returned to that lady's court. This time he did not hang back but resolvedly pushed his way through the crowd, and came face-to-face with her.

Obviously that was what Nina had been expecting. A small, satisfied smile in her expressive eyes was just beginning around her lips. Next, with great condescension, she touched him lightly with her rose. The velvet touch of the petals on his hand and going up his sleeve was an anointing, an unmistakable signal for him to advance and be acknowledged. But Jordan, glancing down at the flower resting on his sleeve, deliberately shrugged it off.

She looked astonished. But not as much as when he turned his elegant form and walked away, as if he'd seen enough and did not care to put himself to the bother of further exploration!

Heavens! Never had Nina De Bonnard been given a cut direct, and at her own party. Thankfully, none of the young or, worse, older ladies were nigh enough to witness and spread it about. The gentlemen merely saw his departure as creating an opening for them to move closer to their goddess. Only Nina was deeply aware of the insult.

Her offered smile hung on her face, dislodged and banging away like a loose shingle. She could not recollect ever receiving a rejection, let alone such a public one. In her shock, Nina missed a compliment from the left side but turned in time to hear the one from the right.

It took her above half an hour to extricate herself from her followers, and Nina then walked purposely toward her family's summer estate, Sea Cliff. She was almost on a run. Her long white train swept the garden and up the stairs to the veranda. Stopping at the top, she looked back, feeling eyes on her. But Jordan had been quick enough to turn about. Her own group of admirers, of course, was staring after, and she stopped to give them a royal wave.

Pleased with his stratagem, Jordan henceforth deliberately kept his eyes from the lady of the white rose, seeking to blot out her image with views of the scenery: green, smooth carpets of lawns, croquet games, couples strolling, groups sitting under the trees. But the sun was beginning to set. The last surge of brightness at the horizon threw out a golden glaze that outlined the swaying trees and the women walking to and fro. Their long dresses trailed across the tips of the grass, hardly making an indentation, as if they were floating just above it. A pink organdy dress here, a mauve one there, and, farther on, shades of sunset yellows and the softest of sky blues. They were lovely, like phantoms from his past drifting between the now and nostalgia. Only Nina De Bonnard seemed a jolt of the present while he was overcome by the feeling of being out of place—even out of time.

To come back to the present, Jordan adjourned to a table laden with barbecued meats and carved birds and took the heaped-up plate offered by the standing servant. Ignoring the special ladies' table of jellied salads, cucumber sandwiches, and shrimps crouched on mounds of ice chips, he paused at the punch bowl. There were pitchers of iced tea and decanters of mineral water, but he needed something stronger. Spirits, he recalled, were kept in the library in cut-glass decanters for the men to sample along with their cigars—out of sight and censure of their wives. It was just about time for that. He could see many of the gentlemen already heading for the house. Swarms of servants were out on the lawn now, clearing the tables of leftovers. As twilight descended, the ladies were gliding toward the verandas and the comfortable rockers.

Jordan himself, after the needed refreshment in the library, strolled around that porch, which was lit by strings of hanging lanterns flickering through red, white, or blue glass coverings. Like a ship's deck, the veranda extended all around the house. In the back were stairs leading down to the beach, and from there, even through the laughter and soft times, came the hearty sound of the surf, insisting on its part in the moment. He remembered swimming with his friends, some of whom were here, with their unfamiliar older faces but always familiar old stories. His father had gone to his "reward," as his mother was fond of saying, making death seem like one more place for society to gather and continue a life of rewards. Since Jordan had last been in Oceana, the most astonishing change was in his younger brother. He'd left Dickie a child and found him a young man old enough to court. Only his mother was the same. He looked affectionately at her on the back veranda, grouped with all the other matrons, sitting in their high-backed rockers. Suddenly Jordan stiffened, shaken out of his soft memories, for Nina was approaching the same area.

This time she was quick enough to catch him looking and smiled as if he'd taken her white rose, after all. In reaction, he rushed to plunge himself into an all-male standing huddle. More patriotic chatter. Jordan had an overwhelming sensation of déjà vu at the sight of their club ties and striped sport jackets, but the American-flag rosettes in the buttonholes were new. Indeed, American flags abounded on poles and halyards or spread across balconies in yards of bunting. Undoubtedly the frenzy was due to this being the centennial year of 1876 and people feeling, by golly, the nation was one hundred years old and had just come through a war that had split it in half, yet the country had survived and come together. Surely a grand reason to celebrate. Indeed, the denizens of Oceana, New Jersey, were determined to prove their patriotism with every last bit of flag waving at party after party. Being so close to Pennsylvania, the state was flooded with the overflow of excitement for the Centennial Exposition. People were coming from Europe to see the exposition's proud display of the best in America—from its inventions to its people.

Jordan waited through the gentlemen's professions of patriotic fervor, hoping for a natural pause to bring the conversation around to Nina De Bonnard. In the past, with the women safely in their own enclave and the gentlemen's tongues loosened by several trips to the library, one could easily unearth all the scuttlebutt. Yet when Jordan mentioned Nina's name, there was a stiffening. Apparently she was not as notorious as his mother had led him to suppose, but was still protected by the rule that daughters of the wealthy families were never openly discussed. He had committed a faux pas. He grinned at their outrage and smoothly changed the topic to the stock market, which soon had everyone relaxing, satisfied that Jordan was one of them after all.

Meanwhile, Nina was similarly ruffling the feathers of the matrons. The women were circled in their rockers like wagons pulled around, protecting themselves from invaders. Thoughtlessly, she had broken into that formation of female chatter for a personal aside to her mother. Most of the women forgave her interruption on grounds that it was always refreshing to see a daughter seeking her mother's advice. But several ladies, with cause, could not forgive any actions of that young woman. There were too many rumors about her. Nothing proven and nothing anyone was anxious to do more than discuss, in view of the De Bonnards' importance, but still, she was definitely "smoky." Mrs. Windsor risked showing her disapproval plainly by fanning herself agitatedly with her palm circle fan. For Nina was the source of her son's unhappiness, and she could never forgive anyone for wiping out Dickie's usual smile. Mrs. Windsor had looked forward to the social life in Oceana: the parties, the picnics, the card games and the leisure walks, and, most of all, the exchange of gossip with friends. Instead, she had had to suffer Dickie's raptures for Miss De Bonnard and the other women's prophesies of doom and their smugness when Nina acted true to form and switched from her son to someone else. The word *flirt* was freely whispered, but Mrs. Windsor used a stronger term: *jilt*.

Mrs. Windsor was disturbed to note that Mrs. De Bonnard turned in a direction indicated by her daughter's almost imperceptible nod. In that direction, Mrs. Windsor noticed with a jolt, stood both her sons. Of course, Mr. De Bonnard was there as well, but it was scarcely likely that a young lady would interrupt her mother's conversation to ask a question about her father. Familial but far-fetched! Undoubtedly that flirt had some new devilry afoot. At last Mrs. De Bonnard patted her daughter's hand and sent her on her way, turning back to her ladies without a word of apology or explanation, as if they hadn't all been waiting on her convenience. At that signal the conversation recommenced, but Mrs. Windsor could not be easy enough to join in. Rather, she followed Nina with the concentrated eyes of a hawk, hooding them in relief when Nina, unbelievable as it was, approached her father after all.

Thus Mrs. Windsor could devote herself to her favorite pastime: admiring her two sons. Their superiority must be clearly evident to anyone who had eyes to see. Dickie particularly was so exceptional that he deserved a special young lady, not one already tarnished! That little-boy charm Mrs. Windsor found so endearing reminded her of her own late husband. Next her eyes traveled to her elder son, the much-traveled Jordan. He was taller, broader, and certainly imposing, but she never felt happy in his presence. His cool, appraising stare could in no way compete with Dickie's all-conquering, open smile. On the other hand, she was proud to see the gentlemen of his father's generation taking to Jordan. His grandfather, the venerable Marshal Windsor, she knew was eager for Jordan to give up traveling about and sending occasional columns; it was time for him to settle in America and take over directing the entire Windsor newspaper chain. Elvira Windsor concluded that that possibility had both pros and cons. As long as Jordan traveled about, squiring every new European beauty, there was less chance she would lose him. Here, he would probably be caught by some manipulating American matron anxious for her daughter to become a Windsor. No, as much as she missed her boy, she preferred remaining "his best girl," as he had put it just this evening. Satisfied that all was well, Elvira turned back and happily plunged into the invigorating currents of gossip flowing around her.

Too soon. Mrs. Windsor should have kept guard. For in the very next second, Jordan was following Nina with his eyes and even taking steps to keep close to her.

Meanwhile, Nina was running through the information she had gained from her mother. The man who had snubbed her was none other than Dick's brother, Jordan Windsor, the very man every young lady had looked forward to meeting all week, since hearing of his return from his years in Europe. Nina had, as usual, not joined in the general reaction. But then she had a strong reason for wanting to keep away from the Windsors—enough to assure she would never have extended the white rose to him if she had been aware of his identity. Even Dick she had attempted to avoid, but he had pushed himself into her entourage. Her only recourse was tolerating him, very much as she once, as a child, had touched a mouse to prove to the boys on the beach that she was as brave as they. Well, Dick was a very tiny mouse, and yet she could not wait to jilt him. Jordan obviously was an authentic Windsor whom she would not touch even on a dare.

While he'd been a gate-crashing stranger, she'd found him worthy of her notice, Nina acknowledged with a rueful laugh at herself. She'd even been sufficiently disconcerted by his rebuff to blame it on her new white straw hat with the wide forward brim. Had it made her look so severe she'd frightened him off? She had almost removed the offending chapeau on the spot, but she'd restrained herself, remembering that a lady ought not remove any item of her apparel in public, and that included her hat.

Yet Nina mentally took off her hat to fate for protecting her from a shocking lapse in her own instincts. The very last thing she wanted was a relationship with a Windsor.

Eventually the sun began to set, gilding the entire affair. It was now permissible to remove one's hat, and Nina, being private, quickly did so, shaking out her burnished gold curls. Her hair was free, as she was free of that gentleman with the knowing, superior glance. Still, one nagging fear remained: that his rebuff might have been a ploy to whet her interest while he planned to renew his advances. She had to be certain that was not a possibility. Walking as she'd been trained by a score of governesses, straight-backed and with small gliding steps, Nina crossed the veranda toward her father.

Awash in financial news and surrounded by his financial cronies, her father took a moment to remember her. It was too much effort to stray even momentarily from the stock market. He was forever taking its pulse and discussing its symptoms, very much as a new mother would hover over each of her baby's breaths. But now he looked up and guessed correctly first time out: "Nina, child."

Nina-child knew she had to speak quickly to keep his attention. "Father, you were talking to Jordan Windsor. What did he say?"

"Said he didn't think much of the commodities market."

"And . . ."

"Good grasp of the market."

"And?"

"And? Ah, fellow did say something else."

Nina sighed in relief. "I thought as much. Tell me exactly what he said, Father, *exactly*."

With a wide smile, her father said quickly, "Said Tilden's soft money policy is going to give us inflation! How's that for a prediction?"

"Fascinating, Father," Nina concluded, and released her hold on her father's sleeve, turning away. For a passing moment, Mr. De Bonnard was brought to consider that, since his daughter had such interest in the soft money–hard money controversy, mayhap he'd take her for a visit to Wall Street when they returned to New York City. He'd make a note to ask her.

As for Nina, with the test at an end, she felt confident that Jordan was indifferent to her, otherwise he would have used the opportunity while talking to her father to bring the conversation around to her. Obviously Jordan had concluded, after a cursory examination, that she was not up to his standards. Nina had to laugh at herself. How could she be both relieved and disappointed at the same time? Yet she was. Not that there was any question that she could ever be interested in a Windsor; the very possibility had her trembling. But she certainly did not relish being found wanting by a gentleman who'd just returned from Europe where presumably he'd been accustomed to more select fare. Well. That led Nina to a reexamination of her merits, just stopping short of running to a mirror to check if she was still herself. Oh stars, she exclaimed to herself, flushing, she would not be influenced by Mr. Jordan Windsor's assessment. She was what she was. She had done very well for so long without this traveler's seal of approval, and she could continue to do so. Nothing would make her waste another thought on that undiscriminating cad!

"What do you think of Jordan Windsor?"

Rolling her eyes in exasperation, Nina turned. Adele, her younger sister, was agog about this stranger. Nina could never bear to quash Adele's enthusiasms. Nor had she ever successfully done so. It was always best to let them run their course.

"Did you see him!" Adele continued. "Dickie's brother? He *spoke* to me!"

"Really! I'm delighted he can do something beyond standing and staring sightless like a statue."

"Right! He stands over six feet! And you're double right: he looks just like a Greek statue! See, see, he's right next to that column. . . ."

"A hairy Samson ready to knock down the world around us, I expect."

"No! His name is *Jordan*! And he's not hairy! Although up close you can see a suggestion of a mustache—that's so . . . devastating."

Imitating Adele's eager tone, Nina continued, "Look! There's a suggestion of devastating punch dripping from his devastating mustache!"

"Oh Nin! There isn't any—is there?"

Nina laughed. "Not that I can see from this distance."

Adele sighed. "Doesn't any man excite you? Come on, Sis, look at him, closer!"

After allowing herself to be dragged a few steps, Nina reached out for a column to stop her movement. "Adele!" she protested. "I can see reasonably well from here. I don't wish to be pushed under his nose! There's a patio gaslight hissing directly above his head, which as far as I'm concerned is quite an apt comment on the gentleman."

But Adele was too preoccupied with attacking one of the blue bachelor buttons that joined the white and red carnations entwined about the column. All over Sea Cliff, a red, white, and blue motif proudly proclaimed Mr. De Bonnard's Americanism; he'd even ordered a flag-draped Gilbert Charles Stuart painting to be brought from the library and positioned on an easel smack on the stairs' landing, where it was constantly bumped into by the people passing into the house.

"He loves me!" Adele exclaimed after depetaling the accommodating bachelor's button, making one of the characteristic little jumps that went with her enthusiastic conclusions. Her pale blond hair, arranged in two bunches of curls on either side of her head, shook like bells. "But one thing he said is really interesting . . . or should be to you, because it's about you."

Instantly Nina was alert.

"He said"—and she paused dramatically—"he hoped you had *conversation*."

Adele bounced away, leaving Nina to consider once more the truth of Jordan's reaction to her. Did that remark mean she was so disappointing in appearance that at least she should have conversational ability? Or did he mean she looked so perfect that he hoped the image would not be ruined by her conversation? Oh, bother the meaning! Bother men! Almost on a run, Nina turned toward the stairs leading to the beach. She would have preferred walking down there, free at last from the weight of them all—from Bobby Van Reyden's sweaty palms on her naked arms to Michael's droning voice in her ear to Dick's wounded-puppy stare and, most of all, from Jordan's enigmatic gestures and underlying threat.

But almost immediately she stopped herself. Of course she could not walk on the beach by herself. Everyone would imagine she was having an assignation, and she would have to be married before she could blink. That must be prevented at all costs. Nina, at twenty-two and perilously close to being viewed as an old maid, was determined not to wed, despite all the unsubtle questioning of her future plans by her mother's friends. She was just able to restrain herself from saying "I'm planning to join a Wild West show!" That would have surprised them. The newspapers wrote daily of the exploits of Wild Bill Hickok, Buffalo Bill, and Calamity Jane, which fascinated her, as did the description of the freedom of the West. But the moment she'd made any such statement her father would be informed of it, and he was so literal he would start giving her the percentages of financial failure inherent in Wild West shows, and it would take her half a month to convince him she was not really planning a western passage. Nevertheless, if she ever did marry, it would not be to anyone of their set. That would mean sentencing herself to a repetition of her mother's unsatisfactory life—which she, more than anyone else, knew was a sore trial.

Walking back to a deserted section of the back veranda and looking out at the darkening sky, Nina was reliving the day. She had expected it to be the same people and the same remarks and the same disapproval, so she'd been prepared, had her tolerantly unperturbed face in place, till she'd been jolted by the appearance of a stranger. Studying him, Nina found much to like, from his imposing height and physique to his challenging approach. She was even near to approving his air of pride—until it had taken the air out of hers. But her excitement went flat, replaced by alarm, when the stranger's identity was revealed. Whereupon Nina coldly reevaluated everything about him. His height indicated presumption. His close-fit clothes revealed him as an impostor by dressing like a European when he was an American and a Windsor. Even his pride was no longer tolerable but unmasked as a shocking fault, while his snubbing her became the crude act of a cad. Nina fervently wished she could take back that moment when she had extended her white rose, shuddering at how close she'd come to making a connection with him. Apparently, fate had offered her what had seemed a shiny red apple and then, at the last minute, had brought the poisoned side to her lips. Sinking down on the glider-swing, Nina rested her head back, allowing the soft evening air to soothe her alarms.

There was a fragility about Nina that might be missed in view of her outward playfulness but was revealed through sudden gestures: eyes closing to hold in her emotions, a hand clutching into a fist during the most commonplace talk or more likely because of it, and most often, as now, two hands going to her heart to still its restless, quickened beat.

This vulnerability was like an aphrodisiac to the clusters of men, serving to keep them alert for her call for help that would transform them into gallant rescuers setting out on some perilous journey to win her back from the blackness that habitually hovered around her. Yet in contrast was Nina's independence, which assured that no help would be sought till the last vestiges of her own strength had been exhausted. How much more heroic then would the men be in their rescue! How much greater their rewards!

Then, too, there was the intensity in her eyes that held many of the men close, wanting a taste of that intensity—competing to reach it, elbowing away competitors; hanging round, waiting for her weakening, which would signal them to act.

Yet now, suddenly, without waiting for a signal, one of them *was* acting. Coming upon Nina in a posture of vulnerability, he was blatantly going beyond the rules of gentlemanly behavior and shaking the swing-gilder beneath her. Swinging it hard. Harder.

Two

ina's eyes opened, searching for the source of the attack, and saw Dick Windsor. Angrily, she signaled him to stop. He did not.

"Dick, please leave me. I do not wish to be rocked."

"You don't wish to do anything with me anymore," he said mournfully, rocking her again—annoying her, annoying her.

"Stop rocking," she snapped.

Instead he moved her faster. The white rose she had tucked into the side sweep of her hair fell out.

"Stop it! Let me off!"

Dick was laughing, swaying the seat almost off its springs, and furiously Nina jumped off and fell to her knees, tearing her white lace and organdy dress. Dick laughed at her sprawl. The next instant Nina was up and furiously shoving him aside, cutting off his laughter, which ended in a grunt. Yet he held on to her hands while defending his act. Self-justification had been Dick's forte since he was a young lad. He always persuaded himself and others that he was the one aggrieved.

"You've hurt me so much! You smile one minute and the smile goes right to my heart. And then next you frown, and I crash to the ground. Well, now you know how it feels being so shaken up all the time! How do you like it?"

Abruptly, he let her go while Nina was pulling away. That had her toppling back on the swing, where she edged away from him as he sat alongside.

His voice was calmer now, talking as if *he* were the one all along attempting to keep their exchange on a civil level.

"Listen, Nina, try to grasp what I'm feeling. Your face has wiped out all my fun this season. Tennis, sailing, are nothing to me anymore. Just you. Just you and your smile . . . that you give away to everybody else while I watch, waiting just for the edge of one. A smile for Greg and two for Bobby. And several for your group. And—and you do the stupidest things. I know you're planning to go sailing with Bobby when he can't properly handle even a canoe, and he'll probably knock you overboard!"

He waited for Nina to respond to that, but she was still so angry she would not even face him. Assuming that, like his mother, she would immediately forgive and respond to his cajoling, he continued in a more confident tone. "I want to take care of you. Protect you from the other guys—but what can I do if you won't let me? If you even let Rupert bring your punch? You see, I had to trip him. I'll trip anybody you favor, so you'd better make up your mind to take me. It'll be better for both of us if you put me out of my misery and say you'll marry me. No kidding."

Nina attempted again to get to her feet, using the swing's arm to help her. Then finally, standing alongside, Nina turned to Dick and, emulating her mother's cool manner, said, "I thought I had made it clear from the beginning that I would not marry you, Dick Windsor. Face that. I don't belong to you. Remember that. I will accept the attentions and compliments of many other gentlemen kind enough to offer such. Accept that. So don't keep on with these pranks. They and *you* are boring me to . . . to my eyebrows! You have no conversation but what *you* want, what *you* demand—like a child banging a spoon at the table. Well, I never was and never will be interested in *children*!"

With that, and with head high, Nina walked to the side entrance and into her house.

She was in a rage. Why couldn't men who prided themselves on being called gentlemen *act* like gentlemen—especially when alone with a lady? Or did one put on "gentlemanly" airs only in society's presence? At that moment Nina vowed she would never again allow herself to be alone with any of these Oceana gentlemen. Dick Windsor proved how correct she'd been to keep to the safety of groups.

Having had enough socializing, Nina felt she could in all good conscience retire to her room. For this special Independence Day event, Nina had promised her mother that she would not retreat to her room midparty as she had on other occasions when struck by an overwhelming desire for privacy. Often her mother had patiently explained that due to the De Bonnards' position in society, Nina's solitary streak had to be suppressed. The only way for Nina to live up to all her social obligations and still keep some sense of aloneness was to be in a group. She the center of the group, of course, with the gentlemen at an equidistant radius from her. That was her protection. As was seeing the humor in people's behavior, even her own. How amusing that she was regarded as flirtatious because she liked the attentions of her entourage, when in reality the gentlemen liked her because she was sportive enough never to take them seriously. Gentlemen, she knew, had a fear of being taken too seriously and thus having to be called to account. Nina let them practice their gallantries on her until they perfected them prior to graduating to serious young girls who would have no memory of their first gaucheries. Sometimes Nina could predict when a gentleman was prime for dismissal, so she'd begin including a likely young lady in her conversations to speed him on his way.

What Nina could not countenance was her defenses being broached. She kept everyone at bay with an air of unapproachability, and when that failed, she backed them off with playful wit or relevant quotes, most of which went over the heads of her suitors. Principally they asked, as all suitors do, for approval of themselves, their yachts, their tennis strokes, their dancing styles, and she would usually answer ambiguously, "It's just what I expected from you." And since she smiled when she said it, everyone assumed it was a compliment.

Only when these ploys proved insufficient and one of the gentlemen strayed too close did Nina bolt away, overwhelmed by a sensation of being groped, held against her will. A memory would strike out at her, which she would attempt to squelch. That effort showed in the whiteness of her face and in her fixedly focused eyes as she carried on her conversations until a socially acceptable way opened for her to make good her escape.

Nina did not know whether these moments of panic were unique to her. She never would discuss them, knowing when they had begun, and that root occurrence was never to be mentioned to anyone. But after a while Nina talked herself into seeing her panic sensations as distinctive shields that kept her safe and pure. It was always best, she thought, laughing at herself and her fear, to see herself from a positive angle—for there were always enough others to point out her negatives.

But in truth Nina had never been like the other young ladies of Oceana, grouping together to chat and gush in chorus over some eligible young man, in this case Jordan Windsor. She had to be alone to keep guard over the memory of that night when she was thirteen and the closing began. Time grew walls of an increasing thickness about that happening until it seemed as if it had never happened. And Nina gilded the walls and insulated herself with laughter and admiration and compliments. Dick's shaking had rattled some of her composure, more effectively because he was a Windsor. But the one Nina's instincts warned her against was Jordan. In any case, she had done her duty for this party: Even her mother must acknowledge that she'd stayed long enough. Already in the hall, Nina was nearing the back stairs when her heart lurched. Jordan Windsor was coming toward her.

She considered backing out, but she had been seen. Retaliating for his cut direct and refusing to give him a further chance to evaluate her "conversation," Nina swept by him as if he were a servant.

Carrying on his own agenda, Jordan stepped directly into her path.

"Stand aside," she muttered, regretting having to speak first.

Instantly, gallantly, he complied, bowing himself aside. Relieved, Nina walked on, only to be obstructed again at the last moment by his stepping back into her path, so that the impetus of her movement bumped her directly into him. She bounced away from their contact. His eyes were alight with challenge, lacking the slightest bit of respect or deference.

That attitude galled, as did his sending her messages of sensuality with each glance. She blinked away his invasions. This boor was not going to force her into running away. This was her house. She was mistress here.

"Step aside," she repeated more authoritatively, advancing with the pride of her mother's heritage.

Nina De Bonnard was beautiful when serene, as she'd been in the garden, but now, agitated, with her eyes flooded with anger and sending out golden glints, she left Jordan gasping. She was a rare beauty who could be quite a coup for his collection. Generally, capturing a lady was easy enough. The true difficulty was finding one worth capturing. This one, at least, was different from the giggling girls of Oceana. Different from the sophisticated European matrons. Different each time he saw her. At first she caught his interest by her unapproachability in the midst of her crowd. Proud. Silent. Determined. Admirable qualities. Then she turned and became the blatant flirt his mother had claimed her to be, extending her white rose in his direction. That disappointed him, and he punished her for it, until she once more did the unexpected by turning away from her admirers, as if bored with the entire game. And now Jordan came face-to-face with still another Nina.

How many personas did the lady have? Determined to unmask her, he whispered with a jesting tone, "Still smarting at my refusing your white flower? Never mind, not everyone is perspicacious enough to see the obviousness of that ploy."

"Is boorishness a Windsor trait?" she snapped, and then, making her complaint clearer yet, "Two of you are too much for one evening!"

Jordan frowned. What had the young ass done? It certainly put a crimp in his style to be linked to his brother. Nevertheless, it also roused his protective instinct, prompting him to change his light response to a blunter sarcasm: "Shocking, how some gentleman go beyond the line. Unless of course the line is deliberately, provocatively, moved to tempt a crossing?"

"And what would you call lurking in a back hall to waylay an unsuspecting young lady in order to *bump* her?" Nina retorted. "Not what one would expect from a world traveler. More the act of a callow, inexperienced youth. You Windsors are all alike."

Flabbergasted by the image of self revealed in the mirror she held up to him, Jordan paused. Confound, she was correct. Assuming that everyone in Oceana would respond only to the least subtle tactics, he had not put himself out and been properly called on it. For the first time in a decade, Jordan felt himself as callow as when he'd left Oceana. Grudgingly, he admired Miss De Bonnard's home thrust. She'd found a soft spot and neatly pinked him there. Sportsmanlike, he inclined his head, giving her the point.

Refusing to carry on their duel, Nina waved him away from her path. Instead Jordan reached for that imperious hand in midmotion, and held on. Rule one for enjoying a dalliance with a young lady was having her stay put. He had to keep her before him, in her place—close and captive.

Unlike the other young women, who usually either blushed or flushed at this unexpected liberty, Nina turned white with panic at his closing in. It seemed impossible that such a sought-after coquette would genuinely feel as terrified as she looked at a mere gallantry. What shabby pretense, he felt, thinking less of her, especially when she cried out, "Unhand me!"

That had him breaking out in loud laughter, and helpfully adding, "You forgot to add 'knave.' Isn't that what ladies say in the stage melodramas? But knaves, you know, take any advantage. As perhaps I am intending to do." When Nina did not respond, Jordan considerately supplied her lines, even mimicking a lady's outraged voice: " 'Why can't gentlemen learn to keep their distance? What has Oceana come to, when a stranger, without even an introduction, makes so bold as to touch one's sacred person!' "

His laughing and foolery began to revive Nina, who was finally seeing him as just another admirer, but one who had twice insulted her. Not forgetting his remark that he hoped she had "conversation," Nina decided to give him a healthy dose of it.

"How prophetic of you to become adept at carrying on a conversation with yourself. That way you will always have someone to speak to when your ruffian manners cut you out of society."

And she cut him in retaliation, as thoroughly and pointedly as he had turned away from her. But Jordan moved swiftly after and took hold of her hand once again, whispering, "That simply raises the stakes, my dear lady. I'll see you and call you." And, bowing over the hand, he raised it to his lips, anointing it with several swift soft kisses, teasing, testing.

"I gather you are figuratively suing for my hand," Nina said, coldly attempting to disengage her hand from his, "but I decline."

"You jump to hopeful conclusions—exaggerating an accepted bit of byplay. I have kissed every matron's hand this evening. 'Tis my European training at fault, I fear. A helpful hint: Don't take everything so *personally*. One might suspect you of spending most of your time admiring yourself in your mirror."

"Gentlemen's eyes are my mirrors," Nina countered, "and I expect I have read yours correctly. You've been out of this country too long. American men don't need to cloak themselves with disclaimers. They're honest enough about their feelings to be direct!"

"Regrettably, I don't do direct," he said with a smile, not intimidated by her charge. "There are more subtle ways of getting what one wants—it all depends if the lady is worth the effort. Forgive me, I'm accustomed to European ladies, mistresses of repartee, who would shudder at the bluntness you demand. Possibly, I mistook your depth."

Eyes flashing at another of his charges that she was not up to his cosmopolitan level, she whispered, "Why don't you adjourn to a private room where the staff can supply you with pen, ink, and stationery to write down all these bon mots you seem so axious to impress upon me and mail them to the European ladies who might not be so direct as to tell you how predictable you are."

"I don't do predictable either," he responded, still grinning, apparently unquenchable. "And as for your suggestion, I heartily endorse it with a minor adjustment. Let us *both* adjourn to a private room where we could enjoy ourselves hugely without saying a single word."

"And I adjust your adjustment by endorsing part of your suggestion. Let's adjourn without saying a single other word to each other. There's nothing I'd enjoy more than leaving you . . . speechless." And, turning on her heel, Nina lightly ran up the stairs, pretending not to see that, although speechless as she'd requested, he was still communicating by throwing her blown kisses. On the landing she once more could not resist a momentary glance down, only to find him still standing there, watching her, satisfied that she'd looked back. Her hand was near a potted plant on the wide railing, and she had a sudden impulse to shove it over and down onto his upturned, grinning face.

Instantly reading her mind, he made an exaggerated lurch backwards, and laughed aloud while she stormed off toward her room. "Insufferable fool!" she muttered, hoping his ears were as sharp as his eyes.

Three

*D*ick had returned to the punch bowl, smarting under Nina's words. A bit of regret was beginning to penetrate through the blinders of his injured feelings. His mother and brother would probably be ashamed of his behavior. He hoped Nina would not confide her annoyance to her mother, who would probably tell his mother. But he did not think she would. She was basically a game gal.

Bobby was there with several others of Nina's court. Between gulps of punch, he was mouthing away about a game he'd played earlier that afternoon with Nina, describing in detail the beauty of her body in motion during the tennis match. And Dick felt a flash of heat, jealous again, especially when he remembered his own tennis match with Nina on the previous day.

He had disgraced himself. So absorbed had he been watching her body in motion—she always put more of herself into physical actions than most women—he had forgotten to watch the ball. Or so he told himself. Of course she had a good serve, but he could never return it because of the distraction of the pull of the material against her breasts when she lifted her arm to toss the ball above her head. She was rather a good player—for a girl. To be honest, she always beat him. The worst part was that Nina enjoyed the win instead of apologizing for it or modestly claiming the luck had gone her way, as all other women would. Hang it, she even jumped up and down, exclaiming "I've won, I've won!" so people in the next court knew the results—which was mighty inconsiderate of her. At the end she'd untwirled the long silk scarf worn wrapped around her hair during the game and flung it out into the air, like a banner to herself and her victory. And even then, instead of being annoyed, he sat down on the court and watched her leap around . . . and enjoyed that more than the entire contest.

Oh yes, he was obsessed with her! And she'd never even let him kiss her: not one for victory, not one for defeat.

So, still stinging from Nina's rejection, he was doubly galled to overhear Bobby claiming that Nina had kissed him that afternoon for his record of ten aces. The only way the entire night's humiliation could be eased would be by punching Bobby's gloating face. Walking up hurriedly and refusing, gentleman that he was, to bring up Nina's name, Dick said coldly, "You serve like a woman, Bobby. Your wrists are . . . limp."

On cue, Bobby took offense. A few "Oh is that so's!" and one "Oh wipe the gum off your lip!" further exacerbated the level of antagonism. Dick pulled it one notch tighter by pushing Bobby away from him. Bobby pushed back. That graduated into each throwing a punch. But almost instantly Jordan was there, stepping between them.

To cool off his brother, he led him down to the beach and threw some water into Dick's red face. And then both were quiet as they sat down on the wet sand, waiting each other out.

Dick broke first, covering his face with his hands and moaning, "I'm so unhappy!"

"It's just a fight. Bobby will—"

"No, not that. It's her. Nina. I was planning to tell her I loved her . . . to ask her to marry me, and while planning it I was so sure she'd say yes. I mean, confound her, we're rich, not like her family, but close, and all the other gals have liked me—a lot. And besides, why can't she understand, I *want* her? But . . . she said, she said . . . *no*. And she said I was . . ." He choked the insult back, unable to let it out.

"You were . . . ?" his brother gently urged.

"I was . . . boring."

A smile twitched on his brother's face. *"No!"* he protested. "Well, how do you like that! I wouldn't say you're boring, kid. Sometimes I find you a bother. Unnerving, annoying, even mad-

25

dening. But boring? No. Why look how you brought the De Bonnards' insipid party to life! . . . Childish, maybe," he acknowledged after a pause.

Jordan was having trouble not chuckling, and when his brother looked up and said "Oh, she said *childish* too," he had to cough back his laugh.

"Well, that's something you're bound to outgrow, isn't it?"

"I can't grow without her. I don't want to grow another day," Dick threatened, and his voice shook and broke. Then, abruptly, before his brother could guess his course, he'd plunged into the ocean. Jordan dove in after. He caught up in a few strokes and fought to get Dick to turn back to shore. Fortunately, Dick was not as tenacious as his brother—even with the emotion of this attempt. Relentlessly Jordan was pulling, pulling, till both were back in the breakers and onshore. There, wet and wrung out, side by side, they rested on the damp sand.

Still angry with his brother's attempt, Jordan pounded Dick on the back harder than was necessary. And then they both lay out flat on the sand.

Jordan resented more than the dousing of himself, the dousing of his watch, and he was trying to dry it, keep a check on his brother against any further moves toward the ocean, and figure out how to get him home without anyone seeing them, when Dick made another sudden move. This time, he folded up into a ball and cried in deep, heavy gulps, as he had when hurt as a child. "Fix it, Jordie," he whispered.

It reached Jordan. He had been years away from home and come back to find his brother grown up. So he thought. Yet underneath, Dick was still the kid who had trailed him everywhere he went, who'd been his ball boy at tennis matches, crewed his rowing outings, waved good-bye at the docks, and seven years later was the first one there to bear-hug him on his return. Throughout the party Jordan had had a strange suspended feeling, as if everyone were coming toward him with bits of the past in their hands, using them as claim checks for his attention.

"I'd like to fix it if I could, fella, you know it. But how do I make a lady love you if she doesn't?"

"She would. She would!" Dick said earnestly. "If she'd just get off her high horse long enough to see how much I need her. But she can't because there's always another guy ready to throw himself at her feet. So she never has even a chance to see what she does to a guy when she walks away. 'Cause"—Dick breathed deeply—"she never looks back. And, hang it, I would like to make her look back. If only someone would make her know how it feels to be dropped. . . ."

Whereupon Dick dropped his head into his hands till a quiet whisper from his brother shot his head up in a snap.

"Now *that* I can do for you," Jordan was promising softly.

Fixated by Jordan's serious face, Dick said wonderingly, beginning to smile, "Yeah, you can! You can make her love you—easy! It's a great idea. And then you'll drop her and . . . she'll come back to me. I'll tell her I understand how she feels 'cause that's how I felt when she dropped me—and, and we'll have something in common!"

Dick was up on his feet, collecting his wits, which was not very difficult since he did not have an overwhelming quantity of them, describing Nina's inevitable speech of contrition and his own gallant reply.

Meanwhile, Jordan was musing over that lady himself, remembering the haughty lift of her head when she walked around her estate, remembering the pleasure of their verbal duel, remembering the glow of her eyes as he held her hand, remembering the life in her—so different from the pale, placid Oceana contentment—remembering her walking up the stairs and looking down as if she would toss a plant on him. He grinned at all those memories and felt a growing stimulation at the thought of further combat with the lady. He had been planning an immediate departure, but Nina had already given him some second thoughts as to how immediate that would be. Now Jordan had a perfect excuse, say rather a noble excuse, for remaining the summer at Oceana—not that it would take that long.

Dickie interrupted his brother's musing with his own. He had just culminated his fancies with his wedding to Nina and was inviting Jordan to be best man, thanking him for bringing it about. "I knew things would go great the moment you came home. You won't be sorry. I know it'll be boring for a sophisticate like you to hang around all of us here, and don't think I don't appreciate it."

"Not at all, dear boy. Actually, I expect teaching that proud miss some humility will not be without some . . . benefits."

"It's a pact, then!" Dick enthused, hurrahing and shaking Jordan's hand vigorously as his brother rose lazily from the sand. And once more Dick gave his brother a vigorous pump for the sheer joy he felt that Jordan was taking this problem in hand.

"Rather an immoral pact." Jordan grinned ruefully. "But yes, a pact."

"What's your plan?" Dick asked anxiously, wiping away the water dripping from his hair. "Will you tell her you're in love with her right away, like I did? Or will you do it Bobby's way, by sending her a roomful of flowers?"

Jordan's smile broadened. "Hardly. I imagine Miss De Bonnard is surfeited with those tactics. I shall have to invent new ones, I expect. Definitely this requires a more subtle approach."

"Aw come on, Jordie, give a fella a hint. I want to be picturing it tonight when I can't sleep again. Just *some* of what you're planning?"

The two brothers began to walk down the beach past the other mansions, toward their own beachfront estate, which lay ahead. They heard the cannon sound. And for a moment Jordan felt they were the target, but his brother explained it was Mr. De Bonnard's salute to July Fourth.

"Rather premature."

"This whole summer's a celebration, with the centennial and all," Dick explained, and was tempted to discuss the exhibition but did not want to distract his brother from planning a strategy against Nina, and once more urged him to give the particulars of his scheme. Jordan finally obliged.

"I see a concentrated, unanswerable, unstoppable campaign ahead for her affections that will leave her breathless. The first step will be to inundate her with love tokens and poems. Fitzgerald's *Rubaiyat* is the vogue in London. Pagan thoughts always appeal to the young. Yes, I'll start with, 'Yet ah, that spring should vanish with the rose, that youth's sweet-scented manuscript should close.' And then go on with the racier quatrains. That should make a good entrée. But the pièce de résistance shall be dazzling her with talk of my own exploits—expurgated, naturally, to be suitable for a young girl's ears."

Dick was confused. He was, as he liked to say, a simple and straightforward guy. There was nothing circuitous about either his thinking or his conversation; therefore, he expected everybody to act and think as he did. On the other hand, his brother's remarks often seemed simple and straightforward but were accompanied by an undercurrent that had him suspecting a trick hinge between phrases that would turn them into something else.

Meanwhile, Jordan was growing more and more enthusiastic. "We'll omit serenading, due to my voice, but short of that, everything will be included. You suggested flowers, and eventually they too will play their part—yes, bouquets upon bouquets of pale yellow roses to match her pale hair. Yes, by God, not a single obvious, tawdry, clichéd act of gallantry and affection shall be omitted!"

"Great . . . great," his brother said, hesitantly. "Except you made a mistake. Her hair's not pale yellow. You said 'pale roses' to match her hair. Listen, Jordie, you haven't confused Nina with some other girl?"

"Oh, didn't I explain? I intend to reach her by an indirect method: through *her sister*, the pale-haired one."

"No!" Dick objected. "I mean, gosh, Adele's a sweet kid, but she's only seventeen years old. Three years younger than me and over ten years younger than you! We don't want to get her involved. Besides, I don't understand how that'll help—"

"Elementary," Jordan said smoothly, slowly smiling in anticipation. "Indifference is the only way to win a young lady overfed and overaccustomed to attentions. I'm going to make her positively ache to be Adele . . . to want to dim the blaze of her hair and step into her younger sister's shoes. I'll make her feel old and unwanted . . . and, most of all, 'passed over.' And just when she can't stand it a minute longer, I'll switch to her. And, presto! She'll sink gratefully into my arms. And not only will she have learned what it means to be jealous, but how irresponsible it is for her to switch from one gentleman to another."

"Yeah, like she's switched from me to Bobby and broke up our friendship. Right. Right. That's perfect. But . . . I just thought. . . ." Dick frowned at an unexpected wrinkle he'd discovered in the plan his brother was stretching out before him. "After you've won her, you're not going to . . . take advantage, and kiss her and such?"

Jordan tried to hide his amazement at that caveat. "Oh perhaps a few casual kisses for the sweet young miss would not be amiss—strictly brotherly," he assured with a grin. And Dick was appeased.

"And then?" Dick prodded.

"And then, I shall hop off back to Europe, where I shall say my fiancée is waiting for me. How's that for total humiliation?"

"Ahh!" his brother answered, closing his eyes and seeing it all as if it had already happened and justice had been served. They had reached their own beach entrance and turned to look back at the sprawling ship of the De Bonnard estate, which dominated the view even from this distance. It was still aglow with lights and activity. Both Windsors were concentrating on the second floor, where only one window was lit up, and both were thinking it was Nina in there, waiting for them and their plan.

"You don't think anything can go wrong?" Dick asked nervously, just imagining Nina's accusing eyes, but his brother was all confidence.

"Trust me," he whispered. "The plan is foolproof. I simply cannot imagine anything that could happen to prevent my . . . eh, *your* perfect revenge."

four

*N*ina woke early the next morning when most of Oceana was still asleep. She liked beating everyone to the day. She dressed in a simple white organdy blouse and blue cotton skirt that was slightly shorter than her usual skirts. In fact, the hem ended at her ankles, which would never do if she were to be seen by anyone, for ankles were clearly points of a lady's body that excited gentlemen to a state of ambling after. Yet this shorter skirt let her walk with wider strides without having to worry about tripping over her hem. She donned it when she went on her morning walks or her escapes to her doll house across the many lawns. She also failed to dress her hair, letting it hang wildly about her face and down her back, just as it fell after she hurriedly brushed out the night's tangles. Oh bother, she thought when she remembered that a lady of her age would not appear without her hair neatly pinned up in a variety of buns, looking more like a hat than the free fall of natural hair. At the last moment, she was circumspect enough to take along a leghorn straw hat. That would disguise her hair somewhat and also protect her skin from the untoward advances of the sun.

Not that the sun was up yet. She was even ahead of nature.

Of a sudden Nina had a desire to see the morning ocean, and instead of walking across the tended lawns, she skipped around the veranda to the back steps that led down to the shore.

Taking a long breath of sea air, Nina ran along the ocean's edge. She lost her hat. To retrieve it, she stepped into the surf, wetting her laced-up shoes. The morning breeze played with her golden-red curls and made them a wilder tousle. Her usually pale skin was flushed with exercise and the joy of abandoning her senses to the moment. As the morning light split the ocean's skin, Nina stood motionless, watching the rays gilding the ocean. The peace and beauty washed her clean of many of yesterday's hurts, starting from a barrage of disapproving looks from Mrs. Windsor to the other matrons, young and old, who had unleashed a bombardment of catty remarks about her not being married that she'd pretended not to hear. But even if she'd been deaf she would have sensed the general enmity. It telegraphed itself from eyes, pursed lips, averted heads, and it struck Nina in the heart. Usually the men's praises protected her from major bruising, but yesterday the men too had been hostile. Witness Dickie practically tossing her off the swing, and, worse, the exalted Mr. Jordan Windsor and his needling messages transmitted by the lift of an eyebrow and the hint of a smile.

The sun was stretching, rising, reminding Nina that her family would soon be up. She had to rush home to dress in her social uniform with ankles completely hidden, hair up and confiningly coiffed, face immobile, and body moving in proper ministeps. Just a few more moments of naturalness remained, and Nina used them to scoop up some seashells, including one find that looked just like a bird in flight. She pocketed them and walked up toward the dunes, where she plucked a tall grass weed with a feathery brown head and used it as a conductor's wand, signaling the crescendo of her morning symphony. The ocean obliged. Nina smiled, satisfied, and, swinging her stalk, hurried back to Sea Cliff's lawns.

A gentleman stepped back behind the rickety wooden steps that led down to the jetty. He'd come here to search for the fob he'd worn on his vest yesterday, assuming he'd lost it when he'd gone after Dick into the sea. Since it was one of his favorite ornamental fobs, made of ivory and hand-carved into the shape of a bird in flight, he'd come back to this beach on the chance it had fallen where he and Dick had sat sealing their pact.

It was ironic, he thought with a grin, that he found, instead, the object of the pact. Nina De Bonnard. He'd stayed back, watching her response to the sun: raising her arms high to the sky, as if in morning worship. When she walked on, he noted with interest her exposed ankles. Well turned, the connoisseur in him decided.

He'd been somewhat regretting that foolish pact with his brother, but seeing its target this morning goaded him to heightened anticipation. Miss De Bonnard's early morning escape attested to her squirming at society's confinement, needing just a nudge to break free. He was, he acknowledged with a twinkle in his eyes, rather a good nudger. He'd pushed many a lady over the brink and enjoyed the benefits of each fall.

The thought of Nina's fall had Jordan smiling broadly. She was clearly a lady chafing at the conventions. It was his duty to turn her loose. And if subsequently she became a loose woman, well, that was her concern. Forgetting his fob, the elegant Jordan, who had not stopped to don the proper morning outfit, rushed home to dress correctly for the courting ahead.

Approaching her mansion, Nina stopped short, for the gardeners were out, getting an early start on returning the lawn to some semblance of order after yesterday's trampling by the guests. Recollecting propriety, she quickly put on her hat. Oh stars! Standing at the door was the housekeeper, Mrs. Wrenfield, who, true to her name, never stopped chirping. That constant flow of talk would ruin the purity of the morning. Making a wide turn, Nina evaded her and the gardeners by cutting through the bushes, then sprinted across the lawns to the wooded end of her father's property, where her own private little cottage was waiting for her. It had been built when she was ten years old as a doll house to hold her collection of porcelain-faced, snooty dolls. Same faces, just different hair colors, and they wore a variety of dresses, of course. Nina was always given dolls, despite being quite vocal about not caring for them. Except one doll, which was broken and which Nina herself had patched up and still kept in her room in Sea Cliff, closed up in a wooden chest with its china blue eyes staring, waiting for the rare removal and sneaky hug. The rest of the doll collection had been given away or relegated to the doll house's dusty shelves, where the majority had been attacked by the family of cats she'd moved in later. Then the cats had wandered off all over the property, forming attachments with others, mostly Adele. Her sister had won them all, except for Spooky, Nina's favorite, who showed his mixed breeding by having mixed loyalties.

Entering the one-room house, Nina fell into the usual coughing it brought on, being stuffy and dusty from neglect. Actually, most of this young lady's possessions were neglected for periods of time. Running around opening windows and shaking out dust-covered pillows, Nina reclaimed her place. It was in here she'd discovered how tall she'd grown when she stretched and found her fingers touching the ceiling that had once seemed way above her. A lesson for life, she'd thought with a grin. One always outgrew things.

No gentleman had ever come to this special hideaway. . . . Strike that, except for Bobby Van Reyden, who had once followed her and barged in, getting a much-deserved bloody gash on his forehead. She'd shown him not an ounce of pity, for this was her private domain where Nina sought solace from society's barbs or gentlemen's barbarisms. This morning she also came to deal with a past memory that had newly erupted and once more needed to be faced down. With a set expression she did so by heading toward the small closet for the model of her father's yacht, the *Nina*. It had been a cherished gift when she was eleven years old, proudly displayed on the cottage's small marble mantelpiece until her thirteenth birthday, when it had been hurriedly removed and hidden in the closet. Her love of that yacht had started it all. Not only was the *Nina* named for her, but her father had promised the yacht would be hers when she was older. Clearly carte blanche, Nina had assumed, to slip aboard anytime, and become acquainted with the crew, pretending she was captain, and when her father wasn't around, she proudly wore his captain's hat.

For her thirteenth birthday when asked what gift she most wanted, Nina had promptly claimed the fulfillment of her father's promise of an overnight cruise on the *Nina*. It was astonishing to the little girl that her wish was denied. "Next week," her father promised, evading with a dismissing smile. But it was her birthday *this* week, she attempted to explain. Yet no one else saw the importance of its being that night. To Nina it was necessary because she was entering her teens and she wanted something very grown-up to mark this threshold. But she bravely put on the best face possible for the child's party her mother had arranged. Afterwards, she gave away most of the gifts to Adele, who always wanted whatever Nina was given. Then when everyone had left and Adele and Mrs. De Bonnard had retired for the night, Nina sneaked out. Camouflaging her identity in the cook's large-sized blue cloak and hood, she made it to the dock undetected. If everyone else failed her, she would not fail herself, Nina swore, promising herself a few hours on the anchored yacht—planning to be back before she could be missed. The moment after twelve struck, when it was no longer her birthday, she would head for home.

Approaching the yacht's berth, Nina realized even from a distance that her plan had failed. There was activity on the *Nina*. Clearly it was being readied for a cruise. The hanging lanterns were flickering on the deck and the sailors were carrying on loads of provisions. Nina was hurt. It was one thing if her father had a business appointment elsewhere, but if he was going cruising on the *Nina* on her very birthday night, why not take her along? Unless . . . yes! Almost jumping with excitement, Nina was struck by a wonderful possibility. What if her father was preparing a party for her? Possibly he had planned to send a crewman to Sea Cliff with a note inviting her and then he and his friends would jump out and yell "Surprise!" She was visualizing the scene with delight until reality struck that there hadn't been a note and it was too late to send one. Not only wasn't she going to be the guest of honor at this party, but she wasn't wanted there. Attempting to stop her lips from trembling, Nina accepted that her father was having his own private party with strangers.

Beginning to turn away, Nina stopped. No, she could not just leave without some attempt. Often Nina had been able to distract her father from his business affairs; she could do it again. So Nina made her fateful decision to make a surprise entrance at the party.

Waiting for the correct moment when the sailors were occupied or below deck, Nina climbed up the gangplank unobserved. Voices were coming from the main lounge and she turned toward them. At the last minute, just about to make her surprise jump into the party's midst, Nina had second thoughts. Perhaps a private appearance before her father might be more advisable. Nina hurriedly retreated when the couples began exiting and making their way toward the cabins. Only one gentleman was left in the lounge, and he was not her father. Nevertheless, something about him was familiar, if she could just see his face more clearly. The man was sprawled on the sofa, singing to himself. Odd. When he stood up, weaving his way to the bar again, she recognized Mrs. Windsor's husband and Dickie's father, Otis Windsor the Third. He was the one who always pinched her cheek and tried to take her on his lap. Yes, the one she always squirmed away from, giving him a wide berth, which she did that night as well, stepping away and setting her course for her father's cabin when she felt a jolt and realized the *Nina* was upping anchor.

Oh stars! Nina said with a private giggle, she was going to have a night cruise, after all. Having put herself in this position, she would do what her father had always taught her to do: tough it out. She was cold and hungry. She wanted to be given something hot to drink and be cuddled in a comforter. Her father would supply both; he always forgave her surprise acts, admiring the brashness that he often claimed she'd inherited from him. It would be fine. She must be bold. Removing the borrowed cape, Nina stood in her thin party dress, ready to make an entrance into his cabin, when a steward approached. Quickly Nina hid. Better wait to reveal herself after the servant had left, she decided. Balancing a tray on one hand, the steward gave a discreet knock. When the door opened, her father was there in the lighted entrance and Nina's mouth opened as well. Mr. De Bonnard was in a state of undress. Even in his bathing suit he'd been more decently attired. Now his chest was bare, and a towel substituted for trousers. He must have been showering, Nina concluded and averted her glance. She was scarlet with humiliation, thinking how her father would feel if he knew she had seen him in such shocking undress. Delicately, keeping her eyes away, Nina waited until he had time to make himself presentable by donning a robe. A second steward arrived, bringing champagne. Unconsciously Nina's eyes followed and saw her father still in just a towel. Even more astonishing was his next action. He turned and offered a glass to someone behind him. That someone laughed. It was a woman's laugh. Next moment the laughing woman appeared next to Mr. De Bonnard, and Nina noted she was also in a state of dishabille, wearing a bright red nightdress in a very thin, see-through material. She leaned against Mr. De Bonnard and whispered something that had him laughing. Never had Nina heard him laugh so softly. He did it again. The two stewards left and the door closed, but from behind the door Nina could still hear the laughter, joined and then abruptly cut off.

Nina retreated. Too appalled to know what to do next, she pressed her fist to her mouth so as not to cry out and then involuntarily began running, just wanting to be off the boat. Off! *Now*—before she could see anything else. But next moment, as she passed the lounge, it was she who was seen, grabbed and pulled within.

It was Mr. Windsor.

He was holding her against her will. In her panic, Nina nearly cried out for her father but couldn't bring herself to encounter him again in his state of undress. Her father, who had always been her special protector, was now "that naked man." No longer was she red just from embarrassment but from anger as well. All the images of her father—teaching her to ride, giving her his captain's hat to wear, taking her to the New York Opera House, escorting her here, there, both so proud—were wiped out. All their past moments were made lewd by the view of him nude and holding an almost nude woman.

Mr. Otis Windsor was talking to her and Nina was brought back to her own more present threat. Bravely, Nina gauged her enemy, the full hulking height of him. His open smiling mouth inches from her. His large sweaty hands on her. Despite the odds, she decided the only course was taking command. "Take your hands off me, sir!" she ordered firmly.

"Call me Otis, little girlie. Otie, if you like." His slobbering smile was coming close again. He kept calling her "girlie," which meant he had not recognized her as Nina De Bonnard. That was good and bad. For while he could not report back to her mother without knowing who she was, his not knowing who she was eliminated the protection of who she was. "What a beauty," he dribbled in a slurred voice. The whiskey smell of him had her grimacing. "Let *go*!" she insisted.

"Right! Let's go to my cabin, pretty little thing!"

Nina squirmed, fighting to slip out of his grasp, but his hands were moving up to her shoulders and down to her chest, where he grabbed onto her budding breasts and squeezed.

"You're hurting! And you smell!" she cried out.

Mr. Jordan stepped back, astounded.

"Now that's no way to speak to the gentleman who is going to give you such a grand time," he whispered and stuck his mouth over hers like a wet rag that had Nina gagging. Fear gave her the added strength she needed, enough to push him away. But his passion gave him a fierceness that had him groping for her again. She picked up one of the sofa-decorating pillows and held it between them as a barrier. He walked right into the pillow and squeezed both it and her in his large embrace. At that moment, with the pillow in her face, an irrelevant thought pierced through her panic: How her mother had been particular about finding the correct lilac color for the pillows to match the salon's motif. Her mother always wanted everything to be correct, persevering until it was so. Nina admired that in her mother. She admired her mother and wished she were there . . . so much so that Nina began calling for her.

The cry of "Mama! Mama!" surprised Mr. Windsor. He dropped away, looking behind him in alarm. Nina was free. When he fumbled for her again, Nina with new confidence hit him with the name of another woman. "I know *Mrs. Windsor*! If you touch me, I'll tell *your wife*!"

That was enough to petrify Otis Windsor so completely that Nina could almost have walked away, but she did not. She ran. Ran.

five

In a blink she was at the stern of the boat looking down. They had moved, but the *Nina* was still within sight of the dock, although it was swiftly getting farther away. Having always been proud of her swimming, Nina had no fear of the distance, but something warned that swimming might be difficult in such darkness. Moreover, Nina was still trembling, not as yet recovered from the man's hands on her. That was all mixed up with the view she'd had of her father. Yet those sights became goads to be gone, and, closing her mouth, Nina jumped.

It was July but the water was cold, seeping in icy splashes though her eyelet dress to her skin. To warm herself she began vigorously swimming, not worrying about the splashes bringing attention, just wanting to get to shore. Her arms were feeling leaden. Nina lifted her head to check how close she had come to the dock, and was disappointed to note she'd hardly made any progress. She swam faster not to freeze. Swimming. Swimming. The waves joined her father and Mr. Windsor in attacking her. The salt water was flooding her eyes, stinging her sight.

She was losing direction. In desperation, since it had worked once, Nina tried it again, "Mama!" This time the only one to hear her call was herself, but still it helped, reminding her of Mrs. De Bonnard's constant evaluation: "You are my daughter, Nina, dear. You can handle anything to perfection."

Yes, she was her mother's daughter. She felt a strengthening. Floated briefly to get her breath. Then she concentrated on counting her strokes. Looking up, Nina saw the moon forming its rays into a long line, like a silver finger pointing toward the shore. She followed it to the surf. She was on the sand.

Nina rested for several minutes. She had missed the dock and come out on a side beach. But that was a bonus because there was less chance she would be observed from there. Moreover, it was closer to her estate; she could walk through the sand fronts and short-cut her way to her own beach area. At the private stairs leading up to Sea Cliff, Nina reconsidered. She could not enter her home so wet and looking such a fright. Any servant awake would report her to her mother first thing, and what explanation could Nina give? The only safety was her cottage. Exhausted, pushing herself the last steps across the lawns to the woods, Nina reached the cottage and fell across the chintz sofa. Alone and unobserved, she began to cry.

For the rest of the night, Nina hid in there, reliving everything that had happened. She overcame the cold by covering herself with the knitted afghan, but the icy images of her father and Mr. Windsor would not go away. They hovered over her. She pushed them off. She could not come to grips with them. She ached to talk about them to her mother and at the same time knew she could never hurt her mother by mentioning any part of her birthday night. It was a dirty little secret. Since she'd been part of it— by being groped by her father's friend—she'd become as shameful as her father. Both of them had let her mother down. The only way to live with that secret, she concluded after a night of agonizing, was to bury it here in the cottage. Symbolically she removed the model of the *Nina* from above the mantel and shoved it in the closet, slamming the door shut. Hidden. Forever.

Only then could she go back to Sea Cliff and to her room to bathe herself clean. For the rest of that summer so perfectly did Nina dissemble that the only change evident to her mother and father was that she no longer had an interest in sailing—that had ended that night. Otherwise Nina was the same, except perhaps less of a hoyden, which pleased Mrs. De Bonnard. Rather than running around and enjoying nature, Nina was discovering the joys of studying alone in her room. Mrs. De Bonnard was a reader herself and naturally approved of her daughter's taking after her. But Nina went her mother one better by developing a taste for writing. In a blink her little Nina was filling up diary after diary.

"But what do you find to write about?" her mother asked in amusement. "Before, when you were active all day, you never wrote a line. Now when all you're doing is sitting at your desk, you've written volumes!"

"It was stored up," Nina said calmly.

Her mother laughed at that. "Apparently so." As tokens of her approval, Mrs. De Bonnard gave her daughter the collection of novels she had enjoyed when growing up: Jane Austen, Fanny Burney, even gothics by Radcliffe, and the poetry collections of Byron and Shelley, and, of course, Shakespeare.

Nina still had those books, as well as her diary volumes, in the steamer trunk in the cottage. The diaries were pushed down by more recent editions, for Nina continued faithfully to record her daily events. When Nina entered her later teens, Mrs. De Bonnard insisted that her daughter come out of her retreat and join society again. Nina's solution: to take her solitude with her, like a protective shield, hiding in a crowd of gentlemen. That kept her self content and her mother pleased at her daughter's becoming such a sought-after young lady. To attest to that popularity, Nina had piles of dance cards also stored in the several souvenir trunks at the cottage.

Each bunch was tied with a different color ribbon for the different years. But Nina had forgotten the key to that color-code and had to look at the cards themselves. Usually a name would clue her in to which year was represented. Spotting Whit Walker's signature, Nina remembered that she and Whit had shared quite a passion, but it was for horses rather than each other.

Whit had gone on to Maryland and become part of that hunting set. She would have forgotten him completely except that he still sent her notes twice a year—on the anniversary of their engagement and on the anniversary of the breaking off of their engagement. Generally the letters had cartoon drawings of two horses nuzzling, under which were different captions. The last was *Please don't keep being a neigh sayer.* Nina looked at it and laughed, as she always did. These little reminders kept Whit in mind longer than her other fiancés.

Her more serious engagements from nineteen to twenty-one had left behind three elaborate diamond rings in a velvet box. She opened that and put on all three diamond rings at once, on different fingers, of course. The oval represented Torence Wilcox III, she remembered. The pear-shaped was Laurence Mason. The heart-shaped one was from Franklin Smithson. Although she'd properly returned each ring at the parting, the gentlemen had properly insisted she keep them. Obviously each assumed she would oft look at the ring and remember with regret what she'd spurned. They were halfway right. She often did look at the rings, often remembered the gentlemen spurned, but never with regret. Subsequent meetings with the gentlemen only reinforced her decision. A case in point was Laurence Mason and his wife at the party last night. He'd held on to his straw hat with more affection than he showed Mrs. Mason. Waving at him from afar, Nina had kept her distance, refusing to be cornered for reminiscences. The way men treated women when they became wives proved to Nina that an engagement was enough of an entanglement. If society was a gilded cage, marriage was unquestionably the lock. She would not be thus imprisoned. Nina nodded in relief at the rings and put them away. More than ever, she held to her belief that a courting gentleman, once assured of his eventual conquest even at the quasi-possession stage of engagement, began to regard the lady as his property, having no importance to him as a person. He was on to other conquests. Even a lady of such a depth of character as her mother could be and had been dropped by the wayside.

As for herself, Nina realized she was being sought after for her place in society and her father's wealth or, if there was anything personal in the pursuit, for her outer body. The Nina within was not only not known—a condition she prided in continuing— but if known would have proven too much of a challenge. Re- acting against this very belief, Nina at times would seek new gentlemen like a caged bird accepting its position, but sporadi- cally—at sudden jolts of memory of blue sky—throwing itself at the bars. There was always the hope that she would find a gentleman who did not follow that pattern, who would prove himself totally unlike her father. But coming from the same pool, they would inevitably be the same species, and again and again she tossed them back, making a habit of breaking off engagements.

When, in dismay, her mother pointed that out, Nina agreed it was wrong to be too predictable. Henceforth, she would no longer look for the ideal suitor or, even more elusive, seek to find herself through another. How infantile had been her hope that in a happy union she would finally regain the carefree self lost on that birthday night.

It was much less onerous not being engaged, Nina discovered with relief. Subsequently, a sort of ease entered her social whirls, for she picked as suitors only those least likely to seek marriage, such as Bobby Van Reyden, or those slightly younger and just playing at romance. To further assure that no one gentleman would break out in expectations, Nina hid behind her entourage, which was not only safer, but also more enjoyable. It was admiration without responsibility.

While the rest understood they had no hope, Dickie was too petted to believe a lady could mean the word *no* when he so clearly wished it to be yes. That explained why he had dared to shake her. Not that any other explanation was necessary for his attack beyond that he was a Windsor. Nina had attempted to keep away from that family. That was difficult since the Windsors and De Bonnards had been Oceana neighbors for generations.

Jordan Nina did not recall, possibly because he had often lived with his grandfather in Washington, D.C., and then gone to college and on to his world tour. When Jordan had first returned, Mr. De Bonnard had gone out of his way at the Oceana Men's Club to welcome back the young man, favorably evaluating him as a "sharp, in-the-know fella!"

It was soon made evident that what appealed so much to her father was Jordan's knowledge of the inner doings of the Prince of Wales and his set. Mr. De Bonnard had passed on some of Jordan's revelations to Mrs. De Bonnard, and that lady, not mentioning her source and with suitable expurgations, had served up a delicious platter to the girls, disguised as a moral lesson. Especially did Mrs. De Bonnard share things with Nina, who, considering her history of engagements, ought not be too surprised by gentlemen's doings. Except that some of the English royalty's doings had shocked even Mrs. De Bonnard; those were the expurgated parts, including the Prince of Wales having a list of restaurants with private dining rooms, equipped with special buttons that when pushed could present a bed on demand. Nor had she imparted another hard-to-believe *on dit* that Princess Alexandra made friends with her husband's "women," inviting them to her private soirees and discussing their children and "other things" they had in common. Indeed, Mrs. De Bonnard resented that her husband had repeated that to her, wondering if he was trying to use that as an example of correct behavior for a wife. Such behavior would not be countenanced here. The most an American woman could do was pretend not to know. To know and to sanction was too European.

Mrs. De Bonnard could also have done without the young Mr. Windsor's comment that the American matron was a subject of high humor in European society. Mr. De Bonnard and the other Oceana gentlemen hugely enjoyed that. In response, Mrs. De Bonnard had given her husband a cool stare, but he was still laughing as he left.

That barb was immediately shared with her daughters, hoping their protest would dislodge it. Nina instantly did so, assuming the insult was meant for ladies such as Mrs. Windsor. Nina had been reading some of Mark Twain's articles in the *North American Review* that mocked the ladies of Baltimore and Philadelphia for demanding that the city's public statues be covered up for decency. Hadn't Mrs. Windsor had the fountain statues at the Windsor estate dressed with silk bodices to hide the nymphs' breasts, lest her impressionable boys assume that a lady's figure was open to general viewing? Laughing at that recollection somehow eased the personal nature of the insult.

All this talk of the Windsors, especially of a new Windsor gentleman coming to their party, did not increase Nina's anticipation of the event as it did for her mother and sister. For Nina did not feel secure in any Windsor's presence. Yet she always managed to keep her composure before them. She was put to the test a week after that birthday night when Mr. Otis Windsor visited her father in her own home. Nina was two feet away from him and she did not flinch. Nor did Mr. Windsor react, although at one point he gave her a brooding look that she could have confirmed by nervously looking away, but instead stared at him so directly that he lapsed back into his usual befuddled state, comprised of two parts drunkenness and one part natural dimness. He was fully drunk the next time Nina came upon him in her father's private den at Sea Cliff, stumbling and waving a bottle of whiskey, offering it around to the empty room. Instantly Nina backed out, just missing her father's entrance. Running around to the veranda, she looked through the window and saw the two of them drinking together. After a short time they left together. She knew what they were going to do and felt older than her mother, who did not—still innocent of the shifting sands at her feet. At the beginning of the following Oceana season, Mr. Windsor, once more the worse for wear, while riding his favorite hunter on the sands, fell into the surf.

Nina was not surprised that he had died. Since that night on the *Nina*, she had seen him as dribbling away his life until he'd drunk away the very last dregs of it.

As a widow in black, Mrs. Windsor came to visit the De Bonnard women overflowing with descriptions of the great love she and her husband had shared, as if she were showing stereoptic slides of their joint trip through life, presenting trays of them while Nina and her mother made appropriate remarks at suitable intervals and Adele jumped up and exclaimed, "Oh my!" continually and often at the wrong time. But when the widow concluded into her wet hanky that she was thankful Otie had died before her because he loved her so much she did not think he could have lived without her, all three chorused Adele's exclamation. Later, when Mrs. Windsor interrupted her sobs to criticize the sponge cake that was Mother's recipe—even suggesting that her cook speak to the De Bonnard cook—Nina felt that was her cue to excuse herself. So much for turning the other cheek to the Windsors. The less she had to do with any Windsor henceforth, the happier she would be.

But Nina simply could not rid herself of that family. Witness

Jordan coming to the De Bonnard lawn party and ruining it with his sarcasms.

As Nina sat in the cottage the morning after, upon having finished clearing out her thoughts of the past and putting away her mementoes, once more Jordan popped into her mind. Nina did not welcome his ungentlemanly intrusion, but apparently he never waited for permission to make himself felt. He did that with his imposing height and dark eyes that peered like weapons. Beyond his appearance, the other favorable thing Nina recalled about him was his being the only man yesterday not wearing a straw hat with a red, white, and blue band around it. Another plus in that vein, Nina remembered with a grin, was that he, unlike the other gentlemen, could sit on the wicker settee without jumping up at each one of the creaks it made when one moved. In conclusion, he was superior to the rest because he was not as inferior as the rest, not because he was unique in himself.

Stop it! Nina ordered herself. Thinking of Jordan Windsor upset her, caused her to feel physically uneasy, so she vowed to block out all other thoughts of him. Except that very attempt had her even more focused on him, to the point that when Nina actually saw Jordan Windsor climbing the veranda stairs ahead of her, she could not credit her senses until he gallantly doffed his hat—a timely reminder to don her hat and tightly tie the cream-colored bands and smooth her hair.

His arms were filled with flowers in obvious tribute to her. That was disappointing. He was behaving just like her usual admirers after all.

Nina approached, waiting for the praises that generally accompanied the posies. But Jordan gave her neither. Instead he rudely subjected her to a long, appraising glance from her hat down to her bare ankles. There, his glance shot back up to her face as if to demonstrate his shock at the unveiling of her ankles! That succeeded in disconcerting her. Nina's only recourse was rushing ahead to the veranda to sit down and cover her ankles. But before she could do so, Jordan turned and continued up the veranda steps ahead of her.

Oh stars! He'd turned his blasted back on her again—the

second time he'd made so blatant a cut. And where was he going when *she* was right there?

"Where are you going!" Nina called, aghast.

He looked back in surprise. "I'm paying a call on the beautiful Miss De Bonnard."

Appeased, Nina climbed up and nonchalantly held out her hands for the flowers.

He refused to hand them over, rather turned about as if looking for someone.

Confused, she stared at him.

"I expect if I ring the bell, a message can be delivered to her that I am calling?"

"What are you saying? I'm already here."

"You are, indeed. How does that answer? I am not calling on you."

With a slight smile at her shock, Mr. Windsor extended the pause and then added compassionately, "I'm certain some other gentleman might be found to pay his attentions to you. That is, I expect there might still be one or two youngsters still immature enough to be interested." But Jordan's dark eyes had a mocking gleam that seemed to indicate that possibility was quite remote. "I'm calling on the *young* lady who lives here. Arabel—a beautiful name for an enchanting girl."

"Adele," Nina corrected shortly.

"Ah yes, Adele. Even lovelier. Do you think she'll like my selection? I spent some thought on it. The roses are pale yellow, of course, to reflect her pale blond hair. The vivid purple irises mimic the intense irises of her eyes. And note the pink peonies; those are for the blushes on her beautiful cheeks when a gentleman speaks to her. She is, in short, a flower of a girl."

Jordan looked fixedly at Nina to note whether she was impressed by his explanation. She was still looking stunned.

"They're for my sister," she finally said.

Jordan could not resist a small laugh and a teasing, "You *are* sharp. That's what I have been saying all along. At last it has penetrated, has it? What's the barrier to your understanding: natural ignorance, morning fog, or just colossal self-absorption?"

47

Nina flushed. She would not passively accept his taunting. Straightening her hat and her motions, Nina responded coolly, "One would need to leap over quite a barrier to accept that you are calling on my *little* sister."

"I expect you're going to have to become accustomed to a horde of gentlemen beating a path to your beautiful sister's door. We all have our day and eventually must step aside to avoid being run over by the . . . eh, oncoming crowd. Am I fortunate enough to be among the first? First, but not last, of course. Do you think she'll receive me and my poor tribute?"

"It's too early in the morning for my sister to receive callers, as you must realize if you had any any awareness of the customs. You may leave your card and your flowers on the doorstep."

He came close and peered under her straw hat at her still flustered face. The huge brim gave her the image of a sun maiden with a lovely aureole, and for a moment Jordan stopped smiling and just stared at her flushed and beautiful face.

Her eyes were golden-flecked, and he enjoyed gazing at them. She stared back at him, sensing his interest, which confused her even further. "What are you playing at?" she whispered.

"I? Playing? Heavens!" he expostulated, exaggerating his response and indignation. "How could you think that of me? I'm always most sincere about my every gesture. Would you could say the same."

"Why have you come here?" Nina asked with an almost desperate desire to know.

For a moment he hesitated, feeling her earnestness, but was quick and slick enough to slip back into his performance. "Why can't you believe what I say? I'm here to court your sister. Come, Miss De Bonnard, it's time to face the inevitable. Some blooms, while beauteous at their peak, begin to drop petals and must make way for the bud on the same stem. Sad, but true. ' 'Tis true 'tis pity; and pity 'tis 'tis true.' "

"You're quoting," she accused, as if catching him in an indecency. "Yes, it's Polonius, I think, the speech about the brevity of wit. Pity you didn't take his advice and shorten your speech, even shorten the length of your appearance here. But I will abbreviate this meeting with one brief word: Leave."

Ignoring her insertion, he continued his previous point. "Would you prevent your sister from having the experiences you enjoy? You've set the example—don't you agree it's time for her to join the sport?"

"My sister doesn't wish to be involved with a gentleman of your ilk!"

"How do you know what ilk she'd like? She and I may be of the same ilk. Even you and I may be of a similar ilk. Ilks of a feather, shall we nest together?"

While making his laughing remarks, Mr. Windsor had placed his bouquet on the doorstep, and Nina, pushing ahead of him, whether deliberately or not, walked over the bouquet. That was a satisfaction she could not resist and found herself retracing her steps on the blooms.

Jordan was pleased she had so quickly exhibited the jealousy he'd planned.

Looking up and seeing him watching her with amusement, Nina felt a desire to walk over his face in exactly the same manner. Putting all the distaste she was feeling at being so close to and so manipulated by a Windsor, she said, "All you *Windsors* prey on younger woman!"

"Curious statement! Considering you are older than my brother! But age did not stop you from toying with *him*," Jordan replied with a cold tone. When Nina just shrugged his brother off, showing no sign of regret or apology, Jordan felt his pact was justified and, carrying on with his performance, he concluded in mocking tones, "But does age have anything to say when the heart speaks?"

Kicking away the crushed flowers in her path, Nina said, "You may send more flowers. These seem to have been run over by the hordes you were predicting."

He threw back his head and laughed, adding with pointed tone, "But will you be *selfless* enough to allow your sister to receive the next tokens of my esteem?"

"You may rest assured they'll receive all the attention they deserve," Nina said sweetly. And this time, neatly overstepping the strewn flowers, she walked into her home, closing the door firmly behind her.

From within Nina watched him whistling as he returned to his carriage, starting his horses with a light flick of the reins and whip. Grimly, she realized he'd been using the same approach on her, flicking her here and there. She felt a wave of fear that a Windsor man had come into her life once more to tear it open so it would never be the same. But she was adult now, she comforted herself, and could control her reaction to any gentleman regardless of his name. Straightening her shoulders, and with an air of composed indifference cloaking her once more, Nina climbed the stairs to her sister's room.

Six

hat do you mean?" Adele asked in surprise.

Once again Nina explained about Jordan's visit. Adele was wide-eyed. "But the flowers were for *me?*" she insisted on clarifying for the fifth time.

"Yes. The elder Mr. Windsor seems to have a turn for younger ladies," Nina had to confess, somewhat bitterly. But then, seeing the delight blooming on her sister's face, she began to smile as well. A strange emotion. Being passed over for her sister. Did it make her feel old? Yes. Did it make her feel jealous? No.

It was a relief to find that was true. Observing Adele's face, Nina further acknowledged that she herself would not have felt so honored by the privilege of Jordan's attentions. To her it would have been mere satisfaction. It was worth more to watch Adele fully enjoying this moment than to have a paler version for herself. The only concern was Jordan himself. Not only was he a Windsor but according to her mother's whispers obviously a *worldly* man—which could mean civilized, but in his case had more negative connotations. Some men treated women as objects of care, others as objects of decoration, but this man treated them—if his attitude toward her were any indication—as objects of challenge. Behind a veneer of dry humor, he was definitely combative. Adele deserved someone caring and genuine, and as enthusiastic about life as she was. Would the jaded Mr. Jordan Windsor crush her sister's spirit, or would *she* awaken him to an eagerness for life he seemed to have lost in his world travels? If he imagined that, he was mistaken. It could be said she had the same experience in her unwitting association with Dick, only to discover that one became a mere onlooker, able to tolerate mere sips from that well of insipidness before having to put down the cup, while others were drinking deep.

Still, maybe Jordan was different. Men seemed to have a life-long capacity for enjoying themselves through younger women.

"What are you doing, Adele?"

"Oh, just fooling around."

Self-consciously Adele changed her hair, which she had just arranged in Nina's style. Nina touched Adele's pale yellow locks. "Yes, you should be putting it up. At your age I had been wearing it up for a while. But not like mine. You should always try to look totally like yourself. If there is any copying to be done, let it be others copying you."

"The way all the girls tried to copy your fringe!" Adele enthused. "All of a sudden, everywhere I went, all I could see was young ladies, girls, and even their mothers wearing that upsweep with a long front fringe that you started wearing at this year's January cotillion. And now, look, you've fooled them all by changing to a front pomp. Why can't I at least wear your fringe—like the rest!"

Nina was smiling. "My 'lunatic fringe.' It's been totally insane seeing Mrs. Bellows adapting it to her skimpy hair."

"Yes, the name helped. Everybody wearing it felt a trifle wild—why can't I?"

"No. You start your own madness. Enjoy every minute of it. Soon enough it becomes . . . redundant."

"That's because . . ." Adele paused, afraid to say what she was thinking, but Nina pressed her, and Adele continued, "you have no heart."

Nina was surprised. "You think I'm heartless to you?"

"No, not to me. Not to Mama or Papa. You're very loving to us. More so than any other sister I know. But to men. All men. And to some of the girls around Oceana as well, you're so distant."

"I have to be distant. When I come close, they attack."

"I don't understand why they would. Or why, when I tell

them how sweet and caring you are, they look at me in such surprise."

"That's because everyone isn't as sweet and adorable as you," Nina said.

"Oh bosh! I'm not so special. You always think I am. You always give me books to read I don't understand. Like the books of that Eliot lady with the man's name, when I'd rather be reading Mrs. Southworth, like the rest of my friends."

"Dime novels!" Nina groaned. "You're as bad as Dick and his Alger books. He's read the entire *Luck and Pluck* series. It escapes me—how he empathizes with a hero who starts out poor and needs luck and pluck to make a fortune when the Windsor sons were born fortunate. And as for reading this Ouida and that Mrs. Southworth, don't you realize they write mainly for people who are trying to imagine what it's like to live exactly the way you do?" Nina threw up her hands. "What's the attraction, then . . . to you?"

"You don't understand," Adele insisted. "It's . . . it's . . ."

"Yes?"

"It's the *feeling* in them! When they love, they love with all their hearts! Even the villains go whole hog in their villainy. It's full-fledged emotion."

"If you like things with no shading, stick to the newspapers." She picked up Adele's reading matter: " 'Deep in Blood—Details of a Frightful Confession.' Heavens! The *Police Gazette*! Where did you get it?"

"Dick. Don't tell Mama. But I think I should learn about life as it really is. Nobody tells me *anything*. It's always 'Hush' or, Mother's favorite, 'That is a matter to be discussed in private.' Or yours—'Who cares about that?' Well, I I care about everything and everyone around me. Including you. And if you'd rather I gave up Jordan because you wanted him—it would hurt me deeply, but"—she took a deep, brave breath—"I would *do it*."

"Thank you, indeed, but what makes you think I would want Jordan?" Nina asked, bristling.

"You always have the best first. I naturally assumed, as did everybody, that he would fall for you right off."

"Well, apparently everybody was mistaken. I don't want Jordan Windsor. Nor does he want me. He was obviously smitten by you the minute he saw you. At least I give him credit for being able to appreciate the finer things in life."

"Me?" Adele asked in wonder.

"You." Nina smiled.

So it was decided. Adele had turned out to be a heroine of the very books she enjoyed reading. The hero was a worldly man returning from foreign travels—with a slight mustache, no less; not a full beard like her father's, but a devastatingly sophisticated suggestion of a mustache. And he also had a gleam in his eye, and that very discerning eye had passed over her beautiful older sister and fallen for *her*. Further, this storybook result had happened naturally to them both at first sight!

The very next day Adele was to have a second sight of him, for Jordan wrote asking permission to call. In despair at the inadequacy of her wardrobe for this grand occasion, she ran to Nina, who gladly gave her free choice of any of her new Paris dresses.

Eventually Adele selected the one with the largest bustle, which Mrs. De Bonnard vetoed as much too avant-garde. The bustle stuck out so far that the designer had claimed a teacup could be placed atop and remain securely balanced even while madame promenaded. Instantly, Adele put the claim to the test, and the cup remained secure through every one of her saunters, even slides, but when she forgot and sat down, it lost its position.

The three women cried out, for tea was spilling all over the beautiful silk, Adele having neglected to empty the cup before putting it on the bustle. Mortified, Adele apologized and Nina bravely lied that she had not cared for that gown . . . very much. Pretending nothing had happened, they went on to pick through the rest of Nina's fashions.

The next loveliest was a lavender gown with a wicked bustle bow. Adele pleaded for that, and both Nina—quickly—and Mrs. De Bonnard—grudgingly—agreed.

Nina even went to the garden for sprigs of lavender to place in her sister's blond hair, since Mr. Windsor saw her as a "flower of a girl." Stepping back to view the results, the two women who loved her applauded. Adele, glowing with anticipation and with the lavender touches, looked like a bridesmaid; no, rather like a wood nymph, Nina thought, absolutely adorable. Sister and mother could not resist hugging her while both hoped Mr. Windsor would not be similarly affected—or would at least restrain the impulse if he was. Adele was the kind of girl people always wanted to hug, for she seemed so susceptible to hugs and would return them in full measure. Indeed, Adele, staring at her new image, almost wanted to hug herself, exclaiming, "I'm beautiful! Do you think he'll like me?"

The next day it was clear that Mr. Windsor did, for after the first visit he asked permission to come again.

Nina had made herself scarce on Jordan's arrival. She heard all about the meeting from Adele later: "He stared at me with smoldering eyes," and "He sighed at me over every word!" And then she heard it from her mother: "He was quite correct in all his attentions. But his manner was somewhat detached, as if . . . rehearsed. I do not know if that is just his style . . . but I am slightly concerned about his sincerity."

Which naturally had Nina concerned as well, and resolving to be present at Mr. Windsor's next visit. But when Mr. Windsor arrived and Adele ran to greet him, Nina somehow found herself unable to enter. Her mother was there. She could handle the suitor. If Nina was present, she concluded, he might change in reaction to her and that would ruin the moment for Adele. So Nina turned away and got a second report from Mrs. De Bonnard. Mr. Windsor had continued in his formal manner, which was commendable.

No intimidating glances? No double entendre? Nina inquired in a roundabout way, and was assured that her mother would certainly not have stood for any of *that*! So Nina relaxed. Apparently his brazenness was brought out only by her. Yet she could not dismiss her unease as she recollected the constant laughter in his eyes that convinced her he never meant a word seriously. What did that mean to Adele, who was the most earnest and sincere young lady anybody could imagine and who took everybody at face value? How could she handle Jordan if he were two-faced? Nina quaked at that possibility.

Two more times that very week Jordan appeared, which really indicated some kind of dedication. Nina maintained her policy of excusing herself. Eventually they would meet again, for Mr. Windsor's interest in her sister did not seem a passing thing. Adele's joy was so palpable that everyone in the house felt it and shared in it.

As for Nina's callers, most of those young pups continued their attendance, except for Dick Windsor, who apparently had gotten the message and was no longer hounding her. At least one of the Windsor brothers was eliminated, Nina thought gratefully. Bobby Van Reyden hung on, dogging her every step. But Nina regarded that young man as one did a flunky, serving his function of attending without needing to have his comments responded to beyond occasional nods or smiles or orders.

Another pre–July Fourth event was scheduled: an Americana bonfire on the beach. It was still June and if the patriotic expression was not yet overdone, she shuddered to think what would happen in July or, worse, on July Fourth itself. Nina normally would have gone to the beach party, but once more she remained unavailable. Frankly, she could not yet face seeing Adele with Jordan. She was so afraid she would sense something wrong, or, even worse, not sense anything wrong with them. Which would mean that her entire reading of Jordan's character and motives was incorrect. And yet she wanted to be proven wrong about Jordan—for Adele. The problem was, she knew in her heart that he was as devious as he was debonair. Then again, her reaction to the Windsors as a whole was not unprejudiced; perhaps she ought not leap to judgment.

The following morning Nina was up once more before anyone else and this time dressed very properly with her hair in its pompadour upsweep. She wore a lime morning dress with full sleeves, for one never showed one's arms, let alone décolletage, before afternoon. Rather than the large, comfortable leghorn straw picture hat that tied under her chin, she wore a smart but uncomfortable chip straw sailor hat with a perky green bow, and brought her groom to drive the donkey cart to the large communal beach where the bonfire had taken place. Signs of red, white, and blue banners, confetti, and bows were still there. Laughingly Nina tied a patriotic ribbon around the donkey's neck and dismissed her servant. She was anticipating a private moment of pleasure, having a long ride on the sand as she was wont to do as a child, when all her expectations fell flat at the appearance of a gentleman.

Naturally, since she had been giving way to a secret enjoyment, who should be there to ruin it but Jordan Windsor? She nearly didn't stop the cart. Decorum and his persistence forced her to a halt.

"If you'll favor me with a few moments' walk on the sand, we can discuss a subject of mutual interest."

Nina focused on his face, assessing his request. He did not appear to be teasing this time. Rather, his air was one of concern. That brought out the concern in Nina as well, and remembering that she'd planned to discover for Adele's sake what there was behind his facade, Nina consented to being handed out of the cart. He tied the donkey to a rock and gave her his arm. She refused it. They walked separately, but parallel, along the shore. This was not done: a young man and young woman alone could only be assumed to be participants in an assignation. But Nina was above general censure, having generally had so much of it, and Jordan would only have enjoyed his share in it. Further, they were too occupied with the impression they were making on each other to bother about an unknown observer's conclusion— which was a mistake. For there was an unknown observer. An obscure relative of one of the wealthy Oceana families whose inability to sleep that morning had put him in a position to repay his free lodging with a choice bit of gossip.

At the edge of the sea, they walked; Jordan beginning to speak, then stopping abruptly and gallantly escorting her away from the danger of an approaching wave that might not only stain her freshly shined shoes but go between the laces and take liberties with her toes. When he had her safely seated on a rock that he had covered with his scarf, he spoke. "Your sister wishes to see the Centennial Exposition. I wish to take her. I understand your mother is thinking of granting her permission, contingent on the correct chaperone."

"And the chaperone is *me*?"

"Precisely."

Nina swallowed the indignity of that and then laughed at the picture of herself in that position. A denial would be easy but foolish, as all easy, first-thought answers are. She thought twice. "Very well. I shall be your chaperone, and you shall be mine."

"Meaning?"

"I shall bring a gentleman with me. Without that accessory, I find it inconvenient to travel to any affair." She smiled blandly to cover the unintentional double entendre, which his twinkling eyes indicated he had caught. "Yes," she continued hurriedly, "we women cannot do without our escorts. Who would pick up one's gloves, signal a hansom, push aside the general public if it intruded on one's privacy . . . or even direct one away from the dangers of a little-bitty wave. Oh, you are too useful to dispense with totally."

He laughed at that, and the two looked at each other challengingly. "Shall not my offices be sufficient?" he parried.

"You perhaps would know best about your sufficiency or lack thereof, but every single lady needs her own attendant to single her out." Facing the sea, she asked it the next question: "Now, whom shall I bring?"

He answered instead. "Allow me to bring along one who, I feel, would be concerned totally with your needs. He is fast on his feet and would never allow a glove of yours even to reach the ground before he had retrieved it."

"Shall I trust you to know my needs?" Nina wondered aloud while he stared at her with his eyes, indicating that he knew the very depth of her needs, but Nina shook her head at him. Nevertheless, not wishing to put herself to the expectations that inviting a gentleman on her own might rouse, she acquiesced.

The waves applauded her action, nature tending to approve erosion of any kind.

Before he handed her back into her cart, Nina asked a question she had been wondering about since their first meeting.

"Are you ever sincere? In your words? Or, more importantly, in your feelings?"

"Are you?"

"I am not expressing, nor have I ever expressed, affections for anyone merely to arouse their own liking."

"And you believe that is what I am doing? Is that because you have too low an estimation of your sister or too high a one of yourself?—assuming that anyone could instantly be caught by you but not by her."

"I make no such assumptions about myself. We are not discussing me. Or myself and you. I am simply concerned whether you are capable of appreciating how deep Adele's feelings are and whether you have an equal depth."

"Which you believe I do not."

"I fear you might be a trifler."

"Ah, from such a known trifler as yourself that is praise indeed!"

So much for civility! They could not even converse without open combat. Shaking her reins, Nina was off, speeding through the sand, leaving a cloud to dust his attire and close his amused eyes. Afterward, Nina was amazed that she'd consented to chaperone a joint event when even a few minutes with Jordan had led to sparring. For his part, Jordan was delighted that he had succeeded in luring her out of hiding, for Nina had to be present for the immoral pact to have any chance of succeeding. She could not evade him during the close proximity of their attending the Centennial Exposition, he noted with satisfaction.

That exposition immediately became the main topic in the De Bonnard home, as it was all over the country. Since the opening in May, everyone had but one question. "Have you seen *it*?"

Nina had not and was somewhat interested in attending. Adele was palpitating to visit it. Mrs. De Bonnard was considering the possibility. Even Mr. De Bonnard himself had heard much good talk about some of the exhibits brought together in Philadelphia to celebrate their nation's one-hundredth birthday. He meant to take his family, but something financial always stood in his way. Nina grimly concluded that he had already been there with one of his interesting companions, and she suffered for her mother but vowed not to let a hint of her suspicion reach Mrs. De Bonnard and certainly not Adele.

Previous to their lawn party, when Dick Windsor had been a fixture in their home, his main conversation had been the Centennial Exposition. He had seen it twice and discussed the exhibits so many times that Nina found her interest diminishing every time he opened his mouth. Everyone had heard him describe the opening ceremonies, which were attended by, Dick said repeatedly, "a whole passel of heavy swells," from Generals Sherman and Hancock down to the President. His enthusiasm faded when mentioning President Grant, who summered in another New Jersey resort called Long Branch and was seen often enough not to arouse more than satisfaction at his continued existence.

Mostly, however, Dick had gone on about the miracle of the Corliss engine. Every time he did so, Adele asked the key question, "How many acres of machines does that engine run at once!" "Thirteen," he always replied and never failed to astonish her, or to derive satisfaction himself out of her astonishment. Even when Dick stopped coming, the Centennial Exposition retained its fascination for Adele. More and more of her friends were going; she was almost in tears at the fear that she would never see the exposition herself. Her hopes flared when Jordan volunteered to take her, making it even more of an occasion, but her mother crushed her elation by deeming Nina not enough of a chaperone for a trip all the way to Philadelphia. To rescue Adele, Nina suggested that her mother come as well, but Mrs. De Bonnard was lukewarm about the whole event. Earnestly Adele attempted to pique her mother's interest: "And from China, you'll see six thousand silk worms all at once . . . eh, doing what they do!" Despite that, Mrs. De Bonnard was not totally put off. Discussing it with her friends, she was assured there was artwork of note to see as well as the controversial Women's Pavilion. Further, people were coming from as clear across the country as California for the experience. Since nothing else was on everybody's lips, the exposition became a thing one clearly could no longer avoid. Therefore, Mrs. De Bonnard reluctantly agreed that Jordan could escort all three of them. They were to go! At that, Nina saw her opportunity once more to excuse herself. With Mrs. De Bonnard present, Nina suggested to her mother, she was decidedly de trop; a couple could manage with one chaperone, but two indicated an excessive degree of distrust. Mrs. De Bonnard could only laugh at that observation and agree in theory, but in practice she thought the exposition would be more enjoyable for her with both her daughters along. Then, too, Nina and she could chaperone in shifts while the other saw some of the displays.

But another glitch developed; it was called Mrs. Windsor. Upon hearing that Mrs. De Bonnard was joining the outing, she insisted on being included, causing Mrs. De Bonnard to open her mouth prepared to cancel the whole trip until she was stopped by Adele's look of dismay. Taking a long-suffering breath, her mother agreed, "Very well, Elvira may come, but *not alone*. I insist we invite her spongy friend Mrs. Spencerville to take in all the gossip Elvira splatters about, so I might be free to hear and see the exhibits!"

Later, although relieved, Adele could not help bemoaning to Nina that a special outing between Jordan and herself had turned into "a full Oceana representation!"

"Indeed," Nina agreed, "it is turning out to be a sorry squeeze. It needs only Dick along to assure none of us has a moment's peace."

So naturally Dick turned out to be the escort Jordan had in mind for Nina. And the party was complete. Upon their arrival by train in Philadelphia, the women stayed at the home of relatives of Mrs. Spencerville while the gentlemen settled at a local hotel.

The next morning, what originally had been a tête-à-tête for two turned into a tête-à-ten, as Adele and Jordan were joined not only by Nina and Dick and Mrs. De Bonnard and Mrs. Windsor, but also by Mrs. Spencerville and two of her female relatives and a clergyman acquaintance. Somewhat lumberously, this select crowd was off to view the Centennial Exposition. As they entered, Nina was hoping to see the display of Bartholdi's torch, part of the Statue of Liberty soon to be built and placed in New York City's harbor, but Mrs. Windsor quickly objected to seeing anything "unfinished," which was promptly seconded by her coterie. That left Nina to suspect that the entire outing was weighted against her. The program would have to suit Mrs. Windsor or, just as daunting, her sons. Anything Nina and Adele and her mother desired would have to be fitted in peripherally. This was not the way she was accustomed to being entertained. Annoyed, Nina watched her predictions come true as Dick unfolded his agenda. But Mrs. Windsor drew the line at viewing Dick's favorite, "Old Abe," an eagle mascot of the Wisconsin Civil War regiment who ate live chickens before one's very eyes and flapped his wings afterward. But she agreed, in appeasement, to his second choice of the giant metal Corliss engine. That wonder was found at Machinery Hall. It loomed forty feet above them, extended like an octopus by pulleys, shafts, wheels, and belts to smaller machinery, thirteen acres of machines moving at once, combing wool, printing newspaper, lithographing wallpapers, making envelopes, sawing logs, cobbling shoes, and more mechanical substitutions for workers.

To please his mother, Dick brought the ladies' attention to an automatic baby feeder. The women were merely amused, whispering to each other that nature had already provided that invention, which the gentleman overheard and blushed about. Attempting to deflect that fiasco, he rushed them to view the gas-heated flat iron, but since none of the ladies engaged in that activity, that also failed to please. As did the rest of the inventions, which Mrs. Windsor concluded were strictly for the benefit of the lower classes, since she and her society preferred such tasks to be performed by living employees who made less clatter while going about their duties.

Indeed, the plebeian air, not to mention the noise, became too much. They must leave, Mrs. Windsor declared. Further, as Nina dreaded, the lady nominated herself their leader and chose their next place to visit. This one none could refuse. It was the Department of Public Comfort.

Waiting outside for the ladies, Dick fumed at the length of the delay, until Jordan explained that a gentleman ought never object to the amount of time ladies needed to seek ease, and showed him the way a gentleman reacted to the waiting by taking his impatient brother to a nearby stand for a lager beer, and then even to have their shoes blacked.

Inside, all the ladies had skewered their brimmed hats with gold hat pins. But Mrs. Windsor and Mrs. Spencerville and the two cousins were further securing their various-sized chignons, which were designed to give ladies not only height but fullness where nature had failed to provide either. Of the matrons, only Mrs. De Bonnard scorned the use of false hair, proud that nature had given her pale locks of such fullness that she needed no help from German peasant girls. Nina was of like mind. Adele, whose locks were similarly full-bodied, nevertheless had tucked a "frisette" at her right temple—just to be in fashion.

For that reason too, Adele had insisted on the maid lacing her corset as tightly as possible in preparation for the outing, ignoring her sister's admonitions that she would not enjoy the day if she could not eat or walk in comfort. Still, Adele wished for the smallest possible waist. B.J.—Before Jordan—Adele had worn a sensibly adjusted corset, leaving space between the lacings of at least three inches or more. Since becoming the object of Jordan's attentions, though, she desperately wished to be worthy of his total attention. Yet here at the exposition, she found herself in something of a dilemma. Her face was turning white, in contrast to her generally blooming complexion. And the thought of attempting to swallow luncheon was nauseating despite her hunger.

"Do you think Jordan observed . . . that is, he already has fixed in his mind how I look in this dress . . . I mean—"

"Yes," Nina broke in, "you have already made your grand impression and shall simply ruin it if you become ill during luncheon. Besides, a slight loosening of your stays will hardly make a difference. You already have by nature the most perfect hourglass figure possible. There is no need to overdo!"

But Adele, who had just about decided that she could do with a little less admiration for a little more breath, suddenly observed Nina's slim silhouette and instead murmured that she was "quite comfortable."

That was the problem with having a sister ahead of all others in style and savoir faire. Of course the five years had made a difference, especially when Adele was twelve and Nina seventeen and already embarked on her career of engaging the young men in their set. Adele recalled watching with clenched fists as Nina paraded about, attending balls, going riding, receiving bouquets of flowers that she indifferently tossed to Adele, who pretended they were for her. In fact, she would fill the schoolroom with them till it resembled a bower and there, confined and constricted, Adele would wander amongst the floral offerings thanking her imaginary gentlemen callers right and left. That was why, when finally Jordan had brought a bouquet just for her—her first tribute—it was so unfair that the flowers had been somehow stepped on by Nina and tossed away. For several hours afterward, Adele almost had dark thoughts about her sister, till Jordan's subsequent bouquets arrived and more than made up for her deprivations. The book of underlined poems she could have done without because Nina insisted that she read at least the underlined lines and refer to them when next meeting Jordan. Adele had meant to do so but had not gotten around to it, and when Jordan said something and paused expectantly, she realized it must be a quote and blushed in panic. Jordan smoothly switched the discussion to the centennial, her favorite topic, and the moment had passed. But Adele had confessed her embarrassment to her sister, who shook her head affectionately and warned, "One has certain responsibilities to beaus. A lady must remember all their sporting records, however minor and, further, laugh at all their sallies and sigh at all their poems, no matter how tempted one is to do the reverse."

"If I'd known there were so many problems to being admired, I wouldn't have been so anxious for it," Adele had answered. And now she had the other problem of suffering discomfort for a compliment. A slight pain from the stays of the corset, which she had been able to ignore most of the day, was now beginning to radiate across her chest, and she found herself occasionally, rather inelegantly, panting. Sitting down did not help, as the corset continued to squeeze. Watching Nina, who never believed in excessive lacing, walking comfortably, Adele frowned. And then as her sister effortlessly handled the long train on her à la mode gray dress, Adele began to regret not having seen that one first. If she were wearing that, with its emphasis on the back rather than the waist, she might not be having problems now. Of course she had picked out this dress herself, begged for it because of its accentuated waistline and lower neckline, and Nina had given it without a murmur. But Nina ought to have spoken, ought to have warned . . . oh well, maybe she and her mother *had* suggested less lacing. But tight lacing made one's "frontal attributes," as Mrs. Windsor called a lady's breasts, so prominent that a gentleman, like Jordan, would not be able to look at any other lady—not even Nina.

Heavens, her lungs were going to burst, Adele thought, grinning at the idea of the news story that would make. She might be put on exhibit right here, with a sign beneath her body reading: LADY LACED TO DEATH!

Mrs. Windsor was having trouble with her chignon; it kept falling, and they all waited patiently while she repinned it. Nina hardly ever primped. Now she was walking about, swinging her train with ease. Adele was certain she herself would have tripped over that train at least three times by now. Instead Nina walked as if she were a bird whose tail gave her balance rather than weighing her down. Altogether Nina cast the aura that any minute that plumed tail might open and reveal a myriad of colors. Undoubtedly Nina kept to gray or lavender or a spectrum of green shades—despite the brash colors decreed by fashion—so her golden red hair would be the brightest note about her. And, Adele concluded, she was correct to keep attention on that beautiful mane. How Nina continually found new hairstyles had to amaze. Already she'd discarded the pompadour, claiming it was too hard to maintain, and devised a look that Adele felt was her most successful coiffure to date. The front hair was a collection of curls while the sides were swept up and clipped at the crown with a bow or ornament, allowing the rest to career down her back in six or seven long, glossy, hanging ringlets. The style mimicked the bow and train line of the dress. Watching Nina in motion, Adele continued to envy that gown, for the subtle seduction of Nina's outfit was really revealed only when she walked. Then the three bows that held the long train tied to her dress winked with each step and the long curls down her back shook like beckoning bells.

When she had first seen the avant-garde gown, Mrs. Windsor had signaled her eldest son for a private exchange. Dutifully he had come and leaned down. "Did you notice the disgraceful state of Miss De Bonnard's train? *Dusty!* In a drawing room where one has confidence in one's floors, that feature would not be quite so objectionable, but here she is merely sweeping the halls, if not the streets!"

"She certainly is leaving a trail of gentlemen behind her. I've had to repeatedly step up and warn them away!" Jordan had replied grimly. That was not what his mother had wanted to point out, and she had had to repeat her observation to Mrs. Spencerville to receive the reply she'd been hoping for. "Disgraceful!" her friend said loudly, and Mrs. Windsor could at last nod in agreement.

These ladies were still raising eyebrows at Nina's train as she walked out of the comfort station before them and joined the gentlemen. Dick's request that they visit all twenty-four state buildings on State Avenue was declined, even the New Jersey entry. The attention of the reverend was on the vendors hawking food, and soon the ladies were acknowledging they would not be averse to stopping for a meal. Dick was horrified at this waste of time, volunteering to bring them food from the stands, which so outraged the ladies that he had to apologize. "A lady never eats in the streets!" his mother instructed. But Adele wanted a lemonade, and instantly Jordan and Dick ran to get her one. Mrs. Windsor knocked the glass out of Dick's hands. "I told you a lady does not eat or drink in the street! Shocking!"

"Please!" Adele said, her face turning whiter and whiter. "I believe I need something to stop me from keeling over."

Hardly had the words left her lips when the very next moment she did keel over and lay flat out on the dirty, busy avenue.

Seven

The consternation of the group was immediate and various. Mrs. De Bonnard and Nina were white with anguish, leaning over Adele and rubbing her hands and face. "Precious," Nina called, and "My baby," Mrs. De Bonnard whispered in a strangled voice. Dick was running around calling for help from anybody he could spot who seemed respectable enough to have ideas on the subject. Jordan calmly went to a fountain and wet his handkerchief and offered it to Nina to bathe her sister's face; Nina accepted the cloth with gratitude, her eyes tearing in private terror. She'd lost her hat bending over her sister and did not take time to retrieve it, whereupon a woman in the crowd pounced on this extra souvenir.

Mrs. Windsor, of course, brought as much attention to herself as she could, claiming that she herself felt seriously unwell, that the halls had been too stuffy and now the streets too crowded. Mrs. Spencerville asserted that she felt a spasm coming on. Her two friends agreed they needed chairs, and the reverend was running around seeking chairs for the ladies. Dick was called by his mother to lend his support and she rested on his arm while he, with a distracted air, fanned her with his program, looking back at Adele every moment. A crowd was forming.

Since no chairs could be found, the reverend was first supporting one lady then rushing to another. Mrs. Windsor had recovered enough from the drama to notice that they were putting on a show for passing strangers and turned red with outrage.

"We are causing comment on the promenade!" she said in

alarm. The other ladies noticed that as well, and Mrs. Windsor, Mrs. Spencerville, her two acolytes, and the very reverend Reverend Twit distanced themselves from the main disturbance.

"Please," Nina whispered to Jordan, "she must be brought to a comfort station. She's laced too tightly."

He nodded and, without further ado, picked up the young lady. Dick, abandoning his mother to the reverend, followed to hold Adele's feet, which was unnecessary but added to the spectacle, delighting the crowd that had come to see all types of spectacles and felt this one was an extra attraction. Nina was holding on to her sister's hand and continuing to fan her while Mrs. De Bonnard, white-faced, was just able to keep up with the pace set by Jordan's long strides. Nina, on her high heels, had to skip occasionally to be parallel with the parade, and so, ignoring the now fading cries of Mrs. Windsor and her crowd at being abandoned in the streets, the party arrived at the nearest comfort station.

Jordan walked directly in and deposited Adele on a sofa there. The ladies within, after a brief flurry of fury, were appeased when they understood his mission. Everyone was clicking tongues and asking questions no one had time to answer, for the moment the gentlemen retired, Nina and Mrs. De Bonnard went to work unbuttoning Adele's dress. Next they hurriedly not only loosened the stays, but removed the corset altogether. Adele moaned and moved her head on the many pillows placed under her, but her eyes were still closed. Mrs. De Bonnard kept massaging her daughter's waist and around the area of the lungs and chest and Nina kept applying the wet towels the other ladies were quick to keep offering. A short lady with a withered face (and a booming voice that was almost unintelligible with its midwestern accent) having come from Indiana to see the exposition, was the most helpful. Quickly, she removed the pillows from Adele's head and put them under her feet. "Let that there blood go to the poor girlie's head!" she ordered loudly. And as if not daring to disobey her, the blood rushed there and put some color in Adele's cheeks. She coughed a bit and began gasping for breath. This time there was no impediment, and fresh air came into her lungs. With a moan of pleasure, she tried for another and another breath until she was breathing fully and freely. Her next progress was fluttering her long lashes and at last opening her eyes. Her first word was, as in life, "Mama!"

Mama was there, holding her child and hugging her, and Nina, with tears in her eyes, was hovering and soon had her chance for a hug.

"You terrified us!" Nina cried, meaning every word, for she was still shaking. Healthy, bubbling Adele was not the fainting kind.

Her mother patted Nina absently and then, with a nod of reassurance that her daughters were well and had survived this day's drama, she stood up and took charge of the issue. "Yes, it's not a moment either of us would wish to repeat. Adele, this is the last time I permit you to lace to such an extreme! You might easily have punctured a lung!"

The hovering ladies agreed and each had a grisly tale to relate of nieces, sisters, or even themselves having collapsed in a similar but much more serious manner and from the same cause.

At last, after drinking several glasses of water, Adele was her old self again. She was up and walking and not feeling the slightest bit dizzy, she assured her mother and sister. Several ladies, now that the drama was over, went on with their own toilettes. Only the midwestern matron stood by. There were two problems still to be dealt with. One was that the dress, being Nina's, would not fit without the corset reducing Adele's waist.

"I'll try the c-c-corset again," Adele said bravely but with terror in her eyes, viewing the flesh-colored object with the steel stays like the torture device it actually was.

"No!" was the instant response, not only from Nina and Mrs. De Bonnard, but from the Indiana woman as well.

"What a fool fashion!" that woman said with a snort. "Can't run a farm tied up like that! A body has to be able to move and breathe, for mercy's sake."

While Mrs. De Bonnard and the Indiana woman were attempting to fit Adele in the dress without the corset, talking of opening seams and such, which was found not to be possible since they were edge to edge, Nina came up with the simple solution.

"We'll switch," she said with a grin.

All the ladies stared at her, not understanding until Nina began undoing the long train that was tied to her dress, and then Mrs. De Bonnard said quickly, "Yes, but that's the same size; how will it help?"

"This one does not feature the waist, so it is quite loose there. The eye is supposed to go to the train."

"But I don't think I could manage a train . . ." Adele began, which showed how much of a fear fashion had put into her, for normally Adele was always eager to attempt the newest styles.

"Elementary. We simply won't tie on that part. You see, the train goes with the overskirt that adds additional draping and forms the extra bows in the back!" And Nina, next moment, stood untrained. The dress was elegant on its own, although not so much of an eye-catcher as the first. Stepping out of that as well, Nina stood unblushingly in her undergarments. Adele quickly accepted the proffered gray gown and donned it. When it closed, with Adele able to breathe comfortably, everybody breathed a sigh of relief with her. Nodding in satisfaction, Nina put on the discarded white gown. While less elegant than the gray creation, this dress was provocatively sensuous on Nina, with the waist so tiny and the bosom so abloom with flowerets that it was certain to evoke a "Shocking!" from Mrs. Windsor. The midwestern woman supplied her own version: "Ain't no man gonna be able to keep his eyes offen them knockers!" That comment had Adele suddenly determined to compete by putting on the overskirt and train after all. Yet when it was all tied on and Adele had tripped a few times, Mrs. De Bonnard had had enough. Under her mother's stern glance, Adele agreed to remove it. "We've come to see the Centennial, not to be *seen*!" Mrs. De Bonnard said in exasperation.

"Well." Nina laughed appeasingly. "We've done both."

There remained now the simple problem of what to do with the skirt-train and the offending corset. Nina wished to take along her train, but the corset was to be left here in the comfort station. The Indiana woman had another solution. She would deposit both at their hotel, as she and her husband were shortly leaving the exposition. Mrs. De Bonnard gave the Spencerville address and, in her gracious way, offered what she said was "transportation fare," giving the woman more than she'd spent on the trip. "And leave the corset—we won't be wanting *that* again. From now on Adele will keep to her own dresses and *undergarments*," she said sternly, and Adele humbly nodded. After the De Bonnards left, scattering many a thank-you, the Indiana woman quickly grabbed not only the train but the corset. Clearly that was the grandest souvenir of the trip. With a wide smile, she anticipated showing it to her sewing circle back home when telling her tale of rescuing some high-toned eastern ladies who didn't have sense enough not to tie themselves up in knots!

Outside, the second major problem that Adele had been dreading presented itself: facing those who had witnessed her humiliation. Dick set the correct note by crying out, "Hey, she's come back from the dead! What did dying feel like? See angels?"

And so the embarrassment passed with a laugh as Adele launched into her version of the experience and Dick his, and Adele barely had a chance to thank Jordan for carrying her to safety. Dick hooted, wanting his share of praise for carrying her legs. Jordan had finesse enough to say merely how lovely she looked with the roses back in her cheeks, which he had sadly missed, and she blushed even more and was content.

Jordan had instantly been aware of the dress switch between the sisters, but knew enough not to remark on it. While Dick, who would have most certainly have remarked on it, did not notice. Jordan was shaking his head privately at the fool fashions that brought ladies to a swoon. In the interim, he had met with the reverend, who had arranged to find seats and drinks for the ladies in a nearby pavilion. When they were all together again, Adele had to withstand a scolding from Mrs. Windsor that Mrs. De Bonnard was quick to end with a cold, "The child has suffered enough for one day, Elvira. The least said about the matter, the best. I assume you have all rested sufficiently for us to continue inspecting the displays."

When Mrs. De Bonnard spoke in that tone, none dared object, and all rose and entered the nearby Memorial Hall, where the artworks were on display.

There Mrs. Windsor and her group had a chance to attack another lady who could not speak back. The source of their outrage was a wax model of Cleopatra in blatant dishabille. What the Indiana woman had called "knockers" and Mrs. Windsor "frontal attributes" were plainly visible to all. One had to push through the crowd of gawkers to be properly offended. Another feature that drew the crowd to Cleopatra was that she actually moved: Her head rolled from side to side, and on one extended finger she held a parrot with movable wings that opened and closed rhythmically. Her other unencumbered arm continually lifted, signaled and dropped, lifted, signaled and dropped.

The Reverend Twit pushed ahead, his bald head and face one shade of red, as he stared, and then, turning back and seeing the outraged ladies behind him, he agreed he'd never been so . . . so . . . He groped for a word.

"Titillated," Jordan supplied helpfully, and Nina had to suppress a smile.

"No sir!" Twit replied. "Shocked was the word I was stretching for."

"It's quite a stretch, indeed."

"I am shocked and, and indignant. For if I am not mistaken, that moving arm is beckoning to *men*!"

"No!" Jordan exclaimed, his eyes twinkling. "How do you know? Do you feel yourself *beckoned*?"

Nina could not resist inserting, "You mistake the lady. She is waving off all men. I see this royal personage as undressing for the night alone in her boudoir, where a gentleman has no place, and seeing groups of men about her has her most disconcerted. No wonder she is waving you all off."

Not able to counter that without saying some home truths to a young lady of innocence, the reverend just said, "Hmph!" and, as he gave his arm to the ladies, they left the polluting presence of the Egyptian priestess and queen.

Adele, her ordinary liveliness in full tilt, had joined with Dick in attempting to lift their arms in time with the statue, making a game of who would succeed first and cheering all the near synchronizations.

With a connoisseur's pleasure, Jordan viewed the Egyptian queen's painted lids and parted lips and exposed breasts. Turning, he stared at Nina's curves, so real in contrast. She'd been almost regal in the gray gown, but now was youthful, nubile, like a dream of his youth. He noticed that she was hatless. There was something about a hatless lady, as if she had removed part of her armor and was no longer ready for battle. That glowing blaze of hair open to the wind and to gentlemen's eager eyes made her more approachable than he ever remembered seeing Miss De Bonnard before. And he inwardly applauded the way she had spoken to the reverend, cutting through his humbug. Now she was unguardedly laughing at Cleopatra's crassness, at an allure so obvious it became unalluring. Compared to that mechanized temptress, Nina was like the sun's heat in contrast to a shaded lamp. Like nature's lily, in contrast to society's gilded ones. Turning away from the painted pseudo-allure, Jordan gazed at Nina in grudging admiration.

Sensing his look, Nina stopped smiling and warily waited for him to speak.

"She's nothing in comparison to you. My picture of the ultimate temptress is at my side at this moment."

Nina was ready to remonstrate when Jordan, recalling his mission, added lightly, as if she'd misread the personal nature of his remark, "Aren't, after all, all women Cleopatras?"

"Aren't, after all, all men asps, eager to jab us to our deaths?"

Jordan grinned. "Then you don't believe in undying love and the union of lovers extending even unto death?"

Nina was surprised by that segue, and even more so by the intensity of his voice, but she could not credit the possibility of his being serious. "That's merely in the minds of men—always assuming women would rather be dead to them than shed of them."

Jordan let out a whoop that attracted Adele, who came bounding toward them, so Jordan quickly concluded, "I'm heartbroken that so engaging a young lady would be so harsh on poor lovesick gentlemen. And I rejoice that my heart is entrusted to the tenderer mercies of a gentler woman." And bowing his leave, Jordan moved to escort Adele to further art displays.

At the supposedly controversial Women's Pavilion, Mrs. Windsor was pleased to note unremarkable displays of the handiworks of women. The ladies nodded in approval over embroidery, artificial fruit, wood carvings, tapestry, and painted china. There was another approving joint nod for the etchings by Queen Victoria herself. All seemed proper. Mrs. Spencerville loudly compared it to the ladies' comfort station.

When they walked into the next room, the good ladies' equilibrium, not to mention comfort, was shattered. It was a room filled with machines weaving, spinning, moving, jarring, grinding. Machines galore! And each and every one of these had a female operator.

"Shocking!" Mrs. Windsor's group said, as they had so many times before. One would think they would by now be shock-proof, or at least shock-acclimatized.

Meanwhile Dick was crowing. He'd smirked all through the women's looking at the artwork, knowing the surprise awaiting them. And now he'd seen the reaction he'd expected. Satisfied, he rushed to the main attraction in this room, Miss Emma Allison, the pleasant and capable chief operator, who was quite willing to answer all questions spoken and implied.

Tending a steam engine, she explained, was no more taxing than firing a cookstove. "Certainly less than caring for a home and children," she added, and the women around the room were uncertain whether to smile or frown. So they did both. One after another. More and more questions were asked. Dick hung around to get his two cents in, asking the same questions he'd asked on previous trips. Jordan looked to see if Nina, having made such a point of needing an attendant, was feeling abandoned by her escort. But she wasn't even aware that Dick was not at her side. Uncertain at his reaction to this, Jordan discovered that he was pleased when he should have been displeased. Jordan could not resist following Nina with his eyes everywhere she went. He had also noted her taste both here and at previous pavilions and had been surprised at how often he agreed with her selections. Now she was reading the eight-page newspaper coming off the press that was headlined THE NEW CENTURY FOR WOMEN. Observing him at her side, Nina grinned impishly and, with all the calculation with which Eve might have handed Adam the apple, she gave him the copy. Warily, he read. Adele, running over to join them, leaned over his shoulder, perfectly willing to help him along by reading aloud, " 'Devoted to the individual interests of women.' "

Every step in the production, it seemed—from writing all the copy to setting the type to running the presses, even to delivering the issues to the newsstands on the Centennial grounds—had been done by women and women alone.

"Did you notice the editorial suggesting equal pay for equal work for men and women?" Nina carefully pointed out.

Jordan merely met her question with his usual twinkle as he blithely expressed himself not the smallest bit in opposition to people, whether men or women, being paid equally. And as for women working, he was decidedly for *that*. Indeed, he had hopes that someday it would be just women working and the gentlemen able to take their leisure at home.

"You do that in any event," Nina riposted, but Adele heard only his approval of women's goals and squeezed his hand exuberantly, saying, "I knew you would be broad-minded enough not to want to put any impediments in a woman's path for self-fulfillment."

"That's been my life's objective, fulfilling women," he replied seriously, and Adele was all smiles and Nina all frowns. Mrs. De Bonnard was reading the newspaper, and she and Adele were going over its contents point by point when Mrs. Windsor arrived and took it from them. She had finally been persuaded by Dick to leave Miss Emma to learn the error of her ways on her own. But a new outrage awaited his mother. When she and Mrs. Spencerville closed heads over the newspaper, both heads shot up in astonishment at the notice that it had been produced strictly by womanpower. Fearful that the reverend might read it, they looked about for him, but that gentleman was still occupied with staring down Miss Emma.

Unable to resist, Dick pointed out the editorial for equal pay to his mother, whereupon she turned purple. "Such things ought not be printed!" she cried, crushing the edition.

"But it *is* printed," Adele insisted, "which proves it can be done!"

Mrs. Windsor sniffed and said, "I didn't say it couldn't be

done; I said it ought *not* be done." She nodded her head, while her bonnet's tall feather nodded along, adding its flourish to her every word.

Dick changed the topic by urging a viewing of the Japanese home in exact scale that was on display and was absolutely not to be missed. The women's objections this time would not be stilled. They would not be urged, cajoled, promised, or petted into viewing one single other exhibit. Certainly not till they had been fed. Or actually, they were fed up and wished to return home.

Dick quickly negotiated with his mother, trading one of his most loving looks for one last look at the Japanese Pavilion. But Mrs. Spencerville and her cousins and the reverend and even Mrs. De Bonnard thought they had seen enough by now. The number one objection was that they simply could not stand up another moment.

"Then we'll have you rolled!" Dick announced, inspired.

That evoked general consternation, until Dick explained himself. Rolling chairs transported visitors through several buildings. There was a religious exhibit the reverend had wished to see, and the rest agreed to be rolled to this, while Dick, Nina, Jordan, and Adele walked to the Japanese Pavilion, promising to meet within the hour at the exit. That arrangement was agreed to by all except Mrs. De Bonnard, who, weighing being alone with Mrs. Windsor's group against the pain in her ankles, decided the former was worse than the latter, and quickly pronounced herself not the slightest fatigued after all. Promptly she joined her daughters' party. The next moment, liveried attendants were paid their sixty cents apiece and half the party was put into chairs and off they rolled, being waved away by the cheerfully liberated five.

The first sight of the authentic Japanese dwelling aroused merely curiosity. It seemed rather small, in Jordan's opinion, which was verified when he had to crouch to enter. Adele and Dick were fascinated by the sliding panels. Nina stopped to sense the peace and individuality of the miniature garden. There were dwarf evergreens all about that pleased her mother, who went off to negotiate for several to be sent to her home. Nina did not accompany her, but walked on by herself, coming upon a small-sized bridge over an artificial pond that she could not resist crossing. Jordan stood back and watched her gliding across it. When she turned and looked back at them from the bridge, there was a moment when he caught his breath.

The sun had just met her hair in small explosions of light, forming an aura that almost pulsated around her head. So perfectly positioned was she that Jordan was almost faint with the need to paint her there and have that moment made lasting. Fearful of revealing his emotions by staring, Jordan broke the connection by abruptly looking down. When he looked up again, she had moved, and that absence he felt for a second within his very self.

Waiting for her return, Jordan was wondering what she was seeing out of his sight. He had an urge to run across the bridge and join her, but he remained stiffly where he was. Eventually she was on the bridge again, walking back. Someone almost pushed him aside and came closer to the bridge. It was a gentleman, sketching rapidly with pastels, and Jordan thought he knew what had inspired him. He approached the fellow and was proved correct. That moment of Nina's pausing on the bridge had been captured after all; Jordan made a quick negotiation for the sketch and had it rolled up in his hands before Nina reentered the house.

She and her mother were discussing the differences between Japanese interior decoration and American style. Looking around, Jordan noted the points Nina was making, and began reevaluating. The simplicity here was startling to eyes accustomed to rooms packed with furniture, ormolu clocks, ivory and porcelain figures, gilt-framed photographs, potted plants in every corner, and walls crowded with framed mottoes or lithographs. Everything here seemed bare at first, but that impression eventually changed to a sense of expansiveness. Mrs. De Bonnard commented that she usually felt dwarfed at home, whereas here she seemed just the correct size. "Dick and Jordan must feel like giants," Adele contributed, and the gentlemen were pleased by that remark. Jordan and Adele exited together, both hoping that Nina was taking notice. Dick and Mrs. De Bonnard followed, with

Dick continually asking to be applauded for bringing them there. Mrs. De Bonnard tolerantly gave him a nod. Throughout the day Dick had had a proprietary attitude about the exposition, demanding acknowledgment if not in exact words then at least in essence: "Yes, Dick, you were quite correct. It was all very amazing. And *you* saw it first."

Nina stayed behind a few moments. No other visitor was there at the moment. She tried to feel what living in such an atmosphere would be like. Would one be more tranquil, or more . . . lonely? Would this clear the world about her, or bring her solitude more sharply into focus? Shuddering, Nina was about to leave when the artist, who from memory had repeated his sketch (this one benefited from seeing Nina closer), handed the new one to her. She hesitated. At first she was annoyed that he had used her as a model without her consent, but when she looked at the sketch, the answer she'd been seeking was clearly there. She was lonely. It showed in her eyes. Accustomed as she was to camouflage, she was shattered by seeing herself so exposed, and would have walked away from the sketch till she was stopped by the young man's mentioning that her tall gentleman escort had already paid for a first one of her, but *this* was his own special tribute—without pay—given by a worshiper of beauty to the embodiment of it.

With that, Nina could do nothing but accept and offer him her smile in return before she hurried along to catch up with the waiting foursome.

At the Centennial Exposition's exit, Jordan was helping the ladies into their carriages, having a special word for each one, particularly his mother. It was, he felt, his duty and pleasure to be charming to women. Duty because women needed to see themselves reflected in the affectionate eyes of a man. Pleasure because he generally found every woman beautiful, young or old. If young, he viewed her as a potential conquest. If old, he viewed her as one who had a history of love and should be reminded by his flirtation of those glorious days, as he hoped one day a young girl would remind him when he had passed his prime.

When Jordan handed Nina into the carriage, he had no attentions for her. He was displeased with her. He had observed her speaking with the artist and holding a rolled-up sketch similar to the one he had bought. Yet she refused to mention it to him or give him the opportunity to explain his actions, to pass it off as a kindhearted act to a struggling artist—as anything but a tribute to her. Also, he wished to see the picture given specially to the model. Was it different from the one he had purchased? And why did she hold it so tightly and stare so fixedly at it, as if it had affected her more than any of his remarks ever had? And why her secret silence? Had she agreed to meet the young artist? A surprising chill went through him at the thought. And he realized, grimly, that he was very near to succumbing to Nina's attraction. Was it possible that he, in attempting to ensnare her, had been ensnared himself—and now was feeling what his brother felt at being tossed aside for another? Had Nina caught and jilted him all in the space of one outing to the Centennial? No—he shook off that conclusion, admitting to a mere momentary pull, nothing more.

While handing her down at Mrs. Spencerville's home, Jordan attempted to regain control by making a light remark and hoping for a smile—she had such a memorable one—but she either did not hear him or pretended she did not. Clutching her rolled-up sketch, Nina entered the house without a look back in his direction.

Adele, staying behind and teasing him to reveal his thoughts, served only to increase Jordan's irritation with Nina. Recalled to his part in the pact, he said the proper words, assuring Adele that she was always in his mind. At which she laughed and bounced happily into the house, slamming the door after her and then quickly opening it to wave once more as he and Dick drove off to their hotel.

That night, while Dick slept, Jordan took himself to the hotel balcony to rethink his strategy. Dick had asked him how much longer must he stay away from Nina, for it had been very difficult not to play her escort when he had the opportunity to be so close to her. He'd so much wanted to take her around and show her everything he'd enjoyed, but instead he had to keep away or talk to Adele, his mother—or sometimes was even reduced to conversing with Reverend Twit!

And all the time Bobby and the guys back home were envying him this chance, which, he reminded Jordan petulantly, he was not taking advantage of. Jordan assured him the point was to make Nina feel neglected so she would leap at any attention Jordan casually tossed her way. But she was difficult to capture, as slippery as a politician. She was always finding needed admiration from passing gentlemen, such as that blasted artist. Yet at her most desperate, when Adele had swooned, she'd turned to him for support—that was some advance. Though not much, he owned. It was all quite baffling.

As an experienced gallant, Jordan had never dealt with so complex a lady. Generally, compliments were all that were needed, for ladies were usually well disposed in his favor. The few he'd had to manipulate to win he had gotten by encouraging their general discontent. He had begun by singling out a quality most sorely lacking in the lady, since that quality would hardly have been much complimented. Thus, his would be the pleasure of discovering a new side of her no one else had ever been devoted enough to uncover, not even herself. If she was garrulous, he claimed her a deep thinker, if dull, he claimed her a wit; if moral, he saw signs of a secret rebel. With Madame Poussin, for example, a French lady who since childhood had exhibited a repressed, subdued personality, he had assured her he saw a secret sparkle that near blinded him.

Then he went on wondering why other people had never seen this remarkable radiance in her before; undoubtedly they had never cared to look deeply enough into her psyche. Madame had eagerly agreed that was true and was resentful that her husband had failed to see all her facets, and she was soon giving this young man her deepest gratitude.

Buoyed by remembering that exquisite triumph, Jordan began to concentrate on a quality lacking in Nina that he could extol. She had charm, wit, intelligence, and even daring, or at least as much daring as a lady brought up in Oceana could have. Ah-ha! That was the ticket! He ought to be attacking her provincialism. Rather than praising a secret asset, he would expose a secret fear and have her determined to prove him wrong by acting more and more rebellious. Yes, at the very next opportunity he would accuse her of being "too Oceana"—in short, a proper prude!

Laughing at his maneuver, Jordan could hardly wait to see her bristle in response. Tossing his cigar over the balcony, he returned to his bedroom, content with himself and his ammended strategy.

Eight

*D*ick *and Jordan* were forced to visit the exposition during the next few days on their own while the women rested after their fatiguing experience. On the third day, the brothers were accompanied by Adele and Mrs. De Bonnard. But Nina refused any further attendance. Staying behind at Mrs. Spencerville's forced her to listen to all the gossip. She attempted deafness, but enough snatches drifted into her consciousness to have her ready to scream.

"Did you hear about Queen Victoria's manservant? The rumor is that that mountain of a man sleeps in the bedroom right next to the queen's!"

The next outrage concerned an American scandal: the revelation that Secretary of War Belknap had two wives at the same time! National and international gossip were just the appetizers. The ladies saved their gusto for the main meal of their own society's scandals. When that was dished up, Nina rushed to close herself away in her tiny room up on the third floor.

To the outward eye, never had a lady more reason to be content than Nina. She gave a good appearance, came from a good family, was socially in good standing. With all this to the good, why did Nina feel herself deserving of something bad happening, writing this dread in her journal, as she wrote all her feelings? These entries had begun with the original secret of learning she could not trust her father. That distrust permeated Nina so thoroughly that her every thought became a secret to be captured and put to rest in her diary, like evanescent butterflies beating their wings against her brow that could only be silenced when pinned down on paper. Eventually all her words broke out into short stories—where there was no confusion. Life in her creative world was clear with solutions, unlike reality, where events and people were often flawed, like fathers, and one had to accept living in confusion and alarm.

Gradually the hope bloomed in Nina that she could be a writer. Yet when she dared to hint at that to her mother, it was not only received with incredulity but immediately dismissed with the unanswerable argument that in their set writers were relegated to the outer tables at the less exclusive affairs. That would not do for a De Bonnard or, even more, for a descendant of the Caroltens, her mother's illustrious family, renowned since the Revolution. That unequivocal response ended Nina's being open about a writing career. It joined the big secrets in her life that could only be shared with her diary. To cover her manuscripts she always kept letters handy to pretend she was engaged in the approved task of correspondence. Since attending the exposition, Nina was inspired to write a short story about it and planned to do so at the first opportunity. That presented itself this morning when Mrs. De Bonnard and Adele departed on a shopping expedition. But her own thoughts impeded her progress, for just before leaving Adele mentioned she was shopping for a dress to wear when Jordan proposed. Nina had been hoping Adele would lose interest. In her heart she knew that Adele's marrying Jordan would be repeating her mother's pattern of having an unfaithful husband. Ought Nina reveal to Adele the secret about their father? No, she answered herself. She could not—not after keeping it so long and after her vow never to reveal it. Possibly Adele would not mind having a philanderer for a husband. Yes, dear God, she would!

The only other solution would be to rescue her sister by deflecting Jordan's interest. Or was she just looking for an excuse because she secretly enjoyed sparring with that cosmopolitan gentleman?

Tossing aside her papers, Nina knew the only distraction for such disturbing thoughts was going somewhere. If only there were someplace to go here in Philadelphia. At home a swim or even a walk on the beach would have rid her of this agitation. Yet here if she just walked out of the door without a chaperone Mrs. Windsor would pounce and insist that she had gone on an assignation. Heavens, it was intolerably claustrophobic living in such close quarters with Mrs. Windsor and her friends. The closeness was made worse by the excessive warmth of the day. Leaning out of her window, Nina caught a glimpse of a miniature rock garden below and a happy smile gave her the solution. She would bring her short story and work on it down there, as well as the letter she had just received from Bobby, as a camouflage in case she was surprised by any of the ladies.

Nina's morning dress was of the very latest shade, "crushed strawberries," a bit brighter than her usual choice of color, but so refreshing she had been unable to resist it. There was a matching parasol, which she used with good effect as she sat on a white wrought-iron chair staring at the minuscule pond in which three, no four, no five goldfish swam around languidly. At this time of year in Oceana, the sea breezes would have cooled the days. Why she had agreed to accompany Jordan and Adele to the Centennial, she could not recollect. Except that she could not refuse either Adele's or her mother's pleading. At least the trip would soon be over. Tomorrow they would attend the July Fourth ceremonies on the grandstand, and then return to New Jersey for the rest of the summer.

Bobby's letter, which she perused haphazardly, was filled with how lonely he was without her while mentioning all his activities, from tennis to yachting to dancing. The very next sentence again claimed his desolation. The hypocrisy of so-called suitors, she thought with a sigh. Look at Jordan, supposedly paying his attentions to Adele and yet using every opportunity to trade quips and looks with Nina and place his boutonniere in her hair so that it might revive itself from "her magnetism." Bunk!

Yet she found herself responding to some of his ploys, especially to his long stares, which transmitted thoughts he never dared say aloud and which could be denied if objected to. A masterful technique, and they called *her* a flirt! But worse—much worse—was that he dared to trifle with Adele. There was no more honest and forthright and generous and decent a person in the world. She deserved a prince and was being given a poseur.

Holding her parasol closer as the sun beat down, Nina was pleased at her success in avoiding Jordan. If he was playing a double hand, she would not be dealt in. While it was up to Adele and her mother to judge Jordan's general worthiness, at least she would not be a partner in his side games.

Her attention was drawn by the welcome sound of the carriages being called for. The ladies of the house were going somewhere all together. Earlier, Nina had heard something about visiting a sick relative who happened to know the inside facts about a young relative suddenly sent south for the summer. No young lady was sent south for the summer unless she had something to conceal, was the consensus, and they hoped Mrs. Parsifal would rise up from her sickbed to tell them her suppositions. Naturally, Nina had declined to attend. Just as she had declined to go shopping, asking her mother with surprise, "In Philadelphia?" One did not find the fashions in Philadelphia, but her mother had been most anxious to go and reluctantly had allowed Adele to come with her at the last minute. Nina had been intuitive enough to allow her mother her private jaunt. Unfortunately, Adele was not as aware and was into the carriage, oblivious to her mother's resigned acceptance.

Bobby's letter had still another page. She had struggled through descriptions of his last two tennis matches and hoped he was not now going to treat her to squash. Really, she preferred Jordan's speechless glances.

No, she had misjudged poor Bobby. The last page was about the indignity of a freshwater yacht attempting to race a seagoing one. And then a P.S. with a rhymed couplet for her: "I send this plea to my heart's Queena,/ Marry me—my very own Nina!"

Gagging at both the rhyme and prospect, Nina was about to toss the page aside when the footman announced she had a guest. Before Nina had time to deny being at home, Jordan followed him in.

Nina was lady enough to dismiss the servant before speaking her mind.

"You have the wrong Miss De Bonnard. Adele and Mama are shopping, and the rest are visiting. I was taking the air."

"Of the three preoccupations, I chose the last. I'll be delighted to take the air with you—what there is of it on this rather close day."

"You misunderstood me. No one's at home!"

"In that berry dress, indeed, you seem like a summer's mirage, but on closer observation one is delighted to see you're very *real* and very present before me."

"Not for long," Nina said composedly. "What is the purpose of your visit?" She rose to show him her intention of withdrawing, so he rushed his statement.

"There's a concert tonight. I thought we might attend. They are playing that piece we discussed by—"

"I have nothing in concert with you, sir."

Momentarily stymied, Jordan was contemplating his next maneuver while staring fixedly at the goldfish in the pond.

"There are five of them," Nina inserted.

Looking up in surprise and then down at the goldfish, Jordan smiled at Nina quickly, as if she had won something from him— and he awarded her with a respectful nod.

"Are there indeed? You have a way of throwing men off balance. I was just preparing myself to say something of importance to you."

"Cancel the preparations. I suggest you keep silent."

"Why so alarmed, my lovely Nina?"

Surprised at his presumption of addressing her by her first name, the young lady stared repressively at him. He did not react to her hint; rather, undaunted, he stared back with his dark compelling eyes, subjecting Nina to a jumble of emotions, culminating in the exhilaration she always felt just before a gentleman made his declaration to her.

He did not make it; rather he was wandering about the small area, lost in thought—then suddenly looked up as if having reached a decision. She waited.

"I've been thinking of the restrictive lives ladies have to endure. You're intelligent enough to resent that, aren't you? I've seen you chafing at the bit . . . bit by bit." He came close to her.

Nina was chafing indeed at the restriction he was putting on her movements by standing so close as he continued. "It's my object in life, I own, to help every woman reach her fulfillment, which is why I intend to help liberate you—whether you thank me for it or not. The way Oceana ladies are forced to live within the bounds explicitly set down by their prudish mothers is downright unnatural."

Relieved at the philosophic nature of his challenge, Nina still had to laugh at that. "Nonsense. To begin with, mothers are never explicit. Nor is society. Everything is either implied or understood, and you are mistaking prudish for *proper*."

"Propriety overdone is *prudishness*," he insisted, "and prudish people suffer for it, denying their own individuality and inclinations—possible for those with manageable inclinations. But some of us"—and Jordan bowed in her direction—"have strong urges that ought *not to be contained*."

Nina flushed at that image of herself. She took a moment to consider the possibility that her keeping several gentlemen around at one time rather than indicating a wish not to commit herself to one gentleman meant a sensual need for several gentlemen, due to an unnaturally passionate nature. Was that possible? She did constantly have to suppress a desire to live life on a fuller scale than was permitted. In confusion she looked at Jordan's eyes and saw deliberate taunting. It was really rather shocking of him to be speaking of "urges" at all in her presence. Ladies never acknowledged having them. Her mother would certainly advise her to deny the existence of such. Yet to call him to task for mentioning them would be to prove his point that she was a prude. Seeing the triumph in Jordan's eyes as he read her thoughts, Nina sensed that the insufferable man had deliberately put her in this awkward position. Smiling archly, she merely switched the point of his remarks to him by asking softly, "When you speak of strong urges that 'some of us have' . . . is that a confession?"

He grinned at her ploy. "Oh, without question, my dear Miss De Bonnard. I have the strongest urges, but I have a long history of exercising my urges; so they are in prime condition and can easily be held in check at my command."

"I am certain all the young women are relieved to hear that."

"While *yours*," he continued, ignoring her aside, "I gather, are *unused* and have become stiff, which, if not soon let free will burst or even worse—atrophy."

"Ah! And I gather you altruistically intend to assist me to exercise them?"

"I will. In keeping with my generous nature," he responded, while slowly removing the white kid gloves that were de rigueur in the afternoon. Then, like a challenge to a duel, he tossed them on the table before her and took her hands, flesh to flesh, and pulled her to him.

Having the beauty close in his arms for a moment exercised his urges to their fullest against him. Just as his lips were near hers, she turned her head so he caught her cheek instead, kissing there, and when he sought her mouth, Nina pulled back, saying calmly, "That is sufficient exercise. Fortunately you warned me that a person with my advanced case of stiffened urges might suffer dire consequence if she gave in to them! How distressing it would be for a gentleman to witness a lady coming apart in his hands. . . . What would he do with a woman in such disarray?"

"You may have the utmost confidence in my ability to handle that situation." And this time Jordan did not allow her to deflect his objective, kissing her ruthlessly. For all his light conversation, Jordan was not prepared for the pleasure that shot through him as he kissed deeply her strawberry lips.

Nina was similarly surprised by an unexpected onrush of sensuousness. But his melding from kiss to kiss brought back another moment when she had been imprisoned like this (Windsor men closing in on her! Windsor men not letting her go!), and Nina began screaming under his kisses, which finally cut through Jordan's bliss sufficiently to have him step back breathlessly.

The lady was gasping as well, but from fear. "You . . . you *Windsor*! Are you drunk? If not on liquor on your own self-conceit? And, dear God, why are you here at all with your phony 'exercising my urges' ploy when Adele is your object! Save your approaches and kisses for her!"

In her flurry of motion as she attempted to leave, Nina dropped Bobby's letter.

Always the gentleman, Jordan retrieved it for her, but not before ungentlemanly glancing at both the signature and the postscript proposal. Of a sudden, all calculation, all sophistication collapsed, and he exclaimed in disgust, "Is *this* your next victim? No wonder you have no interest in either Dickie or myself! You have your next suitor ready to add to your list of witless young conquests! Is that really your preference?"

Seeing him so genuinely flustered, Nina's own panic subsided, whereupon she coldly informed him that there would be no response to so insulting a summation, which had been reached by his boorish act of perusing what was not intended for his eyes.

"That does not answer me," he insisted grimly.

"Correct. I do not intend to answer you. By what rights do you question me? Or force your unwanted presence on me here in this garden? Do I have to remind you that you are my sister's beau!"

He shook off that reminder as if it were of no import. At the same time he found himself shaking off the role assigned him under the pact. Instead he felt an exhilarating thrill to be speaking to her naturally what was foremost in his mind.

"I called on Mr. Fletcher."

"Who?"

"Your artist admirer! I called on him to see if you'd visited his studio—if that explained your sudden unwillingness to be in my company and your implausible desire to stay with the matrons at home. What other explanation but a possible tryst?"

"And you discovered . . . ?" Nina asked with wonder at his daring to act as if there had been an understanding between them and he had the right to call her to account.

"He claims not even to know your name and was anxious to get that information from me. He had made several more sketches of your face. It seems, as with all of us, you have the ability to sear your image into our consciousness. I've hired him to complete a portrait of you."

"What presumption!" Nina exclaimed, walking a bit around the wrought-iron chair. When she had contained herself sufficiently, she continued in the chilliest tones she could summon on such a warm day. "I do not wish you to have a portrait of me. I do not permit it. I deny that I am running around 'searing' my image, as you put it, into your consciousness or anyone else's! I merely passed by the man. As for you, sir, I merely attempted to be conversational with you today and on all other occasions when we have, to my regret, come together. I have offered you no encouragement. Nothing but a . . ." She sought for the word.

He supplied it. "An understanding."

"No, sir!"

"Yes. I've felt our bond since my return from Europe. You fenced with me. You shared glances with me. At the exposition we proved we valued the same art, inventions, even bon mots. We shared laughter. We understand each other today, this moment, and it is time we both confessed it. Say you agree! Say you want me as much as I want you. Say a simple yes, and that will be sufficient."

He was whispering at the end, taking hold of her again. That she would not allow. She stepped back in anxiety, saying, "I'll have to warn Adele about you! She should be warned. All women should be warned against you!" And Nina turned and ran into the safety of the house, leaving Jordan sitting down in a heap. He shook his head. She was, without a doubt, the most difficult challenge he'd ever attempted. And the blasted thing was that she was having more of an effect on his urges than he was apparently having on hers. And yet, for a moment there, the passion, he swore, had been mutual. She might have been reached if it were not for Adele. It was always Adele, Adele, between them. He had damn well overplayed that maneuver. And he had damn well better correct that if he had hopes of any kind for the elder Miss De Bonnard. Good Lord, but her lips had burned into his, leaving not just a sensation but almost a branding. He could not help but think of Shakespeare's line about Cleopatra: "She makes hungry where most she satisfies." Indeed. Blast Shakespeare. And Cleopatra. And double blast his own stratagem.

On her way to the stairs to her room, Nina was stopped by the entrance of Mrs. Windsor and her group. They had returned in rather a sour mood. For a moment as they removed their hats, none observed the young lady approaching, being too absorbed in their barrage of criticism. The friend, apparently, had been too ill to do more than nod and roll her eyes over every one of their questions.

"You'd think she'd gargle!" Mrs. Spencerville was complaining. "There was no excuse for her not speaking to us when we went there precisely to speak to her!"

The unanimous agreement was jarred by a loud "No!" from Mrs. Windsor.

In surprise, Mrs. Spencerville was ready to take issue when she turned and saw the object of Mrs. Windsor's loud negative: Nina at the end of the hall and, coming up behind her, Jordan.

"Don't tell me! Don't let it be true! The two of you have been out alone?" Had they sought scandal abroad when all the time it was rearing its ugly presence at home?

"Not true, Mama," Jordan appeased her. "I stopped by to visit you and, of course, the Misses De Bonnard, and discovered Miss De Bonnard was in the garden. She was just informing me that you were not at home when we heard you enter. Have you been shopping?"

Nina did not bother to wait to see if the excuse was sufficient. She said a general "Good afternoon" to all and went up the stairs to her room. Similarly, any further questions or objections Mrs. Windsor was hoping to emit were left sounding in his wake as Jordan too took his leave, closing the front door on all the morning's confusion.

Nine

*I*s that where the two of you went!" Nina exclaimed. "But, really, it is too bad of you. I should have wished to have attended as well!"

"Oh you really missed it!" Adele was crowing. "At first, because I was there, Mama was going to change her plans and go shopping with me instead. But I said something about Miss Anthony. You know, how we discussed it last night—what was in the papers—about the public parlors for women visitors to the Centennial, and how one could meet with Susan B. Anthony and Elizabeth Stanton and hear what they were planning."

Aggrieved, Nina turned to her mother, who was calmly removing her hat and rearranging her faded blond hair into a more becoming pouf. "Why was it necessary to keep your attendance a secret? I could understand keeping it from the others. But from me!"

"I particularly did not wish either of my two daughters to attend," she responded calmly. "You are neither old enough for rebellion."

"I am so!" Adele insisted. "And there were lots of younger girls than me there."

"Listen, dears. I may wish to be quietly involved in this crusade because of my beliefs, but it cannot hurt me. I am already a fixture in society. I have had my children. And my husband is content with our lives. You are both now of an age to be forming your own lives. Adele, it seems, will be getting married first, and to a sensible, mature man. As for my dear Nina, you have had already too much controversy and disapproval in your young life. I certainly did not wish to put you in a position to receive more."

Both daughters spoke at once denying that assessment, and Mrs. De Bonnard and Adele then paused to inform Nina what had happened and what was going to happen tomorrow at the July Fourth ceremonies. And that anticipation quieted and delighted all. At least, Nina assuaged herself, she could take part in *that*.

While Adele was preparing for bed, brushing out the ringlets with her hairpins flying about the room, Nina checked the morrow's outfit: a navy blue, severely tailored dress and her high-crowned navy hat. Determining that it was in perfect order, she turned next to put some order into her understanding of Adele's feelings.

"I understood from Mother that you are both expecting Jordan's proposal?"

"Oh, yes. His attentions are too marked for him to mean anything less."

"He has spoken to you then of the future?"

"Not exactly of that."

"Of his hopes then for your acceptance?"

"Not exactly that either."

"Has he . . . attempted . . . that is, have the two of you kissed?"

"Not exactly."

"Oh really, Adele! How exactly are you committed to this man, and I stress the word *man*, when he has not made his intentions clear to either you or Mama!"

"He sends me flowers!"

"Good grief! If I considered every man who sent me a posy my intended, I should be engaged to half the population of Oceana, Newport, and New York!"

"Well, haven't you been?" Adele answered with a giggle.

Ignoring that, Nina continued. "Has he made you an offer?"

"No. But he will. And he's perfect for me. Did you see how he didn't object to that magazine, *The New Century*, while Dick had a lot of snickering things to say about it? You know how silly Dick is—calling your train a *tail* and having a giggling fit over that. I mean, Jordan is very serious. And respectful of me. And his eyes when he looks my way do immoral things to me. And the way he says something that sounds perfectly respectable until you think about it and look into his eyes, and suddenly it's not; and I'm all churning away inside. Like the Corliss engine starts everything going when he pulls the lever. Oh, he's everything I could possibly hope for. Intelligent. Romantic. And *mine*."

"Yes, I see."

"Well, why are you so sad? Aren't you happy for me?"

"Yes. I am." And getting up and hugging her sister, Nina said, "You deserve to get exactly what you want in this life. And if I can do anything to assure that, I shall."

"Oh, you're a sweetheart, Nin. But really, I don't need any help. Things are going just swell."

When they had turned off the gas jets, Nina interrupted the dark silence with "He hasn't kissed you?"

"No," Adele admitted. "Just my hand. *But* he kissed the boutonniere he was wearing and put it in my hair and said *there* it would revive."

"Oh, good heavens!"

"What is it, Nina?"

"Nothing."

"Anyway, I was telling you. Marilyn said he'd kissed her. Not that I believe her. She claims all men have kissed her. And I've only had Dick plant a sloppy one on me when we were sailing. And that wasn't so great. But Marilyn said she felt his kiss—down to her toes! So"—Adele was giggling and moving her own toes in anticipation—"I can hardly wait!"

The next morning Nina was hurriedly dressing, and there was no time to think of Jordan.

Adele urged her along, and her mother entered to warn them to keep quiet. "We must needs separate ourselves from the group when the event begins. Understood? There is no need for the news to reach your father's ears."

Although both girls were willing to throw caution to the winds of change, they agreed to move only at her signal.

The ninety-degree heat eliminated half of the party that had been set for the July Fourth festivities. In any case, Mrs. Spencerville and her cousins had vowed never again to attend the Centennial. Mrs. Windsor wished similarly to rescue herself. But there was the question of chaperoning her sons. She could not trust Mrs. De Bonnard to do that, for there was a look in Jordan's eyes lately and a confusion about his manner that reminded her too much of Dick's first reaction to Nina. Of course Jordan was paying his attentions to the younger one, with no history of a jilt—a nice unaffected, bouncy girl—but, *but* she was a De Bonnard. And the women of that clan had a way of making Mrs. Windsor nervous. Thankfully, Nina did not seem to be paying any more attention to her Dick, although Dick was still occasionally sighing after her when he wasn't sighing after the exhibitions! No, she could not chance it. Despite the heat, she would attend. Eternal vigilance was the responsibility of any mother with two such endearing and eligible sons.

The party of six arrived at the centennial celebration in time to have their choice of seats. The wooden platform set up on the north side had a canvas awning overhead, it was a relief to observe. At the last moment, after Jordan had found a perfect spot in the shade and seated the De Bonnard ladies and his mother and Dick was bringing the programs, Mrs. De Bonnard got up, complaining that they were too far in the rear. She then spotted three empty seats farther forward and announced coolly that she and her daughters would take them—if the Windsors didn't mind. Whether they did or not none of the De Bonnards paused to discover, but were off and lost in the crowd.

In a moment their seats were taken by some dignitaries, and Jordan gave up his as well to an extra lady, with one of his gallant bows, which had her blushing. Mrs. Windsor rose and looked for the De Bonnard women but, not finding them, was suddenly alerted to a new danger from the extra lady listening with wide-eyed wonder to Dickie's explanation of the Corliss engine. Her vigilance needed right here, Mrs. Windsor forgot the De Bonnards. As did Dick.

Only Jordan was determined to locate them. Ever since arriving to escort them, he had been suspicious of their actions and manner. And that sense was justified when he spotted the De Bonnards—not even sitting, but standing near the press section. He knew several journalists there and was making his way in that direction when the opening ceremonies began.

One could walk around during the playing of the band music but not during the delivery of the bishop's words. Not till Oliver Wendell Holmes' "Independence Day" hymn was being sung could Jordan move again.

A lady who had been seated in the journalists' section stood abruptly and approached the De Bonnard women, handing them each a pile of papers. They took them up and nodded. There was more conferring.

The mayor of Philadelphia had finished displaying the manuscript of the original Declaration of Independence, and Richard Henry Lee had just completed reading it, when another woman in the journalists' section rose suddenly. She was instantly followed by four others, similarly attired in black. Jordan was holding his breath in hopes that the De Bonnard women would not follow, for he had by then recognized the ringleader. But neither the mother nor the two daughters ventured to the front of the speakers' stand. They obviously had their orders.

At that moment, there was a gasp and a hush from the audience observing the diminutive woman forcefully pushing her way to the front. Then and there, in a clear voice, Susan B. Anthony announced that she was holding in her hands a *new* Declaration of Independence that would include women. It stated, she said, that women were free and independent and no longer bound to obey laws in whose making they had no voice, and, further, that they, as had their original forefathers, objected to taxation without representation. Her ringing conclusion was that there, in the presence of the assembled nations of the world "gathered to celebrate our national centennial," they had come to demand justice for "the women of this land."

While her statement was brief, it seemed long to the audience, who were holding their breath at the audacity. When Miss Anthony concluded, she presented the new Declaration to Senator Ferry. He accepted it with a bow. As the woman and her four followers started off the platform, the De Bonnard women went into action, joined by the other lady assistants, passing out copies of the new Declaration of Independence. There was no lack of interest. Men were standing on the seats, reaching for them, whether out of genuine interest or because they were unable to resist getting anything for free and being part of an "occasion." In any case, while the De Bonnard women were carrying on with the distributing, the demure woman had made her way to the musicians' platform and there Susan B. Anthony read aloud to all her Declaration of Independence for Women, while Matilda Gage held an umbrella over her head and the voice of General Hawley was heard shouting for "Order, order!"

Rushing toward the De Bonnard women, Jordan observed that Mrs. De Bonnard and Adele were standing together on one side—Adele laughing through it all, enjoying it. Mrs. De Bonnard was calmly, imperiously, granting the people the privilege of receiving the paper from her hands. Neither seemed in need of his help. He left them to their pleasure and went looking for Nina. She was easily spotted by a group that had surrounded her, mostly men, pushing in as she distributed the sheets. Gallantly keeping her head up and refusing conversation with those closing in on her, she attempted again and again to step away while directing their attention to Miss Anthony speaking. Finally a young swell with a Vandyke beard and a look of determination held on to the hand that was passing out the paper. She attempted to shake him off—and was seized on the other side by another scoundrel in plaid.

The Declarations of Independence in Nina's hands went flying. Her smart navy hat was askew and tottering over her eyes. But she kicked out. Her struggles seemed to incite the rabble further. Attempting to speak to them in her well-bred tones, Nina asked to be released, but they would not be reasoned with. It took Jordan a mere five seconds to free both her arms, dismiss the crowd, and straighten her hat. When she saw who had rescued her, he read anger rather than gratitude in the glistening eyes. But she managed to nod to him and further adjust her hat, and then, without a word or pause, she bent to pick up the papers and carry on with the distribution.

Jordan was silent in his admiration of her pluck. To show his feelings, he picked up the remainder of the scattered Declarations and, following her close behind, partly en garde, partly because he could not bear to allow her out of his sight, he began handing around the papers as well.

Nina, who at first view of his following began to remonstrate, was silenced by his assistance. And thus they continued through the crowd till there were no more Declarations remaining, except for the one coming clearly from Jordan's eyes and accepted by Nina with a slight smile on her lips.

Ten

When the *De Bonnard* ladies returned to Oceana, Mr. De Bonnard felt that Adele and his wife had benefited mightily from the trip. They both had high color in their faces and a new, set purpose to their steps. Nina, as usual, was unreadable.

He asked them how they had enjoyed the Centennial and Mrs. De Bonnard described some of the new inventions, to which he listened with his usual calculation as to their profitability.

"The Women's Pavilion was the best!" Adele burst in, but at a look from her mother, she was silenced.

"Yes, indeed," Mrs. De Bonnard replied, "it was most interesting. There was a display of etchings by Queen Victoria herself that was most impressive."

Reassured that his women remained in their usual sphere of women's interests, Mr. De Bonnard nodded and left for a day's challenge at the New York stock market.

Alone, the three De Bonnards smiled at each other.

"No mention of the Women's Independence Declaration in the papers?" Adele asked.

"Not in the financial section, and that is all your father reads."

Laughing, Adele continued, "I was afraid Mrs. Windsor would spot us. Not that I'd care. I'm proud of our participation. But better none of the Windsors saw us."

Nina did not dissuade her of that belief. Jordan, of course, knew, but she was certain he would not report to Mrs. Windsor.

"Believe me, if Elvira knew, we'd know by now!" Mrs. De

Bonnard responded with a laugh. "Do you know, I handed a Declaration to Mr. Hayes, the nominee for the Republicans, and he was most gracious. He bowed over my hand and assured me he would read it thoroughly."

"A politician," Nina murmured, but Mrs. De Bonnard bristled at that, insisting that she had had some effect on him, and Adele enthusiastically agreed. Nina remained silent during the rest of the discussion; not that she wasn't hopeful, but she simply wasn't hope filled.

On one of the first five days after their return, the three ladies, dressed in their finery—including twelve-button, elbow-length, white kid gloves, which meant they had to keep their hands to a minimum of motions to prevent creasing and their bodies similarly strictured—went out for a carriage drive. The carriage was as polished as the coachman's shiny boots, and the footmen were in their golden De Bonnard livery with fleurs-de-lis on the sleeves. It was the calling hour at Oceana.

At each of the residences of their society, the carriage stopped and the ladies waited stiffly within while the footman jumped down and, with much consequence and consciousness of his position, handed the De Bonnard cards to the footman of the residence. And on to the next house and the next. At no time would any of the ladies descend from the carriage, since no one would admit to being at home during the calling hour, when anybody who was anybody was out calling on everybody else.

Nina was impatiently twirling her parasol. "This has taken two hours. You do not really expect me to join in the coach parade as well!"

"Certainly. We must omit nothing. Just in case a rumor is loosed, we must be certain no one ever believes we could be guilty of doing *anything* improper."

And so with much inward protest but outwardly sitting up stiffly and correctly, the three ladies joined the parade of couches down Driftwood Avenue, the main Oceana thoroughfare.

So many equipages were out today, from demi-daumonts and victorias, landaus, phaetons, and barouches to dogcarts. One nodded right and nodded left. This went on for fifteen miles, and then at last they could return home.

As she passed the other homes, Mrs. De Bonnard had enjoyed comparing them to her own. Most others were so out of keeping with the setting. For years the homes of Oceana and its environs had been of respectable size, all exuberantly decorated with ornate railings, dormers, gables, and cupolas. Minnie Masters, a friend of Mrs. De Bonnard, had just such an original Victorian house with gingerbread decorations, sea-scrolled carvings, and a huge wooden pineapple atop—a typical sign of hospitality.

Sea Cliff, the De Bonnard estate, had been one of the first to resemble a beached yacht, following in Commodore Robert Stockton's wake, whose home, Sea Girt, in another New Jersey town was almost a replica of the ships he commanded. Sea Cliff was even larger, with decks wrapped around and a lookout point on top, and it was always freshly painted white.

There were several outstanding examples of foreign ornateness, from Regent's Court, the Pynchots' thirty-room estate, to Windsorkin, the Windsors' miniature Tudor castle with Elvira additions such as a Grecian folly, a topiary garden, and an eight-foot-high stone wall that closed around the estate, separating it from the path leading to the beach. For Mrs. Windsor felt that the sea, like everything else about her, should not only know its place but keep to it. She could not understand Jenny De Bonnard's actually standing on her decklike balconies and sniffing in the iodized air, claiming it an anodyne for one's nerves and a tonic to one's spirit. And though Sea Cliff was larger, Windsorkin was grander, and Regent's Court grander and larger still.

But all were dwarfed by a new estate that had been recently finished. This proved that encroaching people built encroaching estates, Mrs. De Bonnard thought as their carriage passed this establishment of at least forty rooms, clearly that of the nouveau riche couple whose name (and it was difficult to credit that actuality) was Richards. They were known to have acquired their wealth in trade and thus could not be invited to the Oceana parties. The stock market was one thing—and even owning railroads was permissible—but it was known that the Richards were connected with a plumbing concern.

It was possible to have a plumbing fixture in one's house but not the maker of it at one's table.

One would have thought the Richards would have had the good sense not to have done their house all in marble, for it so clearly signified their source of wealth. But taste was obviously not something with which they were flush. It was pink marble, no less, which was turned positively bloodred by the setting sun.

No, Jenny De Bonnard could not regret not having left them her card. And when she returned to her shipboard estate, she found one of their cards—pink, of course. It was too much even for a woman of her freer thinking to countenance. And with a small shake of her head, she tore it up and informed her butler that they were never at home to the Richards—should they actually dare to call.

Cass Richards, the eighteen-year-old daughter, had been seen today, driving in a demi-daumont. The carriage had been imported from Paris and was drawn by four horses; it was also equipped with two postilions outfitted not in ordinary livery, but in jockey suits.

Adele had laughed, Mrs. De Bonnard had shaken her head at the gaucherie, and Nina had thought at least it looked original, and later she defended Mrs. Richards by objecting, "The problem with this entire place is that we all tend to be *like* each other. Even this inane ritual of driving about in carriages or leaving cards to people you might very well have seen earlier at the beach. It's a total waste of time. And I for one do not intend to accompany you anymore!"

"Very well," Mrs. De Bonnard said casually, "if you wish to feed the rumors about you. But consider—you've turned down every eligible man here or in New York till you are close to not being eligible yourself. Elvira has whispered the word *jilt*. But for our making certain that no actual act of yours goes beyond the pale, you would have been excluded from social gatherings long before. Up to now it has been all innuendo, which cannot succeed against your father's connections and my lineage. You have to keep to the rules for all our sakes."

Nina looked stricken by the uncharacteristic denunciation from the mother who had always supported her when her father had pressed her to marry. And to speak to her thus—and before her sister, her *younger* sister (who was edging out of the room and had by now softly closed the door)—was too overwhelming.

Her mother looked into her daughter's eyes and shook her head and took her into her arms. "I did not mean to speak so roughly. But we all find the restrictions of society difficult to follow. I know it is more so for you because you have a desire to live a fuller life. I felt that myself when I was beginning my life. Now I accept that we can only be content not to hurt others about us. You're my firstborn. I would do anything I could to make you happy. But you must agree to make life easier for the rest of us, no matter how much you disagree with this society and its mores."

"I'm sorry, Momma. I'll come with you on the carriage ride with a better face."

Mrs. De Bonnard touched her child's upturned face tenderly. "There is no one with as beautiful a face as you have, Nina. When you were a child you had a spirit to match. You could do anything and did it with all your heart. You played the piano enough to make your teachers certain you could have had a concert career. You danced so beautifully. You loved your father and me, a very loving child. Then what changed you into not caring so much?"

"I love you . . . and Adele," Nina objected.

"Is it the young men? Have they become too much of a distraction? Are you not aware that keeping yourself the idol of all men, you lose the chance to find the one man of your heart?"

"There is no man of my heart. There is only settling."

Mrs. De Bonnard led Nina to her private sitting room. Once there, she said earnestly, "What is it, my dear? What are you looking for? I do not wish you to marry against your inclinations. Between us, that was my fate. I dutifully followed everything my father and mother laid out for me while within I was shouting to be free. I have had a comfortable life, despite having married a man who finds most of his pleasures in the stock market, at his club, or on his private yacht with other women."

Nina jumped up in alarm, her face white. Her mother held on to her hand and said softly, "Lately I've begun to sense you have been aware that your father and I are not close. That is correct. We have not been for a long time. If ever. I wished to discuss it but never felt you were old enough. . . . Now it appears you are."

Nina did not feel old enough to discuss it. Of a sudden she felt younger than ever. She was thirteen again. So her mother had known about the yacht all along! In fact, the deceit had been agreed to by both. And, worse, there had never been anything between them to betray. Oh ignoble!

"What is it? What are you thinking?"

"That if there has never been love between you, the only deceit practiced was not on each other but on Delly and me. That the two of you built a false image of family unity . . . as fundamental as belief in God and our society. What did you think would happen to one of your young children when she uncovered that falseness? What would be left for her to believe in again?"

"But that would be impossible. I've spent my life attempting to keep up a good front for the two of you. For everyone. What are you saying? That you knew before . . . that you saw something . . . that led you to conclude our marriage was false?" Mrs. De Bonnard asked with dread as she stumbled over the words.

The whiteness of her mother's face persuaded Nina that she had been correct not to relate what she had seen on the yacht. That would have forced her mother to face that their family secret was generally known to the extent that even her daughter had been long aware of it. After spending her life attempting to make her mother happy, Nina could not in one moment alter that practice, so she quickly soothed her by assuring, "No. Nothing. I mean just something I sensed."

The relief was so strong that it seemed to have caused Mrs. De Bonnard to take a moment to gather her thoughts. She looked down at her hands. The two were silent.

At last Nina asked, "You were never even friends? Never shared some modicum of love?"

"We were . . . we are partners. We supply what the other needs and we have the same goal in mind: the success of our joined pact. My duty and his *acquisitiveness* were the matchmakers at our union. Later when you and Delly were at the ladies' finishing school, I discovered a young man and through him what I had truly missed in my life and how really cruel my parents had been depriving me of any chance of love."

"You found love? You loved this man? Really, and yet you stayed with my father? Why?"

"Because I loved your sister and you more. I could not add scandal to your names. I could not end your chances at a life in society."

"Oh, bother society!" Nina cried out from her heart.

"It may be a bother but it is our life. Where would one be without it? Marriages are arranged, children are reared, boundaries set, judgments made all by its rules. It gives us stability. To break away from it is to give up its strength and support. Even your father, who does not have the background in society that I do, understands its importance in our lives and keeps within its bounds—outwardly . . . and will not countenance his child going beyond them.

"This friendship you have with Bobby Van Reyden—are we coming close to another engagement? I've spoken to you before and made clear you cannot make another connection and break it! The Van Reyden wealth is of such dimensions and Bobby Van Reyden so willing to use its power, he ought not be toyed with! He's not the youngster you seem to think he is. Not only are you both of an age, but the late August Van Reyden was your father's mentor. He helped Philip push his way into our set. Staked him to begin his fortune. Suggested me as the prize of his accomplishments. The possibility that you would marry the sole Van Reyden heir has always been your father's ambition. If you give him any indication that you are willing to accept that connection, he will never allow you to sever it."

"My stars!" Nina gasped. "There's no such connection! That is, Bobby has written me letters making me offers, but I have never responded to any of them nor taken them or him seriously."

"Then you should! Tell him either yes or no. But don't keep him about like a cicisbeo—that's a style only married women are allowed. Thankfully you have dismissed Dick Windsor. There is no need to awaken Elvira's tigress instincts. If roused they could lead to writing you out of society. Even with Adele, against whom not a whisper has ever been spoken, Elvira has been looking about fiercely for some way to discourage her relationship with Jordan. Thankfully, Jordan is too strong to be affected by any of her machinations, but I'm keeping a wary eye on her. I really risked poor Delly's future by allowing her to pass out the declarations, but Adele threatened to inform Elvira about our attending the meeting if I did not. She's so enthusiastic about the cause. God is looking kindly at one of my girls, for it appears Jordan would not object to her interests. I pray every day that he will shortly make his offer."

Nina looked down sharply at her hands.

"What is it?" her mother asked suspiciously. "You are not jealous of your sister's good fortune, are you?"

"No! I wish—what you wish. That he make her his offer as soon as possible. And as for myself, I'll attempt to keep the tongues quiet even if it means countless card leavings and even— even talking with Mrs. Pynchot."

The mention of the dowager dragon of society had Mrs. De Bonnard smiling. Mrs. Pynchot was a seventy-year-old woman who found everything that had changed since her early days a personal offense. In fact, she still dressed in the Regency style of her first season in London, when her father had been an ambassador there. She even continued to address people in the idiom of that time, peppering her speech with "By Jove" and "egad!"

"It is particularly fortuitous that you mentioned Mrs. Pynchot," her mother put in with a slightly relieved smile that they had successfully sailed through the troubled waters of their discussion. "Her Regency fete is at the end of the week; and we shall, unfortunately, have to attend—in full *complement*," she added meaningfully to her daughter.

Nina laughed. "Very well. I'll bring along my vinaigrette and brush up on my curtsies!" And she curtsied low to the ground, fluttering her eyelashes outlandishly, which had her mother laughing but concluding seriously, "Poor woman. Of course I mean rich woman. Yet one can't help but see her as personally impoverished, despite all her wealth and power. Therefore, your father always insists we attend. The sad thing is that she is quite alone and living in her past, which means we have to live in it with her. You've heard about Mr. Marshall taking her over?"

When Nina shook her head, Mrs. De Bonnard described this upstart from somewhere out west making his way into eastern society by attaching himself to the socially important matrons and adding his tasteless flamboyance to the plans for their balls.

Nina laughed and asked how one could add more excess to the mistress of excess and how society could tolerate her.

"At her age and with her standing, Mrs. Pynchot is permitted her excesses," Mrs. De Bonnard explained. "Indeed, matrons and gentlemen may similarly indulge in excesses as long as there is no flaunting. But a young, unmarried lady cannot give even a hint of having gone beyond the bounds. That is why you must use the opportunity of the ball—when all society will be there—to behave circumspectly. You can begin by not allowing any gentleman, including Bobby Van Reyden, to be seen as having your marked favor. No giving away your fan or roses . . . or even special smiles. And no favoring anyone with a second dance. A third one would be practically an announcement. But you know all this. You're not a child."

"Sometimes I feel I am," Nina said, and her mother shook her head at her with a fond smile and said, "My child always."

"I'll sit out the dances next to Mrs. Pynchot," Nina volunteered nobly.

Her mother laughed. "There is no need for such punishment! Have an enjoyable time. Merely don't arouse either expectations or suspicions."

"That won't be difficult. There's no one here I'm interested in," Nina said with a deep sigh that had her mother concerned.

"Perhaps it would be best if you took a trip when the summer is over," she suggested.

"I have been considering traveling. I've been thinking of the West. There's something about a new land . . ." Her words faltered at her mother's look of horror.

"Out west with the Indians!"

Nina laughed. "I have no plans to join a reservation, Mama. I simply wish to see the mountains, the freedom of the people out there, the . . . oh, stars!" She had to giggle at her mother's alarm and concede quickly, "I'll forget the West."

Satisfied, Mrs. De Bonnard rose up. "We'll discuss your destination at the end of the summer. By then Delly will be officially engaged to Mr. Jordan Windsor. And I, with both my girls provided for, can devote my time to our cause."

Nina paused as she was about to leave. "You're certain Jordan Windsor is sincere in his attentions? He doesn't . . . strike me as such."

"Bite your tongue!" her mother admonished. "I could not bear to have Delly's heart broken!"

"No," Nina agreed. "Neither could I."

The next week all discussions, not only at the De Bonnards' but throughout Oceana, centered on the Pynchot invitations. Apparently this year it was not to be the usual Regency ball, which was probably the influence of Mr. Marshall. Instead it was an "American Dream" quadrille. Everyone was to dress as he would wish himself to be in his wildest dreams, but remembering always that this was the centennial year.

Mrs. De Bonnard stared so long at the invitation that Mr. De Bonnard had to speak to her several times and still couldn't get her attention. At last he rose and took the invitation out of her hands and perused it, whereupon he muttered something that sounded like "fool woman," and, though walking out, stopped to say, "Nevertheless, we'll have to attend—blast her!"

By now the girls were looking at the invitation themselves and laughing. Adele, as was her style, was delighted. "I'll go as a bird—because it's always been my dream to fly. And for the Oceana touch, I'll be a seagull."

Mrs. De Bonnard could find no fault with that, provided the wingspan was moderate and there was "just the merest suggestion of a beak."

Adele hotly insisted she wanted a *definite* beak and large wings. And the two left the room, arguing over the dream-costume details.

The next morning Adele was proclaiming her total victory

over her mother and describing her costume, with full beak, on their way to the beach. Rumors that Nina would be appearing in a new bathing suit from France that revealed flesh below the knee were deflated by the reality. A woman in the town of Long Branch had been severely reprimanded and threatened with arrest for just such attire. The white flag was up, which meant it was time for ladies to bathe. Their carriage joined those of the other ladies drawing up on the sand, from which they emerged in their seven-piece bathing suits. Adele had trouble keeping up her black stockings. The thought of skin showing would be enough to give their mother an intense headache, and so Nina helped her sister make the adjustments secure. The De Bonnard girls' fabulous hair was tightly twisted and covered over by oil-silk caps, which were battened down with colored tape.

Throughout, Adele continued to talk of the ball and her costume, wanting to know about Nina's costume, but Nina shrugged, not responding, too eager to immerse herself in the cool ocean. The waves were up today and she dove under, losing her cap as she swam and frolicked with her sister. The two of them were not the slightest bit concerned about the height of the waves, and swam a sufficient distance to be able to float on their backs while watching the other women cringing at the shore and jumping away from every froth of the surf.

Suddenly the women were scattering on the sand as well, running every which way and emitting loud cries, echoed by the seagulls disturbed by all the commotion.

"What is it, do you suppose?" Nina asked her sister when she had shaken her from her floating and pointed to the shore.

Adele did not stop to conjecture. "Let's go see." And she began swimming back. Nina was reluctant to leave. The thought that there might be actual cause for alarm was immediately dismissed as the women were huddling in discussion, rather than running away. Some social disturbance, probably, such as Mrs. Pynchot having lost her hat. Nina's curiosity was not as strong as her desire to swim, and she continued to do so. After a few more laps, she closed her eyes and floated up and down on the waves. She was drifting in delight and ease—when something snaked its way around her waist.

Nina's eyes shot open. She was looking into Jordan's amused face.

"A mermaid, I presume?"

"What are you doing here!"

"I might ask you as well. Ah, mermaid, are you about to turn tail and go back to your siren's home?"

"Not very amusing," Nina protested, trying to look back at the shore. The commotion was continuing there.

"How *dare* you enter the ocean—the flag was white!"

"It was red."

"Then it was changed before its time."

Jordan swam around her, coming up near again and saying nonchalantly, "Apparently some joker changed the flags to disconcert the ladies. Most of them have retired; the rest are busy arguing with the gentlemen."

Nina looked again at the shore. The beach was covered with men in striped jerseys and ankle-length tights. She also noticed a gentleman in his Panama hat—with his pipe—taking his ablutions at the shore.

"Good grief! I'll have to leave now to all their stares—an impossible situation!" Continuing to look, she noted that the women had all withdrawn. Nina bit her lip anxiously. She would be the only woman to pass on the shore with clothes clinging and her cap gone and her hair wet and streaming down her back. She would never live it down.

Jordan sensed her dilemma. "Mother will have such an appetizing story to tell about you. It'll never be believed that you were not part of this escapade—especially since, I presume, it was the deed of one of your admirers, Mr. Bobby Van Reyden."

Trying to decide what to do, Nina kept paddling while watching the shore, which was now thickly covered with men, like nests of seagulls, some ogling out at her. Intolerable. She could not put herself in that position. She'd rather stay here in the ocean till it was dark enough for her to emerge or the gentlemen had the decency to leave. Then a better solution occurred to her. "You swim out and instruct them to leave," she told Jordan.

"Why should I do that?" he asked, smiling at her plight.

"Because *any gentleman* would."

"Perhaps. But that would certainly take the edge off the first entertainment in what has been a deadly dull week."

"You're a boor," Nina pronounced and swam away from him, farther into the sea. In a short time, he was at her side again.

"There's an entire ocean in which to comport yourself. Can't you leave me to swim on my own?"

"Certainly not. I am your official escort. When the moment comes and you have had your fill of this salubrious sport, we'll exit together to assure no gentleman makes a remark."

"That's not sufficient! I don't wish to be seen at all. If you think you're being gallant, why not do as I requested and ask them to leave?"

"Because it would be bringing attention to your plight and most of them would hang around behind the carriages to peek at you. We are, after all, some distance from shore and only the top of your head is visible. We could wait their time out and no one will know for certain. It would only be something one would whisper about, and you are accustomed to that. Are you not?"

Nina considered what he was saying as she swam away from him, and then came back. "There's something to your suggestion. If you weren't so amused, I might believe you in earnest."

"Indeed, I am in earnest. But I'm also in a delightful situation. However you resolve your problem, I'll have the benefit of seeing you in a rather embarrassing position, fitting for a lady of your pride. Moreover, with a lady of your beauty, seeing you at your most natural is a prospect I can't resist."

Nina pounced on him and pushed his head under water, then swam away. By the time he had surfaced and shaken the sea from his eyes, she was nowhere to be seen.

For a moment the humor of the situation was not so sharp. He dove again and again, and only when he was in sufficient panic to consider calling for help did he spot her surfacing from her underwater swim some distance out to sea. And she was continuing her swim farther and farther away. He raced after. She was obviously heading for the rocks several yards to the right. He put on all his effort to overtake her, but she was smooth as a siren indeed. In the distance, he could see her pulling herself up and running lightly across the rocks to the dunes of Pirate's Cove.

With vigorous strokes he cut closer to the shore, and jumped up on the rocks at a nearer point, and thus was almost upon her at the rock wall that fenced this deserted area.

Nina was resting, panting on the sand—just beginning to lift her head. She had made it to Pirate's Cove, where she had played as a child, where rumor had it that Captain Kidd himself had buried his treasure. In any case, it was a wild, unfrequented area where she could rest. Jordan's shadow threw a pall on her self-congratulations. He was standing over her and she, unable to speak, wordlessly flayed at him. But he was furious with her.

"You're a fool! Rather than risk a little humiliation you'd risk your life!"

"You're not aware . . . what it means to be a woman in such a situation," she answered, still panting. Then she rested her head back on the sand and closed her eyes. Half of her face was covered with sand. It clung to her and all over her body, as if the sea had camouflaged her and made her one of its own creatures. He knelt beside her and gently began brushing the sand away. She was too exhausted to repulse his actions. Sensing that, he could not resist touching her. She made murmurs of protest, but he was wiping the sand away from her face with his own face, softly blowing it away, and then almost kissing each individual grain of sand away, and then kissing her mouth and holding the wet, slippery strength of her against himself—but she slipped away and was on the run. He caught her in a few steps and held her again. Both their urges apparently were taking over. By the third kiss Jordan was murmuring words that would have outraged her at any other time, but now she needed to hear them. Strong sensations were overwhelming her body, and just as she'd immersed herself in the sea, Nina was sinking into his arms when her ears heard a familiar voice. Abruptly she turned, looking about. He panted, staring at her inquiringly. There was no sound. Perhaps the voice had been in her own mind, Nina concluded, but it had been timely. What, dear God, was she on the point of doing! Nina had to fight her body's desire to sink back into that sensuous state again as she determinedly separated them.

Bewildered, Jordan demanded an explanation.

Now that her sense was no longer swept over by her sensuality, her fear of surrender emerged as well as the memory that he was a Windsor and, more, Adele's suitor. The last was reason enough for Nina to use in her attempt to keep him at a distance. But he brushed that aside, impatiently pointing out, "I haven't sent her a bouquet since the Centennial. Since I realized where my feelings truly lay."

"Don't say that. Don't even whisper that."

"I haven't even asked her to the Pynchot 'Dream' quadrille. Dick is asking her instead, and I am going with you."

"That's not a possibility," Nina exclaimed. Chills were taking charge of her—chills from her wet attire and chills from his words. "I am going with Bobby," she said positively, through her blue lips. And she sought to put distance between them by taking more steps away, when from across the sand she saw her sister coming toward her in the pony cart. That had been Adele's voice, after all, and in wild fear that Adele would see Jordan, Nina ran toward the cart as if a sea siren were after her, and then the siren was she—running, gasping, as Adele swooped her in and covered her with a warm blanket, and they set off.

Fortunately Adele had not seen who was with her. Jordan had gotten down in the weeds that were riotously sprouting there. Only when the cart had left did he rise and stand looking in their direction.

He shook his head and mumbled something under his breath.

Eleven

*I*t *was the* night of the Pynchot quadrille, and neither Windsor gentleman was to escort either of the De Bonnard ladies. Instead, much to Mrs. Windsor's joy, they were both to escort her. They awaited her entrance, ready to be surprised by her costume. In fact, they had assured their dear mother that they were scarcely able to think of anything else. Whereupon they promptly forgot her in their discussion of the day's events: Custer had been defeated by a bunch of Indians; it was not to be believed! Every few minutes Dick checked his watch, exclaiming at the delay.

"What's keeping her?" he complained. "I want to be there before the De Bonnards or Nina won't have a single dance left."

"You know we're about to be surprised by Mama's costume," Jordan reminded, and Dick just nodded absentmindedly, and then went back to his usual preoccupation.

"What costume do you imagine Nina will be wearing? I bet it will be the best. She's the smartest dresser of all the girls . . . of all the people here."

"I have no idea. But I'm certain it will have a meaning above the obvious. But speaking of Nina, I want you to realize that while she is close to declaring her feelings for me—which would give me leave to jilt her and return to Europe—there is a certain obstacle to my . . . or rather *our* maneuvers."

Dick, who tended to forget what was not his principal topic of interest at one moment, paused to recall the details of their arrangement. "Oh yes, the pact! How's it coming?"

"I just explained to you how it was coming," Jordan answered with annoyance. "I need your help to perform the—shall I say, coup de grâce."

"Well, you can say it, but I don't even know what it means. And how do you need my help?"

"I overplayed my hand with young Adele. My attentions to her were just meant to pique Nina's interest, but I find myself generally believed to be courting her in earnest. And I need someone to move in on the young lady so I might continue our objective toward her sister. In other words, you are to distract Adele."

"Oh, no! Not me! She's just a silly child, almost three years younger than me! Besides, I don't want Nina to think I'm not being true to her."

"*Dickie!* Are you in on this plan with me or not? Are we intending to teach Nina how it feels to be dropped, as you were, or not, so that then she could come back to you? . . . Oh Lord! You got me involved in this idiocy and now I'm forced to explain your own motives to you. Well, forget it. I thought the entire plan was a waste of my time, and lately I am beginning to feel it is totally beneath me as well. I'm relieved not to any longer have to—"

"Oh *no!* We're so close. I just got distracted for a moment. I mean, it's taking longer than I thought. I assumed a couple of days would do it, and then Nina would be mine. But . . . don't give up on it if you feel you're close to . . . Are you telling me you think Nina has fallen for you?"

"I'm certain she has."

Dick contemplated that announcement with mixed feelings. "Well then, jilt her tonight and let me take her home."

His brother explained once more about needing more time for the actual declaration, which he intended to get tonight, and then he would write her a letter in the morning mentioning a lady from England who had a prior claim on his heart or some such. And after explaining again the role Dick had to play in distracting Adele, and after assuring him he had not taken excessive liberties with Nina, they were once again agreed in all particulars and once again shook hands on their pact.

Except that suddenly Dick wanted an explanation of the qualification Jordan had used. "What do you mean, 'not excessive liberties'? What were the nonexcessive ones you've taken?"

At that moment Mrs. Windsor made her appearance, and it was necessary for both her sons to drop their conversation and turn to excessive admiration of her outfit.

"Breathtaking," Jordan assured her, and Mrs. Windsor, gathering her sheets about, was pleased. However, both her sons were uncertain what she was depicting—with all those sheets wrapped about her body, some even around her head, topped by a small American flag.

"Ah," Jordan exclaimed, "I understand. Are you a mummy, Mommy? An American mummy, of course."

Mrs. Windsor was indignant. Nevertheless, lifting her voice over their laughter, she proceeded to explain that she was "the place dreams come from."

"Good grief!" Dick exclaimed, almost unable to get his breath from all his whoops. "Are you a *bed*?"

"Certainly."

At her complacent acquiescence and the actual admission of her attire's significance, the two sons were unable to stop giggling all the way to the Pynchot estate. Once there, however, Mrs. Windsor had the justification of finding several other ladies dressed in similar outfits, and she smugly pointed them out. And further, Mrs. Pynchot had used sheets as decorations, draping several end tables in that manner and placing laced pillows about; all topped by the obligatory American flags.

As for Mrs. Pynchot, it was necessary that she explain her outfit to every newcomer—for it appeared at first that she was a lady dressed in clothes of the Regency period, of course—but, but, one had to look twice to believe: her attire was *wet*.

Amongst the younger set, the giggles were quite clear as one after the other leaped to the same obvious conclusion of her depicting a lady bed wetter.

Unfortunately for all the grinners, that was not the case. She explained: "True to our heritage in this area of shipwrecks, I am 'e faith, *a shipwrecked maid*."

"Ah," Jordan acknowledged, keeping his face as straight as

possible. "But of course. What else could you be? And how, madam, might I ask, does that pertain to the dream theme?"

Mr. Marshall, a man in his fifties who was running the party for her, was quick with that explanation. Apparently Mrs. Pynchot had wished for the theme to be shipwrecks, but he had pointed out that after two or three ladies had dressed in such a bedraggled fashion and one or two men as smugglers or even sailors, the rest of the outfits would have to be repeats. Nor would it be comme il faut with the Americana theme of the entire summer season. It would be almost unpatriotic to combine shipwrecks with the American ship of state! Which forced Mr. Marshall to come up with another unifying concept, or the dream theme. That way, each person, an American, of course, could dress as he or she pleased, and Mrs. Pynchot alone could be the shipwrecked maid—which was bound to make her stand out.

He paused with so obvious a demand for applause at that point that it was only polite to give it, which encouraged him into further explanation, this time of his dress befitting the inspirer of the theme, or Morpheus, the god of sleep.

"But he wasn't American." Jordan could not resist, with a quiver in his quibble.

"But *I* am," Mr. Marshall inserted proudly, and that ended that, with Mrs. Windsor sweeping them into their moment of entrance.

The "dream" ballroom was ablaze with at least one hundred and forty candles in the chandeliers and candelabra. At the edge of the ballroom was a platform holding a small treasure chest. There were delighted rumors that this would later be opened and the contents distributed. But perhaps that was wishful dreaming. Captain Kidd's treasure, it had to represent, for no other pirate was known to be such a regular visitor to the New Jersey shore, nor to have so often left behind his booty.

In keeping with that legend, there were several stockbrokers at the ball dressed as Captain Kidd, indicating that the greatest dream for men of fortune was finding another fortune, even if they had to pirate it from others. Jordan and Mr. De Bonnard, along with others, played it conservatively and appeared in their yachting clothes and captain's hats.

The diverse theme allowed a variety of costumes at the ball. Mrs. De Bonnard had mentioned that she was taking her character from *A Midsummer Night's Dream*. Upon arrival, one glance had her bitterly regretting her unwise revelation, for there were several Titanias, one Oberon, plus here a Puck, there a Puck, everywhere a Puck, Puck. It was Dick's delight to join that casting as Bottom—in his ass's head, which he kept putting on and taking off to startle his acquaintances.

Other costumes would have been decipherable only if one were similarly somnambulant. Quizzed by a lady wearing one such, Jordan intoned, "My dear madam, it could not be more obvious," and then walked away quickly before having either to explain or to hear the explanation.

When the De Bonnards entered, Adele made quite an impression with her seagull outfit; she enjoyed flapping her feathered wings and causing a draft. Dick, true to Jordan's instructions, monopolized her time as the two attempted to outdo each other in animal impersonations.

And then there was Nina. Her costume caused the greatest disappointment. It was nothing extravagant, just a simple Grecian gown, all in white silk with a golden Greek key trim on the train and across the one shoulder. Her hair was lifted high with golden stars and golden ribbons, trailing through it and down onto her naked shoulder. She was exquisite but hardly outstanding, especially when compared to Miss Richards. The Richards had made an inroad indeed. Mrs. Richards, hearing of the Pynchot ball, had learned some Regency idioms and paid a visit to Mrs. Pynchot during which she had discussed London during the Prince Regent's reign as if she had actually been one of his set. Considering both her younger age and lower class, it would hardly have been possible but was enough of an attraction to prompt Mrs. Pynchot to give her and her family an invitation. Miss Cass Richards was dressed from head to foot in jewels: a jeweled gown and jeweled shoes, not to mention the jewels around her neck and on her earlobes. But most outstanding was her jeweled crown in the shape of an American flag with rubies lined up for the red bands, diamonds for the white, and white stars on a bed of sapphires. No man could resist coming close to all that wealth, and thus she was the star of the night as the wealthy danced with their life's object, riches herself. Neither Cass Richards nor her mother stopped smiling all night. Their dreams had come true: not only were they finally accepted by society, but they were ruling it.

When Mrs. De Bonnard saw her husband dancing with Miss Richards, it pricked her complacency a bit. "She's everything he ever desired in life," she said sadly to Nina, who, after glancing over, turned to her mother and said, "Yes, Miss Crass Nouveau Riche," and had her mother cheered enough to accept a young gallant's invitation for a waltz.

Jordan had asked Nina for the same waltz, but she coldly turned away from him and accepted Bobby's outstretched eager hand instead.

Bobby came almost level to her forehead. His short stature was usually camouflaged by outlandishly high hats. Tonight, however, he'd forgone the headgear and wore high-heeled army boots to go with his military attire. With his brown hair and light blue eyes and diminutive form, he ought to have been generally overlooked, except that in his mind he was a general, and anyone coming close or talking to him for more than a moment felt that. Clearly someone tall and imposing looked out from that young gentleman's eyes, which were almost wild with energy and will. Bobby's voice was similarly commanding. His usual question, "Had any *fun* lately?" always erupted out of him with such enthusiasm that others were eager to join in and say "Yes!"

Except for Nina, who had long made it a practice never to answer him in the affirmative, no matter how innocent the question. Now she replied, "Fun? You mean on a par with switching the bathing flags?"

"Oh, did you hear about that! No one's talking about anything else. Even Custer's defeat couldn't wipe that out. The laughs Dick and I had when the ladies came running out of the water, and the men were apologizing all over the place. You should have seen it!"

"I'm sorry to have missed it" was all Nina replied, delighted that her presence there was not generally known. "Is your outfit . . . Custer?"

"Right. See the red paint? That's for the blood." Red stains had been placed strategically all over the uniform and also on the long, yellow-haired wig. An arrow extruded from his back, and Nina was warned not to dislodge it.

"Considering how revered Custer is . . . eh, *was*, would you not say your reveling in his demise is in bad taste?"

Bobby's pale eyes glowed with satisfaction. "That's me. Always leave a bad taste in your mouth."

"Very true," Nina agreed, but could not help tweaking him with a question. "But how do you know he was not scalped? You're not very authentic."

The smile was wiped right off of Bobby's face. He even stopped dancing at the thought of that possible omission in his outfit. "Horsefeathers, the press reports didn't say anything about his being *scalped*! Do you think he was?"

Nina would not commit herself on that point, and Bobby worried about it throughout their dance, shuddering at the chance he'd lost to really shock the crowd ("Gosh! wouldn't that have been great, if I had walked in here with my scalp hanging!"). So distracted was he that he forgot to ask her to marry him—which, of course, had been her objective.

But when she was back with her mother, she was warned, "I thought we had agreed that you were to tell Mr. Van Reyden that his attentions were no longer welcome . . . or did you do so; I noticed he was rather distressed during your dance."

Before Nina had a chance either to deny or to agree, her mother was whisked away for another dance.

"You are Helen, the dream goddess of every man. The woman whose face launched a thousand ships and made men immortal with a kiss?"

Without turning Nina knew that it was Jordan. She walked on and was followed.

"My apologies for the liberties last time. My excuse is your beauty. Which obviously you understand to be a great inducement—as witness your costume. You would not be surprised to have nations fighting for you—or is that your secret dream?"

Goaded at last, Nina stopped walking and faced him. "You see how your lack of understanding leads to further misunderstanding, and then you expect me to continue in that misunderstanding! You're insufferable! As I believe I've said before. I am not Helen, so the rest of your deduction is as faulty as your general reasoning."

"You *are* Helen."

"I am not."

"Then?"

"I shall not explain myself."

"Then I shall guess," Jordan continued, finding himself once more intrigued by her not being the image one would first assume. "Greek you must be . . . but which one? Not Athena—you are not wearing the helmet. Not Artemis—you lack the bow. Aphrodite, without her golden apple? No, too obvious for a mind as faceted as yours."

Nina smiled at that, immediately forgetting her vow to keep away from him, as they both were enjoying each other and their game.

"Persephone, captured by Hades?"

"That would be true only if I were escorted by you."

"Touché!" He laughed. "Hmmmm. You shall send me back to my Bulfinch . . . or perhaps my classics. Medea?"

Nina kept shaking her head through all of his guesses, from Antigone to Sappho.

"You have had all the chances," Nina said as the dance ended and she was claimed by Bobby again. While dancing off, she gloated to the chagrined Jordan, "You'll never ever guess it; you think too much in the *obvious*."

And with that Jordan was totally peeved and piqued. Throughout the ball, as Nina kept refusing him dance after dance and refuting his every guess, Jordan could think of nothing else. He'd tried the distractions of several dances with the dazzling Miss Richards and several other women there, including two with his mother and one strategic whirl with Mrs. De Bonnard. When Mrs. De Bonnard urged him to exchange herself for Adele, he crushed her with an airy "Oh, I would hardly move in on *Dick's* territory" and left her staring after him.

At last he cut in one of Nina's dances and told her, "I know. It is obvious. You are depicting a Grecian woman who taunted and taunted men till she achieved her purpose. And further would have joined you in Miss Anthony's cause."

Now Nina was guessing and intrigued. "Who could you—"

"A woman who knows the power of withholding her affections as you have done to me."

"Lysistrata!" Nina exclaimed joyfully.

"Right!" Jordan responded grimly and continued, "and I am right."

"Wrong," Nina insisted. "Again you mistake me—the true me—and continue with these superficial suppositions."

The music turned into a waltz and, although Nina sighed and said she had given him as many clues as she could and attempted to leave him, he whirled her around, his arms holding her tightly against him as the Strauss strains swelled about them, and through them, and for a moment they merely closed their eyes and enjoyed the union.

And yet he was insisting on another dance, caught totally in her web, and the laugh in her glowing eyes and the feel of her softness in his arms; and she was caught by the joy in having him at her feet, after the many times he had humiliated her. It was sweet. And they continued dancing and laughing together.

"To be honest, my first thought when receiving this invitation was to come as a dark horse."

"Truly a *nightmare* would have been the most appropriate attire for this ball." He laughed. "Certainly Dick would have appreciated it. But naturally you would not be that bald. You chose instead . . ." And then, looking deeply into her eyes, he stopped dancing, and the two of them just stared at each other. Swept by the power between them, whether he read her thoughts or felt it in himself, he guessed it at last. "Psyche."

And Nina was all joyous smiles. "Correct," she said softly, and he felt thrilled at that one word and held her close.

"Yes," he said, "you are my soul—my heart and soul . . . and I am yours."

So filled with the moment and the closeness of him, Nina was about to nod and say the word he was anxious to hear when her glance caught the horrified stare of her sister, and she stepped back. Turning, she found Bobby at her side, and she quickly accepted whatever he had asked her, and when he joyfully escorted her out, she followed; anything to get away from her sister's wounded face.

Twelve

*H*ow could you!" Adele was crying. "In *front of everyone!* My own sister whom I loved so much all my life taking the one man I truly ever cared for—entrapping him, weaving your spell around him so he could dance with no one else all evening and never even spoke to me and followed you with his eyes— everywhere you went and even when you left, he stormed after you and didn't come back. You stabbed me in the heart and made it all so . . . so . . . *public*!"

Her mother had the same indictment in her eyes, although she did not say it, concerned with comforting her youngest child. "There, I'm certain Nina did not mean to . . . did you?"

Nina was clasping the bird mask that had been thrown at her as Adele entered the bedroom with her mother at her side. Now Nina took time to put it down and collect her thoughts as she tried to explain that she had done nothing of the sort.

"Oh, it's just your fatal beauty. Is that what we are to be- lieve! Did you purposely plan to make his transference of affec- tion to *you* from *me* obvious to all—so that you could hurt me in the most devastating way! How else explain it? You know he's *mine*! I told you so often how much I cared for him—how could you . . . ?" Her words were drowned in her tears as her hopes, ap- propriately enough after the evening's entertainment, were ship- wrecked and turned into a nightmare.

For a moment Adele was unable to catch her breath, and both her mother and her sister were running around getting water and fanning her. And finally, when she found new breath, new sobs came out with it, till Nina, sobbing herself, cried out, "I'll go away and never see him again! I swear!" But that just increased, if possible, her sister's paroxysms. Her face was so red that Nina was in terror and leaped for anything to appease her. "But it's *you* he really loves. It must be that he was jealous because you were paying so much attention to Dick . . . and he was paying you back in kind!"

It did the trick.

Adele stopped crying as that new possibility threw a lifeline to her dashed hopes. "You think?" she asked both her sister and mother. At which point Mrs. De Bonnard similarly seized on that as the solution she could most live with, for certainly she could not accept that her daughter who had always been so caring of her sister would have made such a change as to deliberately steal her sister's intended.

"Yes," she said triumphantly, "that explains what he said to me!"

Ordered to repeat exactly what Jordan had said, she did so. "His exact words were: 'I never move in on Dick's territory.' It's obvious; he was simply jealous!"

Adele was rejoicing, apologizing to Nina and laughing and planning how she was going to explain to Jordan that she cared only for him, and both Mrs. De Bonnard and Adele were reconciled that Nina was the loving girl they had always known, after all. And Mrs. Windsor, who had rushed up to Adele and her mother at the ball and pointed out Nina's maneuverings, was now revealed to be a vicious liar—but, more important, she was *wrong.*

Mrs. De Bonnard thanked Nina and, with a look to the ceiling, thanked God—in that order—and led her exhausted youngest daughter out. Having hugged both her mother and sister with extra affection, Nina said nothing more after her declaration. Only when the door closed and she was alone did she sit down on her bed and face up to what had happened, what she had allowed to happen. She was attracted to—no, fascinated, even almost swept up by—Jordan Windsor. And try as she had to deny that fact even to herself, tonight everyone had seen it—even Adele.

Groaning, Nina hugged her pillow to herself, uncertain what she ought to do. Her instincts were to temporize, to say he never loved Adele, so she had not taken away anything that her sister had really had. Except that Adele assumed he did love her. And to be fair, even Nina was uncertain what might have ultimately occurred if she were not in the picture. Oh stars, how had she gotten into this muddle! All along, up to tonight, Nina had been hoping that Adele would tire of Jordan and go on to another, younger, gentleman, as she would have done. But Adele was fiercely loyal. Once giving her affections, she would never let go. Nina belatedly acknowledged that. And she further belatedly remembered their sharing a cat named Spooky. He was all black except for a white face, legs, and belly. Spooky had been a charmer, going to each family member, rubbing against them, and giving meows that seemed to indicate that each was his favorite, and thus coming away with extra tidbits, extra hugs, and an extra bed to sleep on when the old one paled. Adele had wailed when it came her turn to be deserted and locked the cat in her bedroom until Spooky began clawing at the door. Nina had come rushing to let him out, whereupon Spooky, released, bounded to Nina's bed. That had earned Nina a look of accusation from her sister. That betrayed glance repeated itself tonight. Yes, it was the very same look her nine-year-old sister had directed at her when she'd warned, "Spooky's mine!"

"Fine," Nina had replied. "But if you want to keep him, you'll let him be freer to roam. Keep your door open, and he'll always come back to you."

But Adele had scoffed at that, concluding, "That way he only learns to be a roamer!" And she'd pushed past Nina into her sister's room, where she picked up the dead weight of Spooky and took him back into her room, making a big show out of shutting out her elder sister. Nina had shrugged, closing her ears to Spooky's cries, till he stopped crying and settled down, making the best of it. But when Adele left in the morning, Spooky made a run for Nina's bed and almost grinned at his escape while Nina laughed with him, "Got away, did you? That's my good old roamer!"

So what was the point of suddenly recollecting that? It was evidently a timely reminder of Adele's nature. Nina's mistake had been in judging her sister by her own actions. Clearly Adele would keep Jordan, even if she had to lock him in her room. And Nina must walk away, listening to his cries, calling after.

That was the answer, of course. She must walk away quickly. But where to? And with whom? She would not be permitted to go on her own.

The only solution was to turn to her father. Ever since her discussion with her mother, Nina had begun to see her as less of a victim, or at least as a willing victim since she knew what was going on and had made the best of it. And her father had become less of a culprit since he was not breaking up a happy marriage; it had been broken to begin with. Mr. De Bonnard did not spend the summer in Oceana; rather he came at will, on weekends and for important events and social affairs. So it struck Nina that a perfect solution would be for her to join him in New York City.

Leaving the field clear for Adele might turn out not to be so bad for herself, after all. She would have time on her own to make sense of her life. Whatever she had in her, hidden deep down, she was going to let come out. Society taught women to compress their dimensions to fit into the approved form. Well, she'd had enough contracting; she wanted to break out, reach out. In this vein, her first act was reaching out to her father after years of withdrawing from him. Yes, she would take a chance of repeating her birthday night and breaking into her father's party life. Only this time she was asking him to take her into it. Somehow she had to let him know she would not interfere, and maybe then he would let her sail along.

In his chamber the next morning, Mr. De Bonnard was staring at his daughter after her request. He and Nina had been quite a team when she was a child. And when she started growing up, she grew away from him. Became her mother's child. He missed her. Had often wanted to include her in his life. His wife was not handling her right. She looked tired and unhappy, and she should have been married by now. Bobby Van Reyden would make a good son-in-law; there would be no end of ways he could make use of that boy.

But there was more to Nina's sudden desire to join him in New York than met the eye. He remained quiet and stared at her, waiting. This waiting was a technique Mr. De Bonnard had perfected in business. People responded to it by rushing to fill in the quiet with the facts he would have had a hell of a time getting from them by asking.

Another success for his stratagem: Before his steady, expectant gaze, Nina began explaining herself. "I think it would be a good time for me to leave. It would give Adele a chance to shine without me around." Her father was still waiting. "I gather I inhibit her."

Mr. De Bonnard nodded. "Very unselfish. Not a bad idea for you to come to New York. I'll keep my nose to the wind on my trips back and sniff out when it's safe for you to return. If you want to return. Heard the commotion last night. Don't want my girls fighting over the same man like dogs over a bone."

Nina started to protest and then, looking at his sharp eyes, she was quiet. "I'm already packed" was all she said.

"Windsor fella wants you after he's been making a play for Delly?" He summed up it briskly.

"I believe . . . Yes."

"And what do you want?"

"Not to hurt Adele!"

"What do you want?" he repeated sternly.

"Not him. He's . . . been dishonest with us both."

Mr. De Bonnard nodded. "Best to come with me. We had good times together. I'll squire you about."

Nina was stunned at that suggestion. She'd assumed he would not want her about. She felt he was reacting to the moment and might rethink it later, so she gave an assurance without being asked for it. "I won't be going out much. I've been thinking of working on my . . . correspondence."

Mr. De Bonnard dismissed that. "Can't act like you're in disgrace; gonna look like you have done something to be disgraced about."

Nina nodded at her father's evaluation. It would be best to go out with him to some places. She stared at him, remembering his escorting her to the circus, to the opera. She had enjoyed it so much. He'd brought her flowers and called her "my little partner."

He either sensed her thought or was thinking the same things, for he smiled at her warmly and said, "Welcome back, little partner."

The endearment reached Nina, and she smiled tremulously. Her father smiled widely and took her by the arm and they walked out together. "I'll handle it all. Gonna say I need a hostess and your mother had to stay here with Adele."

By afternoon Adele and her mother had heard the announcement from Mr. De Bonnard. Untypically, they did not protest . . . or even question it. That told Nina that both had thought over last night's event and concluded that the easy answer might be too easy, after all.

In fact, Mrs. De Bonnard took Nina aside and asked outright, "Will Jordan ask for Adele's hand in marriage?"

Nina had some difficulty answering that. At last she looked her mother in the face and said frankly, "I don't know. I've been telling him at every opportunity that I had no interest in him. He's used every chance at the Centennial and here to pursue me, but whether he is just a flirt who wants every woman, or . . . whether I've unwittingly attracted him away from Adele, I'm not certain. But . . . I felt the only solution was to go with Papa."

Mrs. De Bonnard sighed. "Yes, that is the only solution. But, dear God, why have you put us in this position? Why could you not have—"

"What? I presume you think I encouraged him. I did not! Decidedly the reverse."

"Your actions last night, dancing so closely with him, the looks the two of you were exchanging—that is not what a lady does when she wishes to discourage a gentleman."

"I . . . could not help that. I was . . . *am* attracted to him. From before I knew he preferred Adele. So I kept away. Even refused to meet him. Ran away from him again and again, I swear to heaven I did."

Her mother shook her head. "But always looking behind to see if he was following? Adele does not know those kind of tricks. How you found them out I do not know. It must be inherited from your father."

Nina gasped. Her mother could not have insulted her more, knowing as she did her father's philandering ways. She looked down with tears in her eyes, and her mother gave her a hug that reasserted their tight bond.

"I know you were not trying to take him away from Delly. But you just didn't try enough not to. Even this leaving for New York is not sufficient. He might very well follow you, and that would disgrace Delly even more."

"Then what? Just tell me exactly what you want me to do. I promise to do it! I can't help being attracted to Mr. Windsor. He says we have a connection. And, God help me, I fear he's right."

"Then break the connection!" Mrs. De Bonnard exclaimed anxiously.

"I am. I'm leaving."

"No! It must be more definite. No loose threads. Meet him and explain you don't wish him to follow you . . . that you'll never submit to any feelings you have for him because he has proven himself dishonorable by courting two sisters at the same time."

"And yet you would allow this dishonorable man to be your son-in-law if he drops me and proposes to Adele?" Nina asked in confusion and some anger.

"Only for Delly's sake. She loves him so. She's been crying all morning in my arms. She sent him a note, explaining her heart belongs to him, not Dick, and he has not even had the decency to respond."

"Dear heavens! Poor Delly. Very well. I'll meet him and say what you want me to say, but I don't think it will work. I believe he has his own plans. I don't know what they are. He's not lightly playing as I was. He is intent upon a course that I fear is dishonorable."

Mrs. De Bonnard turned white at that possibility. "Then when you break with this scoundrel, it will be the best for you as well. *That* life I will not allow you to lead. Your father has a mistress, an opera singer—Camille, she calls herself, after the Dumas novel. But I expect her lungs are in somewhat better shape, for she has been heard singing at the top of them at several recitals that your father has sponsored. I saw her once from a distance. She ducked away. When ladies of decency pass her, she must always duck away. I don't want you to live that life . . . no gentleman is worth it. Men and women engage in the same act of love and the gentleman is unbesmirched but the lady is forever tainted. Do you understand?"

Nina nodded and smiled for the first time. "I have too much of your pride, Mama, to spend my life ducking out of sight."

Her mother smiled back in some relief and the two were able to say their affectionate good-byes, without reservations.

There was no such parting scene with Adele, who carefully avoided her sister. That was Nina's worst punishment. Obediently Nina followed her mother's orders and sent a note to Jordan to meet her at the beachfront of her estate the following morning. He arrived in triumph.

She let him savor his moment, taking her in with a jubilant stare as if relishing every inch of his possession. Then she calmly spoke. "I'm leaving for New York City to finish the summer there with my father. In essence I am leaving the field clear for Adele and you. That's to be understood. All these secret looks and so-called understandings between us—I want you to acknowledge that they are naught but cruel attempts to have two ladies on your string. Therefore, I am cutting mine to you. If you have any decent feelings, you'll concentrate on Adele. You can still win her. Mother doesn't think highly of you, but I expect she will accept you as Delly's husband if you remain honorable in your actions toward her henceforth. That's all I have to say."

Nina was turning away when, coming out of the daze of her words, Jordan sprang close, stopping her. "Blast it! Was that speech rehearsed? And who the devil instructed you to say all that? Your mother? Your father?"

Nina was astonished by the genuineness of his emotion. His previous sarcasm or worldliness were gone; indeed Jordan was looking at her with an urgency built up from the hours apart. But she could only shake her head at him and insist, "I need no one to instruct me to do what is honorable. My own decency tells me that! Where in God's name is yours!"

He stopped to stare at the ocean waves crashing onto the surf. It gave him pause, enough to speak with a return of his mocking self. "Why denounce me, when I've merely followed the fashion here in Oceana? You yourself set the style for playing with a younger, more susceptible person to add to your list of conquests, but breaking off before you had aroused serious expectations."

"You *have* aroused serious expectations!"

"A young girl's expectations are aroused by the first posy."

"You are remarkably callous. Adele is genuinely in love."

"As was Dick . . . and as is Bobby, I presume, if he has any genuine feeling beyond being a poseur."

"It's different for a man who has so many other avenues of life open to him. He expects to play at romance. In any case," Nina insisted, wearily, "unlike Adele at seventeen, Bobby is an adult and even Dick is twenty years old. Besides, there was no separate relationship—they were merely part of my group. And further, I never let either suppose I was in earnest, as you did with Adele. I didn't speak in hushed tones of the roses in their cheeks or send the poems that purportedly made the declarations for me that I was too overcome by emotion to make for myself!"

"No, you merely accepted all of the above, so that one after another of your young men assumed you were genuine in your returning those feelings!"

"That's not so!"

"It is. I have it from Dick himself. Your attending to their attentions, even if it was with a tolerant smile, was *accepting* them."

"And that's similar in your eyes to your full-scale attentions to Adele!"

"Exactly so. In any case it has done Adele a world of good, for she will now be able to consider better if an admirer is sincere in his advances or merely sincere in his admiration for her as I was."

"Then you would say Dick has had the benefit of the same education!"

Jordan stared at her for a moment and then smilingly admitted, "I see. We are to be equally to blame or equally not to blame?"

But Nina vigorously shook her head. "It's different for a woman. If she is dropped, her humiliation is such that society will very likely not give her the chance to find a truer man. And besides, a woman feels it more."

"So you, as a woman, say. And I, as a gentleman, say the reverse. Let me show you how a gentleman feels! I've been thinking of nothing but you since I've first come to Oceana. It's a good idea for us both to go away from this society and its prying glances. We can say you are in New York while in reality you will be with me!"

Nina was staggered by the leap of joy she felt at that invitation. "You will be with me" echoed enticingly. She wanted to be swept up by Jordan, taken far away. So when he took her tightly in his arms Nina struggled only lightly, allowing the pleasurable sweep of emotions to flood through her body until a rise of panic once more struck at the sudden remembrance that he was a Windsor. But this time it immediately receded. He was not just a Windsor; he was Jordan. And his long, slow kisses were easing her fears. She closed her eyes to hold in the passion so she could not see what she was doing. She just felt . . . responded . . . bathed in the overwhelming rush of it all when his whispers changed from sweet words to jubilant crowing. "I have a private yacht where we can go. What say? Are you daring enough for that? Are you woman enough for that?"

Nina's eyes opened as if a bright light had been turned on in a darkened room. She blinked in the harsh glare of it and moved away.

Jordan allowed her to step a full arm's-length distant, assuming that she was considering his proposition. The tawny eyes staring at him turned gilt with inner fire at her startled understanding. She was almost gasping at the unbelievable affront he had offered her.

"Are you suggesting that, I, Nina De Bonnard, become a yacht girl! Dear God! Is that the way you see me?" She paused to take a deep breath so she could continue, yet remained so breathless she could only whisper, "Or aren't you aware of what you are asking me to become? Yes, you know. You know. And now I know how very minuscule your affection is for me, if there is any there at all. I was correct in my first assessment of you. You are naught but a seducer."

"Most men are," he acknowledged with a grin. "Why are you so surprised? It is, after all, the natural state between a man and woman. He to seduce and she to be seduced. Admit it, that is what you've been wanting from me—to be seduced."

Nina was speechless.

Observing that, Jordan pressed home his advantage, adding a coaxing tone to his soft voice. "Confess, between you and me. You're tired of playing the lady. You want to be just a woman, reacting to a man on an elemental level. And God knows I want you in that way more than any woman I've ever met. You want to forget the rules and just let yourself . . . be . . . free."

He stopped and nodded approvingly at her continued silence. Then, coming so close to her that he spoke against the top of her head until she felt his breath through her hair, "Your kisses say all I need to know. They say you want me. You . . . want . . . me. As I . . . want . . . you. And I say: Stay like that—blank, speechless—and let me fill in your answers with *my* lips . . . on *yours*." And he bent to kiss her again.

His audacity finally released the words bottled up in her as she stepped back. "I am not a blank you can fill in, sir. You are reducing me to a naught because that's all you can handle. You're a blank, a surface charmer with no substance, and I deserve more than that. The only emotion I feel now, besides regret, is shame at having wasted even a particle of affection on you."

And she walked quickly up the seven steps to the first balcony of the stairs leading to her house, before looking back. Jordan had not moved. He was still standing directly below, shaking his head in exasperation.

"I gave you too much credit for honesty. Rather, you, like all women, are resentful of honest speech. You want the trappings, not the truth, and you say *I* am surface! Very well"—he sighed—"let's play the game as you want it—with false words borrowed from the Bard. Since you are on a balcony, what could be more apt than we do a Romeo-and-Juliet balcony scene. 'It is my lady! O it is my love! O that she knew she were! She speaks, yet she says nothing.' The next line is yours. Bend over and call to me. Call to me as I climb up and we'll complete the *romantic* scene you seem to crave."

Nina did bend over, but to warn him off. "The very word *romance* turns ironic in your mouth. You play at feelings, feeling none. I was wrong. You are not superficial. You are a cold, calculating, deep-down dastard! And I shudder at the thought of ever letting you near to me and mine." She was on the point of continuing up the steps when that last word reminded her of Adele, and she turned back and somewhat anticlimatically, but dutifully, added in a stern shout, "You propose to Adele today or stop any connection with the De Bonnard family! *Hear!*"

"All of Oceana must be hearing you. Surely such intimate negotiations ought to be carried out face-to-face," Jordan was admonishing as he reached the platform and stared at her face-to-face. His reply seemed to imply that he would discuss proposing to Adele. Her sense of drama and preservation urged her to leave on the high note she had set. But her very purpose for meeting him was to give Adele every last opportunity. She attempted to read his expression, but he made a translation unnecessary by smoothly spelling it out for her—all the while leaning against the railing, physically showing how comfortable he was with his inclinations. "I have long broken off even my pretended attentions to Adele. You and I are the only couple in consideration here. And, as you must have finally realized, Miss De Bonnard, I'm not the marrying kind. For any lady. If and when I decide to alter that proud position, it will be because I've met a lady who could not be otherwise caught or otherwise engaged. Au contraire, both De Bonnard ladies were too easy to capture, falling right into my outstretched palms. Adele one expected to be easy. *She* had no experience. But you have again and again shown yourself as eager to be seduced, so much so that I can only wonder that the other gentlemen have not availed themselves of that opportunity. Or perhaps they have, and it is they who became bored—they who broke your *many* engagements."

He stood away from the railing in anticipation while waiting for the explosion he knew would follow, as one knew a lion would roar if poked. He enjoyed making her jump, roar, feel. She did it so well and always made him feel in response. She'd been looking down, absorbing his blow, and the next moment, when her eyes swept up to his face, he was startled by the golden fire in them and even more startled by her not saying a word. Rather, stepping close, she slapped him with all her might.

To Nina, the sound of the hard slap, not to mention the feel of his face on her hand, brought such a stunning satisfaction that she could only savor it in silence. Breathing harshly, she gloated as he flinched under the blow and backed up, crashing against the balcony rail, almost slipping and going over. But he caught himself and straightened up.

Relishing his almost falling, deliberately making no gesture to help him, Nina waited. Only when he righted himself did she speak. "Pity. You ought to have taken the quicker route down. So much more scenic! It would have been a pleasure for me to see your inflated head bouncing like a beach balloon on the sand below! But at least I got in one blow for my sister . . . and for me. And if you ever dare to come close again, you'll get another. I expect this has taught you to keep your distance from us both."

Free at last, Nina turned and slowly walked up the remainder of the steps into her house, leaving Jordan with a red imprint across his face and a gasping for breath from having banged his back yet unable to cease looking at her with begrudging admiration. She had such an air! Such a queenly aura that he could not help but seek to fix her into his mind as she reached the door into her house and closed it. Like an audience wanting an encore, he stayed where he was, ready to clap, call "Bravo!" call "Encore!" but she did not come back for bows. And it came clear then that the show was over. Jordan had a sudden inexplicable desire to cry out at the ending as the reaction hit him with more force than her hand had struck, that he'd just thrown away something that might have been very precious. Slowly he began going down the stairs to the beach, grudgingly aware that he'd been left with feelings he didn't know what to do with. He felt very much as if he had casually been tossing about a Ming vase to show how indifferent he was to its value and found it crashed into pieces at his feet. Staring at the pieces could not put them back together. Wishing he'd simply put the vase down respectfully on his mantel to have ever after to admire could not mend the slivers. Their relationship was like the Ming vase in pieces; he had seen that in her face when she'd come close to him at the end. He had shattered their connection, and in shattering that, he had shattered, he acknowledged with a curse, some part of himself.

It was surprising, however, that as he walked back to the Windsor area of the beach, there was a sense of lightness. With each step he felt himself being shed of protective, hard-won layers. There went a bit of experience. There, a sheen of cosmopolitanism. Something long dormant at the core was waking up. It was the callow American youth of nineteen who had arrived in Europe ten years ago, hoping for experiences and finding himself the butt of that society's jests. He'd been laughed at for his open ways and childish demands. Had no one taught him the way things were done? One never asked for anything, especially not a lady's favors! One only suggested, implied, until they were offered. So American, they had said, as if that were the most damning appellation. And he had felt callower and callower, until he began to understand the ways of that world. And attempted it himself. His first success gave him confidence and begrudging approval, so he eagerly carried on until he no longer felt eagerness at all. Through the years his experiences coated him, like a pearlized covering, burying the shrinking raw youth deep within. So polished, so glossy did he eventually become that Jordan had turned into a veritable gem of a gentleman. How proud he was of the shiny veneer over his untouched heart! Even here, in Oceana, Jordan had smugly contrasted himself with the bumptious Americans, shaking his head at their wearing their hearts on their sleeves like the proud red, white, and blue boutonnieres everyone was still sporting.

Yet being back in America even a short time had an effect on him, as if the rough American winds and open ways had washed layers off his polish. Old feelings were poking through the veneer of his pearlized self. A feeling of enthusiasm for some of the men even in Oceana who had taken on challenges and begun their own companies had him thinking of going to Washington and joining his grandfather in running the family's newspapers. His youthful self had wanted to achieve something beyond becoming an expert at making, spending, and hoarding money. It was still there under the covering that had begun to be peeled back.

But the most corrosive effect on his shiny surface, he admitted, had been a certain American lady who was so intense she burned through all his protective covering. He'd attempted to ward off her influence by keeping his pearlized surface shining directly at her. He'd even tried to challenge her to join him in a pearlized state. But she was herself, a vital presence that had torn layers of sleekness off him without knowing she was doing it. He found himself vulnerable whenever she was near and angry with her for that vulnerability. He wanted to diminish her to protect himself. And so he'd struck out.

And yet he hadn't been able to make her less, or to make himself want her less. Letters from a countess of past importance kept arriving, urging him to return to Europe as planned. But he sensed they were written to another man. His native land had him going native again, he thought with a grin, had him wanting to stay in America and achieve something. Or to stay with a certain American lady. Whatever the cause, he was different. Lighter. Freer. A *feeling* self. The only trouble was that, now that he was free at last to feel, what he felt most was the loss of her.

Thirteen

In the rows of New York City brownstones, the De Bonnard white stone mansion stood alone. So was Nina alone in that white house—if one did not count the servants. Her father had kept his word about escorting her, but only to one dinner at Delmonico's. After that, apparently, there were no occasions to which it was suitable to take her. The season had not yet begun. Whomever he was seeing night after night were friends he did not wish to introduce to his daughter. She was back to that birthday moment on the yacht, seeing him partying on his own. Which left her on her own and feeling even more alone in her heart, for Adele and her mother were no longer in there as comforting presences, but rather were sore points, bringing up myriad agonized thoughts. Jordan, of course, was not even to be thought of, so it was remarkable that she spared him so many passing observations. Oh stars, she had thought he was cosmopolitan but not corrupt. She had thought he was sophisticated but not insensitive. She had thought he cared for her, but not in that degrading way.

Refusing to bemoan her fate like a ninny, Nina straightened her shoulders and put on a rather fetching white straw hat. Dressed for an occasion, she sought someplace to go and settled for a visit to the local galleries. At least this time there were no restrictions as to which showings she could see, since there was no one now to censor her experiences. If loneliness was the penalty for leaving home and family, then the gain was independence. Another plus was that she could play the piano with no one to comment on her selections. Her mother and father had disapproved of a young lady playing Bach, although they allowed her Offenbach because everyone was humming his tunes. Now alone in the house she regained her fingering and allowed her passion to break forth in loud chords, con brio.

In the back of her mind, fueling her decision to come to New York was a plan to use this time to write a novel. Under the pressure of being watched, Nina had been able to write an abundance of stories and essays. How much easier it would be, she'd thought, when she could write openly. But it was not. Rather, she discovered that being free to do something forbidden made it lose some of its attraction. Further, she no longer needed that outlet when she could go out instead. Her father's remark that all appearance of hiding in disgrace must be avoided had Nina making it a rule to appear somewhere each day—although very few of the De Bonnards' set were in New York City during the heat. But there were always enough hangers-on to keep the rumor mill going, and she had to give them the innocent viewings to report back in their eager letters to Oceana. Taking her maid as a chaperone, Nina daily shopped or walked through the park. When that began to pall, she sought new places worth attending by going through the newspapers after breakfast. The major item was the presidential election. The *Times* was pushing the Republican Rutherford Hayes. Her father was supporting Hayes, for Samuel Tilden, despite being a New Yorker, bore the sin of being a Democrat. There were frequent rallies for both candidates, but Nina could not see herself in a crowd cheering for a gentleman she had not even been introduced to. The New York *Herald* had columns about explorers, allowing the readers to live through these gentlemen's exploits vicariously. But Nina never cared to experience anything secondhand.

The rest of the newspapers were overflowing with reports of an unemployed workers' demonstration in New York City. Fifty thousand men had marched with bloodred banners. Now that sounded like something worth seeing and writing about! But it had already occurred. At length Nina was reduced to reading the sleazy *Police Gazette*, which she'd been shocked to find in her home. Certainly her father had unexpected facets. Sitting at her desk, Nina skipped through that paper. It had so many Personals, many embarrassing, until she came across one that had her laughing aloud. "To a lady: when disembarking the 7th Avenue car on Macdougal Street, was the fall in my lap *accidental*? If not, address, in honor, Bachelor, Box 139." That was a subtle way to get a gentleman's attention—fall right on him!

Turning the page, Nina came across a large advertisement for a spiritual seance. She recalled hearing Bobby talk of going to such a showing by a blond lady, Anna Eva Fay, who had performed before Queen Victoria. This spiritualist was a gentleman with no regal affidavits. Nevertheless, Nina penciled the seance into her schedule as a lark.

Leafing on, the product advertisements were other ripe sources for amusement. But she did not have gout, or hair loss, and if she had female problems, they were not anybody's business and she was shocked to see them even alluded to. Another advertisement, however, leaped out at her. It was a half-page drawing of a lady in a corset trimmed with rows of satin rosettes. That reminded Nina painfully of Adele's corset experience at the Centennial, but she shook off that recollection. In the background was a sketched gentleman giving the lady an approving glance, igniting a flushing fantasy of herself wearing that rosette-trimmed corset and parading before a certain world-traveling gentleman. Thankfully, those thoughts were interrupted by the sound of singing coming from the library. Astonished, Nina rushed in that direction. No maid would take such liberties as to sing aloud with such gusto! Opening the library doors, she spotted a pale blond woman going through her father's desk.

"Stop that!" Nina demanded.

With a slow smile, the blond woman took out her feathered fan and swayed it indolently before sitting down in Mr. De Bonnard's chair.

"Don't get your dander up, my dear. I'm just looking for an address. Philip forgot to give it to me last night."

Nina, her skin tingling, knew without being told who this was. Or rather what she was. She was this year's lady on the yacht. How often had Nina's skin crawled at that memory of her in the half-light of the cabin door. That woman had been laughing at Mrs. De Bonnard, Nina had assumed when the wound was fresh, and often rewrote the moment by having herself jumping in and pushing the lady away to stop her laughter. Later, when the years dulled the memory, Nina saw herself as one day coming face-to-face with her again and coldly, calmly, dismissing her, saying, "You may go." But that had not happened. Only the laughing memory remained, floating around the edges of her mind as either a warning or a model.

And now here was another such woman. Nina eagerly examined her, staring as if the woman were something on a laboratory slide.

Amazingly, her fashions were not noticeably more déclassé than ordinary ladies'. That vibrant shade of royal blue she'd seen even Mrs. Windsor wear. The only clues to her class were perhaps the décolletage being a mite too low for so early in the day and the six rows of opulent pearls that looked as if they'd cost someone a tidy sum. The intruder was fingering them absently while staring in a laughing, challenging way at the young lady. Why did these women always laugh?

"Which one are you?" The woman broke through the silent examination, daring to get personal. "Nina, I guess. Philip calls the other one his baby, so you must be the young lady of the house? Too pretty by rights. T'aint fair that you should have position, wealth, and such good looks in one. But life, I've learned the hard way, ain—*isn't* even-handed. The back of the hand to one and a kiss of the hand for another."

Listening, Nina was shocked to realize that this woman before her was just another human being, not a nightmare come to daylight. The woman coughed and didn't have a hanky on her person, as her mother had taught Nina that every lady should. Another cough reduced her to just a person with problems. Nina removed a hanky from her pocket and handed it to her. The woman took it and blew her nose, and then tucked it into her décolletage. Now *that* Nina would never have done!

"I gotta get a room!" the woman murmured. And Nina was shocked, her emotions surging up from disdain to concern, which must have shown on her face, for the woman laughed again. "Just kidding. I have an apartment. But people always see us as being from the streets, am I right?" She grinned impishly at Nina, who realized with shame that she had indeed been seeing her as some-one off the streets, who might leave a stain on the chairs . . . the way possibly Mrs. Windsor would view her. Reacting against that, Nina was determined to be different and she began by smiling back.

"Hey, now! That's another unfair thing. With a smile like that, you'd have every gentleman at your feet! But then I've heard you do anyway. Although I've often wondered why you bother, since you don't need to. Lotta hard work to get a gentleman at your feet. Even harder to keep 'em there."

Challenged, Nina suddenly wanted to match her honesty, and so she did. "The gentleman you have currently at your feet is my father?"

The blond woman laughed in delight. "I could say I was the new maid, but you wouldn't believe that. Point is, we could pre-tend I did, if it'a be easier on you. Then you could believe what-ever you want."

"I don't need that kind of pretense. I gather you are a friend of my father's."

"Friend? Sorta. I'm Camille. Call myself that after that play. I feels drawn to her, 'cause we're in the same situation. But I'm not dying . . . yet." She winked and coughed some more, and Nina gave her another smile.

"Well, Camille. Do you have the address you want?"

"Dismissing me, hun?"

"No, if you wish to stay for tea, I'm perfectly willing to en-tertain you. Just giving you the option to leave, for you know Jef-fers, our butler, tells Papa everything that happens."

"Oh, Jeffers is on my side. Cute little guy, ain't he?"

"Jeffers! He's ancient and so stiff!"

"To you, 'cause you're quality. To me he talks a lot about the wife he lost. Misses her, you know."

"Well, no, I didn't know. That is, Mother is in charge of the do-mestics."

"La-de-dah! He's been in your home since you were a baby, I bet. See him as just furniture, don't ya?"

"No," Nina replied, but added ruefully, "I see him as just Jeffers. He's an institution here. He always frightened me when I was a child. To be truthful, he's a snitch. Always reports everything I do to either Mother or Father and, earlier, to my governess. I've always viewed him as an enemy."

"No kidding! See how different everyone looks like from different eyes! Yet I can see how he might frighten a little girl. Don't worry about him spilling the beans to anyone. I'll tell him to leave you alone."

"Eh, thank you. Tea?"

So they had tea, served by Jeffers, who, despite Camille's conversation with him, was stiff and shocked in his attitude. That had surprised Camille, who laughingly told him to "loosen up," but he simply stared at her and continued to address himself to Nina.

Shaking her head, Camille said, "I guess I shouldn't have jarred him like this. He's used to everything in its place. And you and I together are real out of place! But you're a nice lady. No hoity-toity airs."

Nina laughed at her slang. "Perhaps because I'm in disgrace!"

"Yeah?" Camille asked with sufficient interest to make her stop stuffing her mouth with small sandwiches and cake. How she ate that much and still had such a small waist, Nina could not imagine. Noticing that Nina was surprised by her third piece of cake, Camille explained, "Gotta eat, you know. I'm singing tonight, and I need to build myself up. Eat up and you get energy. Otherwise, I'd be happy to just lounge around like a lady. Like you."

Nina did not take offense, for that was indeed what she had objected to in her life as a lady. Besides, Nina was going to work soon—as soon as she could come up with an idea for a novel. Was this Camille an artist? With interest Nina asked, "You sing? Opera bouffe? A concert?"

"Yeah, that. I stand up and sing, and your pa pays for the band behind me. You know, like Jenny Lind did a few years back. But I'm not Swedish. Nor a nightingale. I've got a loud voice, but not sweet. Yet I enjoy singing and lots of people enjoy hearing me. I always get a roomful of flowers and gifts after, and they're not all from your pa, neither!" She tossed her light flaxen curls and grinned as she amended that. "Some are. Maybe more than

I think. But these concerts make me feel like I'm special. And then there's that applause. Nothing else equals the thrill of that, whatever else gentlemen say." She winked. "Believe me. I know everyone's gotta do something in this world that says, ain't nobody else in this world can do that just like me. You know what I mean?"

"Yes," Nina said with a sigh. "I liked to play concert pieces on the piano. But as a lady it was considered déclassé to want to perform seriously. You are fortunate you've been able to have that choice."

"Oh, I perform all right!" Camille laughed, but she was shaking her head. "Hey now!" she exploded, staring at the young lady, surprised enough to put down her cake. "A lady like you jealous of what I got! Can you beat that? But wait—I'm not buying the piano thing having put you in the dumps. Gotta be a man!"

Naturally, Nina instinctively denied it, but at Camille's relentless poking, and with the need to speak to some woman about that moment of shame, Nina, between two more servings of cake and a fresh pot of tea, told her about Jordan and what he had said.

Camille listened like she ate, with a ravenous appetite, asking for little details just the way her fingers found extra crumbs on a plate, putting every one into her mouth.

"Okay! So what we got here is a real operator! A gentleman who thinks he can get anything from women and not have to pay. That's the cheapest sort. You can't have nothing in this world without paying for it. You want a lady's favors, you gotta either pay with gifts or a decent proposal. Or . . . and, this is rare, with a genuine return of love for love. But for a fella to think he can take and take and not give back. That's stealing! That's piracy. That's not fair dealing!"

Nina was disturbed at the indignation Camille was showing. She'd hoped Camille would tell her that Jordan wasn't that bad. Now Nina had to admit he was, if even Camille was appalled by him. Further, Nina realized that a lady would have forgiven Jordan more easily or pretended not to see his callousness. There was Camille's honesty again. She was not blinded by Jordan's position or appearance. To her all men were equal: They came to her on an equal basis wanting equal favors. But it also discomfited Nina to realize that she herself had been unfair toward several gentlemen. Had she too stolen from them without paying fair return?

Camille interrupted her musing, asking whether there wasn't any other gentleman. Nina could think only of Bobby Van Reyden. But his name had the most unexpected reaction.

"Oh saints! We all know Bobby Van Reyden! You don't want to get involved with him. He'll drive you wild. Forget everything I said about being fair when it comes to Bobby. He never plays fair and don't expect fair treatment back. He gives a lot but always takes back *double*! Since he was out of knickers he's been hanging around my kind of lady. And he's been getting more crazy, I hear. Comes of having so much money and no ma and pa to handle him, just his trustees, so he thinks he can buy anybody or anything!"

That alleviated Nina's concern about her treatment of gentlemen, for if she need not castigate herself about Mr. Windsor or Bobby, the rest were long married and no longer worth worrying about. Camille was launched into a Bobby story—everyone had one of those—about his buying up every seat in a theater for one evening, ordering the troupe to perform solely for him. Everyone was thinking what a lark, until Bobby began redirecting the performances. At the third redirection, a rebellion broke out, which he quenched by passing out envelopes stuffed with cash. That bought him some goodwill, till Bobby grinned and said, "I was getting on your nerves there for a while, wasn't I? And now, a few bucks and you'll jump yourselves silly pleasing me. Not one of you has the artistic integrity to tell me to go jump in the lake!" Camille was laughing so hard she started to cough, but she concluded, smiling, " 'Course I've told him where to go, lotsa times. And he likes me for it. Bobby's one of the gentlemen who always sends me flowers when I do my singing. Bobby sends so many I made a deal with a street vendor and always gets a tidy sum back for them."

Nina was aghast at that; one did not sell a gentleman's offerings! Except that maybe this woman needed the money more than the flowers. It was a thought she did not usually consider, never had to consider—it made her wonder about many things.

She jumped as Camille yelled, "Hey, where'd ya go?" She was holding out a ticket before her face. It was to her concert, she explained, but warned that no other "lady" would be there, mostly her friends and lots of gentlemen. Yet if Nina wanted to come hear her sing, Camille would love it. Nina declined without hesitation. She could not do that to her mother, or embarrass her father in that open manner, she said frankly.

"They don't care that you're embarrassed. Otherwise how come they both permit *me* to be in their lives!"

And with that, Camille took her leave, as well as the rest of the cake to eat on the way home.

Nina was left with her idea of life in crumbs about her. Why was nothing as she'd originally thought? She could not help but recall the blind men and elephant parable, seeing the whole according to the part each touched. Meeting Camille had shown her that she herself had grown up with a view of the elephant as a firm back that carried her in a life of ease while Camille had felt the trunk and saw life as a snake wiggling its way through her life, ready to strike. How many more pachyderm views were there?

That night, when her father, dressed in his evening clothes, appeared to announce that he was off for a meeting with some friends, Nina was hard put not to say "Give Camille my love." But she played the dutiful blind daughter and responded with a non-committal nod.

Surprisingly, the next day there was coverage of Camille's concert in the newspapers' music sections. Had her father paid for the reviews as well? For they were universally excellent. They spoke of "a clear sound!" and proclaimed, "The beautiful Camille Connors is a joy to look at and almost a joy to hear. She makes one think of a morning bird who wakes up all the senses and yet there is a lack of the sweetness that would make her perfect. But that she is so near perfect is praise indeed."

Indeed. Nina regretted not having been more daring and gone after all. And while she was thinking of being daring, Bobby called. He'd given her a few weeks to get herself used to being alone so she'd be happier to see him when he came. His stratagem had worked. Nina surprised herself by her welcome, yet almost immediately regretted it when he filled her in on Oceana gossip, mentioning, with a devilish grin, that Jordan Windsor had left Oceana and gone to work on his grandfather's Washington newspaper. For all of Bobby's pointed staring, Nina did not respond. So he continued, "He's not the only one who's got newspapers. I've got one here in New York. Worked on it some, but I rearranged things so much they all threatened to leave."

"I know. You paid them extra and they decided to stay, and then you said that showed how few journalistic ethics they had. Right?"

"Hey! This is creepy. How do you know me so well, when I'm still trying to figure you out? I was mad at you for giving me the air at the Pynchot ball. You turned to Jordan Windsor before all our friends. Made a real ass out of me."

Remembering Camille's advice and no longer wishing to appease any gentleman, she said coldly, "You *are* an ass."

Bobby was not offended; rather his snub-nosed, little boy's face was grinning. "That's not me. Dickie was the ass. I'm the guy who goes the limit. Wanna come along and have some fun? I can take you to places here in New York you never dreamed of. In disguise, if you're a scaredy-cat."

Nina did not like to think of herself as a scaredy-cat. Her mother would not approve of Nina being squired by Mr. Van Reyden, although in Nina's mind, Bobby was the safest escort, for she could treat him as callously as she wished and not feel in any way obligated. "I may accompany you to certain respectable places if you have any that would interest," she said in compromise. He snatched that up eagerly.

Bobby had long figured that Nina enjoyed challenges, so he took her to his favorite enjoyment: the coaching races. For many years in New York City every gentleman's goal was to join the Coaching Club, a union of elite sportsmen who each drove a four-in-hand coach. The club was inspired by the English Regency Corinthians, who had made "driving within an inch" an accomplishment of the true athlete and had races to determine the best "whip." Similarly, New York's wealthy sportsmen raced through Central Park wearing huge driving capes and shouting "Spring 'em" at the start of each race. Nina watched a few times and felt green with envy, aching to join. Sensing her need to compete, Bobby took her up on the box when he raced. At one point he let her handle the reins while he sat back and grinned. With that encouragement, day after day she practiced and practiced, preparing for her solo drive. For that occasion, the two arranged for Nina to hide under a driving cape and hat and pretend to be a gentleman. Nina was slightly anxious at first, but when the race began, she forgot about her disguise, having to concentrate on the four thundering horses in her grip, holding them together on the turns. After, despite coming in last, she felt positively exhilarated.

But the next time, when she no longer feared that the others would recognize her, she gave herself to the moment, so much so that she even dropped the cape and stood up as she was, Nina De Bonnard, racing at her utmost, and came in with the five finalists. Bobby was second, having managed to outswerve and outblock everyone else but the winner, a visiting English polo champion. But Bobby's attention was diverted that day: one eye was continually checking out Nina's performance. After the race, his wild gray eyes looked at her flushed face in admiration as he shouted, "You're quite a gal, Miss De Bonnard. A champion to the bone!"

Nina didn't remember ever being that pleased. In gratitude, she let Bobby hold her hand that night. Yet away from the atmosphere of the race, Nina remembered why Bobby was just Bobby, for the hand-holding left her unfeeling, until he squeezed tightly enough to end her normal feeling as well, so she took her hand away. The next day Bobby brought her a coach of her own, with specially designed upholstery and matching livery for her postilions in white with gold stars. "For the gilded, star-spangled lady you are!" he said. That had her frowning as it recalled herself on the night of the Pynchot ball wearing golden stars in her hair. The next race Nina did badly, coming in last again, for she was unfamiliar with both the coach and the four new white horses. Spurred to prove her mettle, Nina practiced every morning with her new team until she felt herself in charge again and able to compete in the next major Sunday race. For that one she arrived dressed to conquer with golden stars in her hair to match her livery. She felt confident of doing well until she discovered an alteration in the course. No longer would the race be limited to Central Park; rather, they were to start from a side street, turn onto Fifth Avenue, and then go down that busy thoroughfare to the park. It was Bobby's idea of a new lark. Some of the more sedate gentleman withdrew, but to the younger contestants the change increased the challenge.

It was bad enough for a lady to compete in a gentleman's race in the park, but to do so in the streets where she might be ogled by peddlers and street cleaners would put her beyond the pale. Yet Nina could not withdraw after all her practice. She had never put herself to so much effort without achieving some immediate gratification. Hesitating, Nina saw the coaches moving off to the new starting point and simply could not bear being left out.

Yet since she had come late, Nina was in a rear position through the beginning of the race, chafing to break out of the crowd. She had her opportunity at the first turn when a young sport, losing his nerve, swerved to a stop. Instantly Nina moved forward into the pack where the pace was breakneck, yet Nina was determined to keep on a par even if she broke her neck doing so.

Past midpoint, the leaders began taking reckless chances and the weeding out began in earnest as one, then two coaches lost wheels and were overturned. The thundering wall of motion made for more defectors, leaving only those who feared nothing but losing. Fifth Avenue had caused a substantial winnowing out. Nina was still in the race, but had fallen back again. Wary of harming pedestrians, she kept slowing on approaching them. Not till she had reached the final clear stretch did she make up ground by pressing her horses onward. Standing up and feeling her hair coming loose, Nina charged on, acknowledging that the added risks had increased the exhilaration, as did being in with the leaders at last. The only one ahead, besides Bobby, was the English polo chap, who did not know Fifth Avenue and thus could not prepare in his mind, as Nina and Bobby mentally did, for the group of produce carts at the intersection. He smashed straight into an apple cart, sending all the apples flying. Bobby ducked under the apple barrage but kept his eye on the prize and smoothly took the lead. Nina was coming in second when the polo chap, whose coach had suffered only slight damage, was up and closing in again. At the park's entrance, he was just behind Nina. The rest were far to the rear. One of these three was moments from victory. The polo chap saw the finish line ahead and whipped his horses forward, bringing him side by side with Nina. Doggedly, she would not give way. Leaning over, he used his whip on one of her horses, throwing her team off rhythm and thereby gained the opportunity to slip by and close in on Bobby. In a blink the two were engaging in a wheel-bunking contest. Distracted with each other, swerving left and right, they unwittingly gave Nina enough space to move ahead. She saw the finish line coming up and cried out, encouraging her horses to extra effort. Hunching forward, she crossed the line first, while behind her the two quarreling gentlemen finished in a dead-heat tie for second place.

Victory! Nina De Bonnard had won the toughest race ever! Standing up in the box, she glanced around at all the losers coming in behind her. Only then did she slowly begin to accept her triumph, and the tears spilled down her cheeks.

The polo chap was heard loudly complaining, objecting to Nina's win, claiming that Bobby had run interference, which was the problem with allowing ladies in their races. There was no room in a race for gallantry. That glorious moment was rapidly being dissipated for Nina when Bobby stepped up to the fellow and said, "You're a damned poor sport, Fotheringale! By rights you were disqualified when you hit the apple cart. And then you oughta have been banished for that whip trick on her horse! What right have you to protest! This lady is the only one who deserves to win 'cause she's the only one who played by the rules. And besides, she's an *American*!"

How the last followed, no one knew, but it made an impression on the rest of the racers, and Nina was given three cheers and even an apology from the English chap. Nina was all smiles again, savoring her win, realizing, as one does at such special moments, that she would probably never reach such a height again.

Fourteen

Of course *Nina* had to pay for her victory. Her father was congratulated on her win by one of the racers, which brought her activity to Mr. De Bonnard's attention. In a huff he gave her a scold and ordered her to cease competing or be sent back to Oceana. Nina could not endure that, so she resigned, appeasing herself with the thought that directly after winning was the perfect moment for quitting. Actually, she felt some relief at no longer being involved, for although she'd relished the challenge, she'd been having second thoughts about the destruction the race had left in its wake. Bobby, as usual, had fixed it. He'd simply paid everyone off until there was no more grumbling. "Money is the real champion," he said with a wink.

But a rival newspaper to Bobby's *Bugle* had gotten wind of the escapade and written a scathing denunciation of "young wealthy gentlemen taking their larks by overturning working people's carts of coal and apples."

"There was no coal cart!" Bobby objected while reading it to her. Nina agreed, but there'd *had* been an apple cart. "Horsefeathers! That old apple woman got so much money outta me, she's given up selling apples and bought a farm in the Bronx. If we ever race in the streets again we'll have apple carts and coal carts lining up begging to be turned over! What's really galling in this fella's article is his making us look like a bunch of rowdy schoolboys when so many of the contestants were older gentlemen, including a world-renowned banker!"

"If you mean Mr. Belmont, he refused to race when you

changed the course," Nina reminded, but Bobby was not listening as he read her an answer he intended to feature in the *Bugle*. It was filled with vituperation.

"That won't make our point," Nina said, feeling some responsibility since she'd been the winner. "First you ought to explain that no one was seriously hurt and everyone's damages were more than compensated for, and then you ought to explain to them the history of the sport and if possible give them a glimpse of the challenge of it!"

"Yeah, sure! I mean I don't think I could . . . maybe I'll assign that to one of my staff, but they don't know anything about coach racing."

"I wrote something, if you'd care to see it. . . ." Nina began shyly. Actually she'd written an essay, a short story, and an article about her enjoyment of racing. That sport had given her back the joy of writing, which she'd missed by keeping herself so occupied going on jaunts with Bobby. That was when Nina realized that writing fed off the emotion one had. Despondent and lonely, she could ease those sensations by expressing them. Jubilant and proud, she could crystallize and memorialize her victory by capturing it on paper.

She felt she had caught the thrill of the race in her short article, and so was not really reluctant for it to be read. After a token demurrer, she allowed Bobby to snatch it out of her hands.

He was silent as he read it. Bobby, who had made complimenting her his daily expression, was frowning over her poor effort. Nina felt some alarm. Was it that badly written? Next moment he had whirled on his heels and left. Well! Nina had thought, that was what dealing with Bobby meant. Too rude for words.

But the next day he was back with a smile, as if he had not affronted her. Nina, who never felt it was worth being angry with Bobby, had forgiven him before he presented her with a gold choker-style necklace with a hanging gold star. It had matching drop golden-star earrings. She was trying on the ensemble, noting how the choker emphasized her long graceful neck and wondering whether a lady ought to accept such a gift, knowing the answer. Of course Bobby had bought her a racing coach, persuading her that the coach was a necessity if she was to be a member of the club. It was just a loan and he had done as much for other members. Mr. De Bonnard would doubtless pay him back once he heard what a winner he had for a daughter. By that process of convoluted reasoning, the coach was made acceptable. It was silly to quibble about the golden pillows he bought next for the coach or even the liveries, because they were part of that original understanding. But this jewelry was an out-and-out gift. Bobby had been creeping up on her morals, making inroads. Yet accepting the jewelry would directly signal him, if not everyone else, that there was more between them than there actually was. His eager, glittery eyes showed he understood her dilemma and had been counting on it.

"No," she said, giving them back, but he refused to take them. Offended.

"Hey, no strings! What kind of fella do you think I am? 'Sides, I wouldn't attempt to buy you so *cheap*. This is paltry—just a prize for your victory!"

"No!" she said steadily.

"Okay, okay, I'm joking. This jewelry is not a prize, or even a gift. It's part payment for your services rendered."

Alarmed and not liking the look in his eyes, Nina demanded an explanation. He responded with a gesture, handing her the *Bugle*. The newspaper was folded back to reveal a two-column article entitled "The Thrill Is Like No Other" and it was bylined "The Star-Spangled Gilded Lily." Below, word for word, was her article on coach racing.

"But how could you put it in the newspaper without consulting me!" Nina objected, uncertain whether she ought be angry or succumb to the delirious thrill of seeing her article in print. The thrill won out. The jewelry was part payment for the article, so it was perfectly respectable, and must be accepted, as well as the usual fee. Nina could have her own steady income if she wrote an article twice a week.

"It'll be easy. Since you write so well. Think of the *fun* of that and how you can spread your fun to others by describing all the events we'll be *engaging* in together!" And he looked deeply at her when using the word *engaging*. She ignored him, too occupied with rereading her article.

"But did anyone say anything about it?" she asked, covering her eagerness with a nonchalant tone. "I mean, for instance, your editor? Did he like it?"

"Oh, sure. Said it . . . now what did he say? Yep, said, 'It has quite a feel to it.' But also he said if it was to be a regular column, you gotta write shorter to fit. He'll send you the wordage and stuff. He's gonna stop by and bring a contract. Gotta get you exclusive, before any other newspaper snaps you up. You're going to be a real star!"

The delight of writing a piece and seeing it in print grew with each article. Nina had at last done something that, as Camille said, "ain't nobody else can do just like me!" Nina smiled. Yes, she was almost proud of herself. Keeping the secret of her identity added to the excitement. Bobby's editor, Mr. Holden, arrived with an aloof attitude, expecting to meet a female Bobby, and was surprised by her maidenly blushes at his slightest praise, which had him doubling them. In fact, Mr. Holden stayed on, discussing his lifelong view of journalism and the recent success of lady reporters, who all used noms de plume, but none of course as original as hers. He was interested to know how Miss De Bonnard had settled on that pseudonym. Bobby interrupted to claim credit. "I put it all together. First she's as beautiful as a lily. Right? Like that Bible quote says about 'consider the lilies.' Nina doesn't need adornment. But unadornment don't fadge in our group. And Nina wore a shower of gilded stars at the last ball we attended. So with all that, and sticking in the centennial and all, I came up with a star-spangled gilded lily."

"Ah!" Mr. Holden said, but Nina objected, wanting to change it to something shorter, like a Society Lady. That was scoffed at, but Nina kept to her wish to drop the lilies, which she didn't care for, and definitely to omit the word *gilded*. "It sounds slightly tarnished. Surely that's the wrong image of me."

"But you *are* slightly tarnished," Bobby said airily. "Or rather gilded. We *all* are in our group. We are the *gilded* society; you are the lily of us all and a star-spangled one. You're not a common society lady!" Bobby jeered. "Don't you wanna tweet them by calling yourself The Gilded Lily? And star-spangled proudly proclaims your American spirit!"

Nina saw the jibe in the use of the word *gilded* but was uncertain. Some version of the name had to be kept, Mr. Holden explained, since it had been established. They compromised on The Gilded Lily, drawn with a star-spangled banner beneath, like a flourish, giving a star-spangled impression without saying it. To decide on her byline took longer than writing the article, but it was done at last. Thereafter, The Gilded Lily wrote columns on topics from an opera opening to a dinner at Delmonico's. Beyond events, she described the pleasure palaces of the rich, such as Pynchot Court with its golden faucets for hot and cold running water and hot and cold running salt water as well. Her most popular columns were those private looks inside her gilded world. At a luncheon at the new posh Fifth Avenue Hotel to which she was escorted by her father, Nina saw some of her mother's set returned from their summer jaunts. After the obligatory nods, her heart jumped at overhearing them discussing The Gilded Lily, attempting to guess who that lady was and how she knew the things reported. The flourish of stars, they whispered, was a ruse to disguise her real heritage, which was not American, but British, possibly a gilded or royal relation of the English beauty and friend of the Prince of Wales, Lillie Langtry. Some connection, obviously.

She almost went up and acknowledged her second persona, having determined that she would no longer hide what she was. A small voice within kept urging her to unveil herself before someone else did. But she was stopped when her father added his speculation that The Gilded Lily was a foreigner, for sure. "Who else would write about our daily doings with such disdain!" Quickly Nina agreed, remembering with a blush that her mother would not approve of her having so public a profession, or any profession, for that matter. To keep her secret, she continued the false assumption that The Gilded Lily was a foreigner by writing several columns revealing inner knowledge of English society.

Those tidbits she got from Fotheringale, the polo champ who was quite friendly now that she no longer raced her coach. In fact, he was racing after *her*, much to Bobby's outrage. An intimate in the prince's and princess's inner circle, Fotheringale exposed the real reason behind the recent fashion set by Princess Alexandra for wearing a broad dog-collar necklace called La Belle Alexandrine. Her Highness had a burn scar on her neck and the dog collar was camouflage. That revelation cinched many readers' belief that the author was English and of the royal circle.

Continuing with that deception, Nina featured the scoop that the Mayfair set had succumbed to the fad of tattooing themselves. It had reached the exalted height of both the Prince of Wales and Czar Alexander II. As for distaff tattooing, the most provocative one was Lady Churchill's small snake tattoo on her wrist. In a follow-up column, Nina suggested appropriate tattoos for certain members of the New York society, including a choice for the writer herself of either a lily or a string of stars; readers were to guess which. That was a hint. Nina's action: Without a second thought, she had a small star tattooed on her right wrist.

"Ah! you're giving the secret away," Bobby objected, but was impressed by Nina's daring and rushed to join her by tattooing an American flag on his own right wrist.

Nevertheless, Nina continued her mystery by covering her tattoo with bracelets, an example of the ambivalence Nina felt: She ached to reveal herself while keeping up her anonymity. She had brief urges to tease her smug social set, who assumed they could be exposed only by a distant foreigner. But that need to taunt was in conflict with her desire for privacy. She attempted to squelch both emotions and concentrate on perfecting her column, for which she felt a growing pride. The more read and quoted The Gilded Lily became, the more Nina was pushed to outdo herself, needing further amusing events to report on, which necessitated her going along with Bobby to shows and affairs. In her whirl of activity Nina had no time to seclude herself and consider what she was running to or away from.

But she did have time to devise a higher coiffure to go along with her higher profile. This was pulling her hair back from her forehead and fastening it at the crown in a round pouf that suggested a halo. She had posed for her photograph in that hair arrangement and wearing a white gown with off-the-shoulder décolletage made less sensational by the addition of a lace shawl. At the last minute, Bobby, inspired, had stepped up and removed Nina's lace shawl, pinning it instead in two arcs behind her on the photographer's backdrop curtain—which gave the effect of wings. The result was a photograph so provocative, such a contradiction of allure and innocence, of sheer purity and sinful seduction, that the photographer had enlarged it and put it in his window. Seeing it there gave Bobby another idea: Nina would join the Professional Beauties. That was an elite group of beautiful women whose photographs were sold in shops. The concept of nominating Professional Beauties had come over from England, where Lady Randolph Churchill, née Jennie Jerome, from right here on Madison Avenue, was one of the main attractions in that line, as was Lillie Langtry herself. At first, the Professional Beauties in New York (or the New York PBs) were opera singers and such, but when just last season some of the daughters of society were included and sales of the photographs doubled, it became clear to the entrepreneurs behind this idea that the public thought the real celebrities of the day were the ultrarich. Just as readers could not get enough of their exploits through gossip columns and social reports, ordinary people felt themselves part of the gilded set by having a picture of one of them in their homes.

Becoming a PB usually began with a photographer getting a picture of a beauty and pushing her as one of this exalted group. But Bobby, who enjoyed using his whims to lead society, decided to make an official list of the leading candidates along with their pictures and publish these in the *Bugle*, making even society ladies anxious to be included.

Originally, Bobby had persuaded Nina to have her photograph taken for her column, to have ready if they ever decided to reveal her face to go with the nom de plume. But when the photograph turned out so phenomenally successful, Bobby's love of exploitation and joy of shocking had him determined to spread her picture to the world. Nina refused, somehow not wanting strangers to have a bit of her in their homes. Bobby used as persuasion not only that the photographer, Mr. Wilson, was already selling her picture, but also that she ought not to be left out of what was becoming a select group. He showed her Mrs. Caroline Astor's photograph, not to mention that of Miss Cass Richards, in her renowned jeweled flag crown, who had included herself at the urging of Mr. Marshall, that same western upstart who advised society matrons on their parties. Still Nina resisted, until Bobby revealed the identity of the newest candidate from Washington, D.C.: a Miss Lucy Perkens, the daughter of George Perkens, who was in charge of protocol there. "Incidentally," Bobby had added slyly, "she's Jordan's current lady. He's been squiring her about."

Knowing she was being manipulated, Nina still could not resist looking at Miss Perkens. Heavens, what a self-satisfied smirk. What little eyes! What mousy hair. Nina had heard rumors that Jordan was involved with some important official's daughter at the capital. So this was she.

Bobby, his wild, light eyes almost whirling in his head as they did when he was plotting, pressed his advantage. "Look at the two of you next to each other. Picture to picture. Now ask yourself would any man go for this face when he'd seen *this*? Let the nation choose which is the most beautiful lady in the world. I bet you'll sell out in a week, a day, while her picture gets left on the shelves!"

Naturally, Nina had been persuaded. Even more naturally, she regretted it upon walking into a store and seeing herself on display as if she were an article of clothing. But Bobby was jubilant. His prediction was correct: Her picture sold out in a day. Interviews, magazine articles centered on her as the lead PB. At which point the very hostesses who had been shunning Nina on their return to the city for the season began sending her invitations as they did to all the PBs—a party not having a chance of success without one present! Bobby came running to show her a note one hostess had added to a party announcement: "Do come! The PBs will be here, including the fabulous Nina De Bonnard."

Thus, Nina in exile had become the fabulous Nina De Bonnard. She kept herself proper by refusing Bobby and Fotheringale and being escorted by her father to every party, which all three gentlemen resented. But there she was, after all the turmoil and threats, Nina De Bonnard at a party with a group of admirers, surrounding her as they'd done at Oceana. Nina had not felt so young and alive in a long time. It was like coming out of a mourning period.

After that, the society pages reported her every appearance as if she were a queen. The main gossip column, "Town Topics," even reported some of her everyday doings, such as when Bobby and she stopped an organ grinder, paying him to jump into their carriage to play his repertoire while they sang all the current tunes and Nina hugged the grinder's monkey, who stole her earrings, and she laughed and let the animal keep them. How anybody knew about that Nina could not uncover until she asked Bobby, who readily admitted he was the source. "Gotta build you up, so everyone will want to read your column when we make the great unveiling!" But after her experience with being a PB and having her picture sold to the mass of people, Nina had second thoughts about more exposure. Even now she couldn't pull an innocent prank without its being discussed at length, such as challenging a group of her admirers to hold their breath while she finished reciting "The Star-Spangled Banner," the winner to claim a kiss. Bobby had won. He would have held his breath unto death to get the kiss. So she kissed him. She became accustomed to kissing him—for winning races, for winning bets, for small, acceptable gifts. He followed her about waiting for the kisses like a hungry dog waiting for a tidbit. Sometimes she kissed him just because he had waited so patiently for it. But she never kissed him because she wanted his kiss.

At first these Nina De Bonnard reportings were amusing. And then when she was being featured as the celebrity of the season, the stories subtly changed. Everything she did was slanted off-color. It was forgotten or ignored that her father was with her at a party where she was reported as attending alone. Or the report was spread that the host had given her a diamond bracelet, without mentioning that all the ladies had received them as favors on their plates!

It was very much like walking down a corridor and coming

across a person at the other end and realizing with a jolt it was a mirror. That unexpected view of self granted a momentary glimpse of what others might see. And for a moment one thought, Oh, I look different than I assumed . . . older, prettier . . . but definitely *other*. Similarly, Nina could not quite recognize herself in print. Defending her real self, she brought up a Nina who had ridden a pony named Blinkie at the age of three, a Nina who loved her sister and mother more than anyone else in the world, a Nina who wanted to have a grand love in her life, and lastly, a Nina who presently wrote a column everybody read and praised for its wit and charm—and even insight.

Nevertheless, Nina could not stop reading these tabloid reports. It was like looking down while crossing a height on a tightrope. She knew she should not, yet did so again and again.

What was most frustrating was that after finding some degree of social freedom in New York, with no one twisting everything she said and did, as they had in Oceana, the gossips were once more having at her, attempting to put her back in the box. It had been a temporary truce. Ah stars, let them write whatever. She would not be pushed into the seclusion they wished. Rather, she would show them they could not keep her down. Deliberately Nina attended a few less respectable parties she'd previously shied away from: those where actors and authors and even politicians were invited. She wore brighter colors so as not to be overlooked, seeking to outdistance the columns, outrun the gossips, flirting on, moving faster than the fast image so it could not be pinned on her. Playing fast and loose to lose it.

And then one day Nina read not a half-truth, but an entirely false report that she had been somewhere where she had not been, doing something she had not done. At first she'd laughed. Then she began to tremble as she realized that her persona had taken on a life of its own.

Why, one needn't go out at all. She could retire to Oceana and allow her dreamed-up double to continue its own frantic, fraudulent, fascinating life. She could send Bobby out with it and not have any problems from anyone, anymore. Except her father kept waving Bobby before her, championing him and accepting his joining in their company. She was expecting another one of his recurrent speeches on the benefit of an alliance be-tween a De Bonnard and a Van Reyden when he took her aside. His face, however, was too serious for a discussion of profit; he was clearly going to mention a loss.

Mrs. De Bonnard and Adele were returning to New York City. Nina felt a first rush of happiness and then, on second thought, concern.

The ladies had stayed away an extra two months beyond even Mrs. Windsor's return. They had missed the entire first half of the social season. The second half promised to be vastly different.

"We're going to have to explain a few things to your mother," Mr. De Bonnard said with an embarrassed cough.

"Such as?"

"That we've been to Mrs. Richards' home. You know your mother was quite emphatic about not recognizing the Richards in Oceana. Since then they've been accepted by Mr. Marshall and even Elvira Windsor. Remember, they were the first to invite you when you didn't have so many invites, unlike now, when you need a special table! Anyway, her daughter is respectable, even if her family is not socially top drawer."

"Say rather, flush bottom," Nina could not resist throwing in. Her reflection on the source of Miss Richards' wealth had her fa-ther grinning, almost against his better sense. But Nina remained suspicious. Could her father have developed an interest in Cass Richards beginning from the night he'd danced with her at the Pynchot ball, when she was covered with jewels and personified wealth to him? And was that why he was so considerately es-corting her to all the functions; not to enjoy her company but to use her as a cover for his interest in another young lady?

Her father waited for her response. She was accustomed to his waiting-out tactic and responded in kind. Each silently eyed the other. An emotion—half anger, half disappointment—rose up in Nina. Was that why Father had been so accommodating about her expenses? She needed a new gown every night, not to men-tion matching fans, shoes, and three to four pairs of white kid gloves a day. On the other hand, rather than a bribe, he could simply be proud of her and want to show her off at her best. Nina had no proof that his interest in Miss Richards was more than just eyeing a healthy, wealthy young lady. Her father won the silent contest, for Nina finally spoke, "Well, I won't mention it, if you won't."

"That won't fadge. Elvira will tell her right off. She gave me such a look it froze me down to the toes."

"Mrs. Windsor's looks always freeze one down to one's toes. What do you suggest?"

Mr. De Bonnard was suggesting several possible strategies and then negating them. This insecurity was unlike her father, which caused a renewal of her suspicion and triggered a remembrance of yesterday, when Camille had waved her to a stop from her carriage. "Your pa ain't been to see me," she had said with no hesitation. "He got another *friend*?"

Nina had been embarrassed, so much so that she pretended her horse was restless and patted it. Then looking up and seeing so much anxiety on Camille's face, she quickly assured her she knew of none.

"I heard he had an interest in some lady. Oh fiddle—a *lady*! I coulda handled it if it was . . . well, you know what I mean."

"I haven't heard anything like that," Nina insisted, staring at the woman. Camille was looking older in the daylight. "Even if true, perhaps it won't come to anything. Father always looks but doesn't always leap."

Camille shook her head. "He wouldn't have left me if he hadn't leaped already. Your pa is always sure to have another investment in the pocket before he sells out on the first."

Nina was quiet. Now her horse had become fidgety. That caught Camille's attention. She stared at the girl in her black riding outfit with her hair in a long braid. She looked so young and beautiful. "I saw your picture sold in the shops. I bought one. Once I coulda been in that group."

"You still can. I know the photographer who does the society portraits. He could take one of you, and I can get you mentioned in the *Bugle*."

"Yeah? You're a nice person, Miss De Bonnard. Nicer than your father. I'm going to have to see him and get a few financial things straightened out and then maybe get out of New York City. Place is wearin' me down."

"Wait a few days, for Mr. Wilson—that's the photographer—to contact you."

"Oh, I'll wait. I'm good at that. Don't you ever develop that as a talent, dearie. Once you become a waiter, others pass you by. You gotta leave first."

Now Nina wanted to mention Camille to Mr. De Bonnard, but she'd heard that Mr. Wilson, as a favor, had arranged for Camille's picture to be taken and Bobby had agreed to put her on the *Bugle*'s list, so she was hopeful about Camille's future.

At last Mr. De Bonnard came up with a solution that would work. "Listen, my pet. You're to say you've become real good friends with Miss Richards. That will explain why I might have been friendly with her at certain balls. And even why I might have been seen with her in the park. A perfectly innocent occasion, that. Met her and gave her a ride in my carriage last week. Purely a chance meeting, don't you know?"

"Was it? Hard to believe anything associated with Mrs. Richards could be by chance. Bet you a dollar Mrs. Richards was waiting in another carriage while you drove off with her daughter."

Her father coughed. "Indeed she was. The whole outing was most respectable, regardless of what Elvira said."

Nina was forced to accept that excuse herself, knowing how often Elvira Windsor had misinterpreted her actions. So she agreed to tell her mother of her new bosom friend, and her father agreed not to tell his wife how many times Nina had been unsupervised. Nodding at each other, both waited for the rest of the family with mixed feelings, suspecting that their easy, accommodating days were at an end.

Fifteen

From the end of September through October and into November, most of the exclusive people who'd lolled away summer in Oceana, Saratoga, or Newport had returned to huddle in the confines of New York City, like snails come back to their gilded shells. These were close quarters, of course, but it was the time to be together. Much had to be reported and opinions expressed. The Centennial Exposition had closed after one hundred and sixty glorious days, during which one of every five Americans had come to see America's wares and worth. The election between Hayes and Tilden had not ended with November. Tilden had won the people's ballots, but the electoral votes could throw it to Hayes. The country, after the unifying of the centennial, was becoming divided. Rumors of fraud, of votes being bought in South Carolina, had both sides bitter and the people restless.

The social crowd was, as always, interested only in rumors about its own. The first summer tidbit had been Nina De Bonnard's doings, centering on her having stolen her almost-engaged sister's beau. That in itself would not have crossed her off the hostesses' lists, considering how many of their husbands did business with her father. But eventually Nina's behavior in New York City, such as racing with the all-male Coaching Club, was enough for even wavering members to consider the ban urged by Mrs. Windsor.

But before that could be done, almost in a flutter of blinks, society itself seemed to change. The old restrictions were dropping, as were the old sedate practices, in a wild competition for the title of the most important hostess of the inner set. Every party could no longer be just a gathering but a reflection of the hostess's importance, demonstrated by the themes that graduated from grand to grandiose. The more accustomed guests became to pomp, the more they sought out pompous. Standing gave way to spending, so Mrs. Richards could not be plumb ignored; she was admitted. Thus, Mr. Marshall, who had come to New York City with Mrs. Windsor, now had two hostesses to influence.

To Dick Windsor, Mr. Marshall was an albatross whose omnipresence made the days drag. On his New York arrival, Dick had been hoping for fun after that fiasco of a summer in Oceana. Even Adele had changed, beginning with Nina's and Jordan's departures from Oceana. She was cold and withdrawn and refused to join him in another supervised jaunt to the Centennial before it closed. He had the sneaking feeling, not being anxious to delve whether it was true, that somehow his pact with his brother just might have had something to do with all that strain and sadness left floating in Nina's wake.

Strolling along the New York streets, Dick felt the bite in the air, which gave a snap to his walk. He stopped to repeat some of his rituals of childhood, such as surreptitiously saluting the wooden Indians before the tobacco shops, particularly a tall one with a hatchet that was his particular friend. His steps increased in speed as he neared Fifth Avenue, where the buildings of red brick and brownstone stood almost in a military line, closing up ranks, till the symmetry was abruptly, gloriously broken by a lone, white stone mansion. Her house. Running up the marble steps, Dick paused to breathe in the atmosphere of being close to Nina before risking ringing the doorbell. But Jeffers would not admit him, and Dick, forced to leave his card, walked down the stairs, retracing his steps homeward in a slow, sad tempo. The scene was repeated often enough until even Dick Windsor got the message. Worse was that Bobby had stolen a march earlier by following Nina to New York. Mr. Marshall snidely suggested that Mr. Van Reyden had bought himself a beauty.

"Horsefeathers!" Dick had retorted, but by the time he'd thought of a more explicit answer Mr. Marshall had left. Fortuitously enough. For how could he prove that Nina had never taken Bobby seriously when he had doubts himself? To clarify the situation, Dick had written Nina a long letter and was jubilant to receive a response. But his hopes sank after the first sentence. Not only did she deny his right to question her, but she refused to see him, concluding that in view of his brother's actions, their two families ought to keep apart. And that was that. The sight of Bobby and Nina driving by was all it took to make Dick's cup of gall brim over.

He was in the wrong state of mind for his mother to solicit help in planning her next ball. Her first party after Labor Day had had the theme "A Farewell to Summer," at which everyone was to be costumed to depict their summer sojourn. Mrs. Windsor dressed as a striped beach umbrella. A couple had draped themselves in the souvenir banners they had brought back from the Centennial. Mr. Marshall had appeared as a bluefish (subliminally revealing his penchant for catching anything blueblooded). Dick had done his best by wearing a bathing suit. But most of the ladies and gentlemen had simply added straw hats to their regular outfits. Reliving the immediate past did not excite. Nor did the party. Disheartened, Mrs. Windsor turned to her son for fresh ideas and heard exactly what she didn't want to hear: "Nina De Bonnard would have sparked up the night real good."

Mrs. Windsor bristled. "I don't care for her kind of sparking! The elder Miss De Bonnard has gone her limit, carousing with the Coach Club members, racing like a gentleman! I wouldn't be surprised if she smoked with them afterwards in celebration. No, I have crossed her and her family off my list!"

When Mr. Marshall returned from a visit to Mrs. Richards, his second hostess, Mrs. Windsor, was sour, claiming she'd kept track of the number of hours he'd spent with her in contrast to those he'd spent with Mrs. Richards and that she had had significantly less of his attention. A professional soother, Mr. Marshall rushed to explain that since Mrs. Richards was new to society, she would naturally need more help than such an experienced and talented organizer as Mrs. Windsor. The lady could not deny that, but she still needed *some* advice. After all, had he not promised to make her the *premier* hostess? Nature had made her that, was his glib reply, but he realized that Mrs. Windsor could not longer be put off. So they put their heads together to devise a theme that would be the talk of the town.

The next day Mr. Marshall met with Mrs. Richards for the same purpose. At least Mrs. Richards always had a concept: Spend, spend, and if that did not work, spend some more. She had spent her way into society; now she would spend herself into universal acceptance. Her theme was in keeping: My Favorite Extravagance. Fittingly, Mrs. Richards was planning the most opulent ball in New York's history. She was buying a full forty-piece gold-plate service for the dinner with matching gold goblets and, in addition, each lady was to receive a fourteen-karat gold bracelet as a gift under her napkin. There was nothing the rich liked more than more riches. Mr. Marshall realized that his inventiveness was not needed. Mrs. Richards' extravaganza could not help but succeed. But Mrs. Richards was taking no chances. Ignoring Elvira's ban, she had sent an invitation to Nina De Bonnard. The entrance of that lady alone would cause the tongues to wag and make the night memorable.

Hearing that Nina was invited and that the preparations were at full tilt at the Richards' had Mrs. Windsor in a tiff. Not only was Mrs. Richards acting like the premier hostess, but she was making the rest look cheap with her fourteen-karat favors. "I'll have to ignore the tawdry and go for the timeless. My theme will be Best Friends. Everyone to come with his or her best friend." She waited for Mr. Marshall to applaud. Naturally, he knew enough to do so. He even bowed to her great sense.

Eventually other hostesses sought Mr. Marshall's assistance, and when he could not spread himself thin enough, other party organizers were found to meet the need. Before long the parties were so numerous they had to be extreme to stand out or wind up in extremity and passed over. Even the more sober hostesses joined the competition, unable to bear being outshone. In short, lavish spending became the real object of all the parties. Fountains flowed with champagne. Other fountains were of perfume with floating gardenias. Orchestras of the very best tone and expertise were hired to play over the noise and gossip. Gilt cornices popped up in every ballroom. Delicacies from around the world were served at dinners with enough removes to boast that no one could eat through it all. The Professional Beauties were another attraction. When Nina became the most successful of those, she was inundated with invitations. Elvira's Best Friend theme had been stolen by an upstart hostess newly arrived from Baltimore. And what was worse, Nina De Bonnard not only starred at Mrs. Richards' party but also accepted that Baltimore hostess's invitation. Mrs. Windsor's only balm was hearing that half of the guests had interpreted "best friend" as their cat or dog and brought along those animals as partners. "It was a shocking menagerie!" she exclaimed in glee. "I imagine Miss De Bonnard brought a monkey!" That was untrue; Nina had brought a book of Elizabeth Barrett Browning poems. Bobby brought the organ grinder's monkey, who continued his habit of stealing ladies jewelry, netting Bobby a profit for the evening, he announced with a wink.

While pretending indifference, Elvira Windsor was boiling at being left behind while other, younger hostesses were scoring points right and left. Worse was that Bobby Van Reyden in his *Bugle* had initiated a practice of rating the hostesses for originality, and Mrs. Windsor had scored lowest for her "Summer" bash. Mrs. Richards was well rated for her extravaganza, but the lady who got top marks was a newcomer who put on a Congo ball featuring snakes in cages and everyone dressed as an explorer.

In desperation and at Mr. Marshall's urging, Mrs. Windsor played copycat of a London party theme: Enemies Unite. Known enemies were invited as dinner partners, and by the end of the evening, the hostess was to bring about peace. Mrs. Windsor's sets of rivals were two competitive railroad magnates, several competing hostesses, and young ladies seeking the same gentleman. Society whispered that Elvira's party would be either a major success or a major fiasco—the latter being preferable. In either case it would be worth attending to see which. Her own enemy, Nina De Bonnard, Mrs. Windsor still refused to relent and invite, but she did invite Mr. De Bonnard, who, unaware of the subtle distinction, simply brought his daughter along.

So except for shutting the door in Nina De Bonnard's face, there was not much the hostess could do once the two De Bonnards entered. She gave them her coldest appraisal, and Nina, her eyes glittering, gave a most beguiling smile. Personifying the theme, the two ladies stared at each other from opposite ends of the room until Nina walked across and extended her hand. Since everyone was watching, Mrs. Windsor had to accept it. Whereupon the guests all broke into applause. That one gesture had decided the outcome of the party. It was a success! Bobby gave the event his top grade. In a cross between gratitude and resentment, Mrs. Windsor had to acknowledge that this young jilt had jolted her ahead of the other hostesses toward her main goal of being the premier party giver. In return and in need, Elvira placed Nina number one on her list henceforth.

"I told you so," Dickie said with a laugh.

When Mrs. De Bonnard and Adele arrived in New York City, they could barely believe, let alone accept, the many changes. If one could credit it, society was being run by not only Mrs. Windsor but by Mrs. Richards. Mrs. De Bonnard did not know at which to gasp first.

A second astonishment: Nina, rather than being in disgrace as her mother had feared, was once more on everyone's most-sought-after list. Further, that young miss was not a mite chastened by what had occurred that summer. Rather, she was filled with a wildness neither mother nor sister had ever seen. Mrs. De Bonnard welcomed this new Nina with concern as her daughter spirited about, always on the move, always breathless in her hurry.

In glaring contrast, Adele had not been able to recover her spirits at Oceana. The few parties she'd attended after Jordan's hurried departure had been too strained an experience for her to repeat. Even Dick's presence brought out painful associations, so she cut him off. Mrs. De Bonnard attempted to distract Adele by keeping her busy. The women's suffrage ladies she'd met at the Centennial Exposition came to Mrs. De Bonnard's aid by enthusiastically responding to her letter and inviting her to join them. Immediately Adele and she took off for Philadelphia. There, since no one was interested in Jordan Windsor or in a lady's blighted romance, Adele soon began to come out of her doldrums in her determination to measure up to their expectations. Voting rights for women became her only concern. On election night all the suffrage workers divided, half going to one headquarters and half to the other, hoping to influence the winner to remember their needs. Yet when the election left no clear victor, they gave up that hope and returned to the original plan of influencing each state legislature. So involved and consumed by constant campaigning were the De Bonnard ladies that they kept pushing off the day of their New York return. Adele pleaded that they remain past Halloween, past Thanksgiving. But eventually Mrs. De Bonnard would stay away no longer. She missed her home and her elder daughter. An inquiry revealed that a women's suffrage unit in New York City would be delighted to have their assistance. Thus with no more excuses, Adele had to agree to join her mother and return to New York City.

Arriving at Fifth Avenue, they were disappointed to be greeted only by Jeffers. Glancing at the two tables in the foyer caused the lady of the house to raise an eyebrow. Jeffers rushed to explain that Mr. De Bonnard had ordered the second table after expressing annoyance that his invitations were getting lost in all of Miss De Bonnard's. The overflow on Nina's pile was evidence of her daughter's popularity. Taking up several engraved vellum envelopes and perusing the handwritten personal appeals, Mrs. De Bonnard's patrician eyebrows arched further. But when she came across one from Elvira Windsor herself, Mrs. De Bonnard had to sit down on the bottom carpeted stair. Elvira had not only invited Nina to her Majestic ball, but she had also included two postscripts: one from Mr. Marshall begging the "Queen of Society" to give this occasion "her majestic presence," and one from Elvira herself saying she was anticipating the pleasure of seeing Nina and if she wished, she could bring her sister and mother along.

What revolution had taken place? Offended, aghast, Mrs. De Bonnard asked Nina that very question as soon as the young lady returned from her daily trip to Brentano's on Union Square.

Nina merely laughed, more anxious to hug her mother than to talk to her, and the lady forgot about society in her daughter's embrace. But by the next day Mrs. De Bonnard could no longer be put off with a hug and a shrug. So Nina explained about the Enemies ball, and how amusing it had been to force Mrs. Windsor to accept her.

"I don't understand. Why does she have to accept you? It is her son who caused Adele such pain. The question then ought be, Shall we accept *her*!"

Nina's face fell. She'd hoped the Jordan episode would not be mentioned. Her mother and sister did not seem to have moved on but were still back as if in the first blow of Jordan's desertion. "Mr. Jordan Windsor, I gather, is living his own life in Washington, with a new lady, Miss Lucy Perkens. We are, Mrs. Windsor told me confidentially but with enough volume for half the ballroom to hear, soon to be congratulating her son on having found the perfect wife."

"The gall! And you stood for that?"

"What would you have me do? You would not wish for me to act as if my heart—or anyone's close to me—had been broken?" Nina continued with astonishment. "Naturally I shrugged off her comment as if of no import."

Mrs. De Bonnard was bristling. "But it is of import! Adele has not recovered from being jilted!"

"I had a sneaking suspicion of that since she still refuses to speak to me," Nina could not resist inserting with a small smile. Whereupon Mrs. De Bonnard urged and Nina agreed to give Adele time to adjust to being home.

Coming from daily selfless devotion to a cause to a New York social scene in the grip of glitter, major adjustments had to be made by the two returning ladies, very much as one acclimatized oneself to a different weather by putting down parasols and cuddling in furs. Yet Adele remained the same, refusing even to note the changing social milieu about her. On the contrary, Mrs. De Bonnard quickly reclaimed her previous place in society through luncheon meetings with old friends. Yet if these friends were to be believed, society had departed from its sedate formality to one spinning off its bearings, and, more personally, Nina had been going about quite unchecked. The whispers had to be answered. Nina was called in for an after-tea talk and presented with each accusation.

Nina was quite open about her larking about with Bobby Van Reyden—at her father's suggestion—and she further admitted to having joined the Coaching Club but added that she'd broken away—also at her father's instructions. "Please don't let your luncheon friends distress you, Mama. They are behind the times. I've graduated from those petty peccadilloes of my beginning days here to being very much approved by society. Truly, dear, I am quite in fashion, beginning from when I became a PB, or Professional Beauty. My picture is seen everywhere!"

That blow her mother did not know how to sustain. Solicitously, Nina assured her, after bringing her a glass of water, that no longer was it required that a lady appear in the newspapers only when born, married, or dead. Now every hostess wanted Nina's name on her guest list for her ball or would risk not being well reviewed. And as far as being chosen a PB, that was now quite the thing!

"So many outrageous things have become 'quite the thing' I hesitate to ask, but is it also the 'thing' to be seeing just one gentleman and not be engaged to him?"

Nina shook her head. "If you mean Bobby, I don't see him exclusively. I am often escorted by Mr. Richard Fotheringale and by a whole group—including a relative of the Astors. Oh, I told you I'm quite acceptable to all. Actually, I most often attend the balls with Father. For, to be truthful, I've decided never to marry and lock myself in that final gilded cage."

"You have decided to put yourself beyond the pale then? And put your sister and me there with you!"

"I am not beyond the pale! I told you: I am accepted by all," Nina shot back, affronted. "You saw the invitations."

Mrs. De Bonnard eyed her daughter sadly. She who loved her could see the unhappiness under all that bravado. Being so involved with Adele, she had forgotten that her beautiful first-born's heart might similarly have been shattered by the same gentleman. She took her into her arms, feeling Nina fluttering like a butterfly who was afraid her wings would be crushed. But as her mother sat her down and began soothing her with words of concern and stroking her forehead to test her health and rocking her body against her lap, Nina stopped fighting, stopped fluttering to escape, and became little Nina, a child at her mother's knee.

"What's worrying you so much? What has you so concerned?" her mother insisted.

Nina could not begin to tell her all, but she could discuss her most immediate problem. "Yes, I want to talk to you about Delly. I don't understand why she is still so angry with me . . . to the point of not speaking to me. Not even token words—hello, good morning . . . even a simple yes or no would be something. I was not the reason Jordan Windsor jilted her. He used Delly to reach me, I own, which makes me responsible for her hurt, but—but I never purposely callously attempted to take Jordan away from her, as I know she believes. He admitted he used Delly to reach me and when he no longer needed her, let her go. He claimed never to have even kissed her or made any untoward gesture beyond gallantry to lead her to expect a proposal."

"That is not true!" Mrs. De Bonnard snapped.

"Has Adele said he was attempting to seduce her? I'd like to know how far he went in his diabolical scheme to hurt me."

"Why is it about you?"

"I'm only saying what he told me. Perhaps he was lying and Delly was his objective all along, but she proved not as seduceable as he thought. Apparently I always misunderstood him. If there is anything honest in that gentleman I suspect it is when he implied he was just attempting to get what he wanted from both of us and was disappointed that we were both so easy. He wanted more of a challenge."

"Infamous!"

"Yes. He enjoyed telling me that, taunting me. I never knew whether he was speaking for effect or because that's what he really meant. His humor is influenced by his penchant for Sheridan's plays—he delights in sarcasm. Only sometimes I felt that beneath that surface glitter there was a heart. . . . Certainly there was a passion beyond any I had ever dealt with. He was the only gentleman—and forgive me for speaking of such things—that I did not find it a positive punishment to kiss."

"You kissed him?" her mother said softly.

"He kissed me . . . and that blended into my kissing him, I fear.

Even when we fought—dueled by wits, by looks, by simply being in each other's presence—at all times that we were together, I felt more alive. He would not allow me to remain safely across the chasm I created between me and all other gentlemen. To him it was a simple step across and he was there with me. Yes, I kissed him back for a moment to hold on to the sensation of what physical love could mean between a man and a woman. But I always came to my senses; I did not forget myself or Adele—she was always there between us. I wish she could understand that and how h-hard I tried to keep her there."

Mrs. De Bonnard remembered her own love affair and understood what her daughter was telling her. And how difficult those feelings were to forget. If only Jordan Windsor had been a gentleman like her Anthony.

With a sigh Mrs. De Bonnard concluded, "It appears he has settled down. I can only hope this new responsibility he is evidencing is sincere"—her voice turned bitter at the end—"and worth the destruction of my two beautiful daughters!"

Nina jumped up at that summation, refusing to accept it. "I am not destroyed! Both your daughters are Caroltens who do not destroy easily. Haven't you told us so often that the Caroltens fought for and formed this country? We are of unconquerable stock. And indeed, look at me, I have already forgotten Mr. Jordan Windsor . . . forgotten all the Windsors. Adele should join me at the next ball. I know a great many gentlemen who'd be devastated by her. Let us show everyone, even ourselves, that we don't need Jordan Windsor, reformed or not. And what does this Lucy Perkens have that she was able to reform him while neither I nor Adele could—No, forget it, I couldn't care less what she has."

"You say that and you mean rather that you care for him, indeed."

"No, no—"

"Oh, blast that man! But Adele has found a new interest and that has helped her to heal. I suggest you join us in the cause. Thinking of others always distracts thoughts of self."

Nina sighed. "Well, I wanted to join you both in that, but back in Oceana I asked Delly if I could help and she tried to dissuade me, making it clear without saying it openly that she wanted something particularly her own, without, and I quote, my 'taking it over.' "

It was the perfect moment to reveal her love of writing, and yet she held back, fearing that her mother would think being The Gilded Lily was too public a profession, and she could not bear giving that up as well.

Mrs. De Bonnard was talking about Adele and all the good work she had done.

Nina interrupted to ask, "Then if Adele has made such progress, why is she still so cold to me? I can't continue to apologize and have her slam the door in my face. It is becoming too redundant. Too childish. Even Papa, this morning, told her to stop acting like a child and pass the jam. I would like us to be sisters again. Persuade her to come with Papa and you and me to the Windsor ball. She needs to show the world, yes, but mostly herself, that there are other men."

"We are attending, but I have to tell you, my dear, a first love is difficult to forget. One always believes no one will take his place."

"I know I could reach her if she would just stop playing this 'I'm not speaking to you' game. But I've run out of ideas how to get past that barrier."

Her mother realized she had been remiss in allowing this rift between her daughters, and took a moment to consider. Then a small smile made Nina aware that she had come up with a solution. "Leave it to me," her mother said. "I believe I have a way to handle this."

Nina sighed in relief, willing to believe, as she had all her life, that Mother could fix anything. When she was alone Nina sat down on a golden damask chair with a wing back. She closed her eyes. She felt exhausted from her conversation. Recently she had built a new gilded persona that she wore over the old Nina, and all this digging around had weakened its foundation. She feared toppling . . . exposure. More, she feared that all the stored thoughts of Jordan would come out and engulf her. She had kept herself strong by not thinking of love or Jordan or anything but laughter and daring. She wished she could borrow Bobby's coach and go for a race. She needed something to distract her, get her safely back into the all-encompassing, glowing covering of The Gilded Lily.

Earlier, Adele had come into the room and spotted her mother holding Nina in her arms—and backed out. In her chamber, Adele allowed herself to consider why she was so distressed, acknowledging a resentment that Nina in a few days was able to reinstate her position as the favorite. How had she done it?

Adele shook her head. As well, she had seen Nina and her father in private conversation, showing they had reached a greater degree of closeness than ever before. And, not content with that, Nina had wedged her way between that special bond she and Mama had formed working together. Wasn't that Nina's way: always expecting the best for herself as if it were her right as firstborn? Growing up, Adele had agreed with that, not even feeling rancor. It was the way things were. But when Adele had the best—Jordan—and Nina wanted *him,* finally, finally she had had to rebel and say, "Enough!"

Further, Nina had not quietly taken Jordan away, but had done it so publicly, making Adele the object of laughter throughout Oceana. Even a previously devoted sister could not forgive that. But what really stopped Adele from forgiving her sister was the look in Jordan's eyes when they were directed at Nina. That look, that glow, was a barrier between them she somehow could not surmount.

From Adele's first day in New York, Nina had been making little gestures. She had bought two dolls, one with pale yellow hair and the other with golden red, and put them together on Adele's bed with a note saying *"Don't let anything or any man put them asunder."*

And while Adele had been slightly moved by that, she could not rush into Nina's arms as Nina had been expecting. One always forgave Nina no matter what she did, because she acted as if you were being foolish not to forgive her—childish even. But Adele had simply returned both dolls to Nina's room without a note. Nina had been surprised by her continuing coldness. Truly

Adele had surprised herself, not believing she could hold out against Nina's smile and promises to take her shopping and the usual things she'd offered all her life—which were really offering to take Adele into her world. But now Adele had another world, working with her mother, and she did not need to succumb to Nina's wiles. Except that Nina continued to talk to her. One day both were alone in the conservatory and Nina began talking about the plants. Instantly Adele made ready to leave, when Nina laughed and said, "If you walk out—that's reacting to my presence. The true way to put me in my place is just to pretend you don't see me and carry on with watering the philodendron."

"I don't need you to tell me how to do everything. You even think you know best how I should snub you. I'm doing it my way!" Adele had exploded.

And Nina had applauded. "Great, you're talking to me, after all."

Adele, chagrined that she'd broken her resolve, closed her mouth tightly.

"Too late!" Nina cried. "You spoke. Please don't continue this. We are sisters. I didn't do anything to you, as I've explained again and again. Jordan did it to us both. We should be joining together and hating him. As I do now."

Adele had stared silently at her sister and Nina had put out her hand and came close and almost hugged her. The smell of Nina's perfume reminded Adele of all the years of closeness between them. She nearly let herself be drawn into her sister's arms but next moment remembered that Jordan probably loved the smell of that perfume as well. Jordan was still there, standing between them.

Nina was shocked by Adele's pulling away so furiously. "Heavens, I never believed you could hold a grudge so long. I would have sworn we were so close as sisters there was nothing we couldn't forgive each other. But I guess you didn't feel that."

"I did!" Adele was tricked into speaking again. "But you ruined it. You didn't feel enough for me to give up one more man on your string."

"He wasn't just one more man on my string! And I *did*

give him up. I told him there was no hope for us because of you. But all he wanted was to seduce me. That was no compliment to me—nor insult to you. I expect he just assumed I was more seduceable. In truth, his heart was never engaged by either of us."

"He was engaged to a lady in England, I heard from Dick."

Adele had the pleasure of seeing her sister's face wounded. But next moment Nina was shrugging and saying with a laugh, "Well, just as I said. We were both his victims. If you know *that*, then it is doubly wrong of you to continue this distance between us. It's worse than wrong. It is childish."

"Everything I do is childish. Okay, I childishly believed his feelings for me were genuine. In fact since he began courting me *after*, I'd obviously won him away from the English woman, which shows the depth of his feelings for me, enough to lead him to propose to me—*except for you!*"

Nina neither refuted nor accepted that. She just looked incredulous—which freshly stung Adele in her old wound. Both sisters faced each other with unsayable thoughts jumping around in their minds. At last the silence and the staring became awkward. Nina moved away first. Adele resented that. Nina ought to have remained and begged her pardon. Begged it, if necessary, on her knees! Then she would have been showing true respect to the injury she had caused, but her restraint was a new affront. It reminded Adele of the other day when she'd heard Nina whistling and Adele's heart had contracted. Nina was happy, she'd realized, and even going on to another man or, more likely, men! The same indignity hit Adele now. "What about *me*!" she nearly cried out to the closed door, until it suddenly opened. Nina was peeking into the conservatory with a concerned look on her face. Quickly Adele pretended to be smelling a plant. Her sister backed out. But some of Adele's anger simmered down. She even felt a mite appeased when she realized that Nina *was* concerned. She'd cared enough to come back to see if Adele was crying. In her heart Adele had to admit she wanted to get back to that closeness Nina and she had shared. She missed Nina. Further, Adele was beginning to suspect that this "not speaking" was childish, after all.

The next morning Adele was surprised to be taken aside and told by her mother that she had discussed this estrangement of her two daughters with Nina and Nina had had the effrontery to blame it all on Adele, claiming she had attempted to reach an accommodation with her sister. "I made it clear to her, as I have throughout her life, that as the elder she must bear the responsibility for any disagreement between you two. I'm out of patience with her for not making more of an effort in your direction . . . and, even more so, I am shocked that Nina dared to publicly take part in a coach race! Yet she doesn't realize how displeased I am! The only way to make myself clear is to adopt your approach. Henceforth, we shall both ignore her."

"Oh."

"Yes."

"No, I don't understand, Mama. Do you mean you are not going to be speaking to Nina either?" When her mother nodded briskly, Adele gasped and began pleading, "I don't think it'll be effective if both of us do it. . . . I mean, wouldn't that be overdoing?" But before she could persuade her mother, the rest of the family had joined them at the table.

Adele was in a flutter. Rather than rejoicing at having an ally, she felt responsible for a major disruption. What had at first seemed a dignified way of putting Nina in her place, now seemed out of place in a loving family.

Mrs. De Bonnard's silence went unnoticed by Mr. De Bonnard. Nina of course had instantly sensed the frigid weather wafting her way from both her sister and mother. She looked concerned, Adele thought with a pang of guilt, made doubly strong by the awareness that this had been her idea in the first place.

Yet Nina had not fully realized the degree of Coventry she'd been sent to until she asked her mother to pass the butter. Then Mrs. De Bonnard made it unmistakably clear by deliberately turning her face away and making no move toward the butter. At that point Nina grasped what was happening and gasped, turning a deep blushing color in mortification—understanding now, indeed. She looked down at her hands and the napkin there. Then slowly, majestically, she rose to leave.

"I expect both of you will enjoy breakfast better without my presence," she said with a trembling voice. "I'll have my meals in my room." She paused. There was no reply from Mrs. De Bonnard, who slowly looked away from her. Adele was eyeing her mother with a pleading look, but her mother did not relent.

"Very well," Nina concluded in a low, shattered voice. "Let it be so. Let there be silence between us from now on. My last words are . . . I still love you both."

Nina was halfway out of the room when Adele sobbed out, "Oh wait! I still love you too. I mean, I'm sorry for not speaking to you. I wanted to speak to you. I *am* speaking to you."

Nina stopped and began walking back toward her sister. When they were face-to-face, she whispered, "Thank you." The two sisters moved at the same time into a long-delayed and needed embrace. After which Nina turned and looked expectantly toward her mother. Mrs. De Bonnard merely nodded and signaled them both back to the table.

At that point Mr. De Bonnard put down his paper and looked at the women in some confusion. "I thought you had excused yourselves. Back for second helpings? Try the marmalade. Dashed good." Expansively, he leaned over to spoon some onto both of his daughters' plates. At the last moment, he was gallant enough not to overlook his wife in his largesse. Then, confident that he had sweetened whatever was occurring, he rose to take his leave. The women waited until he had closed the door, and then they began to laugh in their usual conspiratorial understanding that Mr. De Bonnard never understood them.

"Well, what say, shall we try that jam?" Mrs. De Bonnard said with a happy smile. "Except, Nina dear, please pass the grape jam. Your father has lived with me so many years and not yet become aware I never eat marmalade."

"Oh thank heavens," Adele said, "you're speaking to her as well. I was so afraid I had started something I couldn't—"

"Swallow," Nina said, handing her some buttered toast.

Mrs. De Bonnard laughed at that. In fact the exchanges between Nina and her mother were too comfortable, Adele concluded, sensing in a flash that the rift between her mother and Nina had been too easy to bridge.

Sulking, Adele put down her muffin, "Oh you were teaching me a lesson!"

Mrs. De Bonnard reached over and squeezed her younger daughter's hand. "Just a little demonstration, Delly. Just showing you how destructive it can be to break up what has always been such a close family. And how ch—eh, beneath your good sense."

"You were going to say *childish*!" Adele accused.

"To Mama we are both childish. We are her children, aren't we?" Nina interposed lightly. "Although I must tell you, Delly, until you made it clear what she was doing I was quite crestfallen. Thank you for catching on so quickly and relieving me of my anxiety. It was difficult enough for me to have you not speaking to me. Especially when I want so much to hear all about everything you've been doing."

Adele was appeased by Nina's not being in on the plot. It was just her mother's little example setting. That could be tolerated.

Preening at the success of her venture, Mrs. De Bonnard sat there at table holding the hand of each of her daughters. They were united again. Then Mother, as usual, had the last word, putting everything in correct order. "What I believe we should all three talk about is . . ." She paused and looked around to assure she had their rapt attention and, seeing she did, concluded, "what to wear for the Windsor ball, which we shall be attending in full family complement to show society the De Bonnards have arrived back on the scene—united."

As if to illustrate that point, when the three smiling ladies rose to leave the table, they closed ranks and engaged in a triple hug of pleased reconciliation.

Sixteen

Jordan Windsor and his brother Dick were staring at the decor of their New York brownstone ballroom. It was smaller than Mrs. Astor's which fit exactly four hundred people and thus drew the line at anyone who could possibly be classed as four hundred and one.

"We're even more exclusive, Mother says, since our renovated ballroom fits only three hundred," Dick was explaining to the newly arrived Jordan.

In the five months since he'd seen his brother, Dick noticed a more sober aspect and attributed it to the strain of working, vowing never to indulge in such a rash pursuit himself. To cheer him, Dick attempted to bring his brother up to date on the good and bad changes in New York. Bad: the importance of Mr. Marshall. Good: the parties were wilder than ever. "It's all so much fun! Would you believe a ballroom dinner eaten on horseback? Yeah! And the horses were fed flowers and champagne! Bobby was the host of that one, and everyone came. The *Bugle* reviews and rates each ball, so the hostesses are all jumping to outdo each other, coming up with some real snappers. Speaking of which, there was a Fish for Your Own Supper gala with all kinds of fish swimming in tanks by each table and rods at the ready. And a Deck-of-Cards ball, with everyone dressing as a favorite suit. And also, also, a Mother Goose quadrille. Lots of sheepish folk that night! It's been real swell!"

"Apparently excess is the key to success," Jordan said, looking around at the suits of armor lining the walls of the ballroom. He asked about them with a lift of his eyebrow, and Dick, laughing, rushed to explain.

"Mother's guard. She's coming as Queen Elizabeth. I'm Henry the Eighth, so I can eat all I want and people will think I'm just playing my part. And you?"

"If *majesty* is the theme, I expect I have enough of my own not to need to impersonate anyone else."

"That's cowardly!"

"Not at all. Sensible. Besides, I may not remain for the ball tonight. I just came to do some business with the *Herald* and . . . to see how you're all faring. It sounds as if New York society has been turned on its head. But I never thought *Mother* would be that head!" He let out one of his more open laughs.

All this time in Washington, working on the Washington *Courier* and being involved in reporting on the still unsettled presidential race, Jordan had surprised himself by enjoying his work. He'd gone to Indiana, an undecided state, to interview the Democratic candidate for governor and Tilden supporter, Blue Jeans Williams. That interview had brought Jordan national attention because he had written the entire piece in the candidate's authentic Indiana drawl: "I larned everythin' worth knowing in blue jeans. I went a-coortin' in blue jeans. I'll knock bung outta the Republicans and beat 'em in blue jeans!"

Jordan found the social affairs in Washington more interesting than those in Oceana because everyone talked politics, even the ladies, such as Miss Lucy Perkens, whom he met at a dinner. She had the intelligent ability to ask the right political questions so a gentleman could explain his stand. Tolerably content with his new life, he wondered why in blazes he had come running back to New York City. Something had drawn him. The pull began when Lucy showed him her Professional Beauty picture and made the mistake of asking if she had posed too sedately because some New York lady had caused a sensation with her angellike representation. Without having to ask which New York lady, Jordan knew her identity even before Miss Perkens showed him the New York lady's picture. After that, although his smile of satisfaction had Miss Perkens assuming he was happy to be with her, his almost immediate departure made her wonder. One look had marked the end of Jordan's contentment: He made a dash to buy up as many of Nina's photographs as he could find, and then as soon as arrangements could be made, boarded the train to New York City.

Waiting in the Windsor ballroom, Jordan kept reminding himself he was moments from actually seeing New York's Professional Beauty when Dick brought up the same subject. "The best part is that Nina will be here," he whispered. "She sometimes waves to me or nods. That's all she permits me—'cause of you, I guess. But she delights in forcing Mama to be polite to her and of course Mama has to swallow her pride and do so."

Jordan had to smile. "I might stay to see that." He waited for more information, but Dick had gone on to report with glee that mother had spent ten thousand dollars just for tonight's ball, leaving no gemstone unturned, as would be evident when he saw her costume. Nor was she letting anyone else fall below her standard. "She has a drawer in the foyer filled with fresh white kid gloves for any gentleman so gauche as to arrive without a pair!"

Jordan, impatient with these details, took out a cigarillo and lit it. "How does she look?"

Dick did not have to ask who "she" was. "Beautiful as always. But different. Less like Nina. More polished. More glittering. She often wears stars in her hair. She wears more extravagant clothes. Laughs a lot and rarely listens to anyone long enough for him to finish a sentence. Her eyes are afire . . . like the tip of that cigarillo when you take a deep puff. And yet—yet—you want to take her in your arms and say, 'It's okay.' "

Jordan turned away, asking no more.

But he was there with his mother, Queen Elizabeth, and his brother, Henry the Eighth, greeting the guests. To suit the occasion every person proudly paraded in. Jeweled crowns abounded, some real, others remarkable impersonations—which could be said of the people there as well.

Besides crowns, the ballroom was decorated with peacock feathers, royal purple plumes, and velvets and ermine. Portraits of Queen Elizabeth stared down from the walls along with one of Queen Victoria in her mourning gown. Lots of Queen Victorias danced that night with resurrected Prince Alberts. Everyone, despite their patriotism, enjoyed being royal for an evening. Other guests interpreted "majestic" to include America's founders, George and Martha Washington, as uncrowned heads.

The candelabra were all lit and the gaslight fixtures turned up high, so every outfit could been seen and appreciated.

What a crashing bore! Jordan thought when half the evening was over. All chitchat, no politics, no exchange of ideas—no Nina De Bonnard. She had not arrived. While picking at his meal, Jordan noted a lady staring at him in disbelief. It took him several moments to recognize Adele. Where was the flowery, bouncing girl of Oceana? She wore a sedate black silk dress, and beside her, Mrs. De Bonnard was similarly dressed. Suffragette uniforms, Jordan guessed correctly. In fact, Adele had even center-parted her hair and arranged it in a bun, exactly as Susan B. Anthony wore hers. By contrast, Mr. De Bonnard was giving Dick competition for the best Henry the Eighth. But nowhere near them was anyone who might even possibly be Nina. She had not come.

Miss Perkens, invited by his mother to his surprise, said something that was very sensible, as usual, and he nodded. What she'd said he didn't know, but his nod seemed to satisfy. Adele was standing at his side and Jordan stood up quickly, bowing respectfully.

Mrs. De Bonnard rushed to protect her daughter, so Jordan smoothly turned his attention to her. "You appear to be dressed as the most truly majestic woman of our time, Miss Susan B. Anthony. I did an interview with her about a month ago. Did you by any chance read it? Miss Anthony was kind enough to send me a message about it."

That distracted both ladies from whatever they were going to say. Mrs. De Bonnard made a fitting reply. Adele, not taking part in the conversation, just hungrily stared, until she suddenly blurted out, "Are you engaged?"

Mrs. De Bonnard looked at her daughter with pain in her eyes, and Jordan said kindly, "I am not."

That seemed to appease the young lady, for she stopped looking at the blushing Miss Perkens and walked away. Jordan signaled Dick, who ran after Adele, and a second later, both Mrs. De Bonnard and Jordan were relieved to see the two dancing.

He ought to have let well enough alone, but Jordan could not resist asking, "Is your other daughter attending?"

Mrs. De Bonnard eyed him coldly. "Nina will be here eventually. But she will not be here—for you. I expect you will have the decency not to ask her to dance and repeat the infamy of the Pynchot ball."

Jordan shrugged as the lady walked away. He had no intention of asking Nina for a dance. His only plan was to see her. And then as the dinner was over, and the dancing began again, he saw a crowd of men. Without moving, he knew who was at the center. It was joltingly reminiscent of the first time he'd seen her. As then, Bobby Van Reyden was there, trying to push some of the other gentlemen aside. Tripping one. The top of Nina's head could be seen if one stretched. Jordan noted with pleasure that she alone of the women in costume was uncrowned. Her golden red hair was crown enough. And then as a waltz began and she'd chosen her partner, the men parted and she stepped out to accept that waltz. He caught his breath, and then smiled widely, "Devil!" he whispered, grinning. She was Cleopatra!

Nina's model was indeed that mechanical Cleopatra at the Centennial. She even had a stuffed owl on her arm. It hung from a string when she danced. Her choice was a poke in the eye for anyone who might remember their Centennial experience. But mainly Cleopatra appealed because she had been the leader of half the world, a lady to whom emperors had come and lain their hearts at her feet and who, even in defeat, had determined her own end.

Studying every inch of Nina, who was standing poised beneath the twenty-tiered chandelier, Jordan noted that on second glance she was wearing an Egyptian headdress that clung to the sides of her head in the shape of golden stars. Her hair hung loose all the way down to her hips. That beautifully proportioned body was covered with cloth of gold from high at the throat, sliding down to the fingertips. The glowing material moved sensuously with her every breath. So while it was the most modest of costumes there, considering all the displays of bosom, it was the most daring as well for its caressing of the body within. The result was pure Nina, giving two contradictory illusions at once: modesty and seduction, and laughing if you chose wrong.

Jordan needed to see her closely. To laugh with her over her selection. To share more than laughter. He ached to touch her so he could feel himself alive again after the long drought. Forgetting Mrs. De Bonnard's warning, he cut in. "I'm the host," he explained to the startled Englishman who was not eager to relinquish his partner. Moving quickly, Jordan had the golden lady in his arms and whirled her from the ballroom's center to a private corner.

Nina did not say a word. She stared at him with eyes, as Dick had said, that had the fire of a cigarette tip freshly inhaled, and Jordan moved closer, attempting to inhale her fire into his lungs. "Dear God, you're more beautiful than ever!" he could not help exclaiming.

"And you're as presumptuous as ever. Fotheringale and I were having a very interesting conversation."

"I'm not here to chat," he said, concerned. "I'm here to warn you. No one else but those who love you can see it. But, blast, you're blazing like a firework. And while we're all 'ohhing and ahhing' at your fire, you yourself will soon find yourself spent and in darkness."

"Quite an incendiary observation. Possibly I too, like Cleopatra and Psyche, have divine fire that can never be extinguished."

"You will consume yourself," he warned huskily, but the dance was over. He longed to take her to the balcony, and even made the attempt, but she laughed and ran away, into the arms of her court. They closed around her, and he heard her laughter until she was drowned by their voices, and the music announced another dance.

Jordan walked away, out of the ballroom and up to his room, wondering what the blasted use was pretending. He loved the woman. Would always love her. He'd almost had her. Now thinking of both Adele and Nina, he concluded with regret that they were like the bright star and her dark star shadow, and he, he felt in his soul, was responsible for both their changes. It was necessary for him to talk to Nina out of the glare of society; that dance had not given him enough time. Only at that point did he remember, with a frown, Mrs. De Bonnard's request that he not dance with Nina lest he repeat the disastrous pattern of the Pynchot ball—but he'd done so. He had not been able not to.

Nina was under an inquisition for that very occurrence the next day by both her mother and Adele.

"I did not give him a dance. He cut into Fotheringale's turn. If I'd been allowed to dance with Bobby, I could have used his unscrupulousness to match Mr. Windsor's gall, to trip him or push him, but Fotheringale, being English, when told Jordan was the host, bowed away. His manners are too impeccable. As for me, what could I have done else? I considered screaming or fainting but assumed that would draw more attention to a moment that ought to be made as unimportant as possible."

"But it was of major importance," Adele gasped. "It was my first attempt to get back into society after the major humiliation of seeing you dance with Jordan in Oceana. How could you have allowed that very scene to be repeated. Yes, you ought to have simply walked away from him!"

Nina attempted to justify herself. "I don't believe he would have let me go so easily. He was set on speaking to me and if I had protested and not listened everyone would have stopped dancing and focused on us."

"They did anyway," Adele said.

Her mother thought it the correct moment to interrupt. "Nina is correct. A lady must always do her utmost to avoid a scene."

"Further," Nina insisted, taking Adele's hand, "what he wanted to say was not complimentary. He merely wanted to predict my destruction. Does that make you happy?"

Adele turned away. "At least he wanted to speak to you." Then she turned back and faced Nina. "I guess you can't help shining. Why do we all want to black you out? I guess because you black us out. But in a way that shining came in handy last evening because if Jordan had any intention of marrying that Miss Perkens,

I'm sure seeing you again convinced him not to settle. Although if he were going to settle why couldn't he settle for me?" And Adele ran out of the room.

Mrs. De Bonnard was torn between running after her or staying with Nina, whose white face was showing her distress, as much as she attempted not to reveal it. Yet that proved that Nina could handle her emotions, and so Mrs. De Bonnard chose to go after Adele.

Nina sought her usual solace: her pen. She began an article on the ephemeral nature of majesty for her Gilded Lily column. It concluded with the comment that it was better to have a shiny moment of ruling than never to have shone at all. Which was an answer to a certain gentleman's dire prediction that had disturbed Nina more than she acknowledged even to herself. Jordan seemed less brittle, less sarcastic—even his insult had a sincerity to it, as if his remarks came from concern rather than the usual attempt to score points or whatever had been his ulterior motive before. There she went again, trying to see Jordan in a favorable light! She was as hopeless as Adele—and poor Miss Perkens following him with her anxious eyes all evening. Would women never learn not to be attracted to dangerous gentlemen?

A certain gentleman was regretting having spoken so unguardedly to Nina last night. But this was the new Jordan who would never again speak for effect and say words he didn't mean, even if the words he meant came out wrong. The following day, he was reading the *Bugle* and came across the column by The Gilded Lily. One paragraph in, he nearly dropped his morning cup of coffee. This article was a direct refutation of the remarks he had made to Nina. Who had been there to overhear? Or was it just a fantastic coincidence? Immediately he rushed to the office of the *Bugle* and read as many back columns of The Gilded Lily as could be found. Jordan Windsor came away a happy man. She was not so frail, after all. There was a core. She was laughing at them all. They were the ones likely to flare out. Very likely she did have eternal fire. By God, was it possible to love her even more? Because he did. It was essential for him to stay in New

York and attempt to communicate with her. In the interim he arranged with Mr. Holden for her column to appear in his Washington *Courier* and several other papers in his chain. "Who discovered her?" Jordan could not help asking, cursing when he heard it was Bobby. Would that blasted pest ever let her go?

Bobby had no such intention. Waylaying Nina returning to her home after her morning ride, he followed her in and informed her there was a Wild West show in town and she had to see it for her column.

"I don't care for circuses and Wild West shows," Nina replied, remembering her mother's edict, but he convinced her this was not the stagy Buffalo Bill stuff of shooting demonstrations and such, but an actual depiction of *authentic* Indian life on a reservation. That had Nina interested enough to forget her mother's warning and agree to attend. But first she had another appointment that could not be canceled.

Bobby was suspicious. "If you're meeting Jordan, I won't stand for it."

Her eyes widening, Nina stared at him. "You won't what?"

Realizing he'd gone too far, Bobby amended sheepishly, "I'll . . . eh, sit it out and wait my turn." He showed his good faith by sitting down, but Nina informed him she had no time to chat; she had to change.

"You are continually changing. That's what's so intriguing about you."

Since he was going to discuss how intriguing she was, Nina felt she could spare him a few moments, until he said, "I want you to marry me."

Annoyed that he was discussing not her but what *he* wanted of her, Nina prepared to rise.

"You have to marry me. You have no other choice."

"Why do you assume that?"

"Because *I* am what you really want. I am *society*. They're following where I've already trod. I am society's child. I prank while they pose. All women would rather marry society than a man. With me you get both."

"Assuming I want either," Nina threw in with a smile, but he was too wrapped up in his argument to be sidetracked.

"Who brought you back into society's acceptance? I did, by changing society. You enjoy being its heroine, don't you? But don't make the mistake of wanting a hero. That won't work! A heroine becomes secondary when the hero takes over. A heroine like yourself demands too much of a hero's time. Oh, he'll save her—in order to build up his image as a hero. But after a while he wants to go on and build an empire—a newspaper chain. He wants a Miss Perkens type, content to be a secondary player to his heroic role."

No longer amused, Nina cut in impatiently, "What are you saying?"

"Just that you'd better not marry Jordan, if that's in your mind. Jordan's not enough of a challenge for you. He gave up too fast. I never would or will. I'll devote my life to making up for my unworthiness of you!"

"If being unworthy were sufficient reason for my marrying someone," Nina said matter-of-factly, "I should have married most of the men in our society."

"You almost did, getting engaged to one fella after another. You keep making the same mistake: picking a worthy gentleman. Don't you know worthy gentlemen don't want unworthy women? That's the reason you're so right for me and for this gilded society. You like to shine and outrage. That's our bond. You offend society to lead it. I lead society and make it offensive." He giggled at that juxtaposition and continued rapidly, "Another thing we've got in common: we're not followers. The rest are all scared of being classed as *outsiders*. They fall over each other's feet to keep in lock step. So that's how I became society's leader. I always go to the head of the line. If you link up with me, you'll have your own newspaper to publish everything you want. Or have other writers jumpin' to your tune. Like they do to mine! My motto is: He who follows the crowd never leaves his own footprints."

Nina, feeling some of his thoughts attaching themselves, had to shake off those tentacles quickly. Yet persistently he sent more her way, whispering in a soothing voice. "Think of being the queen of us all."

"You're a snake!" she inserted, laughing.

"Sure. But it's better slithering around with me than having an Adam ruining our fun! What do ya say?"

"No! Get away, you tempter! I don't want a newspaper. I don't want to rule society."

"Yeah, you do. You wanna be outside of society but ruling it, laughing at it . . . being admired by it. You want applause, all the time not valuing the ones who applaud. I can give you every-thing: followers—a whole society of them—gowns, wealth, plea-sures, jaunts, adventures! And I'll always keep you laughing."

"And love?"

"Golly, there's no one who loves you as much as me! As long as you don't bore me—and you never have—and as long as I don't bore you—and I never have—we'll be happy together. We're fellow outragers!"

Nina, about to dismiss him with a laugh, realized by his plead-ing look how serious he was, so she responded truthfully, "This is a temporary waiting period for me, Bobby. I'd never spend my life *pretending*! I'm searching for something that really matters to me. Mother may be correct. Perhaps I, even *we*, ought devote ourselves to helping others. Anyway, I'm going to try that today. Mother and Adele and I are going to bring soup and other things to some poor people."

Bobby's eyes went wide before he fell into a fit of giggles. "Lady Do-Good, *you*!"

Nina was offended. Bobby rushed to explain, "Aw, Nina, my beauty. Think of what you're doin' to these poor folk! I'd choke on the soup! I'd toss it in your face! You, a beautiful, rich lady stopping by, and when you leave, they've had a little soup and a *lotta* humiliation, 'cause you've shown them how lowly they are. Better send a servant with this hundred-dollar bill," Bobby of-fered, taking one out and handing it to her. "Then see how happy they'll be! With this they can buy real food and have enough left over for some fun! Here, give 'em two of these bills, and they'll be blessing your name forever after. Build an altar to you! Money's what counts in this world. And *I* am money. Think about that when you're so quick to turn me down! I'll pick you up this afternoon for the Indian show to get your answer."

After Bobby's exit, Nina hardly had time to think about all

he'd said. Her mother and sister were rushing her into the carriage. Mrs. De Bonnard was talking about their destination. "We shall not venture into the Bowery, even with John escorting us." she pointed to their burley servant who was riding with the coachman. "It's a common area for beatings, even murder. Although the ladies have entered it for the *cause* and not been harassed, which is more than can be said for other more respectable areas of town!"

Nina had lived in New York City all her life, except for her times in Oceana and Newport, but there were parts of this city she'd never seen, with which her mother and Adele had apparently become acquainted. Strange that they knew things she did not. She remembered them differently back in Oceana. Now they were efficient, dedicated, concerned about the effect of hoodlum-gangs roaming around certain areas, stuff she'd read about in the newspapers but didn't assume she could do anything about. And they talked of *her* changing! Mrs. De Bonnard's voice brought her quickly to attention. "I was saying, Nina, we've chosen for your first attempt a family of a slightly higher class, if one can use the word *class* with the poor."

"Mother! You don't mean that," Adele inserted. "This family, the Rafertys, are fine people. As are many we've met. But others don't speak English, you know, in the Italian, Russian, even Chinese sections. So many different people!" Adele's eyes sparkled at the variety. Nina nodded.

"Yes." Mrs. De Bonnard agreed approvingly. "We've seen them all. But the Rafertys, as I was saying, were chosen because the father works. He makes a dollar a day for a six-day week. But sickness has set them back. In the winter diphtheria or pneumonia sweeps all through these families. Already the Rafertys have lost a grandmother, and Mr. Raferty himself has been poorly. As have some of the children. We're praying for them, but especially the father. To be frank, once the father goes, the children here are doomed to orphanages." She sighed and shook her head. "That's incentive for us to keep them well. See how important your volunteering is today?"

Nina nodded again. Her strange new mother and sister and the different world she was nearing were leaving her speechless.

Naturally one felt sorry for a family who had hanging over their heads the threat of the children going to an orphanage. That would appall anyone. Yet when her mother and sister were silent, Nina had second thoughts about being here. What right had she to oversee other people's existence and, godlike, solve their problems? Wasn't it putting them in a position of children? She could remember how frustrating it was to be handed somebody else's thought-out solutions when maybe, on her own, she would have come up with a whole new problem! And worse, what if they looked to her for answers and she had none to give—did God ever feel like that? She flushed deeply at daring to feel sympathy for the Almighty.

Looking at her mother, Nina relaxed. Her mother would know what to do. She always did, and Adele was becoming a lot like her. Both so certain of their courses. Of course. Of course. It was that confidence, especially in her mother, that had reassured Nina when she worried about the Richards' party on the following night. Mrs. De Bonnard would be attending, and for the first time she would actually see her husband with Cass Richards. Nina was hoping her father, unlike other times, would keep his distance from that young lady. Also she had to remember to pretend to be Cass's friend, even though that lady's constant flaunting of her wealth grated; she talked of having ninety gowns and fans to match just for this season alone. But more, there was something about Miss Richards's eyes that made Nina wary, a beady look, like a goose ready to pounce on its next piece of bread. The only comparable expression she recalled ever seeing was on her father's face when discussing a financial deal. Nina shuddered at that similarity.

But again she squelched all concern about that situation with the reassurance that her mother was home now and would put a stop to anything untoward happening—at least publicly.

"Why are you frowning, Nina?" her mother asked in concern. "Are you frightened for your safety?"

"Oh, no! Just hoping I'll know what to do."

"Nonsense. My daughters always know what to do, *instinctively*," Mrs. De Bonnard pronounced.

Nina nodded again, hoping that her instinct was in good

order. But in case it failed, she decided to imitate Adele, who was actually looking forward to barging in on these people's lives. She smiled as Adele smiled and followed Adele's quick exit from the carriage, but could not follow Adele's quick entrance into the house. Nina was stopped by her shock at the heaps of filth in the street. On all sides were rows of two- or three-story houses that had people erupting from every opening: people on the stairs, in the windows, on the sidewalks. Most astounding was the din coming out of the houses. As Nina had known them, except during parties, houses were generally silent. Here, these boxes held shouts, cries, laughter, and curses. Looking about, Nina realized she was alone on the steps and rushed to catch up. Going inside the small, noisy box, Nina was presented with another assault, this time to her nose, and she quickly sought the protection of her gardenia-scented handkerchief. Mrs. De Bonnard smiled at her daughter's holding a hanky to her nose.

"Don't do that," Adele said. "They'll know you think they stink."

"Don't they know they do?" Nina asked in surprise.

"No, they've become accustomed to their smell. They live in a world of bad smells. But what do you expect? So would you smell if you couldn't afford soap, or coal to heat your water. And if you had to share a latrine and had nothing to wipe your bottom—"

"Adele! Do we have to be so graphic?" Nina protested. But the whole situation was graphic in extreme. And she was dressed incorrectly. Her mother and sister were wearing the old black dresses they used for suffragette work while she was in her lovely green taffeta with a train that was already dragging over an eclectic selection of rubbish on the stairs. But she wanted so much to succeed at this. Resolutely, Nina put away her hanky and got an approving nod from her sister. Once inside the one room, she regretted having done so as she was overcome with the additional smell of three people ill in bed, one retching. Nina nearly made an about-face. Mrs. De Bonnard gave her an encouraging nod of her head, so Nina bravely stayed.

"We've brought you some soup, Mrs. Raferty," Mrs. De Bonnard called.

"The saints preserve you!" came from a dark corner. Her mother and sister, forgetting Nina, joined a woman in a mob cap at a table. John pushed past Nina, bringing in the large basket. The woman was joyfully emptying it. Aside from the jar of soup and sandwiches, there were matches, coal, soup bowls, and napkins. It began to look like a picnic! The whole family, three adults and five children, sick or not, came running for them. One of the girls, about seven years old, had some dignity. She hung back and just stared. Shaking herself out of her shock, Nina went forward and filled a bowl and brought it to her. The youngster had immense blue eyes that clearly had the sky in them. Those sky eyes stared at Nina and her green dress. Fascinated, the young girl came forward to touch the taffeta, stroking it. The soup was getting cold. The blue-eyed girl's mother admonished her from a distance, "Don't be bothering' the lady. Eat up." Nina presented her with a sandwich, which she took but ignored. Rather she was still gazing raptly at Nina, as if afraid she would disappear. The beautiful visitor gave her one of her rare Nina-smiles, and the girl put down the sandwich to devote all her energy to drinking in the apparition. Between large blue eyes and glowing gold-brown ones a linkage formed.

"My name is Nina. . . . What's yours?"

"Deirdre," came out with effort.

"A lovely name! Sounds like 'Dear One,' doesn't it? I predict you'll have a life of people calling you that. Would you like being admired and praised and told how lovely you are?" The little girl nodded eagerly. "Well, I predict you shall be. Won't that be fun?"

Again the red-haired Deirdre nodded. Her breath, however, sounded harsh, and Nina realized with a jolt that she too was sick. A wave of compassion and fear for the child spread over her. In one of her impulsive acts, Nina reached over and took Deirdre onto her lap and rocked her. The little face was attracted by the gold star necklace Bobby had given Nina, and she reached for the shine. Nina removed the necklace and placed it on the little girl. Flushing with pleasure, Deirdre kept trying to bend down to see it, which brought on a coughing fit. Her mother came running to hit her on the back. Then she gave her some of the hot soup. When the mother was called to another of her children, Nina finished serving Deirdre the soup. The girl was perspiring, but that was understandable: the soup had been hot and the room was getting warmer now that Mrs. De Bonnard had brought enough coal for a real fire to get going in the brown potbellied stove. Apparently she and Adele had brought that stove on a previous visit. John had been carrying in barrels of other supplies that had the adults exclaiming. During that distraction, Nina looked down and saw Deirdre attempting to sneak back onto her lap, and she lifted her up again and began singing to her, ignoring the times the girl coughed in her face, wiping the child's lips with her gardenia-scented hanky. Deirdre kept sniffing it with such pleasure that Nina gave it to her.

One of the popular songs currently being sung in her crowd was "Nita, Juanita," although the gentlemen turned that to "Nina, Juanina" when singing it to her—and that's how Nina sang it, with Deirdre echoing a word or two. Then there was "Endearing Young Charms," and Nina sang that several times while Deirdre closed her sky-blue eyes and hummed along, then just breathed along, a harsh sound that had Nina assuming she was snoring. Smiling, Nina continued to sing and rock her. She stroked the damp dirty hair from the forehead that had seemed so warm before, but was now cooler. Nina was pleased by that. The others had finished eating and had come and taken the sandwich Deirdre had not touched. Nina noted with satisfaction that the child was sleeping peacefully. She kept humming and holding her. But there were signs they would soon be departing, so Nina began to make little motions to waken Deirdre. After a bit she started softly singing some of her childhood favorite songs to rouse the child. None of them did. Deirdre was getting heavy in her arms. At length, Nina was forced to adjust her position. When she did, Deirdre's head rolled down on her chest and stayed there.

A stab of terror went through Nina as she sprang up with the girl's body in her arms, crying, "Oh dear God!"

The mother came running. Others. The child was seized from Nina. Screams erupted all about. Mrs. De Bonnard was there, pushing Nina toward the door.

"Is she . . ." Nina began, unable to say it.

"Yes, dead," her mother said with annoyance at having to put the obvious into words, as she joined Adele in rushing to comfort the family. Both De Bonnard ladies were openly crying. Nina just stood there, tearless. Then slowly she took out the two hundred-dollar bills Bobby had given her and put them on the table. Backing up, she hit the door and then turned and stumbled out and down the stairs.

Seventeen

The coachman was waiting. Nina jumped into the safety of the coach and huddled there. Images of Deirdre pushed in and filled the seats around her. Deirdre listening. Deirdre with her sky-blue eyes and Nina's star necklace around her neck. Deirdre dead. She'd died clutching the necklace and Nina's gardenia-scented hanky, listening to promises of a glorious future and the courting songs of future lovers who would never be. Nina did not cry, but she could not stop shuddering. A bunch of children Deirdre's age were fighting across the street. They were dirty. Deirdre had been dirty too. But her blue eyes were clean. And now she had gone to join the heaven blue of her eyes. Dear God, she was better off there than living in this squalor! Nina herself would rather be dead than have to exist in this dark world. Shivering, Nina vowed never to come to this place again. Never! Never! Bobby was correct. Money was king and queen and the whole blasted deck of cards.

Mrs. De Bonnard and Adele entered the carriage. Her mother hugged Nina, who looked so forlorn. "Thank heaven I have my two little girls," she said, hugging both affectionately. "Did you leave them that money?" she asked Nina.

"Yes, it's from Bobby. He said he wanted to contribute."

"Well, it couldn't come at a better time. They can have quite a wake with it. They didn't want to touch it at first. They thought you'd brought death to Deirdre. When you hugged and kissed her, they thought . . . oh well, I know it's your good heart. But . . ." Mrs. De Bonnard did not concluded her statement.

Nina looked confused. "Are they accusing me of killing the girl?" she exclaimed, fury rising her out of the sunken pit of her shock.

"No," her mother exclaimed. "Of course not!" She gave Adele a warning look, but Adele was already explaining. "It's just that you're so beautiful in your green gown, and they thought you were a goddess who could make Deirdre well, and then when she died and you left the money, they were whispering that you took her soul."

Nina laughed ironically at that. "I've got enough soul of my own, thank you." She was quiet and glum and unhappy and angry and frightened and swearing never to interfere in other people's lives ever again. She had enough trouble with her own.

In commiseration, her mother and sister assured her that other places they would take her would be different, and that she ought not allow this unfortunate first attempt to deter her. Nina did not reply, feeling inept, out of place, wanting to run to some safe place or safe person where she could belong. But the person waiting for her was Bobby, set to take her to the Indian show. Nina, having previously decided not to attend, now felt that Bobby was at least a distraction from the guilt she felt. Guilt had been her partner since that birthday night on the boat; now she had one more thing to regret. But she hadn't taken Deirdre's soul. She had tried to give her part of her own. Nina had to shake her head vigorously to clear it of the pictures that clung there: Deirdre coughing, Deirdre smiling, Deirdre attempting to sing "Nina, Juanina" and dying with a small smile on her white face, clutching the star necklace.

"I gave the star necklace to a little girl and then she died," she told Bobby as he escorted her into his carriage.

"Did you take it back?"

Nina gave him such a look. Sometimes Bobby shocked even her. Inconsiderately, his next speech was a marriage proposal.

"I've decided never to marry," Nina shot back sharply. "The thought of having children and seeing them die makes me feel sick! Best you marry a Lucy Perkens too, and have lots of children, so you can join them in being one happy family of children."

"I don't want children," Bobby said seriously. "I'm child enough."

Nina had to laugh at that. He *was* a child, and she suddenly felt so old.

In a small clearing in Central Park, there was a disappointingly meager exhibition of an Indian reservation—with only one tepee and a handful of Indians standing around. A totem pole, not quite secure, kept swaying in the breeze. It seemed hurriedly arranged. She said as much to Bobby.

"Righto. I just had it set up this morning to please you. No time to get the proper stuff from out west." Complacently, he placed a white and black-tipped feathered headdress on his head and preened about in it. He handed her a pair of moccasins and several jade necklaces that went well with her green dress and took the place of that star necklace. That brought back a momentary thought of Deirdre until Bobby pushed Nina toward the tepee. Obligingly she entered, ducking under the flap held up for her.

Inside, there was an old parchment-faced Indian man squatting and smoking a pipe. Eyes dancing, Bobby sat next to him and took a puff of the pipe. Nina watched his face as he absorbed the smoke. Then, with a contented sigh and great ceremony, he handed it to her. Nina's eyes went wide. There had been times when she'd occasionally taken a whiff or two of a cigarette, but she had never enjoyed it, having done it for the dare. Bobby put his dare into words. "Go on, scaredy-cat. It's an insult not to smoke his peace pipe! It's like saying you don't want peace with his tribe."

Nina considered, and then, squaring her shoulders, took a small puff, but that wasn't enough for the Indian; he kept urging her to take another. His black eyes insisted, so she took one more puff, and then a long, deep drag. It was heavy, strangling smoke. Nina, like Deirdre, tried to cough herself clean. Almost choking, Nina coughed as much smoke out of her lungs as she could, but it had gone into her bloodstream. One minute she was there coughing and the next she was rising to the top of the tepee where the sticks came to a point and the soft skins covered all pointy, sharp things in life. The skins settled around her. She floated, looking down at Bobby. He was staring at her with the same satisfaction he had shown when she had won the coach race. Had she won again? Gone higher in this tepee than anyone? It was exhilarating being up there, exactly what she wanted to happen to her since Deirdre had died. She needed to get away from the world. And so she stopped resisting and let herself float on. She was out of the tepee, having somehow gotten through the top points. Ah, she was rising up above the trees on eagle wings. "I am an eagle!" she cried out. "I have sharp eyes to see the world, but I float above it and beyond it."

Deirdre was there in the sky, the color of her eyes, and she was healthy and laughing. But Nina could not stop for her; she merely waved. Her journey was a long one and she renewed her speed by flapping her eagle wings, gliding now . . . reaching toward the stars. And then. Then she was falling into darkness. Someone had touched her.

Nina was on the ground. Her head was flat down. She heard a match being lit and half opened her eyes and saw a small flame attaching itself to a candle that floated along in the dark space, coming closer to her. Someone was holding the candle over her head and staring down. She opened her eyes wide and stared back. The candle jumped in the person's hands.

"You're awake," Bobby said, pleased.

He was shadowy. He brought an oil lamp in and turned that up and Nina could see him sitting cross-legged next to her. She was lying on a fur on the ground inside the tepee. She attempted to sit up, groaned, and let herself sink back on the fur rug, closing her eyes again.

"You asleep?"

"I'm attempting to keep my body and head together. What in the name of heaven happened?"

"You took too much peace pipe. Knocked you out. Shoulda just taken a whiff, like me. Chief Long Journey said you'd be okay. You'll be better than that 'cause you got the chance to see your future. What did ya see?"

Nina opened her eyes at his cheery sound. Yes, he was grinning, ready to be entertained. She would have liked to knock him flat, but she didn't have the energy to lift her hand.

"Take me home," she said after a long silence.

"Can't. Normally, anyone bringing you home like this would be made to marry you. And that would be great. But you've triumphed over reputation. So your mother will probably prohibit you from going anywhere with me again. Which I can't allow. Your mother's already stopping us from dancing. I had to do something."

Slowly Nina forced herself up, but not without a wave of vertigo. She had a sense of urgency, of needing to have her wits about her, as she said hurriedly, "I'll enter on my own and make an explanation that doesn't involve you."

Bobby did not respond, nor make any gesture of help when she struggled to her knees. At that point she looked down at her dress and suffered a shock. It was not the green taffeta she'd been wearing when she arrived. A loose kind of dress made of thick leather hung over her body, exposing a great deal of leg. It was beaded in many colors and she had bead necklaces hanging around her neck. Her instincts warned her not to ask Bobby about this until she was safely out of his control. She ignored her dress and the moccasins on her feet and stood up. She swayed for a second, but then willed herself steady enough to duck out of the exit flap.

Bobby followed her. It was dark in the park. Nothing of the reservation remained. No Indians. No totem pole. A deserted field. Nina's heart was pounding as she looked about for another person. Even the waiting carriage did not have a driver. Taking a deep breath, Nina walked toward the carriage and the snorting horse. It whinnied as she patted its long neck. She leaned against it for a moment, revived enough by its warmth and life to attempt what would normally have been the easiest maneuver and now took every ounce of strength: entering the carriage. It seemed higher than any carriage she'd ever been in.

"Come back and lie down, Nina," Bobby said, and she jumped. He was right behind her, trying to lead her back. She bristled and pushed him away.

"I'm going home!"

"You won't make it without my help, and I'm not giving it to you unless you're willing to listen to a few facts and stipulations."

"I am never willing to listen to anything *untimely*."

"I don't get that."

"Precisely. You're not getting your way when I'm not in prime condition to combat you. Obviously you've done something disgraceful . . . to me and to my best interests, but I can't discuss that now. Tomorrow we'll have a thorough examination of tonight's events and repercussions."

So positive did Nina sound that Bobby was in confusion. He had not planned for this, but Nina always surprised. That was why he found her so intriguing. She surprised again by making it into the carriage in one bound, taking up the reins, and setting the horse on the move before Bobby could jump in. He was running to catch up. But her weeks of training in the Coach Club stood her in good stead. She had her horse at a galloping pace and did not slow down for all of Bobby's cries.

Recognizing the area of Central Park she was in, Nina found the correct path. Once she lessened the pace to get her balance. But the next moment she heard noise in the bushes, spurring her to set the horse moving. Fifth Avenue was not far away. With deep breaths and keeping her eyes focused, Nina made it out of the park. The streetlights were still lit; they had not yet been extinguished, but on the horizon she could see daylight beginning. She had been gone the entire night. Disgrace was the least of her worries. She would face that when she had overcome the tendency to sway and fall. At least the horse was a placid sort and willing to be led. Two blocks more and she would be home. There was always the possibility that Bobby had another faster carriage of his own and would waylay her. She looked quickly behind her. There was no carriage following. But that movement of her head made her feel as if she'd been turned on her head. She slumped, nearly lost control, but pushed on, gritting her teeth, until the De Bonnard mansion was ahead. She was home. Going around to the mews, Nina left the horse and carriage tied to the back gate. No one would answer the front door at this hour. Down in the servants' quarters, there was activity. The maids were up to lay out the morning fires. Jeffers was his usual unflappable self as she walked by him. In her mother's calm, composed tones, she ordered, "Have someone take care of my horse," and nonchalantly walked to the stairs leading to the upper floors. Jeffers was following her, so she asked him, "Are my parents still asleep?"

Jeffers replied that Mr. and Mrs. De Bonnard had been concerned at her absence. Mr. De Bonnard had retired, but her mother was awake in her sitting room.

"Oh dear, did I forget to tell her about the morning breakfast that was to conclude the costume party? How thoughtless! Thank you, Jeffers, I'll go immediately and reassure her that all is well."

Whether she moved with a lady's grace or stumbled Nina could not be certain, but she had done all she could to repair what would in any case be whispered about in the several servants' quarters before the sun was fully up. Nina took a look at herself in the hall mirror and gasped; she decided she could hardly wait on her mother in this condition. There was a red paint mark on her forehead. Her hair was loose and tangled. The Indian dress was more embarrassing than being seen in her nightshirt. All she lacked was an arrow in her back.

Adele was waiting, sitting on the edge of Nina's bed, and rushed up and took her in her arms as she staggered in.

"What happened?" Adele asked in alarm.

"I've become an Indian," she said, laughing lightly. Urged to be serious, she haltingly explained that Bobby had taken her to see an Indian show and given her some puffs of an Indian peace pipe. "That's the last I remember until I woke up a half hour ago and made my way home."

Adele was furious. "Dear God, did he . . . ?" She couldn't put it into words.

"No," Nina said. "But I am still suffering from the effects of the smoke, whatever that was. Can't understand why the world keeps spinning. And there's a pain in my chest."

She sat down on the edge of her bed. When she placed her head in her hands, that gesture pushed her over to the floor.

Adele cried out and attempted to pick her up.

From the floor, Nina looked up at her sister's loosed long

blond hair and wide clear blue eyes. "Did anybody ever tell you you're as beautiful as an angel?"

Adele's eyes rounded. "Nina, darling. *You* have told me so— over and over. And this is not the moment to repeat compliments. We have to get you out of this outfit and into bed before Mother sees you."

"Right."

"You're slipping, Nina."

"Sorry," she mumbled, unable to keep herself upright. How was it possible that she was dizzier now then when first waking? A new effort roused Nina from the floor, and she was back on the edge of the bed. She looked up at her sister for approval.

"Yes, very good." Adele laughed. "Are you certain you didn't have anything to drink?"

Shaking her head caused the room to spin and Nina was back on the floor. She started to cry. All her efforts and she was back where she'd started from. "I fell," she said forlornly.

"That's all right. We'll get you up again. Don't cry, pet. You'll be better when you wake up. I could call Mother, and between us—"

The mention of her mother roused Nina to attempt another push. This time she landed across the bed and stayed there. Adele shoved her straight. Then, bringing a comforter, she quickly covered up the Indian dress. Drifting toward sleep, Nina could hear her sister singing as she bathed her face, removing the red markings.

Nina sighed, content to be in the sky again. That's where she wanted to remain. She was back being lifted up on the wings of an eagle. Back to being an eagle herself. Back soaring toward the sun. So hot. So hot. She blazed out into its center and burned to a crisp.

Eighteen

*H*er mother was staring at her in concern. Nina moved her head to the side and saw her sister staring at her in concern. At the foot of her bed was her father. He was staring at her.

Nina tried to speak to them. Her voice cracked, but she got out one word: "Eagle."

"What?" her father asked crossly.

"I was on the back of an eagle," she said laboriously, pushing each word out of her mouth like a heavy weight, relieved when she was rid of it.

"Don't bother talking, darling," Adele whispered. "You're better. Whatever was in that peace pipe has gone from your system, the doctor says. But you caught a cold. So you need to rest and not worry about anything."

Her mother nodded her agreement to all that.

"What do you want done in regards to Van Reyden? I can have him arrested," her father said sternly. "Confound, I can't believe this of Augustus's son, but if he purposely made you ill and took advantage of you in any way . . ."

The last part came out gruffly; he was looking at her with desperate questioning. Nina shook her head. "Prank, I suppose. Forget him. But . . . don't want him . . . near me."

All three answered in unison, "No . . . Never. . . ." Her father added an insult he'd never used before his daughter, and walked out.

It said a lot that Mrs. De Bonnard did not offer a reproof to Mr. De Bonnard for his language. Most of the day her sister and mother walked around, serving Nina cool drinks, cups of tea, and lemon or maraschino cherry ices. Nina was having difficulty swallowing anything. Her mother and Adele brushed her hair, talked cheerily, smiled comfortingly. Nina relaxed under their ministrations. "Two angels," she murmured and her mother and Adele laughed.

"You're my angel," Mrs. De Bonnard said with a choking voice and held her around the shoulders, rocking her against her breast.

The next morning both her keeper-angels wanted to bathe her. She accepted that, although it seemed unnecessary to bring more heat to her already overheated body. Nor did she have the energy. Just to get to the tub she needed help from her maid, Maria, and both her mother and sister. Plopped in, she nearly drowned as her head ducked under and all three women frantically went fishing for it. Promptly her mother took charge and got on her knees beside the tub and held Nina's head up out of the warm water while Maria washed her. Nina had just enough degree of alertness to protest a gardenia scent that Adele was preparing to add to her bath. So Mrs. De Bonnard picked up another bottle next to it and Nina was soon floating in the aroma of lilies—her signature scent obviously, Nina thought, and lay back, becoming a quiescent, floating water lily in her copper tub.

"Bobby was here," Adele said the next morning while Nina was attempting to sip her morning cup of tea. "He had the audacity to call and leave flowers. Mama received him. He insisted she give permission for your marriage or he would spread the word you were inebriated in his arms all night."

Nina cried out at that, and Adele rushed to embrace her. "I didn't mean to alarm you. But I could sense you were worrying and it's okay! Mama informed him that on the night in question she and her husband were with *both* their daughters visiting a relative. She just stared him down, you know the way Mama does. And he laughed and said, 'Aw, Mrs. De Bonnard, don't you want your daughter to marry a rich, loving fella? I gotta force her to say *yes*, 'cause she keeps saying *no*.' So Mama said, 'That little boy charm never was very effective with me, Mr. Van Reyden, nor with my daughter, I gather. Both of us are interested in responsible, mature, *honorable* gentlemen.' "

Nina smiled, adding hoarsely, "And he said, 'You won't find any of those in our set,' correct?"

Adele was flabbergasted. "How do you know?"

Nina just shook her head.

"Anyway, Mama let him know she'd given orders that he was never to be admitted. Nor will any messages from him be accepted henceforth. So he was considerably chastened. Father spoke to him as well. I don't know what went on between them. But there was shouting. Papa says the matter is settled, and we can forget about Bobby. Let's turn our attention to other gentlemen. Look at all the flowers from all your beaus! Reminds me of when we were growing up. These are from Mr. Fotheringale. He stopped by. As have others. But mother explains you're ill and not receiving anyone, and thanks them for the flowers. I ate Fotheringale's candy. They were caramels."

Nina smiled.

"You're not worried about anything?" Adele continued, anxiously.

Nina shook her head and held on to her sister's hand. The room felt hot. Her brain had blanks in it, like a sponge with lots of holes. "Don't care about . . ." She shrugged, unable to finish her words. "Tired," she concluded, and her sister let her rest, stopping to kiss her brow.

Feeling better that afternoon, Nina attempted to dress, but she didn't have the energy to go beyond her sitting room, when she was startled by the unannounced entrance of a delivery boy bringing in flowers. She wondered how he had gotten past Jeffers. Before she could ask, he looked up from under the brim of his cap with a little boy grin on his face. It was Bobby.

Nina gasped.

"If you scream, it'll attract the servants and start the gossip your mother and father are trying so hard to prevent."

"Out!" Nina managed to say, going to ring for her maid.

"I'll tell her you invited me here; she'll believe it because no one let me in."

Nina felt the small ounce of returned strength ebbing out of her. She sat down quickly. "Why can't you leave me alone?" she whispered.

Bobby shook his head sympathetically. "I can't. And I've just begun to pursue you. Better if you just agreed to marry me. Otherwise I'll have to make certain you're so disgraced no one else will have you but me."

In an eruption of fury she spurted out breathlessly, "That'll never happen! Even if you turned me into Lucrezia Borgia herself . . . and, and women all crossed the street when I passed, and grown men shuddered in my presence and, and children cried to hear my name, even then *I would not marry you!*"

"I guess you're not ready yet," Bobby said with a plaintive sigh and walked away. He closed the door, and then just as she'd relaxed and was getting back her breath, he opened it again and peeked in with an extra good-bye. "See, just when you think you've gotten rid of me—there I am again."

This time when he closed the door she remained stiffly staring at it for a while, and then struggled to walk across and open it to assure herself he really was gone—only to find him patiently waiting there, whispering, "I'm always here, closer than you think."

Nina was trembling visibly. That shocked reaction was what Bobby had been seeking during the entire interview. Nodding in satisfaction, he finally skipped away. This time Nina stayed at the doorway, watching him leave, before she at last closed her door. And yet, after walking a bit, pacing back and forth, she still occasionally went to her door and opened it for reassurance that her house was free of him.

Around teatime, Adele stopped in and Nina jumped when the door moved. That had to be explained, and Nina, attempting to make light of it, reported Bobby's latest act.

"But that's impossible. The staff has strict orders not to admit him. You must have dreamed it."

In confusion, Nina stared at her sister. Normally she would have been annoyed at anyone dismissing her conclusions, but she was not feeling or seeing things normally since the time at the tepee.

"He brought flowers," Nina whispered, hopefully.

Adele looked around. "All of these are the ones I arranged," she said sympathetically, looking at her sister with unease.

It was true. He must have taken the flowers with him. But Nina did not remember that he did. Perhaps the whole thing was an illusion. There was one red rose on the carpet. He'd been carrying red roses. She had never liked them; they reminded her of drops of blood. Nina reached down to pick it up to show her sister and prove her point, but as she bent, the floor came up and hit her.

Mrs. De Bonnard was there when she woke up, her face anxious again. She was calling Nina "Baby." That reversion was a bad sign. She must be sicker than she realized, Nina concluded, unable to think beyond that point. If there was any point beyond. She made no protest about being put back in bed, nor did she disagree with her mother's assessment that she had rushed her convalescence, though she must have been rushing something because she was panting. Her mother sat by her side. "Tell me a story," Nina whispered, and her mother smiled tolerantly and began recounting her day. Nina shook that off, wanting her favorite childhood tale about two sister trees that embraced each other with their leaves when they were in trouble . . . she'd forgotten how it ended. Mrs. De Bonnard, pleased at Nina's remembering, came close and taking Nina's hand in hers, infusing her own strength into her child, began the sister-trees story, during which Nina fell asleep and never did find out the ending.

Nina was better next morning for having slept through the night. But by afternoon her temperature was rising again. Adele and Mrs. De Bonnard had an important meeting in which Adele was going to give her first report. When they expressed reluctance to leave her, Nina urged them to go, assuring them she would be fine.

Nina was well enough to sit up on the settee, she concluded. Putting on her lavender robe with froths of lace at the sleeves gave Nina something to do; she was playing with that lace, imagining it was ocean foam and she was floating in the surf, when Maria brought in a gentleman's card.

For a long time Nina stared at it as if she could not quite read the letters. Then with effort she spelled them out and a small wave of delight went through her. "He's here?" she asked the waiting maid. When told he was downstairs, Nina signaled that he was to be admitted. Her hair was down and loose. Nina remembered enough propriety to attempt to go to her dressing table and put it up. But she simply couldn't rise. Closing her eyes, Nina prepared herself for the sight of him. When she opened them, Jordan was standing before her. She smiled but did not indicate that he was to stay.

"Am I permitted to sit in Her Majesty's presence?" he asked in his remembered mocking way, but this time he used it to camouflage his concern at her wan appearance. When Nina did not react, just stared helplessly at him, he frowned and sat on a chair close by. He'd expected this to be their usual sarcastic duel of wills. But she seemed will-less. "I heard you were poorly. . . . I had to see you," he began awkwardly. Never had he found himself at such a loss for words. Nina was not helping by supplying any herself. Sometimes she looked in fear at the door and then back at him, as if reassured. Her anxiety communicated some alarm. Protectively, he came to sit next to her on the sofa.

"Are you really ill? There have been all kinds of rumors. I assumed you would not receive me, but I took the chance to leave you this letter. And then, last moment, I thought, persistent chap that I am, that I'd make a push to see if I could actually give you the letter myself."

He waited for her to ask for the letter. She just looked back at the door, and he sensed a need to rush. "I gather we do not have much time together. But this moment, being with you, is worth whatever will come across that door." He said the last with a grin, but Nina looked concerned again.

"Don't be frightened," he soothed. "I won't let anyone hurt you . . . but me."

Nina smiled at his attempt at humor or just at him.

"My God, I'd forgotten that. That smile! I mean, I haven't forgotten your smile—just how it feels when you do it. The hit in the solar plexus, if you'll excuse an inelegant comparison. But there's no other way to describe how overwhelming it is just to be near you. That beautiful face is like a diamond, shiny with new facets every time one looks at it. Although, to be frank, my beauty, there is a quieter glow about you than usual. What is it? Tired?"

Nina nodded. She took a deep breath. This time she opened her eyes slowly and saw him still next to her, and she almost laughed, as if she'd been given a present.

Jordan was frowning. He moved closer to her, his dark eyes fixing her with an expression of such intensity that she could not turn from it—and did not want to turn from it. She reached for it as if it were an energy that she could use.

"You're really here?" she finally whispered.

"Yes, my dear heart. I am." He gave her his hand to verify it, and that had him frowning even more. Her white, delicate hand was trembling in his and, further, was decidedly warm to the touch. And those brilliant eyes he remembered, with all that fire in them on the night of the Majestic ball, were now subdued, as if they'd changed to liquid form, yet he still felt their warmth reaching him, overwhelming him. In response Jordan felt a rush of love for her, stronger than the passion that had been bedeviling him. He did not think it was possible to love her more. But he knew then that he did. Ignoring conventions, Jordan took both her hot hands and kissed their palms.

It was a surprise that she did not rebuff him, but rather closed her fingers over the kisses, holding in his touch and giving him another loving smile.

"Dear God, what's happened? Not that I'm not delighted . . ."

She did not explain, just waited serenely for his next words. That encouraged him to continue. "This letter is an unleashing of all the feelings I've been attempting to restrain. The beginning is an apology for my idiotic behavior the last time we met at Oceana. It should actually be filled with apologies. I offer you them verbally as well. Sorry, sorry . . . so blasted sorry. Do you accept my profound regret?"

Nina nodded as if uncertain what he had to apologize for, indicating by her hurried manner that he was wasting time when they had more important concerns. She was using her golden eyes to go over his face, feature by feature, almost memorizing each line as if she would draw him and when she'd had her fill, only then did she lay her head back against the pillow of the sofa, content.

"What, love?" he murmured.

"Where have . . . you been . . . for so long?" she managed to say softly.

"God knows," he said honestly, "wherever I was, I was wrong to be there." She was silent, so he assumed she wanted a fuller explanation. "Tried to make a life in Washington, despite knowing all along my real life was you. Tried to make myself believe we were best apart, but the PB pictures being sold at the shops showed me how much I'd been fooling myself. I was enraged, ran around like an idiot buying them up . . . came to New York, hoping—for my own sanity—that when I saw you there would be a sense of both of us having gone on. But one look at you at the ball and I was consumed. You were all fire, and I feared you were consuming yourself as well, recognizing that lost darkness in the center of your eyes. . . . Even in that we're together. I'd been in that dark drifting space myself until recently when I took over Grandfather's newspapers and discovered the satisfaction of accomplishment. Gives one back one's pride. Enough to think I could win you back in the face of what I'd said. Presumptuous of me. Yet I had to presume because I *had* to have you back, so I stayed in New York, hoping for a chance to make clear to you that, despite our separation, we have never been completely cut off. You feel that connection, don't you?"

He waited for Nina's reply, but she made none. He was thrown into confusion by her lack of response.

"Have you heard anything I've been saying? No? Very well, don't listen. Just feel what I feel. Let my heart talk to you." And without asking for permission, he placed her hand against his chest. "Feel the love that has been pounding through me for you for so long now."

Her hand fell off. He flinched as if she had slapped him; so much was he certain that if she felt what he was feeling she would respond. To have her simply fall away from him as if it was too much effort to touch him, or even listen to him, left him stunned. Then he was even more astonished by her leaning back against the pillows and closing her eyes.

"I apologize for boring you," he said shortly.

Eyes opening to slits, she murmured, "Saw your face . . . at times. Reached out . . . but . . . never there." And experimentally, she reached out, gingerly touching his lips, whereupon he kissed her fingers.

A surge of energy went through her and she opened her eyes wide as if forcing herself alert to hear his next words. Jordan, sensing he had to say the right thing, felt his tongue falter. Having so often used words to deceive, now when he had need of them they were worn, unusable things . . . leaving him with silence and the one word he murmured again and again: "Love . . . love . . . my love."

She smiled a bit and that encouraged him. He had so continually imagined this meeting, down to her every expression, that now he was at a loss. It was not happening as he'd scripted. She was not ablaze with emotion that allowed him to feed off it, so that each word would flow through him and ignite her.

Yet, looking about, he acknowledged that being in her rooms was a major advance, especially since she was accepting him being there. He felt himself becoming part of it—as his feeling for her flowed out of him into everything about. Nina lived here. Nina saw that watercolor of the sea each morning upon rising. Nina slept in that bed with the gold satin canopy. Her flower scent was redolent through the room, a lush exotic aroma that played with his senses and never left his memory. He basked in it all, feeling that if he stayed there, still enough, he would blend into her.

Abruptly Jordan laughed at himself for wasting time, looking at her setting when he had the woman before him. But he was too bemused by being so close to her after living that possibility so often in his fantasy. Turning in her direction, he still played it safe by concentrating on her outline: on her figure, the lace edging of her robe, the golden halo of her hair. Then, taking a breath, he concentrated closely on her face, from the closed eyes to the slightly parted lips, and he kissed them lightly. She was too breathless for more than a touch, so he held her against him.

"Rest in my arms, my wild girl, rest against me, get your strength from my strength."

Nina sank against him, feeling his arms closing her in, as if she had been on a long turbulent sail and had arrived safe at harbor.

Their bodies were fusing together, their breaths synchronized. He moved to get a better hold when she, in alarm, whispered, "Stay . . . with me."

"I've been with you from first sight," he confessed, and kept her close, promising in his own breathless whisper, "We'll walk by the sea when you're better. Each wave striking on the shore will be a pledge. No words will be as strong as that sound of our two hearts. No other pledge as elemental. Can you hear each wave? We are unified by the sea . . . and what nature has brought together, no man can put asunder."

"I wouldn't be too sure of that!" a man's voice said with a laugh.

Jordan looked up in surprise. He gave Nina a quick, reassuring hug and turned to face Bobby Van Reyden.

"Get out," he said quietly but sternly. "Miss De Bonnard is not to be disturbed."

The young man stared at Nina's white face. Her eyes were closed. He bit his lip for a moment. "She feels good in one's arms, don't she? I held her all night on the bare ground of Central Park. We were in an Indian tepee. I had on a chief's headdress of white feathers. She wore a maiden's dress of beads and moccasins on her feet. We pledged ourselves together that night as you assume you're pledging yourselves now. But she doesn't mean it. She won't remember tomorrow. Will you, my own?"

Nina did not respond to Bobby or his words. An instant ago when Jordan had let her go, she had murmured in protest. No longer being connected to his strength, Nina felt herself loosed, falling; her eyes fluttered and images of her room descended on her. She saw Bobby and shuddered.

"Tell him you were in my arms in the tepee! Tell him you pledged yourself to me," he insisted.

Nina shook her head weakly, using her hand to fend him off.

Bobby warned Jordan. "She'll be pushing you off like that tomorrow!"

Jordan rose up in annoyance. "I told you not to bother her. Do I have to pick you up and throw you out?"

"Aw, come on, Jordie. I'm your brother's best friend. Or I was till Nina came between us. Now why would you believe her, rather than me? Ask her, though. Ask her mother and her father. They're trying to hush it up. But we were *together*, if you get what I mean. She can't be yours. Because, buddy, she's been mine first."

Jordan, his face flushing, looked just for an instant at Nina, not to seek the truth of that, well, maybe just for a brief instant of doubt, but he remembered Bobby's talent for trickery, and also remembered that it didn't matter. "Even if true and you fooled her in some way, or whether she forgot herself for a moment, doesn't matter, because, Bob, old chap, Nina and I belong together. Nothing that happened before has any effect on that. Nothing that can happen—ever—can change that reality." He was finishing the words back on the sofa, saying them to her, and Nina laughed in pleasure, her eyes accepting him back into her sight, and she relaxed against him again. Jordan was whispering, "It's okay, my heart; he won't part us, not by words nor any act. Nothing can part us . . . now."

He was rocking her against him, listening to the sounds of her breath getting harsher like the ocean. The two clung, so absorbed into each other that they forgot the existence of anyone else; no longer aware of Bobby's presence or even hearing the entrance of two other people. But Jordan was brought to his senses by a woman's cry and by being shaken.

"Release her! In the name of heaven! Are you two gentlemen mad! Nina is ill. What are you doing in her room?"

Jordan was apologizing to Mrs. De Bonnard. He had a brief glimpse of Adele staring at him with wounded eyes and he felt the need to apologize to her as well.

Bobby was trying to make the worst of the situation. "I caught him embracing her and told him he had no right. I told him about Nina's having given herself to me the night on the reservation."

"I told you to keep your blasted mouth shut about her!" Jordan cried. "Whatever you say or invent has no meaning when people are truly in love. Maybe someday when you've stopped seeing only your own emotions in life, you'll discover that. Nina and I will always be together, and you are never to attempt to interfere with her life again. Not as long as I stand between her and all harm."

"You do not stand in such a position with my daughter," Mrs. De Bonnard said coldly. "I'll thank you not to make any such assumptions on the strength of a lady's being too ill to push off your attentions. Dear God, are both of you so blind you cannot see her condition for yourselves? Leave her alone! Leave the entire family alone! Especially you, Mr. Windsor. I would have thought your own decency would have made it plain that your presence is not welcome by either of my daughters. You have played your last callous game here!" And she went to stand before Adele, whose eyes were rooted on him.

"Believe me, Mrs. De Bonnard, I never meant to hurt Adele. Ask her! In all honesty she must admit I never proposed to her or did more than flatter and admire her for the young, lovely girl she is. There was no mention of love between us, for the simple fact that there was no love between us!"

Adele interrupted his assurances by emitting a deep sob.

Jordan cursed himself for having said the wrong thing.

Bobby was laughing at his discomfiture.

Suddenly the footman, John, and Jeffers were there. They'd arrived at the sound of the raised voices.

"Thank heavens, Jeffers," Mrs. De Bonnard said, her face white in indignation. "These gentlemen wish to be escorted out of this room and off our premises. Neither is ever to be readmitted."

Bobby was willing to leave, especially since John had him by the arm and was pushing him out. At the last minute he looked over his shoulder behind him, feeling pleasure at the anger, despair, and outrage on the three faces. Nina's face had no expression. Her eyes were shut.

Jordan attempted to whisper to her, but Mrs. De Bonnard had had all she could stand from that gentleman. She did what she'd been thinking of doing since he'd first jilted Adele. She gave him a box on the ear and pushed him out, aided by a dignified Jeffers holding the door.

"Let me know how she is, in the name of heaven!" Jordan cried out as the door was slammed in his face.

Relieved of two of the culprits' presence, Mrs. De Bonnard

turned to Nina. "Are you all right?" she asked, alarmed. "This door should have never been opened to them! Where is Maria? But it's my fault. We should never have left you alone!"

Mrs. De Bonnard was pointing at the door with anger as Nina opened her eyes and followed her mother's arm to the closed door. What had the door done that her mother was so riled against it? Then she turned and saw Adele crying. Adele had accused her of opening her door to free Spooky. She had denied it then. Denied it now.

"He was scratching and crying," she whispered, "But I didn't open the door and let him out. I swear it. Don't be angry, Delly. I miss him too."

Adele stopped crying and Mrs. De Bonnard looked at Nina's pale face and heard her voice sounding so hoarse and breathless; her alarm escalated.

"She's talking about Spooky," Adele explained with a gasp.

"The cat? But that was years . . ." They stared at each other, sharing their confusion, and then both abruptly turned as Nina began a paroxysm of coughing. Jeffers was called and ordered to have the doctor there as fast as John could bring him in their carriage. Adele, in a whirl of her own emotions, still pushed them aside to stroke her sister's head. "She seems a great deal warmer, Mama," she whispered.

Mrs. De Bonnard bit her lip in consternation.

"Letter," Nina said, looking around for something on the sofa.

"What is it?" her mother murmured.

Adele found the letter on the floor and gave it to her. Nina clutched it and held it to her chest, like a talisman, and closed her eyes into unconsciousness.

Adele and the maid carried her to her bed. Nina was still holding the letter in a fist. When her hand loosened and the letter fell in a crumpled ball on the pillow, Adele picked it up. Later, while the doctor was examining her sister, she opened it and groaned, realizing it was a love letter from Jordan.

She read just two lines, then skimmed for a mention of her own name. There was none. The only name was Nina, Nina, Nina, Nina. A reflex of self-preservation swept over her and she acted. She didn't know how she could have done such a thing, but it was done before she could regret it: She threw the letter into the fireplace.

While waiting for the doctor's conclusion, Adele paced. To stop herself from thinking of Jordan and his letter, she remembered Spooky. As fresh as if it had happened today, she felt the anguish of Spooky's loss. He was always going to her sister when he was *her* cat, and Nina was always welcoming him. So her disclaimer that she hadn't opened the door couldn't be believed no matter how often she said it. Adele was positive of that—then and now! She was especially positive when recalling how often Nina had said Spooky needed to be free. Well, he'd freed himself of them both by running away—which was probably the answer for Jordan. It was best if neither sister had him. The sight of Jordan, as always, had sent Adele into a rush of wild hope and then into a plummeting of despair. How could he look at her as if she were nothing when she'd given him every bit of her heart?

When her mother came in to report that the doctor was seriously concerned, Adele forgot her recently stirred-up resentment and ran to help.

"She must have gotten it from the night in Central Park . . . or from Deirdre," Mrs. De Bonnard concluded, her voice low and hopeless. "Fate always chooses Nina. I should have considered that and left her home. But even here she wasn't safe. Lord help us—half unconscious, she had two gentlemen fighting for her hand, causing an unspeakable scene. We have to protect her from them as well. Between Mr. Van Reyden and Mr. Windsor spreading heaven knows what tales to society, we're on the brink of a scandal of unscotchable proportions! Not that that matters now. What am I saying? Let them talk! Let them rip her reputation to shreds as long as she recovers to laugh at them all." And Mrs. De Bonnard rushed out, ostensibly to consult Mr. De Bonnard but actually to get herself in control.

As the day sank into twilight, it was obvious that Nina was sinking as well. All Adele could do to stop what was happening was to cry out for it not to happen. She came close to her sister and whispered a confession: "I burned the letter from Jordan. Couldn't help it. But at least he wrote it to you—that shows he still cares about you. And I love you. And Mama loves you. And

Bobby and Dick probably do too. Isn't that enough for you to want to come back and love one of them back? Aren't I and Mama enough? Even Papa has been pacing the floor downstairs. Is that what you really want, after all? You off in heaven above us, and us down here crying? You can't be mean enough to want to leave so many of us . . . alone. . . ."

It seemed that Nina could be mean enough or selfish enough or just plain sick enough, for day by day she left them farther away.

Nineteen

cross the street from the De Bonnard mansion there was a tree and a bench that became Jordan Windsor's position during the days following his expulsion from Nina's presence. He focused on the room he knew to be hers, sending her thoughts of healing, of need, of love.

The doctor's carriage arrived twice a day, and Jordan always waylaid him for full reports. The first week the doctor's grave face gave Jordan sinking thoughts of losing her. He flew into rages of castigating himself for all those blasted wasted hours in Washington, keeping apart from her . . . only to discover that she might be apart from him forever.

Dick came to sit with him and was enlisted to pay calls and bring flowers to the De Bonnards, assuming he'd be admitted. Nothing loath, Dick became a faithful caller, reporting back to his brother on the bench.

"You love her a lot." Dick said, looking at Jordan's sleepless red eyes. It took Dick a while to see the obvious, but once he saw it, he acted. "I'll try to get Adele to understand about you, I mean that you're not such a skunk, so she and her mother will let you in. But, you know, pal, we can't see Nina. All we do is talk to Adele and sometimes Mr. De Bonnard. Fotheringale spoke for a bit to Mrs. De Bonnard. She likes him 'cause he's English and knows how to be real smooth with her. She likes that Astor relative too, Jacob, but we call him Jack. She tolerates me. Adele is nicer. She understands that we want, you know, hope. She gives it to us by talking about Nina, how she always was a fighter and stuff like that. But it's bad. Pneumonia, I think. Got it from visiting some poor people, you know, bringing soup and stuff. Why do women do that? Mother has a day set aside each month for 'good works.' Is it buying their way to heaven or just because they're used to taking care of people who need help, like children, so poor people are like children to them too?"

"Dick, I'm not interested in philosophizing about philanthropy."

"Hey, I wasn't doing that!" Dick exclaimed, offended. And then, thinking again, he smiled. "Was I? Pretty good, when I don't even know what that means. But I know, I know, you want to hear about Nina. She's having difficulty breathing. They have her room all closed up, with the drapes drawn even during the day so drafts won't get at her in her weakened state. She's also being bled. Normally, this doctor doesn't believe in bleeding 'cause it weakens already weak patients, but he feels in Nina's case it's advisable because she's restless, turning and calling out, and that prevents her from getting sleep, which is healing. So he's deliberately trying to make her weak."

"Confound the idiot!"

"Yeah, I don't like the sound of that myself. But Mrs. De Bonnard agrees with him. She says Nina always had too much energy. And she is better since being bled. I can tell you something disgusting, but—"

Jordan looked up at him sternly.

"Okay, when she was bled, would you believe, Fotheringale wanted them to dip his handkerchief in her blood so he could have a drop of it as a memento! He said it was quite proper, that Byron had kept Shelley's skull, and I said, 'I don't care what your friends do, you're not going to take a drop of her blood to wear as a trophy!' And Adele agreed. Fotheringale's words shattered her. I had to take her into the conservatory to tell her how I would do anything to help her and that she mustn't tire herself, because Nina wouldn't want her to get herself sick too. You know, I care for the kid. She's an old friend. And I got her laughing, after a while. I talked her into coming for a ride with me tomorrow morning just to have a break. But Fotheringale overheard and he wants to come too. And would you believe, she accepted both of us."

"Don't waste my time gossiping, blast you! What about Nina!"

"Okay, take it easy, Jordie. I told you, she was bled and she's quiet now. But weaker."

Jordan was up, pacing. "They need a better doctor. And more experienced nurses! In England that profession has improved considerably since Florence Nightingale set the standards about twenty years ago. But here in New York, the nurses are no better than charwomen!"

"Don't get riled up! The nurses are good, and besides, Nina has her mother and Adele."

The next day Dick reported on his ride with Adele and Fotheringale, and Jordan had to cut him off again and get him to the point.

"Oh, Nina's the same. But that's an improvement. I mean there was a period when she was sinking rapidly. And I heard Mrs. De Bonnard say to her husband, 'She's slipping out of our hands,' and the old guy started to cry."

"When? Why didn't you tell me that?"

"Aw, I didn't want to push you over the edge. That was a few days ago—things really looked bad. Adele and her mother stayed up with her round the clock and told her stories. She gets better if you tell her stories. I volunteered for that. Gee, I got lotsa tales, if they'd only let me sit by her side. I know every one of Horatio Alger's books! But Adele said Nina likes the stories her mother tells her about when they were growing up at Oceana . . . and about trees and stuff. So I said, I don't know any tales about trees, but I can talk about Oceana. Fotheringale interrupted to say, 'Dryads! I'll bring my Bulfinch and read it to her.' Anyway, they didn't want any of us. Jack put in his two cents that ladies always get better with their rooms filled with flowers, so he's sending her bouquets of them. So have I. But it's Bobby who's filling the house. You've seen him on the stoop. They ordered him off. So he's got his carriage in front and sits there all day."

"I've seen him," Jordan said grimly. "I don't want to hear that either!"

"What the blazes do you want me to say!"

Jordan had been staring at the ground, but at that he looked up, and Dick was shocked at the change in his brother. Jordan Windsor, once a fashion plate, fanatic about having a fresh cravat, had not even shaved. His clothes were askew and his red eyes no longer had even a hint of their usual twinkle. That had Dick fretting about him and sorry he'd yelled, so Dick repeated softly, "What can I say?" His brother was mumbling, so Dick leaned closer to hear.

"I want you to say . . . she'll live."

Dick patted his brother on the back. "She will. Nina's too alive to ever die. Of all the people, men and women, I've ever seen, she's got more energy, more sparkle, than anyone else. You saw her at our Majestic ball, all in gold. She blazed as she passed. I wanted to put out my hands to warm them on her, and I did. She saw me and laughed and then blew me a kiss I felt across the room." Dick's face lost its usual cheerful expression. It crumpled in on itself as he concluded. "She won't die. She's got too many people pulling for her."

But there was no noticeable improvement. Then a setback. Then Dick came bounding across the street. Jordan stood up in terror.

"She did it!" Dick shouted, coming close.

"What, blast you, what?"

"She's outta danger!" Dick said, still shouting, although by now he was standing next to his brother. The two Windsor boys punched each other on the shoulder, almost knocking each other over. Jordan, who had not shed a tear all along, let out a sob that Dick smothered in another stranglehold. They held fast until the sound of a loud "Wahoo!" had them turning. It was Bobby, standing up in his carriage and raising his hand to the sky.

Since Nina was now merely recuperating, Mrs. De Bonnard put her foot down and would no longer allow Bobby Van Reyden's carriage to be parked within a block of her house. "We don't need to be made more conspicuous." And she sent her friend the block policeman to move Jordan Windsor along, as well.

So the vigils ended. But Dick still reported to the house to talk to Adele and take her driving. That was permitted. The news he brought home to his brother was progressively positive: Nina had opened her eyes. Nina was sitting up. Nina had taken some nourishment. Nina was asking for books to read. Nina was sitting up at her desk for an hour a day and answering all the many notes of inquiry.

Jordan kept waiting for a sign from her, an answer to his letter, as well as to the notes he'd sent since her improvement, in which he referred to the long declaration that was his original letter. He spent hours at Brentano's, picking out the books she'd enjoy, such as the new Mark Twain because they had both laughed over one of his. There was never any acknowledgment of his gifts.

At last, unable to wait any longer, Jordan got Dick to tip him off on the exact morning Mrs. De Bonnard had a meeting, and then arranged to have Dick take Adele out for another drive. That left Jordan with the least formidable of the obstacles: the butler. Jeffers had been making enough from Bobby to retire, but once corrupted, he became greedy and eager to accept Jordan's lesser bribe, wanting every dollar for his nest egg. He agreed to take up the book of poems and the note. Jordan, however, was not permitted to wait for a response. That would cost double what Jordan had on him. The lady would write her response, if she had any, Jeffers said, pointedly showing him the door.

In her sitting room, Nina undid the package wrapped in a silk scarf of a deep golden shade like the center of the sun. Within was a book of poems. She admired both. But the scarf slid down between the sofa's cushions as she opened the volume. The poems were by the controversial American poet Walt Whitman. She had heard that some cities had banned his works, alleging him obscene. Nina would not have dared to purchase his poems for herself. She wondered who had sent them. There was no note. Not even a word.

Quickly Nina began reading. So swept up by the emotion of the poems, she was too absorbed to notice Adele rushing in until she heard her gasping and looked up surprised that so much time had passed. Adele's face showed alarm as she asked with indrawn breath, "Where did you get that book?"

"Jeffers brought it up to me. Someone delivered it. There was no note, however. Do you have any idea who could have sent Whitman's poems to me? Seems above the level of anything Fotheringale or Jack would pick. And as for Dick—"

"Oh sorry!" Adele interrupted. "That book is mine! I bought it and forgot it in the hall. But you can read it if you—"

Nina was confused. "Delly? You never liked poetry. How come—"

Quickly Adele took the book and said with some defiance, "I've been changing. . . . I'm interested in art and poetry. This seemed . . . interesting."

"Ah, well, you won't be disappointed. In fact, I'd appreciate another glance at Whitman—when you're finished with it, of course."

Adele was holding the book tightly against her breast, breathing hard. Her eyes had a look of injury that roused Nina's suspicion. There was something familiar about that expression. It was the way Adele looked when there was some connection with Jordan. Nina's instincts told her Jordan was involved here somewhere. Or possibly she herself was bringing in Jordan because that's who she'd immediately assumed had sent her the poems, especially since there had been no card. She even went further, concluding that Jordan himself had brought it while paying a call of inquiry about her health. She'd been planning to consult Jeffers when Adele had walked in.

Now, staring at Nina, Adele was sensing the direction of her thoughts. To distract she burst in, "Oh, Nin! I can't believe how wonderful you look! I mean, you seem so improved."

Nina was distracted enough to turn and look at herself in her cheval mirror. She'd lost so much weight she would hardly need lacing. Her glowing hair was dimmed. None of her admirers would admire her now. Nor would anyone believe she was a PB.

Adele's ploy had worked: The two ladies were discussing appearances. Adele praising Nina's and Nina praising Adele's glowing new looks, and somehow the entire topic of the poems was forgotten. Adele blushed at what she had done. Nina interpreted that as modesty and hugged her sister, who held the book of poems in one hand behind her and hugged Nina back with the other. Another satisfaction for Adele was that her sister felt less frail than before, a tactile affirmation of her improvement.

Throughout Nina's convalescence Adele felt as if Nina were the youngster and she the adult. They had changed places: Adele had become Nina. She felt that particularly this morning, having been escorted by two of Nina's gentlemen while her sister was at home waiting for her return and her report about the outing: what was said, what was worn, and the compliments given. Next Adele was looking forward to teatime, when her two escorts would come for a cup and conversation. She was contemplating the stir she'd create when reporting that Nina was up and dressed. But at the next moment, her sister was giving too much evidence of improvement.

"Suppose I surprise Dick and Fotheringale and come down for tea!"

Adele flushed at that possibility, quickly protesting that it was too soon. "The doctor insists you not rush your recovery!" she said. So adamant was she that Nina looked at her in confusion.

"Very well, if you think I should wait another day. We might schedule it for tomorrow. I think I would not mind even a ride in the park—the weather is so lovely in April. To be honest, Delly, I need a view of nature. Of life!"

Adele was insistent she wait until at least the end of the week, when the doctor would come to give her a checkup. She talked rapidly of relapses and finished with a moving plea that she and Mother could not stand another siege of sickness.

Nina looked down at her hands in guilt. "I know I've been quite a problem to you both."

"No, no, I just meant better safe than sorry."

"I'm not the sorry kind!" Nina said with a laugh. "I mean, some things are worth being sorry for. But stop fretting. I'll wait until the doctor gives his permission."

Adele looked relieved. Seeing the poetry book still in Adele's hands had Nina back thinking of Jordan; something about the verses reminded her of him. Using as much tact as she could, considering the topic, she asked, "During my illness, did I have inquiries or visits from any other gentleman besides Dick and Fortheringale . . . and Jack?"

Adele's face grew flushed. "If you mean Bobby," she temporized, "yes, he was here, but we threw him out."

"I don't mean Bobby," Nina said, eyeing her sister carefully.

Adele was silent.

Nina was forced to have to use that name herself. "What I mean is . . . that is . . . is it possible . . . I'm sorry to give you pain, but I've had a dream of a certain gentleman talking to me, saying things I can't remember . . . it's all vague. But I keep having this sense of a strong emotion from him, possibly concern. Could I be picking up some of his actual feelings? Oh bother, I'll have to just ask it straight out, with apologies for the pain, but . . . Adele, dear, did Jordan Windsor pay me a call while I was too sick to remember it?"

Adele faced her sister bravely. She could not admit to burning the letter or what had led from that one act, such as hiding additional letters and instructing Jeffers to confiscate any gifts or notes from Jordan. How he had let this book of poems slip by she would have to discover. Nina was looking at her with so much hope that it strengthened Adele's resolve to continue eliminating Jordan's influence on this family. He brought nothing but pain to them all. Yet she could not out-and-out lie when asked directly.

"Yes, he was here," she said with trepidation. "I didn't want to bring back an ugly memory, but Jordan Windsor and Bobby Van Reyden broke in on you when you were ill and created quite a scene. Mother and I caught them harassing you and dismissed them. Mother ruled you were not to be reminded of their grossness by any mention of it. Bobby gave us problems. He paid off one of the staff, I am certain, for he was allowed in here while you were unconscious. He had almost two hours at your side while you were tossing and groaning, and I may say, coughing in a very inelegant manner that a lady would not wish to be seen by a gentleman."

"How awful. But I don't care what Bobby thought. I hope you're not implying I looked so unpresentable when Mr. Windsor was present."

"You were not yourself. You were sitting on the sofa there, and when mother and I entered, Jordan was sitting next to you and Bobby on the other side, and your eyes were rolling in a most unbecoming way. And you were groaning. Mother took charge, as I said, and threw them both out."

Nina covered her face with her hands. At last, when she lifted her face, she asked in some anguish, "Was he laughing at me?"

Adele could not go that far. "Of course not! You were obviously ill. He was sorry for you. We all were and still are."

"Good heavens! I will not be an object of universal pity!" She walked about. "You are to tell Jeffers to get my horse ready today . . . well, tomorrow. I don't need anyone to take me for a drive. I shall ride myself and see the trees. I want to see the spring!"

Her mother came in at that point and put a stop to Nina's tantrums. She was not to go riding. Heavens, her lungs were still not clear. She was not to strain herself, nor allow herself to get worked up in that manner. And Mrs. De Bonnard rushed for the cough medicine the doctor had left, putting some in a glass and giving it to Nina.

"I don't want it," Nina said sulkily. "There's opium in it, and I feel strange when I take it."

"There's opium in every cough medicine. And in the drops the doctor gives me for my female troubles. It's most soothing. You ought to rely on it as millions of women do. Please, dear heart, till you are well, suspend your independence, your wanting to do things your way—when the general way would make your life and that of those about you more . . . comfortable. Come, be good, for Mama's sake?"

With a hopeful smile, Mrs. De Bonnard handed her the glass and Nina, after first swallowing down her rebellion, swallowed down the portion.

Left alone, Nina felt that disembodied state again. She did not like feeling out of control. Obviously Jordan had paid an obligatory sick call and had left either revolted or amused at her condition. Oh stars, she didn't know which would be worse. But he hadn't followed up that visit by sending flowers as would be expected even from a new acquaintance. So much for her feeling that he was trying to reach her! Yet on the strength of that fantasy, she had put Adele through the pain of recalling that gentleman. Inexcusable!

How much better off the De Bonnard sisters would have been if Jordan Windsor had never come into their lives, she thought with a groan as she sank onto the sofa and found, the next moment, the yellow scarf. She must remember to return that too, to Adele. Absently, her fingers stroked the silk of the scarf while she squirmed at the image Adele had fixed in her mind of Jordan feeling sorry for her. Oh heavens! Why did a lady need gentlemen callers before whom one must always look one's best lest they hold her in disgust? Forget them all. She no longer needed the protection of a wall of gentlemen about her, she concluded. She could stand up to the world on her own. Those Walt Whitman poems were clearly by a man who went his own way. No form, no conformity. She'd begun writing poems in something like that style before becoming ill. One was about a seabird sailing alone in the sky. She might finish that. And then she must write some columns for Mr. Holden. All this time he had been running her reserve store and that was getting low. She would have liked to write a column about how it felt to be near death, but that would be unsuitable for The Gilded Lily. Anyway she was too tired and breathless to do anything . . . but sleep. She slept.

In that state she had several dreams—all jumbled together, of eagles and seagulls banking and soaring in formation. Her last dream before waking in the morning stayed with her in some detail. She was on a boat and the boat was filled with laughing couples, eating, drinking, embracing, dancing, pointing out others, shaking in the wind that came up and swept them off the deck; and Nina was alone, lying prone, drying in the sun. The golden light dried her wet gown in a jiffy and she was set to disembark, but the boat would not dock, sailing on. From time to time, new passengers would fill the boat decks and begin their rounds of dancing and laughing until they too were swept away and always Nina was alone. And always it was better being alone.

Alone, Nina awakened and shrugged off the feeling of unease left over from that last somnolent scenario, assuming it was hinting for her to alter her life in crowds. The dream could also have been nudging her about the columns owed to the *Bugle*. But what could she write about having been of late out of society and not really interested any more. Nina's solution: She found a few rejected columns, fixed them up, and sent them to keep Mr. Holden satisfied for the time being. That left her free to write what she wished. She wrote of simple things—of flowers and the sea . . . and the kindness of loved ones. She wrote of the joy of being able to breathe an unconstricted breath and of pushing back drapes to let in the sun. She wrote till fatigue overcame her and she sat back on her chaise longue reevaluating more than her past columns but her past life.

For so long she had sought sustenance from admiration—first from single gentlemen, then from crowds, then even from hostesses—till she had been gilded over by so many approving glances that she seemed admirable even in her own eyes. Yet gradually her glistening cover, growing thicker and shinier, became oppressive. She wanted to break out of it. But she was afraid that once she did, there would be nothing under the gilded covering but a self half formed, so evanescent it could be blown away by the first wind.

After her sickness and having so long been without gentlemen callers and social approval, Nina became accustomed to living sans that shiny existence. It was not essential, after all. There was life outside the gilded cage and gilded society—here with her family, where she would stay, writing and seeing an occasional gentleman caller—one needn't break off that habit completely. But she no longer craved a crowd when she had Adele. Clearly, Adele was enjoying her outings with Nina's friends. Wouldn't it be a happy solution, since social life had paled somewhat, to rediscover it through Adele's eyes. Yes, Adele and she, like true sisters, would join in receiving callers, and later even join in going to parties. Then, together, the two would talk about them, share them. Nina already enjoyed hearing every detail of Adele's present adventures. In fact, Adele would soon be returning from a picnic with Nina's admirers, Jack Astor and Fotheringale. Nina grew cheerful in anticipation of the two chatting about that. The moment she finished the chapter she was reading, she would go into Adele's room to wait for her.

Mrs. De Bonnard was also alert for Adele's return. Hearing her coming in, humming as she ran up the stairs, her mother, pleased at those happy sounds, rushed to her youngest daughter's bedroom. Her first words were a contented "I heard you laughing at the doorway, Delly. Who was amusing you? Fotheringale? He seems much taken with you. Even Jack Astor in our chat yesterday was very complimentary about you."

Adele's face showed pleasure at that. But next moment she was abruptly crestfallen, saying sadly, "They're making do with me until Nina is better. Then I'll be pushed aside. She's already talking about joining them for tea. Soon she'll be taking my place in our daily rides."

"It will be all right," Mrs. De Bonnard soothed. "The two of you will jointly receive the visitors."

Adele shook her head. "You know that won't happen." The young lady was silent for a moment, ambivalent, fearing to reveal her feelings, and then she broke out with "Oh Mama! I can't bear being pushed back into oblivion again! I love Nina, but I can't keep up with her. Yesterday at Millie's party—you should have seen me. I was much sought after. I never had a proper season. Before I had a chance to discover who I was, Jordan came. And whatever I was to be was stunted. I became his."

"Forget that man!" erupted from Mrs. De Bonnard in such anguish that Nina, already on her way to chat on the veranda she and Adele shared, was near enough to come running at her mother's cry. But at the door she paused as Mrs. De Bonnard repeated in a softer, more pleading tone, "Forget that man."

"How can I forget Jordan?" Adele countered. "He is always in my heart. Only meeting other gentlemen dulls some of his claims. In fact, at the party yesterday I almost forgot him. I was surrounded by admirers—oh, to a lesser extent than Nina, but I felt somewhat what it must be to be her. And it was exhilarating! I never felt so important. But all that will go, for you know, you *know*, Mama, once Nina begins socializing, I'll be pushed back into her shadow. She blots me out . . . like a sun."

"You don't have to be Nina. You are special in your own way."

"I don't really want to be Nina, for she doesn't appreciate being praised as I do. I enjoy every minute of my success—if only she will let me have a little more of it."

"She will. She will. Everything will be just fine."

"Mama, how can you fool yourself like that! You know the problems we'll be facing the moment Nina starts going out again. Mrs. Windsor has spread the most vicious remarks about the cause of Nina's illness!"

Her mother crumpled onto the settee, in sort of a heap, softly acknowledging the truth of that. "Yes, it is just as I feared. Mr. Van Reyden has spoken out of turn. And Elvira has seized on that and spread the worst possible rumors. Which we shall have to face once Nina is ready to go out and take on this situation. But we can handle them. Although with that and Bobby's intrusions as a distraction, regrettably, I admit your season will be . . . damaged. Heavens, as much as I love Nina, and she is in my heart's core, I have to admit she creates turmoil." Mrs. De Bonnard sighed deeply, not knowing which daughter to protect first. Adele's staring at her with tears in her blue eyes decided the matter, and her mother said softly, "Perhaps the two of us could visit your father's relatives down south. It will be fresh territory, and the rumors probably haven't reached there yet. Yes! Let's do it!" She put on her cheery, confident voice. "Didn't you once say you wanted the adventure of traveling?"

"That was Nina," Adele said, forlornly. "And I don't want to leave here! Not now when I have all these friends. What I want is—" Abruptly Adele was silent. Her mother's expression had stopped the words in her mouth. Both women knew what had been on the point of being said, and Adele began to cry for nearly saying it, while her mother's eyes were shiny with unshed tears.

Outside the door, Nina, her face paler than it had been since she'd begun her recuperation, stepped back and fled to her room, where she put into words what they could not, whispering, "They want me to leave."

After an hour of pacing and defending herself with remarks such as: "But I was planning for us, as sisters, to go to parties together—as a team. I wouldn't block her out! Other women around me compete. Miss Richards. Even Lucy Perkens. I'm not the only society young lady that the gentlemen pay attention to. Besides, I've already left Oceana for Adele once before. Why didn't she use that time to have her season?"

But next minute she'd answered that question herself. "She couldn't because of Jordan. And I'm the one who brought him into her life!"

What was the point of these weak defenses? Nina knew from the moment she'd heard Adele crying and the concern in her mother's voice that she could do no less than leave.

For the next hour Nina, having decided what to do, planned where to go. As much as she still wished to go out west, that trip had to be postponed. Outdoor exploring would need too much energy for a lady still convalescing. Oceana was a possibility, but before long Adele and the rest of them would be coming, and she would just have to leave again. Nina could not keep running away as if she were some kind of pariah. There had to be someplace to go that would be right for her and right for her family.

As if in answer to her dilemma, Nina looked down at the George Eliot novel she was currently reading and thought: *England!* Yes, she exclaimed to herself with a sigh of relief, she would visit England. Surely that would put enough distance between her and all the people she wished never to see again—from Bobby to Jordan Windsor and, particularly, Mrs. Windsor. What were the rumors that Mrs. Windsor was spreading about her that had so overcome her mother and Adele? Nina frowned. Concentrating on that lady, she remembered Mrs. Windsor and her friends in Philadelphia. Weren't they on a crusade to prove that a young lady was pregnant simply because she was indisposed? That must be their usual charge—which meant that's what they were attaching to her as well. Oh stars! She could not immediately leave, after all. First she would have to make one more appearance to prove by her slimness that she was not in the family way. Pacing, Nina considered. Was that sufficient? And she decided it was not. She had to go beyond a defensive move. She needed an offensive strike that would quickly give everyone the impression that London was her great opportunity. To accomplish that required showing a great desire to meet the Prince and

Princess of Wales, not to mention Jennie Churchill, and even Lillie Langtry. Especially essential was making Adele and Mama believe that so they would not feel guilty for wanting her gone. Yes, yes, they must be completely convinced—to the point of rejoicing with her that she was going to a better place. Except for heaven, there could be no more exclusive place than London. And if Nina remembered correctly, Mrs. De Bonnard at least had some entry in the latter locale. She was always talking about her young American friend, Louisa Collins, who had gone there, married a nobleman, and become Lady Moncrief. Amazing how things fell into place. Lady Moncrief would be the one essential key to making Nina's move not only believable, but even enviable.

Planning her campaign as if she were Napoleon, Nina sat down at the desk and outlined her course of action. First she would persuade her mother to write to Lady Moncrief and subtly suggest how much a pleasure it would be for her to have a visit from a total stranger. Well, that could be phrased better. Her mother would know how to put it. Next, her mother must spread the word to the ladies with the longest tongues that Nina was going to mix with royalty, and add as an aside that a Worth gown was being made for Nina's presentation to the Queen. Whether that presentation was possible, Nina didn't know. All that mattered was that everyone else see her new destination as a coup of major magnitude so there would be no possibility that anyone would ever believe Nina did not really want to go: not the ladies and gentlemen of New York and Oceana society, not the particular gentlemen who had pretended to care for her and humiliated her instead, not any member of her family, and, most of all, not even herself.

Twenty

*I*n *London Nina* De Bonnard became yet another person. In America she had had a series of personas. She had gone from being a sister and daughter to a young belle to a femme fatale to a madcap searching for her next prank to a writer of some praise and then an invalid, lost in her body's pain and her mind's confusion. On the long voyage to England, she was a languid convalescent gaining strength by resting on a deck chair. And now in England she was the American lady, with all the responsibility of America's faults and acts on her graceful, silk-encased shoulders. Often she attempted to shrug that off and be just Nina. But to the English, she was an American. Regardless of her father's income and her mother's standing at home, she had no standing in England. She was, after all, a commoner. In the Old World, titles were all that entitled one to respect.

Lady Louisa Moncrief was accepted because she had married a nobleman, but even she was still viewed as an invader. Her ladyship explained her adopted countrymen to Nina. "After fifteen years, they still assume I grew up in a wigwam. At a recent archery contest, my name was entered. The host simply wouldn't accept that I'd never used a bow and arrow, convinced that all Americans are trained by Indians! Entre nous, Lady Randolph Churchill doesn't help since she looks like an Indian herself, with her dark hair and strong features. Thank heavens I have blond hair and you reddish." She paused for a hurried breath. "Another thing expected is that we're all rich as Croesus. I am constantly put down for fabulous sums for every lady's charity, until I put it to them that my husband, Lord Moncrief, has full charge of my money, and then the hostess has second thoughts, knowing that an Englishman who marries an American woman for her money will not part with a penny. The truth is that Alfy just wanted a comfortable life. Just as he has a steward to care for his estates, he has me to manage our money and pay his gambling bills. I assure him things are going swimmingly, and he is content. Englishmen are accustomed to delegating and being deferred to; once a wife understands that, she can control him by pretending to defer and taking over all responsibility. Unlike American men, who always want to take over themselves. I'm raising my son to be just like his father."

She took a deeper breath, during which Nina wondered why she was being told all this. But Lady Moncrief was direct to a fault and, without waiting to be asked, replied, "I assume you're here to marry an English lord. I know you are wealthy, extremely popular, and not satisfied with American men, having jilted so many of them. You want a lord you can control. I have the perfect candidate. And I shall enjoy watching you outshine some of these English ladies who see us as upstarts!"

Nina considered inserting a denial, but then shrugged her shoulders. She had not come to marry, but she would not be averse to having an English lord or two at her feet. Besides, she discovered shortly upon her arrival that it was pointless to attempt to get a word in edgewise with Louisa, who talked as if she'd been locked up in a box for several years and had to gush out all her thoughts upon release. Part of her loquacity was due to finding a "fellow American" who understood her. Obviously, understanding was a quality that was universally desired. Growing up in Oceana, Nina had looked for people to understand *her*. In New York she didn't care whether anybody understood her or not. Then, gradually, she had begun understanding everyone— starting with her father and then her mother and then her sister—understanding, understanding to the point of once more sentencing herself to exile. Therefore, Nina did not see why presently she should discriminate against Louisa and not make the attempt to understand her as well. What she realized about Louisa was that she just wanted the appearance of an audience.

So she supplied that, pretending to listen while engaging in her own thoughts. Yet after a week of steady chatter, Nina was ready to do anything to get away from Louisa, even meeting Lord Nelson Brindsley, who was Louisa's candidate for her hand.

Since it was June, the season was practically over, with only one or two important social events still to come. Some of the Mayfair set had already retired to Bath, Brighton, or their country estates. Lady Moncrief bemoaned that Nina had come so late but, regarding the spectacular young lady in her peacock blue gown with a crown of peacock feathers framing her blazing hair, she was certain Nina De Bonnard would not need more time to make her mark.

Lord Brindsley was quick to raise his monocle at her entrance. When assured by Lady Moncrief that she was an heiress of no small fortune, he became Nina's constant attendant. The trouble was that with her appeal and the rumor of her wealth, other English lords began attending her as well. That had his lordship and Lady Moncrief quickly conferring—and settling the problem of competition in a trice. Nina was not to remain in London. Rather, Lady Moncrief and Nina De Bonnard were invited to spend the end of June and beginning of July at his lordship's country seat.

Nina did not wish to make herself so exclusive. But since her hostess had already accepted for her, the young American visitor could only grin and bare her complaints about his lordship to her diary. Lord Nelson Brindsley was amusing but not intentionally so. Further, the statement that he was almost a double of the Prince of Wales, she discovered, upon seeing His Highness, could only be considered a compliment by the English, who obviously preferred mutton faces and sheepish manners. As for his lordship's conversation, it carried British understatement to the point of an undertone. So silent was he throughout their first dance that he was almost nonexistent until realizing that something had to be said, he granted her a haughty nod and one word: "Pleasure." Whether that referred to his pleasure or hers, Nina was uncertain, so she murmured something indistinct to leave him equally confused. He did not learn from her lesson but, proving his obtuseness, continued his obliqueness. Later, while other gentlemen were complimenting her on her beauty and peacock gown, he blurted out, "Shot a peacock, once." "Why?" Nina asked, and that had him retreating back into shocked silence. The British never needed an excuse to shoot a bird. Afterwards, she complained to Louisa that his lordship's Vandyke beard came to a point sharper than his conversation . . . and, parenthetically, that his pointy beard tickled when they danced.

Louisa would not be deterred. If forced, his lordship would trim his beard. Nothing must stop this planned alliance. "I have already written of its possibility to your mother and received a letter of encouragement. She says, in effect, that she had hopes of just *such a match!*"

Nina frowned. The last thing she wanted to do was be Lady Brindsley in permanent exile from home and those she loved. That would be carrying understanding to a fault. Actually she could see that fault opening at her feet—and regretted having gotten herself into a situation out of which she'd have to make quite a leap to land safely and home free. Not till she viewed his father's estate, Mayberry Castle, did some of Lord Brindsley's charm to the English finally become evident to Nina. She had known he was the son of the Duke of Mayberry, for Louisa talked of nothing else and the invitation had come from the Duchess of Mayberry herself, but she had not been aware of the grandeur that title imposed until she stood and gazed at the massive Mayberry Castle. It showed what impostures the faux castles in Oceana were—giving suggestions of past grandeur with present plumbing and recent shine. The real thing just *was*—holding the majesty of antiquity in every stone. The turrets were real, where archers must have stood to defend their lord's domain. The dungeons were real with actual chains and locks. Nor were the grounds neat parks, but a countryside with forests and a private lake and even a private village. Within, the castle continued to fit the authentic with suits of armor before massive fireplaces and generations of portraits in the family galleries. Nina was awestruck. Gradually, Lord Brindsley, himself, in his own surroundings looked more imposing; even his monosyllabic speech grew more pregnant with possible nuances.

The other guests were the duke's friends: the local squire and his rotund wife, and Lord Rackenridge and his countess. All four were in their fifties and not exactly the exciting companions Nina had expected to find on an English estate.

She had been hoping for a Lord Byron type with whom she could discuss poetry, or engage in witty conversation. But there was no one svelte and subtle here, but rather suet-faced and senior. The entire party, not to mention several of the servants, looked depressingly like the duke. His Grace, upon hearing that Nina did not gamble and preferred a book to cards, dismissed her not only from his thoughts but from his sight, turning away. The duke's only passion in life was playing for high stakes, with the result that he had not only gambled away most of his negotiable assets but even borrowed heavily from the entailment.

The duke had recently been forced to relinquish the Mayberry jewels to his bank creditors in order to clear his most pressing gambling markers, giving him entry once again not only to the gambling establishments but to the friendly games amongst his friends. The greatest loss of all was of the Mayberry crown, for it had been in the family since the days of King John. And, in private, the duchess often bewailed it.

Those circumstances explained her son's having to lower himself to court an American girl with no title, no history, and, in fact, nothing but a father with plump pockets.

The duchess walked about as if she were smelling something, particularly when she saw Nina. Her words to the young American were just barely this side of civility, and often slid over. A small woman, Her Grace had an air of expecting curtsies whenever she appeared; Nina was amused by her. She made Mrs. Windsor seem almost human. "I'd love for Bobby to see her. He would lower her dignity a notch or two," Nina said with a laugh.

"Bobby who?" Lady Moncrief asked.

"Oh, bite your tongue. If you even mention him, he has a curious tendency of popping up." And turning to laugh at her own dread, Nina found herself staring at a face in the distance that could only be Bobby Van Reyden's.

She put up her hands to ward off the sight. He had not yet spotted her.

Louisa insisted she be told why Nina was turning white. Did

she feel a recurrence of her illness? In response, Nina could only point at the gentleman walking with Lord Brindsley toward the maze.

"Oh, that is Mr. Van Reyden, who recently arrived in London," Louisa said. "He often comes here for the yachting races. Always well received. Belongs to most of the exclusive gentlemen's clubs. The secret of his being so much in demand is that he not so secretly pays off many of the lords' debts. Did it again this time with Lord Brindsley. Further, he took the duke to the races and banked him. Small wonder he's so welcome here. The duchess wanted to invite a young English lady for his entertainment, but he assured her she was all the entertainment he could possibly want."

"Good grief, I'm returning to London! That man has made it his mission to pursue me!"

Louisa laughed, assuming that Nina was jesting. When it was clear she was not, her ladyship just shrugged, concluding, "A little competition will make Nelson come up to the mark much quicker."

"You don't know Bobby. When he's around, everyone and everything spins off its axis."

"But I do know him. My family knew his family in America. You mistake the fellow. I recall his always being eager to lend a hand to everyone. Been rather helpful to me already. Entre nous, dear Nina, I've a certain gentleman I wished to include in our gathering. Lord Brindsley quite pigheadedly refused, wanting no more gentlemen about. But Van Reyden persuaded him that distracting the chaperone, me, was a smart move if unsupervised time was wanted with a certain American lady. As a result I have my young gentleman here to keep me amused."

Nina groaned. "Bobby always arranges things. But now he has you in his debt and, believe me, he'll want a favor in turn."

Louisa looked uncomfortable.

"Ah, I see. He's already demanded a quid pro quo."

"It's a very minor favor. Just to hand you this letter." And she did. It was, with Bobby's usual use of overstatement, his promise not to harass her. Could they just meet as "old friends"?

After that Nina was not surprised when a servant came with a gentleman's request for a meeting in the rose garden.

At the point of deciding against complying, Nina had second thoughts. It would be best to see Bobby privately because the English would not understand some of the choice things she was going to say to him. Bobby had a way of making her forget she was a lady, and the duchess was already eyeing her with grave suspicions of that fact.

Sitting on a marble bench in the rose garden, Nina looked up at approaching footsteps and saw not Bobby Van Reyden but Jordan Windsor.

Assuming it was another hallucination, she simply stared until he was directly before her.

It *was* Jordan.

She gazed at him in such astonishment that Jordan could not resist reacting to it. "Yes, isn't it amazing how we keep bumping into each other? One could assume fate is drawing us together."

"Say rather Nemesis."

He grinned. "Sharp-tongued as ever. I'm delighted to see you've recovered your wits. The last time I saw you—"

Nina jumped up, not wanting to bring to mind that embarrassing occasion when, according to Adele, she had made such a spectacle of herself. "The less said about that moment the better. In fact, if you were a gentleman, you would not allude to it!"

Jordan was not smiling anymore. His eyes were puzzled, on the point of anger. "But how could I not remember it. That moment is all that gives me hope. I relive it over and over. . . ."

"Good God, have you no sense of decency!"

"You regret your moment of weakness, then?" he asked, grimly.

"Of course! But I hope you understand I was not myself."

"Ah, that is to be your excuse. Anytime you show your true emotions, we are to forget it. Well, I won't forget it. You wanted me there, close to you. You clung to me! We were both at long last honest about our feelings for each other. And yet, directly after, you denied me the right to see you again. Well, this time you'll have to deny me to my face."

"I not only deny you, I deny any memory of what you are saying. The last time we had any conversation was at the Windsor ball when you accused me of burning out . . . which was rather prophetic of you—sensing I was soon to be ill."

"We, in essence, *pledged* each other," Jordan insisted, speaking over her words.

"I recall no such pledge. Unless you're making a curiously inappropriate reference to that idiotic Romeo and Juliet scene we played in Oceana when you were good enough to call me a 'yacht girl.' And if you are still continuing with that infamous proposal—"

Jordan, in a whirl of astonishment, broke in. "But we had passed that point! You must remember. I had apologized for that, explained it all to you. Not only orally but in that original letter. You must have read it. Blast it, you must have read one of the letters or notes I sent you. The Elizabeth Barrett Browning poems? The Whitman poems? I didn't send flowers because Van Reyden was filling your house, but I sent you, with each note, a single white silk rose."

Nina was quiet, listening to him now. Something was echoing in her memory but she repelled it, sticking to what she knew to be the truth. "I was told Bobby and you were in my room *laughing* at my condition while I was going in and out of consciousness."

"Dear God in heaven! How could I laugh at your illness when the sight of your wan face cut my heart in half!"

"Pity is just as bad," she inserted, although shaken by his certitude.

"If there is anyone to pity, pity me—for opening my heart to you as I have never done to any other person. Pity me for feeling my life was being torn up by the roots because you were so ill. Ask Dick! Ask anyone! I waited a block away on the bench for Dick's daily reports. I wasn't permitted to come near you again. But I was near you. Although stopped from physically being next to you, my thoughts, my love, were with you every moment."

Nina turned away from his ardent eyes and concentrated on the fan in her hands. She used it to stop the heat his words had called to her face. And she thought. She remembered. There had been that something about Adele's attitude while she'd talked about Jordan's presence. But if Jordan was telling her the truth, it would be necessary for her mother to be in on the conspiracy. "No one told me you had sent me anything. And the proof that you are once again manipulating me is that I had no letters, no notes from you—not a single message!"

Jordan groaned and came close to her, in his agitation forgetting to keep a gentlemanly distance or address her politely. Rather, he broke out with "Confound you, Nina. I put *in your hands* a thick letter that took a blasted week to write, that reviewed our entire relationship, step by step. But that main letter wasn't all. I sent followup notes referring to it. A single white silk rose accompanied each one till I'd reached a dozen. Ask Jeffers. And I sent other things as well that I mentioned in the notes. Novels. Anthologies. The last was the new collection of Whitman poems. It was wrapped in a silk scarf that I picked because it was the exact golden color of your hair."

Nina gasped. She remembered the golden scarf. How could he know about the poems being wrapped in it—if both had not been sent by him? But to believe him meant to disbelieve Adele! Not Delly. Not Delly, she prayed, and in answer, next moment, a thought came that exonerated her sister. In relief, Nina said coldly, "You are lying to me now to my face. You say you gave me a letter during a time when I was too sick to remember, but if that is so, where is that letter? Why do I not have it amongst all the other messages of concern from my friends? *All of which* were given to me, put on my desk so I could respond during my rehabilitation. Rather, I believe you were curiously remiss in your correspondence." Upon seeing the effect her words were having on him, she temporized, "Perhaps you meant to give me a letter and forgot to do so."

He was fuming. Not willing to accept her face-saving compromise. "You were holding my letter in your hands," Jordan insisted unflinchingly. "You had it as I was pulled out of the room by your servants at your mother's instruction. But it was not I who upset you, as your mother assumed—it was Van Reyden!"

Something fluttered in her memory. Nina felt that whatever it was verified him, but the thought dissolved as she reached for it. Staring at her so closely, Jordan sensed a softening in her conviction and in reaction took a quick step toward her. But Nina stepped back in alarm and said quickly, "Whatever you say . . . just possibly might have some truth in it. Perhaps Mama and Adele were trying to protect me from any further connection with you and confiscated your letters. I'll write and ask them. But what is the point at this point? We'll assume you wrote. Gallantries are your forte, so you probably did send the poems, and I thank you for them. But where does that leave us? Except where we were before my illness: at an impasse."

There was a finality in her tone that shook Jordan; it overwhelmed him. And she continued, turning to him with an expression one would give to a memory, wistful and sad, as she concluded softly, "There is too much in the past between us. For the present let us keep it in the past and be civil to each other . . . at least for the short time we are here together."

She was moving away in dismissal when she was stopped by his holding on to her. "No," he whispered with a quiet vehemence that could not but get her attention, "You can't be that heartless."

"If the truth is heartless, then so be it. We must turn to truth! There have been too many games and too much distrust between us. Even talking together like this is wrong! I've explained to you countless times and will do so one last time to make it crystal clear. I could never hurt Adele. I left Oceana for Adele. I left New York to give her a chance to flourish out of my hurtful presence. Would I do all that and then, for a passing dalliance, wound her once again? If you were my life's mate and I loved you past all distraction I would still turn away from you . . . for her." And turn away she did, almost running down the garden path, but then he reached her and led her in the opposite direction to another garden path into the maze to continue their conversation.

"I *am* your life's mate. And I will never let you turn away from me again—not for anyone, not my brother, not your sister, not even when you put an ocean between us."

Nina was in the center of the maze before her amazement cleared enough to protest Jordan's maneuver. At the next moment she was being seated on the bench within the marble Grecian gazebo. Gathering her wits together, Nina got up to leave.

He stopped her with a single plea. "Just one moment more! I brought you here where we won't be interrupted to give you something to read."

"This is hardly the moment for poems!"

He was reaching into his pocket and pulled out an envelope. "It is a letter. And, I swear to you, after you read it, if you still wish never to see me, I'll let you go," he pledged.

"Is this the letter you say you already gave me?" she taunted.

"Ah, Nina, Nina, why won't you ever give me the benefit of the doubt! You must remember some of our closeness . . . some of the things we said when we were together. . . ."

Nina sat back down on the bench and was quiet for a moment and then admitted, "Moments come back. But they could just be dreams from my delirium."

"Was I in them?"

"Yes. You're talking to me. We're standing by the sea . . . and then we're not, but I still hear the sound of the surf," she laughed at her confusion. "It's a jumble. But I feel you near. And I hear the sea."

He laughed with her. "But that's right! I spoke of our going to Oceana and pledging ourselves before the sea. And the sound of the ocean—please, please remember—must have been the beat of my heart as I held you against me."

Nina started; a sliver of that memory, tantalizingly close, made her almost succumb to the plea in his eyes and the sound of her own heart, but she pulled away at the last minute, groaning in despair. "I don't know where I stand with anybody anymore!"

"You stand with me as you always did, from first sight, in the very center of my heart."

Reacting to that with some of her old hauteur, Nina exclaimed, "I hope you're not playing games again. That sounded dangerously close to the remarks from our days at Oceana. I no longer have the need to duel and tease and taunt. When I felt myself at death's door, I began to think of life's purpose. I don't know what mine is, but it is not to be insincere."

"Dear God in heaven! I say I love you and you think I'm insincere! I've done nothing but follow you about since Oceana, waiting for a sign from you. I even followed you to England, and you think I've done all this because I am not in earnest?"

"Maybe you are. Maybe I want you to be. But . . ." She looked down at the letter in her hands and quickly looked away. Only one word was written on the envelope: *Nina*. Offense that he dared to address her so personally in a written epistle vied with her desire to see what the letter said but, next minute, getting back her resolution, she shook her head, pushing away her curiosity at the same time as she pushed away the letter toward Jordan. "I explained to you about Adele."

"And that is all that is standing between us?" he asked with such a fierce look that she sensed a trap and carefully sidestepped.

"That and other parts of our past."

"Those other things in the past may be prologue. But mainly it is Adele that stands in our way, isn't it?"

Forced to answer, she admitted that Adele had always been her main concern. The moment she said it, he burst into a cry of triumph. "Look at the letter! Look down! Don't you know the script?"

Warily, Nina took another look and recognized with a jolt her sister's handwriting. "It's from Adele," she said with a gasp.

"Yes, from Adele," he responded with satisfaction. "I believe she will explain everything better than I can. I'll leave you to read it on your own." And, bowing, he calmly took his leave of her, turning back at the entrance to add, "And then, and *then*, dear heart—we shall meet again to talk about our future."

Twenty-one

O vercome with confusion yet filled with expectations, Nina opened her letter. She had just determined that it contained above seven sheets written on both sides when Jordan suddenly came rushing back. Astonished, Nina was about to question him when he made it clear that they would soon be joined by others.

"I wanted you to have a chance to read it without interruption," he added in regret.

Quickly Nina was putting the letter away into her lavender reticule, when she was once more overcome by surprise. It was Louisa and Bobby walking arm in arm, chatting conspiratorially.

Sitting down next to her, sotto voce, Jordan said, "Here comes the snake, making this our Eden complete."

Nina could not help but smile, for their feelings about Bobby were in accord.

Entering the gazebo, the two newcomers were agitated enough at seeing Nina and Jordan sitting together on the bench, but seeing them sharing a laugh that looked near to a secret understanding, giving them an aura of being joined, caused cries of dismay.

"How the heck did you get invited to this shindig?" Bobby demanded, running up to Jordan. "I told Nelly boy—no other *Americans*!"

Before either Jordan or Nina could reply, or do more than rise, Louisa added to the furor by groaning and calling out, "Oh, help heaven! How is it possible! I haven't even introduced you two and he's already your *admirer*!"

Nina looked at Louisa's mortified face and at Jordan's mocking shrug and felt a flash of understanding. "*You* are Louisa's *friend*?" she asked directly.

"I was at one time. I sent a note asking if she could arrange for me to be invited to the duke's."

"You let me think . . ." Louisa began, red-faced and silencing herself. It was quite obvious what he'd let her think.

"I did not," Jordan denied. "Any such recurrence we both know has long since been impossible." Jordan turned to Nina, saying earnestly, "I'd once rescued her from a difficult situation. This was to be a mere repayment of one generosity with another." He turned back to Louisa. "Isn't that the case?"

Louisa remembered her pride. "Of course. That's what I assumed." But her resentment broke through her pretended indifference. "Then if it wasn't to see me again, why did you want to come here so desperately?"

Laughing, Bobby supplied the answer. "Nina. It's always Nina. If I had known your friend was Jordan, I would never have persuaded Nelly to let him come. Not that it matters. Maybe it's good to have him here for our final challenge. He thinks he has a chance with Nina, but no one does because she's mine."

Louisa objected. "She's not yours. Nor yours," she said threateningly to Jordan. "She is going to marry Lord Brindsley."

Both Jordan and Bobby turned in unison and anger toward Nina at that pronouncement.

Nina, using her fan to ward off their glares, said casually, "I'm not marrying his lordship. Nor do I belong to any of you. Would you all kindly desist from making my future an open topic. Have none of you any delicacy?"

Whereupon Nina walked off in a huff.

The three remained to argue their positions, but without the lady present there could be no resolution. And when Nina was seen walking back to the castle with Lord Brindsley, both American men were bitter and brimming over with plans to separate and rescue the American woman from English usurpation.

Nina was dressing for dinner, keeping Adele's letter close by. It was so thick Nina decided to save it for after the evening meal, when she would have time to savor it: an after-dinner sweet, she promised herself with quiet pleasure. Knowing from a previous warning by Louisa that it was a serious faux pas to be tardy for the formal march into dinner, Nina rushed in order to be on time. She was curious about who would be her escort, only to discover in disappointment the sudden appearance of three lady companions, which led to Nina's marching in alone at the end. Further, she was seated beneath the salt, which gave her an inkling of the duchess's estimation of her worth.

As for the duchess, she was still recovering from the humiliation of having to entertain *four* Americans. One, she could tolerate; two endure; three, rise to the challenge of—but four was an invasion!

That Van Reyden young man did not even know when he was being snubbed, her grace concluded, irritated by the way he laughed at her every remark. He continually demanded that she repeat what she had just uttered, ordering silence so everyone could get an earful.

"I am not on exhibition, Mr. Van Reyden," she objected. "I do not speak for your enjoyment, nor for that of your friends."

"Call me, Bobby," Bobby urged in delight. "Isn't she great! Just as if a picture, one of those Van Dycks, jumped off the walls and started talking!"

After a time the duchess, unaccustomed to such open admiration, began to enjoy Bobby's attentions. She could not help playing up to him a bit. By the end of the evening she'd unbent enough to call him Bobby and to grant his wish of planning some entertainment for the "whole group," which he assured her would be "great fun."

When they had gathered for a game of cards, Jordan took the opportunity to move discreetly next to Nina and ask if she had read the letter. She explained her need to have time to absorb it, and he urged her to read the news at first opportunity. His use of the word *news* made Nina eager to retire. Much to the disappointment of the gentlemen, she did so forthwith.

And it was good news. Great news. Overwhelmingly positive news in fact: Adele was engaged to Dick Windsor!

By the third reading Nina was over the shock and accepting the wonder of the announcement. Dick was apparently the perfect man for Adele. He had all the good qualities and none of the bad qualities of Jordan. Adele had found herself sought after by several young men after Nina's departure, but while this experience was pleasant, she soon began to realize that each gentleman was lacking in some way. They were not as entertaining or charming as Jordan. She almost stopped going out, but Dick would not be denied. He listened to her and agreed that Jordan made all the men look like nothing and confided he'd always felt he was nothing next to Jordan. They shared that sense of not being able to live up to their brother or sister, and from that revelation began to share other private thoughts as well. They began to relive all the times they'd played on the beach from childhood, how they'd always chosen each other as partners. It struck them, with satisfaction, how much they both enjoyed each other's company. Even at the Centennial their common interests had been marked. Dick was concerned about her going for the cause into neighborhoods where even the police would not enter without being in full force. He began making it a policy to escort her on her assignments. And before he knew it, he'd been drawn into the cause himself. Shortly, Dick became everyone's favorite brother. The very next step—would Nina believe it—was that Dick joined the suffrage movement. Wasn't that clear evidence of his unselfishness and the correctness of their union? "At first Mama was concerned I might be looking for a junior Jordan, but once she saw us together for several outings, she acknowledged what we have finally understood and what was there before us—all this time! We are clearly meant for each other."

Nina's eyes were overflowing with tears of relief. She put down the letter and savored the news. Then, little by little, she began to think what else this union meant. First, that she had not ruined Adele's future, but rather had done the correct thing to leave her to have her chance. Second, that Adele and Dick had somehow cured the sadness and gulf between the De Bonnard and Windsor families. Acknowledging that the two had the same chord of innocence and goodness, she realized that only they, in their innocence, like angels treading where the rest feared, could have effected that unity. Nina was in agreement with her mother's postscript: "This is a marriage made in heaven."

Putting down the letter to absorb all she had read before continuing, Nina struggled for composure but, realizing that no one was there to observe, allowed herself to bubble over in gusts of giggles and tears. When she was spent, she took up the letter with a fixed smile on her lips and a sense of perfect satisfaction, that sometimes life or fate or God could do it right.

Adele had explained the reason for her entrusting this letter to Jordan: It was a sign that she had finally gotten him out of her heart. Aside from a momentary pang that he seemed to be so delighted to be rid of her, Adele acknowledged at last that she and Jordan would never have been happy together. Further, since he was to be her brother-in-law, and since she had Dick, she could now admit that Jordan had written *several* letters to Nina and that she had burned them—unread, of course. But she had done it for Nina's own good. She had not admitted this even to Dick, and certainly not to Jordan. Rather, it was an act she could not even write now without blushing and having to beg Nina for her understanding, which she knew Nina would always give. To recompense Jordan, Adele gave him this letter to deliver to Nina in person. Wasn't it amazing how quickly Jordan decided he had business in England? He would beat the mail, he insisted, and she agreed, feeling that she owed him the letter, having destroyed so many of his. Adele's last line was her hope that Nina would be as happy for them as she and Dick were for themselves.

Having read the letter enough to know it fair by heart, Nina offered a prayer to God that nothing would ruin this one happy union. A negative thought struck as she lay on her bed that a Windsor and a De Bonnard, coming from such unhappy couplings, needed every good wish to succeed. But the next moment Nina chastised herself for ruining this perfect moment by worrying that the perfection might not continue until happily ever after.

The following day, after breakfast, Jordan and she stepped aside to rejoice privately over the happy news. He had no reservations whatsoever about the bliss of the union of their brother and sister. And with his confidence about it, she allowed herself to trust in that hope.

"You realize this means," Jordan concluded with an air of elation, "that nothing stands between us anymore."

Nina would not go that far. "We have had so many twists and turns in our adventures together, I suggest we start fresh and see who the other is and how we really feel without having to take into account past deeds."

Jordan shook his head. "Why can't you simply act as you're feeling!"

"You'll have to be patient until I trust it . . . and trust you."

Jordan's dark eyes were begging her to come into his arms. He considered taunting her with being too cautious, a cowardly little wren instead of the bold seabird he always assumed her to be. But she was waiting for his one misstep. It was a sign of his deepening love for her that he nodded, caring enough to wait for her to catch up to the pitch of his feelings.

"I'll woo you, Miss De Bonnard, step by step. But at the end we shall arrive at the same destination together. Because that's where we've both been heading from the beginning."

The one topic about which Nina and Jordan found themselves of one mind was Bobby. When informed that Mr. Van Reyden and the duchess were closeted making plans for a special surprise, they wondered whether they should warn the duchess that she would regret allowing him to take over any arrangements, only to agree that her grace probably would not listen to them.

As for Louisa, Nina had to endure her alternating between acting cold and giving her a scold for stealing Jordan. So any sympathy Nina might have felt for her evaporated under that constant assault. Time and again Nina attempted to explain: "I had no idea Mr. Windsor was an old *friend* of yours. What would you have me do? His feelings, like yours, have evidently altered. Didn't you tell me about *several* other gentlemen who had your favor?"

Louisa could not deny that. She had expected Jordan to have affairs with other women after her, but what riled, Louisa privately acknowledged, was that this gentleman who had previously been impervious to any genuine feeling for other women, such as herself, had become such a lovesick follower of this young lady. Moreover, there was the concern that if Nina responded to Jordan, what would happen to her remunerative agreement with Lord Brindsley? So Louisa would not be stilled, warning Nina, for her own good, and for her ladyship's own relief, that when Jordan seemed most sincere, he was the most to be feared. Why else, did she assume, had he held the record for broken hearts?

With a tolerant sign, Nina agreed to take the warning to heart, and then her heart promptly forgot it.

For Nina and Jordan, the days at the castle began to take on fairy-tale dimensions. Together they roamed through the maze, delighting in seeking out new paths to their Grecian temple. Together they rode through the grounds. Together they sat at the tea table and side by side after dinner for the evening entertainments. All in all, they were reluctant to be apart.

Often they engaged in pleasurable rowings across the lake. On their last one Nina was dressed in a green sheer voile dress with trailing sleeves that fluttered in the breeze as Jordan handed her into the rowboat. He bowed her in with such obvious pleasure it seemed as if she were acquiescing to escaping with him into a dream as Jordan rowed them across the lake to a small island known as the Willows. It was surrounded by weeping willows whose curtainlike green branches shielded anyone entering beneath from reality, revealing a special world, plucked unfinished from the dawn of each day to exist just for them.

This is our world, their glances said. When we leave, it will still be ours, for we will take it with us.

Jordan rowed, never looking away from Nina across from him. Rowed and watched. Then he put up the oars and let the boat drift under the protective willow shield, where they banked. The only sounds in there were those of far-off birds and of the breezes through the willow windbells transforming them into soft lovers' sighs. The only sights were the willows themselves, for the sun could only randomly penetrate the boughs. In the open lake Nina had been holding a golden parasol, but once ducking under the weeping willows, she lowered it to rest behind her where it collected all the refracted rays and centered them on her sun-infused hair.

Jordan drew his breath and exhaled it slowly, trailing breathy words: "I'll 'make me a willow cabin at your gate, and call upon my soul within the house,' " he began quoting, and she smiled and encouraged him, as he softly carried on, "Holla your dear name whilst standing on guard; till all the world shouts, Nina De Bonnard!"

Nina shook her head at his misquote of *Twelfth Night* and her presence in it but was silent, watching him rise and come closer to her, carefully balancing each step.

"You're going to capsize us," she warned, but her voice was low and not much concerned. She even smiled as he leaned closer and kissed her sun-warmed lips and gathered her into his arms. They lay together side by side in the boat with the leaf canopy above, through which the sun in serrated rays stroked the couple as they kissed again. In rapture. In reconciliation. In union. In love.

But they kept their love on the same uplifted, enchanted level as their isle. Kisses that grew too warm were cut off with soft laughs. It was all a promise not of present gratification but forever faithfulness as, kiss by kiss and look by look, they made a willow cage to hold their joint hearts and keep them safe through all the blows of fate to come.

But there was one more twist ahead that was not foreseen. Returning from their outing, they entered the castle, rushing to avoid being obviously late for tea and give cause for more comment than they had already occasioned. After tea they made an appointment to meet in the garden to say good night properly, and both were anticipating that throughout their conversations with others. Stopping at her room, Nina found a new letter there from Adele. More pleasure! Her cup was running over, Nina thought while opening it, looking forward not only to reading it herself but also to sharing it later with Jordan. But while glancing at the opening page, her smile stiffened in place at her sister's news.

"We have both been shamefully used," Adele wrote with no softening preamble. "For Dick's part, I can only say there's some justification, since he felt himself so abandoned, and since, further, he did not really expect his brother to take him seriously. In any case, he has the advantage of confessing this *shameful, immoral pact* that he and his brother entered into at our lawn party last July. Dick has shown total contrition. He assures me that he often forgot about the 'pact' and had to be reminded by his brother to live up to it. So I have forgiven him.

"But what can one say about his brother, who was old enough to know better! Jordan Windsor deliberately used my feelings to rouse your interest! From the first, assuming you were too jaded with attentions, his plan was to use me to teach you the pain of being passed over. The Pynchot ball was to be his next step of dropping me and turning to you. In gratitude, you were to confess your love—whereupon he would teach you a deserved lesson by jilting you in turn!

"It didn't happen then because you wouldn't accept what he did to me. Your eluding him doubly goaded him to keep coming back to conclude his plan of tossing you aside with a jeer of prior commitment. Dear, dear sister, this selfish man has often attempted to come between us. Even when you were ill he maneuvered his way into your presence and your heart while you were too weak to fend him off. The one benefit of that dreadful fever was that it burned him out of your affections, leaving you free to break away from him and start a new life. Mother is relieved and Father positively rubbing his hands in delight at the news Lady Moncrief has written of your becoming Lady Brindsley and eventually the Duchess of Mayberry. I can't think of anyone who deserves and who looks more as if she ought to be a duchess! Dick says Jordan is still pursuing you. For such an accomplished flirt, I guess he can't admit defeat. Or he might have a more sinister motive that I can't put down on paper and even if you were here could not whisper it. But he is not, I am told, a gentleman who can bear not to have his lust satisfied. He has kept a list of his conquests and still gloats over each one. He proudly told Dick about his time in London as a sought-after, style-setting gallant who didn't consider a season complete until he'd defeated a competitor in that gentleman's favorite sport, captured the affections of a friend's lady, and organized a much-talked-about outing, inviting people he scarcely knew while excluding his closest friends, just to outrage them and amuse himself. So too has he been laughing at us here. I shudder to think how much I once admired him. In conclusion, I warn you to be alert. He is a false gentleman. False to you as he was to me. He has been puppeteer to us all long enough. Thankfully, Dick and I have cut the strings. I pray, my dear, dear sister, that you haven't entangled yourself in an irrevocable way. God bless you, and I hope soon to be sending you congratulations on your engagement to your noble host!"

Her hand shaking, Nina put down the letter carefully and went to the window, looking out at the garden where Jordan and she had pledged to meet for a private rendezvous tonight. She stared at the part of the garden visible below. She could see the huge urn that topped the marble stairs that led toward the hedged enclave. Somewhere beyond that was a marble bench. That was to be their meeting point.

A full hour she waited at the window. It was darkening outside and soon she could no longer see the urn or the marble stairs. Nina was forced to imagine the gentleman waiting on the white marble bench. With each breath, with each echo of her sister's words, with each winged stab of thought, Nina felt an icy persona forming within her and coldly using her own eyes to watch the dusk dissolve into total shadow. No moon came out to reveal whether anyone was waiting. And then, yes, yes! a pinpoint of light, like the point of Jordan's cigarette being flared with each breath. And then it went out. And there was just darkness. At that, Nina closed the shutters and the heavy drapes and retired to her bed to lie down and read the letter through the night.

Twenty-two

Where were you? I waited. Not a message. Not a signal. I felt like a proper fool. The only excuse was that you were ill again, and I didn't know whether to wish for that or not."

"Rather my illness than your humiliation? Is that it?" Nina laughed.

"Well, of course not." He stared at her in confusion. Her face was the same and yet not. "What is it? Why didn't you come to me?"

"Did we have a rendezvous?" Nina asked, horrified, and then laughing at his confusion. "I really can't recall."

"What kind of game are you playing? Is this all I'm worth to you?"

"Forgive me," she said superficially. "I got involved in something else and simply forgot."

He demanded to know what had detained her, and she first said "a book" and then "washing her hair" and then she laughed and said she could not recall exactly what, but she assumed it must have been most important, if she could just recollect what it was, and then smilingly assured him it would come to her "eventually" and walked away before he could do more than bluster after her retreating figure.

She was unavailable the rest of the day, occupied with riding with Lord Brindsley. He confronted her at last in the hall after supper and insisted that she meet him tonight and explain her actions, whereupon she assured him sweetly that she would not fail. He was somewhat appeased, until the hour for the appointment.

Once again she did not appear.

His fury was now unbridled, and he sent her an icy note, which she received with her morning cocoa. She sent him a note in reply explaining simply, "I feared the night air would not agree with my complexion."

Complex, complex Nina! Jordan cursed her inwardly, and outwardly considered leaving. Then he reconsidered, determined to discover the reason for her actions.

The next day was the unveiling of the much awaited special entertainment Bobby had been arranging. Money was scented by those who where always on the scent for it, and excitement by the others in hopes for that. Which left Nina and Jordan on the scent for each other.

Last-minute details were worked out by Lord Brindsley and the duchess in the early afternoon. Nina stayed in her room and then, before dinner, took a stroll in the garden. Dressed in her most becoming violent muslin, she appeared a lady in her first season. When confronted with a now almost frothing Jordan, she looked properly frightened and even retreated as he advanced.

"What *Nina* is this? The inexperienced young 'miss' joining the callous 'flirt' and the mentally vapid 'vamp'? Or are you all just facets of the one main Nina, known throughout Oceana for jilting young man after young man?"

"I have as many facets as a star. Are not you similarly multi-faceted, my dear sir? Even multifaced? Or double-faced?" And her anger broke through for a moment but she quickly camouflaged it with a smile, as if she were teasing, and picking up a white rose from the vase on the way to dinner, gave it to his lordship as he escorted her in.

After which came the formal entertainment.

While waiting for it to begin, Nina sat on the damask divan, pretending to be reading a book of history. Louisa, tired of the coldness between them, sat next to her, attempting to chat. Since Louisa did not need much in the way of encouragement and Nina was polite enough to supply her the necessary sighs and "Oh my"s, Louisa felt she had won Nina back to her side, and, more importantly, to Lord Brindsley's side. All the while Nina was thinking of Jordan's pact with his brother. What especially galled was the memory of Jordan's rowing her across the lake, stroke by stroke, and she leaning forward feasting on the small, intimate smiles Jordan threw her way until she was eating out of his hands, ready to do whatever he asked. And then, almost as if she'd been tipped overboard into the lake, came the cold splash of the letter and its revelation, awakening her out of her dream. Oh yes, he'd tossed her in, while he sat snug and dry at the prow! Interrupting her thoughts of that gentleman, that same gentleman came and sat next to her on the divan. Louisa pointedly left. Nina forced herself to remain. Evidently he wanted the game to continue. Well, if he would play at jilt, she would show him first how it was done—by an expert. And she gave him the smile he always complimented her on and came flirtatiously close ostensibly to smell his boutonniere and whisper that he was overpowering a poor defenseless woman with both his wit and ways, till he was enraged by her falsity.

"Where is the genuine wit and sparkle, the honesty that I respected?" he asked. "What is all this simpering and idiotic flirting?"

"Ah, perhaps I'm just conforming to your tastes. Like to like—don't you like me that way?" Nina asked innocently.

"What do you mean?"

Nina was tempted to tell all, culminating in a demand for a full explanation, not that she expected him to do anything but deny it—as all men did when caught. And then that other manipulator in her life, Bobby, approached, announcing that the moment had come for the special entertainment.

After a brief reflection, Nina was not displeased by the interruption. For, in truth, she'd learned often when one assumed that telling all would clarify a situation, it served rather to introduce new situations. So there was no ending to it.

Putting a stop to their tête-à-tête, Nina hurriedly rose, following the guests into the drawing room, where the duchess was seated on a velvet-tufted mahogany chair of gigantic proportions that dwarfed her small figure into a comic caricature. Yet the caricature had a voice of such volume that its pronouncements reached the entire room, especially Louisa and Nina.

"Ah, Miss De Bonnard, I hear Louisa introduced you to our Wedgwood and you bought a set for your mother. Most commendable. American women, I daresay, want to buy everything from England—including husbands."

Jordan, staring at Nina, was startled to find himself addressed by the little woman. "What do you imagine is lacking in the American man, Mr. Windsor?"

Collecting himself, he responded calmly. "Obviously we lack the willingness to be bought, your grace."

"Not likely, judging from the American political muddle—with electors indiscriminately selling their votes. Is it any wonder that your women are taught to *buy husbands* . . . and your men that money can buy their way into *any* society. Even one of the very highest!" And she looked with great disdain at both Nina and Bobby, not only to illustrate her point but to hammer it into both their heads.

"I have always thought," Nina answered, stung, "that both buyer and seller are equally at fault. One puts up only money—which is yours, mine, everyone's—but the other sells himself, which is something that should never be other than freely exchanged."

Jordan smiled at her almost with palpable relief, as if the real Nina, the one he recognized and loved, had come back again, but before he could respond, Bobby cut in. "Aw, everyone, man and woman, lord and lady can be bought. Just a question of price. Some demand money, some title, some excitement, some . . . power. . . . Speaking of which"—he rose and rubbed his hands together—"it's time for *our* little game, ladies and gentlemen!" And he quickly explained that the order of questioning was to be determined by lots. "It's just a little question-and-answer game. Whoever hedges or refuses to answer will be excused. He or she who answers falsely will be excused. Till we whittle down to one: the victor, who wins—are you all sitting down?—ownership of . . ." he paused dramatically before ending loudly, "*the Mayberry Crown*."

The faces of the listeners went from disbelief to interest to a growing gleam of rapaciousness. The Mayberry Crown was the crowning glory of the Mayberry jewels.

"Oh yes, I bought it back from the bank," Bobby said with glee. "And here it is." Whisking out a velour sack, he held it up before them like a magician opening his bag of tricks. Naturally, he made them wait, swaying the sack a few times before their mesmerized eyes. Then, languidly, he signaled a footman, who came forward with a velvet cushion and placed it before Bobby, on the floor. Opening the drawstrings of the sack, Bobby disrespectfully spilled the object—*plop*—onto the cushion. It only stopped shaking when righted by Bobby's booted toe. The Mayberry Crown glinted before them, all golden with a giant ruby on each spike tip and banded with several circles of diamonds. Glittering, glowing, gathering gasps.

Patting it paternally, Bobby said to it, "Now stay there and shine. Get all these good folks' attention and let 'em think how swell it would be to own you!" Leaning back in satisfaction, he began humming and then singing softly to the national treasure. " 'Believe me if all those endearing young charms were to fade . . .' Yep, folks, you might lose this little bauble if you play it safe . . . or play it false. You've got to play the game the *right* way: *True Blue.* Our good duchess here"—he pointed to the usually stiff and reproving face, which was trembling with the emotion of actually seeing the crown, once lost and now within her grasp—"has given me the raw goods on all of you. She's the official holder of the proofs. And get this: If none of you are left at the end of the game, the crown reverts to the house. Or duchie here gets her hands on this hollow crown. Any of you who don't want to play, speak now or forever hold your peace; but if you stay and speak later, you may forever hold this piece." He held up the crown directly under a candelabra, and the gold glittered mightily till there was a sound of indrawn breaths in unison. Bobby was basking in it. "Okay," he concluded, "we've all agreed to play my game."

"Not *all.*"

Bobby turned, shaking his head. "Why did I know you'd be the only one to give me trouble? Beautiful, bold, and bewildering

Nina." Jordan rose as well. "Aw, come on, Jordie. You know I'd like to have an American here to support me. Can't you two hang around? I'll sing a few choruses of 'The Star-Spangled Banner.' "

Even that, apparently, was not sufficient inducement, as both Nina and Jordan were halfway out of the room. They were just stopped from leaving by Bobby rushing before them and whispering to Nina, "Speaking of stars, not only will I reveal certain 'starry' facts about you to your friends and family in America that will turn their faces *lily* white, but I'll cancel those 'gilded' effusions of yours. Second thoughts?"

That gave Nina pause. She had to admit to herself that she did not want Bobby to uncover her as The Gilded Lily to her family or New York society. She ought to have done it herself rather than waiting and giving Bobby this opportunity to do so with his sleazy slant. Even his threat to cancel her column gave her a jolt. She had come to rely on it as her secret justification. That's what had given her confidence in her decision to walk away from Lord Brindsley and the offer he kept hinting he was going to make. Since she would not be returning to Oceana as a future duchess, she was hoping to reveal something commendable about herself, such as being the writer many people in her set were reading and quoting. But yet, yet—no longer would she permit gentlemen to manipulate her.

Sensing that she was ready to refuse, Bobby added quickly, "I'll sweeten the pot! I'll send a letter to Mr. Marshall and admit I've been lying about you and me in the Indian tepee. Your appearance at the opera before you left only proved you weren't with child *then*. But after you left, you wouldn't believe how many people were led to believe your illness was a coverup for a *miscarriage* of our child—thanks to Mrs. Windsor and myself. Weren't we devils? But what I start, I can also scotch. And that's what I'm promising to do if you'll stay to the end of the game. Not much to give—to get so much? Right?"

Nina was disgusted. Jordan was riled, needing one look from her to knock Bobby down, but Nina put out her hand and stopped him.

"I need no champions. Mr. Windsor. I've had enough of gentlemen thinking they can control my life."

Jordan was insulted that she would link him to Bobby and dumbfounded when Nina wearily turned to Bobby and agreed to play his game as long as he held his hand in the threats and used his hand to write the promised letter to Mr. Marshall. "If it will lighten some of the blackness you've thrown my way, I certainly want a modicum of reputation left when I return home," she finished with a small forlorn sigh that had Jordan inserting, "Get it in writing."

"Aw, Jordie, you hit me to the quick. Don't you trust me? As one American to another, would I lie to you—expatriationally speaking."

"Get it in writing definitely . . . and preferably in your hands."

"Yes," Nina insisted. "I want the confession written and handed to me."

Before the words were out of her mouth, he had removed a piece of paper from his vest. "Why did I know you'd ask for this? Must be something unique about me that I never leave a single angle uncovered. Ah, Bobby, Bobby, you're a wonder!"

Nina ignored both his words and his giggles while reading it through. Then she looked up and, seeing in Bobby's eyes how very much he wanted her participation, Nina realized she could get something more from him, something she'd been wanting with all her heart. "This is not enough!" she said crisply. "On second thought I wonder whether denying your own rumors might not bring them back in the open, and so you get what you've always wanted—linking us together."

Bobby refused to admit that as his objective, but there was a sly look in his eyes so Nina quickly added, "No, the only way I'll stay and play your game is *if* in addition to the other agreements, you give me your sworn promise to stop following me. To, in short, leave me forever alone!"

"I can't do that!" Bobby cried, letting out a groan. Nina made a move to the door. "Okay! Okay! I swear, before so prestigious a personage as Jordan here, that if you stay, you'll be rid of the greatest burden a young lady ever had to endure: a man madly, wildly, inconsolably in love with her! I promise, as you said, to, in short, leave you alone!"

There was an impatient call from the duchess for their getting on with the game, and all three Americans walked back, Nina slowly, Jordan grimly, and Bobby bouncing.

And the game began.

The lots had fixed the order of the questioning. The squire's lady was first. Expecting something such as her opinion of one of the other ladies' dresses and preparing to be diplomatic, she was stunned by being asked to reveal her exact age. She lied quickly, and just as quickly was caught up by both the duchess and Lady Moncrief—and she was out. She remained for her husband's turn, and, when he was asked to reveal the pedigree of his new stallion, he hardly had the words out of his mouth when the duchess removed from her rather large reticule a paper with the correct particulars. With affronted dignity, the squire gave his hand to his wife and the two exited.

"We're whittling down to a nice cozy group! Eh, what? Duchess?" Bobby concluded with his eyes gleaming.

Everyone was now viewing the duchess's reticule with respect. Obviously she was prepared to go all the way to retrieve her crown. There was a nervousness as the next one was called to play the game.

The reticule also contained Lord Rakenridge's military records, attested to by a superior in the Lifeguards. He saw her patting her reticule when a certain question was asked of him about a favorite story of his courage under fire, and in an appropriately lordly way simply refused to dignify the question. One more gone. Next. It was assumed his wife would be leaving with him to join the duke in a friendly game of whist. But the lure of the Mayberry Crown was too much. The countess insisted on taking her chance, claiming she would answer anything asked with perfect candor, only to be faced with a question as to whether her first child was in reality *premature?* Again the duchess made a significant move toward her reticule, and the countess made a significant move, in superb silence, out of the room.

"Well," Bobby said, rubbing his hands together in satisfaction. "This is going faster than I thought." Looking around, he pointed at Louisa. "Ah, Louisa, you're next and we're going to get you *easy*! For again, it's the age-old question of age. And remember,

I was ringbearer at your *younger* sister's marriage. So I have your exact age in mind, as much as your beauty belies the truth."

Louisa looked at Jordan, to whom, amongst others, she had lied about her age. And, in truth, she had lied about it so often, she had quite forgotten what it was. A rapid calculation, however, soon gave her the total, and she exclaimed, "Good heavens! Forty-five!"

It had escaped her before she could think, and, in great consternation at her own betrayal of herself, she turned to face them all, expecting shock and smirks, but the moment was too tense for them to care about her exposure; only whether she had been eliminated or not counted. They all turned to Bobby.

"'*True blue!*'" he exclaimed joyfully. "Our first truth-teller. So that puts you in first place, and with one hand practically on the crown!"

Delighted at the outcome of her outcry, Louisa looked territorially at the gleaming thing, pushing her admission to the back of her mind, as well as the years ahead of denials. Bobby was continuing. "Now Lord Brindsley, you're next. How many illegitimate children have you fathered?"

A purely American question, assuming that he would be embarrassed to admit even one. But instead the exact number was pridefully acknowledged. Chagrined at having wasted a question, Bobby shrugged and moved on to the next victim—the one he really wanted to nail. "Okay Jordie, here's your question: During your stay at Mayberry Castle, it's reported that you've been visiting the rooms of not one, but two, different ladies on two different nights. Isn't that so?"

Nina was not as shocked as Bobby had expected her to be, nor was Jordan, who casually said, not even blinking in hesitation, "It is not."

Bobby laughed. "So you say. But there might be witnesses to your entering and *exiting*. One of the ladies might even admit it herself!"

"Then she would not be 'true blue,' would she, Bobby boy? Because you made up this entire supposition merely to have a certain lady here conclude it *could* be true. Play True Blue yourself and admit it!"

"That's true blue, I did!" Bobby agreed, nodding and laughing at having been caught. But undisturbed, he continued, "Nearly got you. But the point's yours. Come to think of it, I ought to get a point too, for my *truthful* answer. So in round one we're down to the last participant." He whirled around. "Lovely Nina! Did you think I'd forgotten you? I never will." He paused to add drama to the moment by inserting a pleading warning, "Remember, you have to tell the truth. Your question is: Did you ever love me even a little?"

"No."

"That's a lie!" Bobby insisted. "You answered too quickly. If you want a chance to think . . ." but his voice faltered as she stared back at him, unmoved. "Fine," he said testily, "since I can't prove differently, you get a point. All right, my fellow Americans and my good lord and duchess, we're down to four finalists. Let's get rid of Louisa next. The question is: Have you ever, while married, had an affair with anyone in this room? And don't forget, that while honest Jordan will probably not reveal your lie, there's another in here who'll tell all—being more of a lord than a gentleman."

Louisa was beginning to feel that no amount was worth the humiliation she had already endured in admitting her age, but once having risked so much, it seemed she should get something for it. Then again, *this* admission would be not just an embarrassment, but it would lead to the disruption of her happy existence with her husband. And, looking at Lord Brindsley's face, she knew she would not get away with a lie. They were watching her. Abruptly she stood up in high dudgeon.

"The question is an impertinence! I certainly refuse to continue to lend my presence to this farce. Jordan, will you escort me out?"

"Oh take a damper, Louisa," Lord Brindsley put in, "and let's finish this beastly thing. You're out of the game. Either go to your room or join the others playing whist."

Louisa gave one look at Jordan, who, rising to the occasion, rose to escort her.

"That leaves—with Jordie gone . . ." Bobby quickly began calculating, when Jordan called back from the door. "I am merely escorting the lady. Not all of us are as callous as you—you little twit."

Laughing with great gusto at Jordan's insult, he warned, however, "If you walk out, you lose your chance at the crown."

"I don't want the ugly thing," Jordan snapped. "I'm not participating in this fiasco. I'm returning to see you stick to the rules."

"You mean you'll be back to watch over Nina. With me here, she doesn't need you for that."

"I don't need either of you!" Nina was inserting when the duchess, resenting any side issue when so much was at stake for her, ordered them to continue.

And Bobby, though nodding, put in defensively, "Not my fault everybody has so much to hide. I never hide anything. I believe in admitting everything . . . in being *true blue*, and that's why I named this game that. Yep, true blue is the good old American way. . . ."

"Get on with it!" Lord Brindsley demanded.

"Right, right. And with Jordan and Louisa out, we're down to two. You and Nina. You first. Give us the reason you were expelled from Boodles three years ago—and, remember, I have an eyewitness account in my pocket."

Lord Brindsley turned white.

"And . . . part two of that is also how you contrived to be readmitted."

"You beastly little cad! You know I told you that in confidence . . . and in my cups. You'd think you'd have too much honor to use that!"

"You would, wouldn't you? But I don't. Never scruple to use anything that comes my way to add a little charge to the evening!"

Lord Brindsley began perspiring. As much as he wanted the crown, both for himself and for his mother, there was no possibility he would admit the events in question—not before his mother and before Nina.

His mother stood up. "There is nothing you could have done that would surprise me at this late date," she urged. But even as she spoke, she knew that, just as had her husband throughout their married life, her son, when it came to the last moment, would let her down. And he did.

"I shan't dignify what is known to be slander—not for a crown, not for a kingdom!"

Jumping up and down, Bobby grabbed the crown, and was inches from pressing it on Nina's head when the duchess intervened. "That gel has not given her second answer! There is the possibility that if she either does not answer or answers falsely, the crown reverts to . . . me."

"Righto. There, duchess, m'gel." Bobby laughed, lapsing into a pseudo-British accent as he had done several times to annoy her. "I say, we shan't let this peerless American take away *our* crown! Dashed unfair, what! But then, don't ya know, Nina always wins."

"Cease this levity! This is a question of the Mayberry heritage, bequeathed to us from ancestor to ancestor! And to think we've come to *this* to keep it!" The duchess was quivering with the indignity.

"Then why did you sell it and then spend the money? You can't do that with one hand and then pretend it's so sacred to you. 'Tain't fair, old gel. Not very sporting. And I've been more than fair: I've given your family a double chance to get it back, and I've already paid you a great deal just to have this party. Haven't I, Mumsey? Now, back to Nina and, ladies and gentleman, how much hangs on this lovely young lady's next answer . . . not that Nina ever answers—she just looks at you and—"

"You're going beyond the rules!" Nina snapped. "No editorializing. Just ask the question!"

"I'm just putting it in proper context," Bobby said, injured.

"No, you're relishing our discomforts—looking forward to seeing us all massacred like Custer and his troops."

"Yes, indeedy. Me Crazy Horse! That's Sitting Bull," he said, pointing at the duchess, and then to Lord Brindsley with head in hands, "And there's Custer, defeated."

The duchess had gotten up and was standing next to the crown, prepared at a moment to snatch it up. "Finish it, man," she ordered.

"Devilish improper of me to be jesting at such a moment in history!" Bobby acknowledged. "Your questions, Nina, are twofold, to be fair, since Lord Brindsley had two parts and also because I couldn't decide which answer I most wanted to know. Part One: Did you run away from New York City to avoid disgrace or to buy a British lord? And Part Two: What did you see when you smoked the peace pipe? That foretells your future."

Jordan had reentered in time to hear that question and was just as interested in the response as Bobby.

Nina considered. "No, to both false assumptions about the reason for my leaving New York."

Bobby leaned forward. When it became clear that was all Nina was going to say he protested, "You can't just answer no. You have to give the real reason! What was it?"

Facing him unflappably, Nina said, "That would be a *third* question. Do you prefer that to the peace-pipe one? You can't keep raising the ante and not be called on it."

Bobby concentrated and decided he didn't care why she left New York. But he did want to know what her future would be—to see if he was to be included in it. And he agreed that she should stick to the original Part Two.

Nina closed her eyes and remembered herself in the tepee. The image came clear and she considered whether she wanted to share it. Then she shrugged, and described it, "I saw myself transformed into a bird with large wings—flying solitary across the sky."

Jordan was disappointed that the image was of her alone. Bobby ignored that part and concentrated on what was to his own interest. "Great! The bird with the large wings has to be an eagle. That means you stay in America! Red, white, and blue . . . true blue! A true-blue answer! And with all others eliminated, you win!" Turning to the group, Bobby announced, "Ladies and gentlemen and . . . lords, the new owner of the crown is Nina De Bonnard!" With a flourish, he presented it to her.

The moment the crown touched Nina's head, the duchess cried out, as if up to that second, she still had hopes of retaining it. Reaching for her chair, she sat down, of a sudden, like a shattered bit of old porcelain, there in shards, while her son rose to signal the footmen to escort her to her room.

"Oh, here!" Nina said generously, holding out the crown to

the old woman as she was being escorted past her. That gesture miraculously restored the duchess and she rose to receive it. But Bobby was faster. He had it in hand.

"You can't *give* it away to another member of the game. That's invalidating the whole procedure. If you insist on it, the crown reverts to me!"

"You can't make up the rules as you go along!" Jordan put in, disgusted by Bobby yet moved by Nina's gesture and wanting it all to end on that high note, followed by his taking Nina out of this room, out of the castle, out of the country.

"Yes, I can. I always make up my own rules," Bobby said with such finality that no one doubted him. He was putting the crown back in the sack when Lord Brindsley cried out.

"The rules are the crown goes to the winner! It is *hers*. And everything she has might possibly become someone else's." He turned to Nina. "Louisa has explained that your family is expecting you to marry a lord. I daresay you will not find another one who would admire you as much as I. Nor one who can make you, an American, into a prospective duchess!" Turning to his downcast mother, he urged, "Tell her, Mumsy, what an honor that is. And how much we'd all welcome her into our happy family."

It took a moment, but the duchess weakly assured her it was so. For Nina as a daughter-in-law, especially if the crown came as part of the dowry, seemed a little less American.

"You don't have to marry this weakling. Good God! I've been leading him by the nose ever since I first met him!" Bobby cried in outrage. "What's in a crown? I bought it for you. I'll give you loads and loads of crowns, and you wouldn't have to have a comic mother-in-law looking down her nose at you. We'd be free to play—with the world as our playground! What say! Marry me!"

Jordan, although loathe to get in on this public auction, could not allow his claim to go unheard. "You don't have to compromise at all. You know where your heart is—with me. Let's stop this entire game between us once and for all, and go home together."

Nina turned from one to the other. "Come to think of it, I don't need any of you. Nor am I interested in society anymore.

Or my position in it. With this"—she picked up the sack holding the crown—"I'll probably be able to live quite comfortably on my own—as the lone eagle I am meant to be. So the answer to all three of you is *no*. If this is mine"—she took it out and plopped it on her head—"then I'll keep it. And as for myself, I'll keep *myself free* of you all as well!"

And smiling and with the crown glittering on her head, Nina walked majestically out of the room; the footman rushing to open the door for her and shut it after, all but bowing as she passed.

Twenty-three

*I*t *was downright* discombobulating to be back in Oceana, Nina thought as she walked about her old room. Heavens, the last time she'd been in there was the morning she'd left with her father in a mad dash for New York City to give her sister an open field with Jordan. But he'd shown up there and been responsible for her second exile, this time to England. And subsequently Jordan had set her running again from England. She'd traveled to Paris and Rome, writing articles until she forgot she'd ever known Jordan Windsor. Apparently he had a similar memory lapse, for he hadn't followed as expected, depriving her of the pleasure of refusing to see him. Frustrating. She'd rehearsed speeches and never had to use them. He was an infuriating opponent. How could one combat an absence?

Another maddening contemplation was wondering how such a manipulating man capable of devising such a heartless pact could have seemed so sincere at Mayberry Castle. He had behaved as if she were the very air he needed to breathe. What a performer! Small wonder he'd almost won her and won his pact. Louisa was right. Adele was right. Her mother was right. Only her stupid heart still clung to a remnant of a hope. Thankfully, she met new people on her travels who distracted her. She even wrote an amusing column on how gentlemen flirted in different countries as well as one on the universality of anti-Americanism.

The most satisfying development was breaking her contract with the *Bugle* and signing a much more lucrative one with a newspaper chain that would carry her articles throughout the

United States. There was even a side arrangement to publish a collection of them in book form, which Nina worked hard to complete.

She was holding the finished manuscript in her hand, preparing to skim through it for one last time before sending it to her publisher. Sitting down in her old rocker, Nina rearranged the pillow behind her. It caught her attention. This was the very pillow she'd struggled to petit-point under the direction of her governess, who had insisted she'd never be "finished" without a fine sewing hand. That pillow proved her unfinished nature, Nina thought with a grin, for the flowers on it did not have stems; she simply had been too impatient to needlepoint them in. Staring, Nina realized she actually preferred the flowers free-floating. And as for her tendency to leave things unfinished, she'd broken that pattern by completing her manuscript, hadn't she? In a few moments she was proudly putting it away in her desk drawer when she came across a souvenir fan from the Centennial Exposition, lithographed with lighter-than-air balloons and the dates 1776–1876. This room was filled with memories. Underscoring that was the sound of her two favorite music boxes, which Nina liked to play together so the two different Stephen Foster melodies blended into a tune that was familiar, yet unfamiliar, as the sounds jingled on, then groped, then lapsed into silence. Like a memory of a past happiness dragged into the present against its will when it was best dead and forgotten.

Well, she was home!

Lord Brindsley had continually written to her throughout her travels, but Nina had dismissed his proposals, attributing his desperation to wanting his crown back. On first arriving in London, Nina, having decided she couldn't keep the crown, placed it in the bank's keeping with the proviso that neither the present duke nor his heir, Lord Brindsley, could sell it, but rather that it be kept for the future line. She wrote the present duchess, hoping to relieve her sense of loss, and received a curious response. "Americans think they can buy everything, even gratitude. But you have bought mine."

But actually Lord Brindsley was seeking not *a* crown, but crowns, pounds, shillings—or a fortune. Since he could not wed for it, he fled for it, following Bobby on his gold-mining expedition to Africa. What Bobby's ulterior motive was in taking his lordship into the interior, Nina was unable to imagine. Actually, she was too relieved to be rid of both gentlemen. Particularly heartening was the fact that Bobby had kept his word and had not followed her. As her last bit of unfinished English business, Nina wrote a letter to Mrs. Richards about the availability of a certain future duke, adding that he was currently on the market and could be bought for a reasonable sum. How would she like being the mother of a duchess? She'd signed the letter, "The Gilded Lily." In truth, Nina was killing two birds with one stone. Adele's letters had hinted at Mr. De Bonnard's open liaison with Miss Richards. Which explained a slight edge to her mother's letters to Nina, indicating that while not blaming her, Mrs. De Bonnard was still under the assumption that Cass Richards had been her friend. Originally Nina had gone along with that subterfuge only because she could not possibly see that young woman as a serious threat. But when it appeared otherwise, Nina acted, wondering what Mrs. Richards had done in response to that letter. Staring out of her window at the Oceana surf, Nina concluded that meddling in other people's lives left a God-like impression of one's self, until God stepped in and showed that He always had the last word.

Look at this marriage between Adele and Dick Windsor, Nina thought. Now that it was about to take place, it seemed so natural, so inevitable, it could only have been made in heaven. "Would you believe it's been almost two years since the Centennial July Fourth parties, when we were all together here?" Adele exclaimed with a sigh of wonder as she and Nina were being driven in the De Bonnard carriage back from the train station to Sea Cliff. Catching up Nina with the rumors, Adele reported with glee that the natives were spreading suspicions about the urgency of her wedding to Dick. "It's over a year since our engagement and so we have waited the proper time. Yet they still want us to wait for autumn in New York City, where weddings are done properly and formally. But Dick and I decided we wanted an outdoor ceremony—here, where the two of us grew up together. Independence Day seemed so fitting. For while most women give up their independence upon marrying, with Dick's interest in suffrage, the two of us shall be sharing our independence and turning it into interdependence! Further, Dick can enjoy himself, adding fireworks and patriotic stuff. Anyway, what's the point of waiting? If something's right, do it. Otherwise all kinds of side issues intrude and mess it up for you."

"Talking of side issues," Nina could not help but insert, "I could stand aside if my presence in the wedding party would make it awkward for anyone. Or *he* could stand aside."

"You mean Jordan? That's all forgotten. I've forgiven him. Besides, Dick couldn't bear it if his brother weren't his best man. And I couldn't bear it if you weren't my maid of honor!" Adele's eyes began to twinkle. "I'll admit I did have a momentary thought of not having you in the wedding party, not for Jordan's sake, but because I figured everyone would look at you rather than the bride. Till it struck me that I no longer cared. I have what I want. I love Dick, and he loves me. I have my suffrage cause and a husband who backs it. So it's peripheral who people admire. That's living on the surface. I'm living from the heart."

Nina had been pleased and displeased by that summation. Surely there was an implication that she lived on the surface. But Nina shook off the insult in her joy at her sister's having such a complete life. If one loved another, Nina realized, one wanted to be told they had not only present happiness but a secure and contented future. It eliminated some of the responsibility of that love; one no longer had to make that person happy at the expense of one's own life. Freedom, Nina thought with a smile. Henceforth, she could be as disreputable as she pleased. Not that she really wanted to be disreputable, but daring, perhaps. And it also meant no more exile. She might even finally admit to her family that she was The Gilded Lily. At least she'd try it on Adele and see her reaction.

Adele had gone her own way, Nina thought, remembering fondly the little girl following her about. Nina picked up a box from the bottom of the closet. It contained her childhood collection of shells and bits of colored glass and quartz stones, made precious by sojourns in the sea till they glittered on the sand, waiting to be found and imagined as the real thing. "All this was

Captain Kidd's treasure," she had whispered to her sister, who viewed it with total belief in her little girl's eyes.

Her sister came bouncing in. She was holding the maid-of-honor dress. Nina had volunteered to purchase hers in Paris, from Worth, who designed most of her dresses, but Adele had wanted a similar look for all. She had planned her wedding down to the smallest detail. Guardedly, Nina looked at the dress. It was more Oceana than New York, and definitely not Paris. The yellow silk slip gown was overwhelmed by an overhang of thick fisherman's net. Adele waited for her reaction.

Nina forced herself to speak. "It's a very suitable maid-of-honor dress."

"You mean, commonplace?" Adele asked anxiously.

"No, correct," Nina assured her, meaning commonplace.

Adele relaxed. "The other dresses are like this only pink and blue."

"Indeed? That sounds . . . even more . . . suitable."

Heavens, Nina thought. Why hadn't she remembered that her sister didn't have an ounce of style! Well, it was her wedding.

"Try it on for the fit. If you want to make any little changes, that's okay."

"Okay," Nina agreed. "I might add or detract a few touches, if you won't mind?"

"Oh, no," Adele assured her. "I'll go get the seamstress. She's here just finishing my gown." And Adele scooted out.

Nina attempted to suppress a shudder. An Oceana seamstress! Things were going from worse to much worse! Out from under Adele's watching eye, Nina allowed her face to show her dismay. What a thoroughly average, average gown! First thing that must go was the balloon-like overdress of net! It even had loops at the back that supposedly simulated a bustle but in reality looked like a fisherman's catch. All it needed was a flounder hanging out and a discreet crab claw.

When the seamstress arrived, Nina chatted about everything but the gown shouting its presence between them. At last Miss Wilton was forced to ask if there were any changes Nina wanted and Nina agreed there were. "Just remove this catch from its net." At the uncomprehending stare, Nina was more precise, asking that the entire net overdress be unstitched from its yellow base. When that was done, the yellow gown showed it too had a large plump bustle, but that, thankfully, was removable, since it tied on like a flounced peplum.

"But Miss De Bonnard," the elderly lady said in astonishment, "then there will be no bustle at all!"

"We need not create a bustle over that! Bustles are falling out of fashion," Nina said with a friendly twinkle, as she slipped into the inner yellow slip. It was a mere shell, but at least not a shock. The fit could be better, Nina concluded, and looking through the chests that had just arrived from the station, Nina found her favorite Worth creation and showed the seamstress how a dress should be shaped. With round eyes of wonder, Miss Wilton turned the gown inside out, marveling at the seams, and the over-all smoothness, proceeding on her own to take in some of the sags in the yellow dress. Nina smiled, satisfied that she had not had to tell her.

The Worth gown had a shawl of delicate ecru lace that added a touch of exquisite finesse and Nina borrowed that to wear over the long, narrow yellow slip. She declined the headdress of fisherman's net, and the seamstress left, dejectedly holding the net overdress, the net bustle and the net headdress in a pile. Out of the pull of Nina's smile and gentle words, she realized with a shock that her design had been eviscerated. She took her complaint to Mrs. De Bonnard, explaining that she herself did not mind an alteration of one dress, she was accustomed to that, but this change ruined the symmetry of the wedding party gowns. The mother of the bride shrugged. "Nina is always different. Don't worry, Miss Wilton, you have all the other ladies caught in nets. Let's just assume one got away."

Not a very satisfactory reply. So Miss Wilton took her protest to Adele. But the bride was similarly undisturbed, adding, "You're lucky she didn't make you redo the whole thing. We got off pretty easy with just her throwing away the overdress. I have the feeling she's swallowing her pride to be wearing any part of it. But don't fret. I'm happy with your creations; after all, they were all my suggestions. I wanted a sea look to go along with the sea decor of the wedding. Of course, Dick would throw in the Americana theme because it's July Fourth, but I've kept that to a minimum, just a few flags and such. A little of this and a little of that, and everybody will be happy. That's the main thing. This is an occasion of great joy for me, and I want everyone who is part of it or coming to it to feel equally happy!"

Nina was not happy. She dreaded seeing Jordan again. Thankfully, he had not yet arrived from Washington. Neither her sister nor her mother seemed to have any difficulty with his pending presence. Since Adele's life was in order, they no longer had any reason to resent him. Order and peace was all her mother had ever wanted for both her daughters.

"You're happy, Mother?" Nina asked her on the terrace as she and Mrs. De Bonnard were strolling about the decks, looking out toward the sea.

Mrs. De Bonnard assured her everything was just as she wanted it. "Of course, I would have been happier if you had married Lord Brindsley. But I've long resigned myself to the conclusion that you will never marry. And frankly, I don't see why it's a necessity. If you wish to remain free, I can't fault you for it. Your father was furious. He'd been announcing all over New York that you were going to be a duchess. Then a letter from Mr. Van Reyden arrived denying all the charges he'd made about you, which was not helpful, for it brought back rumors that had long since lost their titillation. But with Mrs. Windsor no longer heading the whispering campaigns, they soon faded." Suddenly Mrs. De Bonnard laughed and revealed an added reason for her complacency. "Actually no one is talking about anything but Mrs. Richards and her daughter suddenly leaving for England, almost in a rush. As if they had to beat someone there."

Nina smiled in the coming dusk and made no comment.

Her mother, however, was honest enough to admit that she'd found Mr. De Bonnard's fascination with that young lady more than she could continue to countenance. "I was beginning to think Mrs. Richards was aiming for her daughter to be the second Mrs. De Bonnard. But even if she wasn't, I was near to initiating a divorce. Either way—" she paused and with a slight degree of admonition concluded, "you would have found yourself with an old bosom friend as a new mother."

Nina merely laughed away that possibility.

"It was not such a laughing time for me," her mother said. "But from your father's scowls, I'm assuming his hopes in that direction have finally ended. And with Adele married and my involvement in the cause, I have very little to worry about except my constant concern for you."

So Nina took that moment to ask her mother if she'd ever read any of the columns by The Gilded Lily.

"Every one I can get. I enjoy them so much. They have a style, a satire about them that one rarely sees." Nina was suffused with pleasure, almost blushing, especially when her mother continued, "There was a period when the Lily was not writing and I was concerned. And then, come to think of it, she began writing from England. Why do you ask about her?"

Of a sudden her mother pulled Nina back into the sitting room, where she could turn on the gaslight fully and stare at her daughter's twinkling eyes. "Good heavens! And then the columns came from the same countries you traveled to. But it cannot be!"

"Yes. I am The Gilded Lily. In the larger dailies traveling reporters traditionally have colorful pen names, such as Hawkstaff, but mine outdoes them. Actually Bobby's original idea was The Star-Spangled Gilded Lily. I at least toned it down, although 'star-spangled' was visually kept in by the banner below the name. Anyway, I'm stuck with it. But no longer with Bobby. I've been finishing off my contract with the *Bugle*. I am already writing for several other newspapers in America. And in England."

Mrs. De Bonnard's eyes were shining as she hugged her daughter. "I should have known. The columns have your humor. Which is actually *my* humor. Your grandfather on my side wrote a collection of limericks, you know. I'll show you. But first we must tell Adele. She reads you too. And my ladies—I must report it to them next meeting! They're always so pleased when a woman has her own career and is successful at it. You must come and read some columns to us. I'd be so proud."

Nina was astonished at her mother's jubilation, which was not at all what Nina expected. She'd thought she might possibly receive censure. Disbelief, certainly. Not this easy acceptance of a fact she'd kept guarded so long. As if it were not really that earth-shattering. But what Nina really sensed from her mother was re-lief that now Nina had her own niche in life. It was almost as good as having her married.

When Adele came in, Mrs. De Bonnard cried out without a blink, "Who do you think is *The Gilded Lily?*"

"Mother!" Nina objected.

"Nina," Adele said calmly. "I knew it when she was sick, and I was putting her things away. Besides, look at her wrist. There's the tattoo of the star, a real giveaway! I bathed that every day, even asked the doctor if it were possible that she'd gotten ill from the ink having seeped into her system. He assured me that was not the cause, and I could be easy."

"Does *everybody* know!" Nina gasped.

"Not Papa, I'm certain. And I haven't even told Dick."

"Thank you," Nina said, uncertain why she felt so dismissed. What had she expected to occur if everyone knew? Nothing. It was not such a major revelation. Maybe only to herself.

"Well, you, of course, would know," she said to her sister, who laughed and gave her a hardy hug. Her mother hugged them both, and the three De Bonnard ladies went down to dinner with satisfaction in their eyes.

Mr. De Bonnard was not smiling. He had just read a letter that displeased him. He turned to his eldest daughter and struck out at her. "Well, you wouldn't take him, and so Miss Richards did! She's going to be Lady Brindsley and a future duchess, by damn!"

"Really?" Nina said with studied indifference. "I believe she'll be very happy in England. She's exactly what the English think American women are, and I predict Mrs. Richards and the pre-sent duchess will find themselves well matched."

"Humpf," was all her father said to that, reading the letter again. "She owes it all to that woman writer, would you believe? That Gilded Lily lady."

"How?" Mrs. De Bonnard demanded in astonishment.

"Apparently she wrote to Mrs. Richards suggesting that she sail over there and get this lord because he was up for grabs . . . on the market to be bought cheap—blast her! Who asked that interfering lady to stick her nose in other people's business? Just because she tells everyone what's fashionable and what's funny, she thinks she can break—" He shut himself up, staring at his wife, who was laughing and hugging her eldest daughter. Adele was doing the same.

"What's going on?" he asked gruffly.

"Nothing," his wife said. "We're just so happy to have Nina home. She has a way of making things happen."

Oceana had similar expectations of Nina De Bonnard, assuming that with her return, the De Bonnard–Windsor wedding was bound to be more significant. Nina's slightly tarnished reputation trailed her like a patched train, but Nina had a way of giving it a stately swing. A few of the Oceana ladies had some reservations about welcoming her, assuring each other with pleasure that they were going to be insulted by the mere sight of her. Yet they were all eager for that insulting presence. The more Nina delayed her return, the more eager they were to see her. It was soon clear that rumors, rather than making her unpalatable, had just added sauce to the saucy minx. "Like a well-buttered chicken," Mrs. Windsor said, "whenever she falls into the fire, she just emerges more crisp and tasty." Everyone wanted a taste of her.

Mrs. Windsor and Mr. Marshall, having scheduled a lavish party for the engaged couple, were a duet of resentment at Nina's not returning for that grand event. Even more were the Oceana hostesses affronted that, after her arrival, Nina went into immediate seclusion at Sea Cliff. In retaliation, the word went around that Nina was no longer the Professional Beauty everyone remembered. One lady went so far as to claim that Miss De Bonnard's face was scarred, swearing to have seen it as Nina had been driven from the railway station. That bit of gossip enlarged itself, becoming the explanation for Nina's having broken off with Lord Brindsley. It must have been his lordship who had done the jilting. For how could an American young lady whose father had all but announced her being a future duchess have been the one to end the relationship? Instantly the scar story was contradicted by Mrs. Windsor, who, as an in-law-to-be, was in a position to know. She also reminded everyone that Nina De Bonnard had a tendency to jilt. It would not be the first engagement she had broken. Nina had behaved true to form. There was some satisfaction in that.

The men, once of her court, were anxious for the pleasure of seeing her again, and the younger boys, who might have thought her too old to interest, were so often warned against the arrival of this "flirt" that they were roused as well.

Indeed, all Oceana was poised to make a pronouncement on its wayward beauty. And still Nina kept them waiting, not attending any of the pre-wedding affairs where she could have been thoroughly eyed and judged, heightening the anticipation of the actual wedding ceremony itself.

But Mrs. Windsor could not content herself to wait for a brief glimpse on that occasion, especially since she expected her eyes to be so teary on *that* day that she could not get a clear view of anyone. Therefore, the moment she was informed that Nina was actually in residence, she arrived at Sea Cliff, unannounced, for tea, only to be disappointed of her quarry.

Nina had gone out for a walk on the beach. Mr. Marshall, who, as usual, accompanied Mrs. Windsor everywhere she went, exchanged condemnatory glances with his patron. They stayed and stayed, hoping for her return, despite Mrs. De Bonnard's constant hints that she had so many last-minute details to arrange, and finally her rising and claiming she had to remind the chef (brought specially from New York for this occasion) about last-minute changes. Mrs. De Bonnard was free at last, never to return while Mrs. Windsor remained. Poor Adele was thus left to fend off the interrogation as best she could.

No, Nina had not mentioned her being engaged to anyone from Europe. Yes, Nina looked the same—just as beautiful as ever. And yes, she was afraid that Nina might take a good deal longer to return, for she sometimes liked to just sit on the beach and gaze at the sea.

Mr. Marshall and Mrs. Windsor were exchanging further glances over that when the door to the morning room opened and both the Windsor boys burst in. Mrs. Windsor could not help smiling; she did it automatically even at the mention of Dickie's name. His presence kept the smile there for as long as it took her to become aware that Jordan, against her instructions, had come a day earlier from Washington and had allowed himself to be persuaded to visit the De Bonnards.

Pointedly, Mrs. Windsor asked Jordan if he had brought Miss Perkens with him, even though she knew that Jordan had long since stopped seeing the Washington lady.

Jordan almost answered that there was only one woman he was interested in seeing again, but he just remained silent, thinking of that one woman. Actually, Jordan had continually thought of Nina from the moment he'd boarded ship, all the while vowing never to think of her again. Instead, Nina became his traveling companion throughout the sail, for he was unaware that anybody else was onboard. Upon his arrival in Washington, D.C., the phantom Nina came along with the rest of his baggage and was there in his home waiting for him when he was alone. Good God, he acknowledged, she was rooted into him, and he could not pull her out without taking half of himself out with her. Daily she became more inexorable. Every place he turned, he saw her. Relaxing had not rid him of her, so Jordan attempted to exorcise her with exercise and work. Not surprisingly, those means proved similarly ineffective. The only way to carry on, he realized, was to pretend that the separation was just temporary. He even began buying paintings for his brownstone in Washington with a view to her approval, and proceeded to decorate the rest to suit her as well, almost persuading himself that she would soon be there to view the results.

And then the announcement came rewarding his expectation. It was a formal invitation, setting July 4 as the date for the marriage of Dick and Adele.

Jordan closed his eyes in relief as his ordeal of waiting was coming to an end. He would see Nina not in his imagination or dreams, but in the flesh. They would meet again in Oceana, the very setting of their first encounter. Life had a way of circling and circling and then closing the circle around one. And the occasion for their meeting couldn't be more apropos. What better push toward a reconciliation than a wedding uniting his family and hers? At such a formal occasion, Nina would be forced to be civil, which was all he needed—just to have her stand still for one moment so he could make his move. He soothed his impatience with pictures of capturing Nina, despite her darting, fluttering ways—like those of a beautiful butterfly. Obviously she had a fear of being caught and pinned to the wall, which explained why, inevitably, last-minute, she flew away from any connection. Couldn't that also be the reason for her contradictory behavior at Mayberry Castle? Confound, he ought to have followed her on her European jaunts and told her he understood her need for flight. Instead, like a fool, he'd stayed apart all these months, assuring himself he would soon be indifferent, passing meanwhile through all emotions but that. Anger at the beginning, which had fueled his initial mistake of getting on the ship for home. Then grief throughout the voyage. Then fear that he would never see her again. Then brooding over ways to reach her. Then a peace had come over him as he felt a certainty they would be together again. He would not give up the idea of her, not when she had become part of him—in his breath, in his bones; his own eyes reflected back all her images stored in there. It was inconceivable that the two would not eventually, inevitably, be joined.

And then, as hoped, fate completed the natural order of things and gave him a chance. All he had to do was to give fate a final push so when the circle closed, Nina and he would be united within.

On her scheduled arrival in Oceana, Jordan cautiously remained in Washington, planning to arrive a day later so as not to frighten her with the impression he was lying in wait. And even once there he was still careful not to cause her to flit away from him. It would be best if their meeting was casual and in the midst of a group. So Jordan accompanied his brother on his scheduled stop at Sea Cliff.

As planned, a group was there, but Nina was nowhere in evidence. Casually, Jordan glanced about. Dick, who did not have one subtle bone in his body, came right out with it. "Looking for Nina?"

Demurring, Jordan grimaced as that caught his mother's attention, making obvious what he hoped would be done subtly. There was no earthly reason why her son would be searching for

Nina, Mrs. Windsor protested. "No one is at all interested in seeing that young miss!"

That in the face of Mr. Marshall's and her own coming just to see her.

To smooth the situation, Jordan said quickly, "Naturally I should be delighted to see her again where she belongs—in the heart of her family."

He was surprised by Adele's embracing him for his sentiments, and Dick made some obvious joke about Adele's changing her mind and preferring Jordan again, which would have been merely good-naturedly laughed off if Mrs. Windsor had not again made the situation worse by indignantly insisting that Adele was not like her sister, flitting from man to man.

This elicited a long-suffering sigh from Jordan. He'd almost forgotten the peril of trying to engage in a conversation with his mother present: One constantly had to be jumping up and changing topics or adding qualifications to her strong pronouncements—with the results that one generally emerged worn out and not improving matters. Dick had a better way of dealing with her: He simply sat back and laughed at everything she said, enjoying her, and she, seeing his enjoyment of her, mellowed herself.

Jordan let his mind wander as his mother began asking Adele about certain wedding gifts. The talk was all of candelabra and tea and coffee services in Baltimore silver when Dick leaned over and whispered, "Bobby's back in town."

Jordan jumped. "What's he doing here?"

"Oh, he brought an English lord with him, and there's talk of his building a club that would permit entrance to ladies—at least for tennis and at certain times."

"If that's the reason he came, I should be very much surprised."

"Yeah, you think, like everybody else, he came for Nina . . . at least to see her again."

"What are you two boys whispering about!" Mrs. Windsor demanded, and her youngest son confirmed her worst suspicions by admitting with a smile, "Nina, who else?"

"How that young woman has the nerve to expect us all to be sitting here waiting for her while she traipses about the beach like a . . . a—"

"Ah, here she is," Mr. Marshall said and stood up, adjusting his monocle.

Twenty-four

And, indeed, Nina, at just the correct moment, had walked in on a crowd of people ostensibly having tea but in actuality waiting for her entrance.

She was carrying a long, swaying weed and her white muslin dress had seawater stains on the hem and her hair was wildly disarranged by the sea breezes. She looked, Mrs. Windsor thought, like something the cat dragged in. Like something a man, lying on the beach, would dream of coming toward him, Dick thought, feeling a momentary pang that was quickly wiped out by the reality of the bouncing, adorable girl at his side.

Like *Nina,* Jordan thought, exactly as she'd first appeared to him on that day long ago when she had been surrounded by the Oceana young men and turned and saw him and extended a white rose and touched him with it. Now she was carrying a weed. Perhaps that was symbolic of the change in their relationship, he thought with a smile, but he could not stop watching her and the surprise in her eyes as she glanced around at the gathering. But, being Nina, she did not nervously laugh or try to arrange her disheveled hair; she simply walked in and sat on the arm of her sister's chair without acknowledging the crowd or making any reference to the time of absence, merely commenting, "The seaweed carts were full and carting away all our dresses, Delly."

Adele laughed and explained how she and her sister used to rush about the beach and deck themselves with seaweed, pretending they were mermaids and how unhappy they were when the seaweed carts came by and messed up their play.

"You'd be surprised at all the changes that have taken place at the beach in the two years since you've been here," Adele offered. "Everyone now sticks to their own ocean access. Which means less swimming."

"Right," Dick plunged in, wanting to be talking to Nina again as soon as possible to bridge the strangeness of her being there. "No one bathes together anymore—of our set, that is. It's not a social gathering spot; only those who really want to swim indulge in it. And, as Delly said, in our own surf."

Mr. Marshall chose this opportunity to explain what had come about largely through his own dictum. "Ocean Beach, or the general beach, I fear, has been overrun by people with whom one might not feel *comfortable* in mingling. One's fastidiousness is offended, don't you know?"

"To which *people* are you referring?"

"Excursionists," he whispered, stressing each syllable of the word to stress the offense of the subject. And then, almost shuddering, he leaned across the tea things to shock her further with the inclusion of additional horrors. "And, on Sundays—*servants.*"

"Indeed!" Nina laughed, "One must not risk that! One might pick up all kinds of servile inclinations."

"Exactly," Mr. Marshall agreed, and then took a moment to rethink her remark, which had Jordan smiling and Adele giggling. And then Mr. Marshall nodded knowingly, as if he had understood her deepest meaning and it was exactly his own. That very "confidentiality" was his route to all his connections.

The thread having become tangled, Mrs. Windsor jumped in to make it and the point clear. "The entire beach area of New Jersey is become . . . suspect. Strollers are taking the space away from people with carriages. Not to mention *pavilions* having sprung up everywhere—that reek of chowder. One sees wrapping paper abandoned to the wind. And, *and*"—she drew breath for the final indictment—"lunches are secretly munched."

At that, although Dick and Adele began it, Nina and Jordan were not far behind in their whoops of laughter. Adele recollected that the lady was soon to be her mother-in-law, and she began quickly to distract her with details of that ceremony-to-be and all the advice being offered to prevent anything going amiss.

She'd barely introduced that subject when Mrs. Windsor was quick to pick it up. Jordan was the first to sense the danger, and he made a valiant attempt to prevent what was coming by rising and commenting on the sunset, but Mrs. Windsor refused to be distracted. Dick caught the peril, but merely sat back laughing, as his mother was by now well launched into the description of her own wedding with the oft-repeated story of her carriage's runaway team. Adele and Nina, also having heard the story before, and even Mr. Marshall (during this last week of wedding preparations) having had to sit through three renditions, and all recalling the length of it, each attempted, individually and together, to budge her from proceeding. But she was firm, and, her voice rising above all of theirs, she carried on with the total description of her wedding dress and the comments of all her bridesmaids and how she had been inspired to mix her historical periods and had an Elizabethan gown—up to the ruff, and had added a head covering with several rows of tulle cascading down—that owed its inspiration to feudal times, in that it was tall and towering.

"Like a dunce cap," Dick put in, but she was not listening to anything but herself. She had reached the point of the greatest drama when, as she and her father neared the carriage to take them to the church, the lead horse turned and stared at her in a "most peculiar way," as if he would tell her something, and then bolted off—with the stable hands running after—

Jordan, unable to hear the tale to its finish, inserted, "Father told it differently, claiming it was your outfit that spooked the horses and that when you came down the aisle with that swaying tower on your head, he nearly did the same."

As was Mrs. Windsor's custom, she ignored all interruptions, especially from Jordan. "And I recall the moment vividly, for just before the animal bolted, it drew up its front legs and began slowly, slowly to shake its head at me—"

"Obviously the original neigh-sayer," Jordan once more risked, which had Nina laughing with him; and they exchanged their first direct glance.

". . . and I took it as an omen, and I said to my father, 'Father, perhaps I should reconsider this step,' and he said to me, 'No, Elvira, I'm not going to allow an animal to decide my daughter's future. *It isn't done.*'" She paused there for the drama of the moment to sink in on them, and then continued triumphantly, "Of course he was correct. So I lifted my head and proceeded with the procession."

But "It isn't done" had so undone the listeners that they were unable to still their bursts of amusement and to keep serious for the remainder of the evening, constantly concluding that this or that *wasn't done.*

All and all, Nina and Jordan were grateful to Mrs. Windsor for bridging what might have been a difficult time. Instead, they were talking naturally—except for the strained sub rosa conversation that continued between them in hesitant glances and long stares that Nina constantly cut off. Jordan's eyes were becoming too eloquent, especially during dinner when Mr. De Bonnard had made an unfortunate mention of The Gilded Lily. Nina's mother had been alarmed and Adele giggled, but the stare that really enraged was Jordan's quick, concerned glance her way, clearly revealing that he knew. Blast him!

After dinner Jordan and Nina were briefly, unwittingly, left alone on the veranda, and instantly he took the opportunity to lean forward and gaze his fill of her without having to worry what others thought about a blatant demonstration of his feelings.

Nina moved away from the urgency coming from him, which was rousing a similar excitement in her. She turned quickly, tossing her long hair, worn as she had in Oceana, pulled up on the sides and hanging long to her waist in ringlets. He wanted to touch one of the curls, cut one off and keep it. But when he touched her, she recoiled, and he said soothingly, "Relax, dear heart, a gentleman can't resist reacting to the flirtation of a moving curl, not to mention those long dark lashes that lift suddenly to reveal golden rays of light. And as for your lips—"

"Stop that talk! Just because we're back in Oceana doesn't mean we're back to playing your mocking games! And stop what you're doing with your eyes as well."

Jordan grinned in satisfaction. "What am I doing with my eyes?" he whispered, coming close enough so they were almost eye-to-eye.

From the first moment of coming from the beach when she'd suddenly seen Jordan again, Nina, although pretending indifference, had felt herself gradually softening. And yes, it was all the fault of those black eyes; the black coal heat in them had reached her frozen veneer. She had to stop his brazen assumption that he could melt her, mold her his way. Yet every time she looked up, the heat of his stare was on her, always there. *That's* what he was doing with his eyes, she could have told him: closing in on her, entangling her, like a butterfly being caught in a net.

Rather than answering, Nina used her own eyes to fight back, to push him off. Then, able to direct their communication, she stood up and asked frankly, "Why did you look so concerned when Papa criticized The Gilded Lily? Are you an admirer of hers?"

"I admire everything you do," Jordan responded with his slow, maddening smile. "Yes, my dear heart, I not only know you're The Gilded Lily, but I've been publishing you in the *Courier* since my syndication arrangement with Holden your first winter of appearing. And now I'm publishing your collection in book form."

Nina's face went white and she was almost speechless. When she recovered somewhat, she asked coldly, "Are you telling me that I have not achieved my success on my *own* . . . that I owe this syndication to another lustful gentleman who is using it merely to—"

"To what?" he urged, his eyes twinkling now. But she would not supply the missing verb; she just sat there, gasping in bitter disappointment while he supplied a selection for her to choose from. "To make you his own? To put the gilded lily in a gilded cage? No, beautiful Nina, I have no ulterior motive unless, of course, you insist on making that part of the arrangement. Then, of course, I'll acquiesce. However, the truth is I recognized superior talent and operated strictly as a newspaper owner and editor who wanted the best for his paper. In short, I wanted to possess The Gilded Lily, not physically, but editorially."

Nina felt some return of pride at that. She wanted her success as The Gilded Lily to be the one thing not connected to her other persona: Nina De Bonnard, the Professional Beauty.

"Incidentally," he was continuing, "why do you sign yourself a lily? Gilded you may be, you know best about that, but haven't you always resented any assumption of yourself as being earthbound, let alone stuck in the mud? Or are you revealing yourself as happily making mud pies to toss at your readers?"

"Ah, the mocking Jordan, back to his old ways of trying to bury me with mudslings and arrows."

"No, no," he denied, fending that off with a laugh. "I'm just seeking to understand your nom de plume, which might be apt as a symbol of resurrection or even as your being 'too beautiful to gild.' But, I've always seen you more as a butterfly or a bird flying free."

"I don't do animal impersonations," Nina inserted sharply. "I am none of those. Not a flower. Not a butterfly. Not a bird. I am a *woman on her own.*"

"You are never on your own. I am always with you."

To cut off his personal remarks, Nina abruptly changed the topic. "How did you know I wrote the columns?"

Willing to be distracted since he could reach her as easily from this road as the other, Jordan responded, "I knew you were the author the moment I read half a page of your column. Your inner voice spoke out so clearly, I was surprised everyone else couldn't see it. I knew you then. I know you now. We are connected."

His taking quick, determined steps forward had her, similarly, step-by-stepping back until she'd been backed out onto the balcony and from there to its railing, before Jordan caught her by the arm, warning, "Back away, run away, but we'll always meet again. Because every path will lead to the center of the circle that encloses us. When you see that, you'll know the truth about us: that we are . . . joined."

The confidence in his voice, and his closeness, inches from stepping against her, left Nina with only two courses of action: surrendering or screaming. She screamed.

Dick and Adele came running out.

"What happened?" Adele cried.

Jordan bowed to Nina, as if indifferent to her explanation. And Nina turned away from him and said calmly, "I nearly fell . . . over the railing . . . or someone was railing," she added in a mutter, and walked away into the house to the sound of Jordan's laughter.

Nina made certain that she did not find herself alone with Jordan the next day, which actually was so rushed, with so many last-minute preparations, that neither of them had time to send any more messages, verbal or through their more effective means of communication, eye-to-eye. Even when the moment came, during the last-minute rehearsal, when Nina and Jordan had to step in for the bride and groom, both carried that off with a modicum of interior conversation.

The night before the wedding, Nina had a few moments to allow her suppressed thoughts freedom. It gnawed at her that Jordan was responsible for the widespread distribution of her column. The only way she could make herself feel better was to remember that the American syndication had not been the only competitor for her articles. So he had won her, but he had not made her. It was somewhat appeasing that Jordan had recognized her inner voice. The many personas that she was had one central core—and she was pleased he'd recognized the source of all her selves. Perhaps he too had a central core she could admire. At times when he stopped his games and spoke to her, soul-to-soul, she felt that he did, that they were united. Nina finally fell asleep and dreamed an answer to her question, but she was awakened too early by her sister, and the dream and its answer slipped away.

Adele was shaking her alert.

"It's my wedding day!" Adele was saying, jumping on her bed just as she had on Christmas mornings. And Nina had hugged her and rushed to get up. That day Nina and Mrs. De Bonnard ran themselves into frazzles, assuring that everything was prepared and putting Adele to bed for a noon rest, only to disturb her continually by peeking in to see if anyone or anything had disturbed her.

That had Adele grinning and the three of them laughing together. It was concluded that Adele did not need to sleep. "I don't want to miss a minute of this day. I want to take part in all the arrangements." It soon became clear that Adele could handle her own wedding best, since she'd done most of the planning anyway. She made quick and hard decisions without blinking or bemoaning difficulties. "Skip the hors d'oeuvres; we have more than enough to feed a regiment!" "If the doves won't fly on cue, it's okay. They don't have to underscore the final pronouncement. They'll make their point whenever they come out!"

So she carried on, seeing it all as a lark instead of an ordeal, and shortly her sister and mother began adopting the same attitude, and the wedding proceeded without a major mistake. The orchestra under the tent did not miss a cue and the rain and chill that had been predicted by Mrs. Pynchot's gouty toe did not materialize. It was perfect outdoor wedding weather. Neither Mrs. Windsor nor Mrs. De Bonnard was upset to discover that both were wearing blue. Each felt that her shade of blue was the correct one for the occasion; Mrs. Windsor wore a definite royal blue that gave her royal airs and Mrs. De Bonnard an ice blue that kept her cool through the ceremony.

Each remembered their child as a baby and cried as she watched that baby marching down the aisle.

The ceremony began with a stream of pink and blue bridesmaids, all caught up in net bustles and bursts of net headpieces, looking either like confections if you were romantically inclined, or fishermen's nets if you were more realistic. Their bustles bumped down the aisle as they moved along at a quick speed. Then, after a pause, with gliding steps, came the moment the gossips had been awaiting: the arrival of the maid of honor. The simple yellow gown clung to her form so that Nina seemed almost daringly sensuous as she moved down the aisle, causing the gentlemen to lean over to follow her every step. She had decided at the last minute not to compete with her sister's theme. Not only had she left off her lace shawl, but she'd donned a straw hat draped lightly with the dominantly used fisherman's net, dimming her face from all who were looking closely to see signs of dissipation. Those ill-wishers were disappointed when Nina reached the altar and pushed back the net as she turned to face them with laughing eyes. One glance proved that she was still the reigning beauty.

Whatever sensation Nina caused was quickly blotted out when the chords of the Spohr Symphony announced the bride's entrance. Adele's gown was enough to outdo any sister simply dressed. It was an authentic masterpiece of matrimonial excess, gilded era excess, and, lastly, patriotic Oceana excess. Her fully crinolined white satin gown had its hem, bodice, and poufed sleeves fringed with bursts of lace. Then there was a ten-foot train, to prove to Nina that she could handle one. The train stemmed from the bustle, which, like those of her bridesmaids', was a tangle of net. The bridal bouquet was of long white lilies that were entwined with star-spangled golden ribbons. Similarly, the headdress, an explosion of tulle, had star-spangled golden stars on golden ribbons hanging beside her face. Even the traditional long white kid gloves, instead of pearl buttons, kept to the July Fourth theme with golden star buttons—a full eighteen of them. Nina had been the one patiently to button each one, making a game of it, and adding a happy wish with each closing. "And this one is for many children . . . and this one is a sister's wish that everyone will think *you're* The Gilded Lily and not me! And this one's for your mother-in-law's sudden decision to explore darkest Africa with Mr. Stanley!" And her sister was giggling over each blessing.

The rector had just reached the part: "For as much as it hath pleased Almighty God . . ." when the doves prematurely exploded heavenward and Adele gave a slight smile to her sister's despairing glance. But then Adele's smile grew wider as the doves came back down and fluttered over her head with menacing intentions. Both Nina and Adele were delicately attempting to discourage them, to no avail, till Jordan stepped in and, by waving his tall hat, sent them soaring up to heaven, appropriately, just as the couple was pronounced "Man and Wife." At that point, Dick, suntanned and golden-haired, let out a whoop that had all his friends smiling and Adele laughing, and the two, clasping each other, made their way speedily down the aisle exactly as they were embarking on their new life—together and in high spirits.

Jordan gave his arm to Nina and they followed sedately, both overcome with the emotion and meaning of the day, moving to the moment and the occasion, as one would to music, and thus, the wedding triumphed over all.

It was when Nina had danced with everyone and only once with Jordan that Jordan began to have a piercing sense of déjà "rue." In fact, Nina danced twice with Sir Nevel, Bobby's transported lord (not Lord Brindsley, as Jordan had assumed), and even laughed with Bobby for two dances, forgetting her ban. Bobby quickly explained that he'd met her condition, since he had sworn, "In *short*, to leave her alone." So he had left her alone for a short time.

Nina was too mellowed by the wedding to take him up on his equivocation. "You're an absolute knave," she said with a laugh. To which Bobby happily agreed.

So overpoweringly agitated was Jordan by her once more being surrounded by young gentlemen that when Nina caught the bridal bouquet—which was actually handed over by Adele—he could not resist reverting to his old, hard, mocking self.

"You scarcely need *that excuse* to add another man to your collection," he sniped.

"Nor do you need excuses for your acts, merely a pact," she said coldly, walking away. Instantly Jordan caught up to her, demanding that innuendo be explained. Whereupon Nina lifted the wedding bouquet and pushed it at him. "Take this bouquet, Mr. Windsor," she said with disgust. "I assume you need it more than I do. It's the perfect grave cover for that *infamous pact* you and your brother made . . . and let the games and all connection between us finally end!"

With that Nina hurried away, slipping through the crowd and joining Adele, who was ready to change into her going-away outfit. Not once did Nina glance back at the stunned gentleman left holding the bride's bouquet crushed against his chest.

A sudden sense of two ill-matched edges clicking into place overcame Jordan. "Confound that insufferable menace!" he growled, and in a spurt he was off, making his way toward his brother.

Cornering Dick, Jordan pulled him toward the beach where

they had first contrived that pact. It did not take long before Dick readily confessed he had already "confessed all" to Adele. "In fact, you know, Jordie, there's a real pleasure in confessing to women—they're so little accustomed to truth from men that it totally disarms them."

Jordan, momentarily distracted by such an out-of-character remark from his brother, asked suspiciously, "Where did you get that?"

"From you," Dick happily answered. "I remember every word you say. But I found this one especially true. For Adele and I have never been happier. You gotta be honest or you can't expect to be happy together, you know."

"Really! It is regrettable for both Nina and myself that that wasn't your attitude just about two years ago when you begged me to make that pact to save your life."

But as usual and particularly today, Dick was too happy to be reached by sarcasm and merely agreed. His brother went on to ask if and when Adele had informed Nina about the pact.

But Dick, looking at a seagull, was distracted by recalling the doves menacing his wedding and would have spent the next few moments reliving that when his brother grabbed him by the collar of his morning coat and brought him back to the point, "*When did you confess!*"

"Take it easy, Jordie, if you mean when Adele wrote Nina about it, I think sometime around when you were both at Mayberry Castle."

"Blast," his brother whispered, instantly letting him go and turning away, walked toward the sea.

Dick would have hung around, but he had a simple matter of leaving on his honeymoon to attend to. So he shouted to his brother something about "rice," which recalled Jordan to his duty, and the brothers, with smiles on their faces, one full, one forced, rushed to rejoin the wedding party.

The couple was well riced and sent on their way. That departure left the celebration rudderless. And not long after, Mrs. De

Bonnard retired, feeling she had done all she could; the remainder of the guests, who did not have the good sense to leave when an affair was over, were on their own.

Mr. De Bonnard felt the same and gathered some of his cronies into the library to discuss the policies of "Queen Victoria in britches," as President Hayes was called, forgetting the wedding before the door was closed behind him and assuming that the servants would magically wipe away all evidences of the occasion before he came out. Only Nina, having now removed her hat, was walking forlornly through the remnants of strewn petals, overturned champagne glasses, and souvenir collectors, when Jordan found her and, taking her by the hand, led her out and down to the sea where they could be private.

"I don't want to come with you, Mr. Windsor," she said breathlessly as he pulled her along toward the beach.

"There's a part of the ceremony we have yet to complete," he said matter-of-factly as he took off his frock coat and placed it on the sand for Nina to sit on. He was still holding the bouquet and she sat down to take it out of his arms, thinking of the day, of Adele, of marriage, of a hundred pressing thoughts, while Jordan sat next to her.

"It's a time-honored tradition for the best man to take the maid of honor aside and in an appropriate place"—he bowed to the ocean—"tell her the truth and have her speak the truth back to him, as if they were exchanging vows of their own."

"I've never heard—"

"Shh . . . you're hearing of it now. And there's more to it. Open your hand."

Hesitantly, Nina did so, and he placed a small piece of rice in its center and closed her fingers over it. "That's to wish on. . . ."

"No." Nina began trying to disengage herself, but he held his hand over her closed fist and insisted, "Yes, we are now going to wish on this *together*. On this and this bouquet! I wish I had never made that immoral, imbecilic pact with my brother. That's what made you suddenly change toward me at Mayberry, refusing to meet me that night in the garden, and then acting so differently, so falsely—wasn't it?"

Nina nodded. "Since you were going to jilt me, I did it first. I'm an expert at it, you know," she said with a proud lift of her head.

"You didn't have to jilt me first, for I had no such intention! Blast Dick. He began it right here on the day of your pre–Independence Day lawn party when we first met. He threw himself into the sea in desperation. I fished him out and promised I'd win you for him. I was going to show you what you'd done to him by doing it to one of yours. But almost before the day was over I knew the game was no longer about Dick, that I'd found a lady I wanted with all my heart. Not that I'd used my heart for some time. I myself had become an expert at playing a role so long that I thought winning was all. Till there was you. You set me free to feel. I thought we both understood that in Mayberry. But you've always known it from the first. Listen to the ocean. Remember our pledge. And my further pledge to you is that the love I feel for you is the love of renewed faith in being and purpose and life; it is a love that cuts to the bone and will never be at an end. As long as I am . . . it will be."

Over the sound of the waves, Jordan's deep voice was reaching her, influencing her like the sea, throbbing along with her own senses. Nina was listening now to him and the ocean. But she still held back, not willing to dismiss so quickly the months of thinking him false to her. "Why didn't you explain about the pact before I had to hear from others?" she protested.

"Why would I even bring up what was long since *invalid?* Surely we were close enough at Mayberry for you to have shown me the second letter and given me a chance to explain. Why didn't you?"

"Because I believed you were false to me—as you'd been to Adele and to me before," she whispered.

"As God is my witness, I swear the pact was long dead and forgotten *before* England . . . *before* New York and your sickness. Nina, Nina, you had to have felt the truth of our feelings during those times. Especially at Mayberry. How could you not have trusted them?"

Looking down at the grain of rice in her hand and up at his

anguished face, Nina said with a sigh, "Because I'd become accustomed to not trusting you . . . to caging my feelings for you."

"Don't cage them! What separates you from the rest is that you've always beaten at the bars of society's gilded cage, breaking free of the rules through your laughter and writings, through your risking, searching. . . . I know that not trusting can't be you. I know it! I've been following you—watching, guarding, longing. Listen, dear heart," he implored, and tightly squeezed her hand over the grain of rice once more as he exclaimed, "I wish to God I'd never agreed to that idiotic pact. Or that Dick had restrained himself and never confessed it to Adele when it had long since ceased to be. It was not there between us when I held you against me in New York . . . not there when we lay side by side under the willows. It had long since turned into merely an embarrassing memory. But Dick's spilling the beans at the wrong time had us losing our third chance in England. And now, if this one small grain of rice can't change the past, let me at least wish on it— that this, our fourth chance, does not pass us by as well."

Nina opened her palm and stared at the bit of rice for a long time while Jordan waited anxiously. And then she rose up to her knees and flung it into the sea.

"Let's give it the power of the sea," she whispered with a laugh. "And we'll see what develops."

He bent down and kissed the palm that had held the grain, and she smiled and let him kiss her lips.

As he helped her up, Nina turned back for the lily bouquet and untied the gilded, star-spangled cage of ribbons, leaving each lily pure and white and untouched. She went toward the ocean and threw in one lily after the other. "Star-spangled no more," she said. "Gilded, no more. Caged, no more," she concluded, as the last lily rode the waves. "Free to be . . . just free."

One of the lilies, however, came back on the waves and stayed on the beach, as Jordan and Nina walked arm and arm back to Sea Cliff.

The gentleman who had been following them picked up the lily. Bobby Van Reyden sighed. It looked now, as he'd always suspected, that Nina was going to marry the hero, after all. He wouldn't mind moving to Washington and paying court to a married lady. A few months married to true-blue Jordan would surely have her ready for a life of gilded pleasure, after all.

That night a bright opulent full moon gave a gilded look to all the people below. Two lovers were married, two more were veering towards possible marriage, and one lone young man was set to carry on with his turning society and all happy unions upside down. He walked off with galaxies of plans bursting in his head while Nina and Jordan sat on the glider-swing on Sea Cliff's veranda. Whatever glance they could spare from each other, they gave to the sky and the July Fourth fiery display, exploding above. But mostly Nina and Jordan waited for the return of the undisturbed sky and its centuries of steady silver starlight that was outshone only by the glow in the depths of each other's eyes.

Everything gilded is not necessarily false—the moon on the ocean gives it a gilded sheen and the faces of those united are gilded with love.

So the days of gilt end with a night of steady light shining above . . . and within.